A CONSPIRACY OF WOLVES

A CONSPIRACY OF WOLVES

Candace Robb

CRÈME de la CRIME

This first world edition published 2019
in Great Britain and the USA by
Crème de la Crime an imprint of
SEVERN HOUSE PUBLISHERS LTD of
Eardley House, 4 Uxbridge Street, London W8 7SY.
Trade paperback edition first published
in Great Britain and the USA 2019 by
SEVERN HOUSE PUBLISHERS LTD.

British Library Cataloguing in Publication Data
A CIP catalogue record for this title is available from the British Library.

ISBN-13: 978-1-78029-115-4 (cased)
ISBN-13: 978-1-78029-607-4 (trade paper)
ISBN-13: 978-1-4483-0224-6 (e-book)

All Severn House titles are printed on acid-free paper.

Severn House Publishers support the Forest Stewardship Council™ [FSC™],
the leading international forest certification organisation.
All our titles that are printed on FSC certified paper carry the FSC logo.

MIX
Paper from
responsible sources
FSC® C013056

Typeset by Palimpsest Book Production Ltd.,
Falkirk, Stirlingshire, Scotland.
Printed and bound in Great Britain by
TJ International, Padstow, Cornwall.

For my readers.

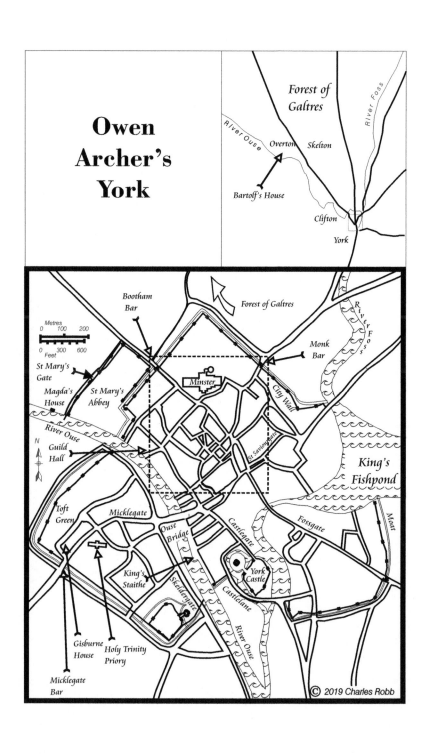

Owen Archer's York

Forest of Galtres

River Ouse
River Foss

Overton Skelton

Bartolf's House

Clifton

York

Bootham Bar

Forest of Galtres

River Foss

Metres
0   100   200

Feet
0   300   600

St Mary's Gate

Monk Bar

Magda's House

St Mary's Abbey

Minster

City Wall

River Ouse

N

Guild Hall

St Saviourgate

King's Fishpond

Toft Green

Micklegate

Ouse Bridge

Castlegate

Fossgate

Moat

King's Staithe

Skeldergate

Castlegate

York Castle

Castlelane

River Ouse

Gisburne House

Holy Trinity Priory

Micklegate Bar

© 2019 Charles Robb

1. Fenton House
2. Swann House
3. Braithwaite House
4. St Helen's Churchyard
5. St Helen's Church
6. Lucie and Owen's House
7. Lucie's Apothecary
8. York Tavern
9. Chandler's Shop
10. Jehannes's House
11. Honoria's Brothel
12. Poole House
13. Tirwhit House
14. Christchurch

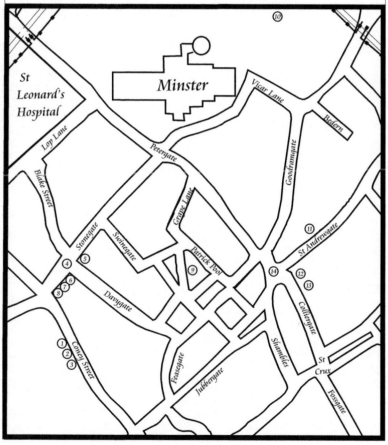

Dramatis Personae

Owen Archer's and Lucie Wilton's household

Owen Archer (Captain Archer) – former captain of guard and spy for the Archbishop of York
Lucie Wilton – master apothecary; Owen's spouse
Gwenllian, Hugh, and Emma – Owen and Lucie's natural children
Jasper de Melton – Owen and Lucie's adopted son and Lucie's apprentice
Dame Philippa – Lucie's aunt, recently deceased
Kate – Lucie's housemaid
Lena – the children's nurse
Alfred and Stephen – former members of archbishop's guard, Owen's lieutenants
Tildy – Kate's sister, formerly Lucie's housemaid, now wed to the steward of Freythorpe Hadden

The Riverwoman's household

Magda Digby (aka the Riverwoman) – midwife and healer
Alisoun Ffulford – apprentice to Magda Digby
Rose and Rob – temporary caretakers; Kate's twin siblings

The Swann household

Bartolf – patriarch, coroner of Galtres
Hoban – merchant, Bartolf's son
Muriel – Hoban's spouse
Olyf – Bartolf's daughter, Adam Tirwhit's spouse
Joss – servant
Cilla – servant

The Braithwaite household

John and Janet Braithwaite
Paul – son, married to Elaine
Muriel – daughter, Hoban Swann's spouse
Galbot – Paul Braithwaite's dog trainer
Alan – servant
Ned – bailiff's man, temporary servant

The Tirwhit household

Adam Tirwhit – merchant, brother-in-law of Hoban, son-in-law
  of Bartolf
Olyf – spouse, daughter of Bartolf Swann
Wren – housemaid

The Poole household

Crispin – merchant, former soldier
Euphemia – widow, Crispin's mother
Eva – servant
Dun – servant

Residents of Galtres

Gerta – daughter of charcoal-burners
Warin – poacher, and his children

Churchmen

Jehannes – Archdeacon of York; Owen's good friend
Brother Michaelo – former personal secretary to Thoresby
*John Thoresby – former Archbishop of York (deceased)
*Alexander Neville – newly appointed Archbishop of York
Dom Leufrid – secretary to Archbishop Neville
*Abbot William – abbot, St Mary's Abbey
Brother Oswald – hospitaller, St Mary's Abbey

York residents

Bess & Tom Merchet – owners of the York Tavern
Old Bede – regular at the York Tavern
Winifrith – Bede's daughter
George Hempe – city bailiff and merchant, wife Lotta
*Gerard Burnby – coroner for York
Honoria de Staines – owner of a brothel near the Bedern
*John Gisburne – merchant, MP

Royal household

*Geoffrey Chaucer – in York on a mission for Prince Edward;
   Owen's friend
Antony of Egypt – member of Prince Edward's household

*real historical figures

'*Humans are inclined to see our own species as embattled;*
we are locked in an eternal struggle in which we defend our
own "culture" against the elemental, animal forces of
"nature." And for millennia, our fellow apex predator, the
wolf, has been forced to serve as a symbolic stand-in for all
of nature, red in tooth and claw.'
                                                    – Laura D. Gelfand

'*What do folk see when they see a wolf, Bird-eye? The animal?*
Think again.'
                                                    – Magda Digby

ONE

The Dogs in the Night

York, Autumn 1374

The river mist curled round Magda Digby's rock in the Ouse, dimming the reds and golds of sunset, distorting sound, creating shifting shapes that danced at the edge of Alisoun Ffulford's vision, chilling her fingers until they were too stiff for the close work. She gathered up the feathers, arrow shafts, and knife with which she had been fletching and returned them to her work basket, then paused, her hand on the door latch, listening to dogs baying. Upriver, she thought, in the Forest of Galtres. 'May they be safe,' she whispered. Like St Francis of Assisi, she felt a bond with animals, so much so that Magda handed over to her all animals brought to the house on the rock for healing. Alisoun preferred these patients to the human ones. Their needs were clear, they did not try to mask their illnesses, and, once healed, gladly departed without complaint or blame. She strained to hear the sounds beneath the dogs' baying. A man's angry shout. Another. The same voice? She could not be certain. The dogs continued as before, which she took to mean they were unharmed. Good.

She lifted her gaze to the blank eyes of the upside-down sea serpent on the bow of the ship that served as the roof of Magda Digby's house. A cunning choice of building material, the part of the ship with the figurehead. The sea serpent was widely believed to have magical powers. Not that Magda ever confirmed or denied it, but as folk had the same suspicion about her, their unease about the sea serpent and the Riverwoman gave them pause about crossing either one. Nodding to the enigmatic carving, Alisoun whispered, 'Whoever disturbs the night upriver will not dare trespass here.' A subtle draft and a warmth on the back of her neck, as if the figurehead responded in a gesture of reassurance, felt rather than seen. There had been a time when such feelings had frightened her, but that had passed as she learned to trust to the mystery of Magda Digby's healing gifts. Now, she took it as a blessing.

Stepping inside, she traded the damp chill and rich, earthy scent of the tidal Ouse for an aromatic warmth, the brightly burning fire teasing out the scents of the dried plants and roots hanging in the rafters to dry. Earlier, she had escaped from its warmth to the cool, fresh air without; now, chilled by the mist, she was grateful for the heat, and the homely familiarity. But she was not at ease – the dogs baying in that eerie mist . . .

She steadied herself by calling to mind the remedies for dog bite and checking her supplies. Although Magda said folk knew to give guard dogs a wide berth, there was always a first time. *Betony for the bite of a mad dog, pound in the mortar and lay on the wound. Or plantain. Vervain and yarrow to be mixed with wheat. Burdock and black horehound need salt. Calendula powder in warm water to drink.* She had plenty of betony and calendula powder. Though unlikely to need it, she arranged them on the work table, preferring to be prepared.

Now to her evening meal. The fragrance of the stew pleased her. She had learned to use herbs to season her cooking, making almost anything palatable, even a coney that some would have rejected as too old and gristly for the stew pot. With Magda away, Alisoun felt obliged to stay close to the small rock island in the tidal river, so that she might not miss those who came to the Riverwoman's house for healing. She dared not range too far afield in hunting for food, making do with fish and small prey like the aged coney that had appeared on the riverbank nearby.

She paused with her spoon halfway to her mouth as a lone dog began to bark, an angry sound, and then a man's startled shout, followed by a loud curse, a few more cries, more pain than anger. Then silence. Alisoun lowered her spoon, bowed her head, and pressed her shaking hands together in prayer. She stayed there until she felt the tremors quiet.

Though Magda scoffed at prayer, she encouraged Alisoun to use her apprenticeship to develop her own skills as healer, not become a second Magda. *All that goes before shapes thee. Even thy habit of prayer. Magda honors that.* Alisoun had little faith that her prayers were heard – God and the Blessed Mother had stood aside while she lost all her family to the pestilence. But something in the words, the ritual, comforted her.

According to Magda, to pay attention to how Alisoun felt about her choices was to heed her inner wisdom, whence came her gift for healing. Her gift. Long had Alisoun yearned for even a morsel of encouragement from Magda. The faith implicit in this instruction had been hard won. In the beginning, Magda merely offered Alisoun shelter, let her observe as she might, and then sent her away to serve as a nurse for Captain Archer and Lucie Wilton's children, and as a companion to successive invalids. Praying that they were tests, Alisoun had done as she was told – though not without frequent complaint. And though Magda had warned her time and again *Thou hast fire in thy eyes, and it is blinding thee*, she continued to invite Alisoun to observe her, and, in time, to attend her. The turning point had come at the deathbed of Archbishop Thoresby, where Alisoun had served as the Riverwoman's assistant. From that time forward, Magda referred to Alisoun as her apprentice – and sometimes simply as a healer.

Looking back, Alisoun wondered at Magda's patience, and did her best to deserve her gift. She was keenly aware of the trust Magda placed in her, staying behind to see to all who came to the Riverwoman's rock while she was away. So far Alisoun had done well, challenged only by her usual doubts about her ability, her calling to be a healer. Not when at work – when tending the ill or injured she thought of nothing but how she might best serve. Her doubts arose in the quiet moments. Pray God that was the worst of it. If she disappointed Magda, she did not know what would become of her. Magda steadied her, coaxed her into believing in herself. Without her . . .

Too much thinking. She finished her modest meal and tidied up, then settled on a stool by the fire and tried to empty her mind, listening to the fire snap, the house creak as it settled for the night, the drying herbs rustle above in the draft from the unglazed windows. With the tide out, the sounds of the river receded to a soft gurgle. Until this evening she had welcomed this part of her day. But the solitude wore thin. She missed Magda and looked forward to her return.

The Riverwoman had accompanied Lucie Wilton and her family

to her late father's manor to the south, Freythorpe Hadden. It was a somber traveling party, escorting the body of Philippa, Dame Lucie's aunt, for burial. The elderly woman had died in her sleep after a long decline, cared for all the while by Dame Lucie. Most fortunate woman. When Alisoun served as nursemaid in that household she had at first chafed under the old woman's watchful eye, but in time she had grown fond of her. Dame Philippa loved to tell tales, and would hold Alisoun's hand in both of hers as she reached the conclusion, leaning close and looking straight into her eyes. The tales had taught her so much about the important families in York that the city felt less foreign to her – having grown up on a farm upriver, it was a gift.

So many gifts, so undeserving.

Alisoun was roused from her reverie by the clatter and squelch of someone stumbling on the slippery rocks that led from the riverbank on the north to Magda's rock at low tide. The earlier unease returned, and she fought the impulse to string her bow and ready an arrow as she rose to fetch a lantern. But recalling Magda's training steadied her. Those seeking a healer should be greeted with open arms, not an arrow aimed at their heart.

In response to a firm rap on the door Alisoun swung it open, lifting the lantern high as she intoned, 'All who seek healing are welcome here.' Magda need not bother with such greetings. Her mere presence reassured the supplicant. But Alisoun did not yet have that gift.

A man stood on the porch, blocking the fading light. 'I seek the Riverwoman.' Pain constricted his voice. He stood slumped, one arm cradled in the other.

'I see you are injured. Dame Magda is away, but she has entrusted me with the care of those who come seeking her,' said Alisoun.

Adjusting the lantern so that she might look at the arm he favored, she recognized him when he glanced up and bobbed his head at the figurehead, a ritual of respect he performed whenever he called on Magda. Crispin Poole. A merchant recently returned to York, he had consulted Magda about the pain he suffered in his stump of an arm, the injury long healed, but still troubling him. Tonight he cradled it as it bled through the sleeve of his jacket.

Saturated, she found when she touched it. She felt him trembling, smelled his sweat. 'A knife wound?' she asked.

'Bitten.'

She remembered the baying. 'I heard several dogs, then one.'

'Several? No, only the one.' He said it as if he would brook no argument regarding the number. 'A hell hound.'

'No doubt it seemed so when it sank its teeth into you.'

'A wolf, I think, though I am told the sergeant of the forest rid Galtres of them.'

Not quite. In winter a small pack came down from the moors, seeking food. But they did not harm folk unless threatened. And it was not yet winter. Alisoun might reassure him of this, but Magda's instruction was to *say only what thou must. Thou art here to listen.*

'Whether dog or wolf – or hell hound, the remedies are the same,' said Alisoun. 'I've readied all that I need.'

'When will the Riverwoman return?'

'I am not sure. But I do know your wound will not wait.'

'Mistress Alisoun, forgive me, but are you not still an apprentice?'

She might say much to that, but she chose her words. 'I have seen to a variety of wounds, and as Magda is not here, you would be wise to let me see to yours.' She stepped aside to allow him into the house if he so chose.

He hesitated, then ducked beneath the lintel, and entered.

As she was closing the door Alisoun looked out into the gathering darkness, puzzled by the absence of a horse on the bank. Most chose to ride, not walk through the forest, if they had the means, and Crispin Poole was wealthy. Or so they said. So he had been on foot when attacked. Doing what? She imagined Magda standing before her, a bony finger to her lips, shaking her head. *Thou art a healer, not a spy.*

Crispin had settled on his usual bench near the fire. That would not do.

'Forgive me, I should have said – for this you must sit at the worktable.' She led him across the room, conscious of how he must hunch over to avoid the rafters and the hanging herbs. Tall like Captain Archer, yet otherwise so unlike him.

Lighting a spirit lamp for the close work, she instructed him to rest his injured arm on the table. With care, she slipped a hand beneath it so that she might move it about in the light to study the wound. The dog had sunk its teeth in deep into what remained of his forearm, a four-finger expanse. The teeth had gone clear to the bone. 'How did you manage to get it to release you?'

'I – shouted and – I could not tell you what convinced it I was not its dinner. All I could think of was retrieving what's left of my arm.'

'You did not attempt to attack it in turn?'

He looked at her as if she were a half-wit. 'I should think it plain my fighting days are over.'

'Forgive me for my thoughtless question.'

'We locked eyes as we each backed away.' He shivered to describe it.

The experience had unsettled this large, powerful man. She wondered what he had done to so anger the dog for it to attack. And the earlier baying. Why did he deny what he must have heard?

She reminded herself that a healer must put the good of the patient before her curiosity. He must not feel compromised. She took a deep breath. Enough talk.

'Some brandywine before I clean it and stitch the flesh together? My ministrations will worsen the pain before relieving it, the worst of it.' And the brandywine should calm him. She needed him steady.

'I would welcome it.'

Slipping away to pour him some, she also fetched warm water for the calendula drink. With such a deep wound, best to give him that now, and send him home with enough for a day, as well as packing the wound with a paste of betony. And boneset, in case the bone had been damaged.

She sensed his intense eyes following her hands as she worked, but he kept still and silent. Nary a jerk or a wince, as if accustomed to sudden, sharp pain. Well, the arm. Of course.

It was only when Alisoun was tying the bandage that he spoke again.

'You are young to have such skill.'

'Our queen was younger than me when she took on the role of the king's helpmeet and mother to all the realm. And Princess Joan—'

'I did not mean to insult you. I wish only to thank you for your gentle, healing touch.'

Alisoun was glad only her hands were in the lamplight as she blushed. Apparently she was too quick to recite her litany of females who had been treated as grown women by the age of sixteen.

'I pray you,' she said, 'I would thank you not to mention my outburst to Dame Magda.'

Crispin nodded. 'And I would ask that you tell no one of this incident,' he said. 'Not even Dame Magda.' He neither raised his voice nor seemed excited, yet he made it clear he expected her to agree. Something in his eyes.

'That will be difficult if she returns before you are healed.'

'I am confident that you will find a way.'

'But why? People should know of the danger.'

'I have my reasons. I pray you, respect my request.' A slight smile that did nothing to warm his wide, dark, thickly lashed eyes. An interesting face, unscarred, yet with the uneven color and roughened texture of someone who spent much time at sea. His heft was characteristic of a muscular man going soft as he aged and grew less active. Magda had called him *a merchant adventurer – though more the latter*, suspecting he earned more of his wealth by eliminating his partners' competition than by his eye for a bargain. For such a man to be so disquieted by an encounter with a dog, and now this secrecy. What had so shaken him? And why must it be a secret?

Secrecy added cost to treatment for those who had the coin – Magda's rule, as it afforded her the means to care for those who were unable to pay her.

And, indeed, when Alisoun named her fee, Crispin did not object, drawing the silver from his scrip without comment.

She handed him the pouch of calendula powder, with instructions.

'I am grateful to you, Mistress Alisoun. May God bless you for the work you do.'

She stepped out the door after him, glad to see that she had worked quickly enough that the tide was just beginning to come in and his crossing should be easy even in the dark.

'Did you encounter the dog nearby?' She hoped it a sufficiently innocuous question. 'I thought to forage for roots at dawn. But having tasted blood, it might be keen for more.'

'Near enough,' he said. 'But if you have foraged in the forest all this while without mishap, I should think you will be safe. May God watch out for you, Mistress Alisoun.'

Crispin bowed to her and set off across the rocks, his boots getting only a little wet in the slowly rising water. *I should think you will be safe . . .* Why? Had someone set the dog on him? He'd said he would have been a fool to challenge it. Yet why else would it attack? And why had it not simply kept its distance as wild animals commonly did in such encounters? All this, and his denial of the earlier baying, unsettled her.

As she lingered in the doorway staring at his back, she caught a movement to her left, upriver. A figure stood at the edge of a stand of trees. Forty, fifty paces up the riverbank. Watching Magda's house? Or Crispin Poole?

When he did not seem to notice the watcher she thought to warn the injured man, but he had already reached the bank. She might wade across, but why? He'd not endeared himself to her, with his selfish refusal to alert the community. She had fulfilled her duty as a healer, tending his wound.

Glancing back toward the stand of trees, Alisoun saw no one. 'My imagination?' she asked the sea serpent. No response. Not a good sign. Once inside she strung her bow and set it near the door, with a quiver of arrows. The tide might be coming in, but she would take no chances.

A week later, Alisoun woke shortly after dawn, having dreamt of Crispin Poole being savaged by a hell-hound, a giant creature, black, with blazing eyes. Shivering, she stoked the fire, lit a lamp, and checked the young woman on the pallet by the fire, grateful for an absorbing task. Young Wren's head was cool. No fever, God be thanked. A miscarriage, the bleeding afterward perhaps more than what might be expected, nothing worse. And, for this serving girl, a blessing. A child would bring only grief.

Gently shaking the girl awake, Alisoun helped her sit up so she might drink the honey water laced with herbs to stop the bleeding.

'If I hurry, my mistress will never know I was gone the night,' said the girl in a hoarse whisper. Her throat was dry from the herbs. The honey in warm water should help that.

'Drink that down,' Alisoun said. 'Then we will talk.'

The girl tilted back her head and drank it down, holding out the empty wooden bowl for inspection, her pale eyes watching Alisoun's face for a sign of argument. 'I need the work. I've nowhere else to go.'

This is how it was. 'Of course. You've no fever. Let's see if you can stand.'

With Alisoun's assistance, the girl swung her feet down and rose with nary a wobble, even taking a few hesitant steps. 'Oh!' She lifted her skirt, saw the watery blood trickling down the inside of her short, fleshy legs.

'Tend it as you do your courses and no one's the wiser,' said Alisoun. 'Your womb is empty.'

'Was it—?'

Alisoun shook her head. 'Too early to know aught.'

'Will you help me to the riverbank?'

She would prefer that the girl lie abed for a day. This was the hardest part for Alisoun, keeping her counsel. *Thine opinion is naught but interference*, Magda would say. *If thou wouldst care for her again, do what she asks and no more.* She must allow the girl to return to the house where her master lay in wait, and he would continue to lie with her until she again conceived a child and carried it long enough for his wife to discover her condition, tossing her out onto the street as a Magdalene.

Unless the charm worked. Alisoun had whispered it over the girl as she slept, a charm said to render a man impotent when he touched her. Magda was not here to chide Alisoun for using it. Even so, she had shivered as she whispered the words, imagining Magda's sharp eyes watching from afar. No one knew the extent of the Riverwoman's powers.

A risk. But Magda had said that Alisoun must find her own way . . .

'Will you?' the girl repeated, tugging on Alisoun's sleeve with the dimpled hand of a child.

'If that is what you wish, come along while the tide is low. I have prepared a powder for you to add to ale or water and drink down if the pain returns.'

'I cannot be lazy . . .'

'This is not so strong that you cannot work as usual. You need not be in pain.' Alisoun pressed it into the girl's hand.

Once she had escorted the child safely through the ankle-deep water, Alisoun returned to the hut and sat down by the fire to dry the hem of her gown while planning her day. She should see Muriel Swann, make certain that the flutters she had felt days ago were indeed the child moving in her womb. Not a young woman, this was the first time Dame Muriel had carried a child long enough to feel it quicken, and the experience had both excited and frightened her. Alisoun added to her basket a calming potion for Muriel's headaches, and a tisane to increase her appetite.

A memory teased her, dogs barking in the night, and a man's cries. Terror. Agony. The girl had awakened, calling out in fear, and Alisoun had risen to comfort her, assuring her it was just a bad dream.

But it had been no dream. Had she been alone, Alisoun might have stepped outside, listening in order to gauge whence came the cry, then set out at first light to see if she might be of help. But the girl had been her first responsibility.

Now she gathered the same remedies she had administered to Crispin Poole a week earlier. As it was light, she might walk upriver, see if she came across someone lying injured. She placed the basket with all she might need on the small chest by the door, then fetched her bow and a quiver of arrows. Poole had not returned, nor had she seen him or heard anything of him, and that silence, that absence made her uneasy.

A soft rain in the night had freshened the late-summer foliage in the meadows and woodland along the road from Freythorpe Hadden to York and tamped down the dust, for which Owen was grateful. He knew the misery of riding for hours blinking away the dust in his one good eye, a scarf protecting his nose and mouth. For Lucie and the children, riding in the cart ahead of him, there was still the discomfort of a bumpy ride, but he heard no complaints.

For a while they had traveled behind a group of players who serenaded them with songs and japes, a felicitous arrangement, though he hoped that his eight-year-old daughter Gwenllian would forget the bawdier lyrics. Now that the players had moved on, the monotonous rattle of the cart and horses was punctured occasionally by sounds of reapers and gleaners in the fields, though not as many as on their journey to Freythorpe. Harvest was almost over.

Adding to the monotony, his companion droned on and on about something – Owen had stopped listening to Geoffrey a while back. Chaucer was shaping one of his poems aloud, replete with mythical palaces, gods, fantastical creatures, which might be entertaining but for his pauses to play with language, trying a phrase this way and that. Owen was perhaps to blame, having insisted that Geoffrey not address the mission that had brought him to York until they returned to the city. He'd hoped the man might ride in silence, but he'd know that was too much to ask of the chattering jay.

In her wisdom, Magda Digby might have found a way to delay Geoffrey's departure. *Thou art needed in the city*, she had told Owen as they sat beneath an oak the previous evening, drawing down the day. *Depart in the morning.*

But Lucie . . .

Agrees with Magda. She has readied the children.

How do you know?

Not the question, Bird-eye. She had turned to him, pressing her forefinger to the spot between his eyes. *Open thine eyes. Trust thyself. The wolves circle their prey. Thou hast the sight to see what awakens.*

He'd questioned the wolves. They came only in winter, the wolves that the steward of the Forest of Galtres swore no longer bided in the land.

What do folk see when they see a wolf, Bird-eye? The animal? Think again.

Magda Digby, his guide, his tormentor. In his mourning for John Thoresby, Owen had sought her out, confided in her all that was in his heart. Long she listened, holding his hands, looking into his eye. *Open thine eyes*, she repeated, and corrected him when he argued that he had but one. He did not understand, and she did not explain. Her last words to him on departing Freythorpe, *Trust thyself, Bird-eye. Thou art called.*

Trust himself. Open his eyes. He was called. Called from a year of mourning, a year of doubting his judgment, his worth, a year of questioning all – all but his devotion to his family. He had failed in his last task for Archbishop Thoresby, keeping the peace at his deathbed. Failed by missing signs of a trusted comrade's discontent, so certain was he of the man's loyalty when the impending death of their patron rendered his future uncertain.

He'd spent the past year grieving for Thoresby and the end of a career that had given Owen purpose, and now he mourned the death of Philippa, a woman of strength and heart who had endeared herself to him over a decade. Philippa's death had taken him by surprise. Though she had suffered for years of a palsy, her strength and memory failing, her end was sudden. One morning she simply did not rise from her bed. She was missed.

Wolves circling their prey. The sight to see what awakens. Something that had already been stirring in York before Philippa's death? He had been preoccupied with his own life the past months, helping out in the apothecary and the medicinal garden while Lucie sat with her failing aunt, riding out to familiarize himself with his new property, a manor in the gift of the Bishop of Winchester, the deed transferred to Owen on the late archbishop's urging. Thoresby's last gift, and, as ever, a double-edged sword. He must clear his mind of all that now.

He had a vague memory of a rumor of wolves in the wood. There were always rumors of wolves in winter, but this time it had continued through the spring and summer. Wolves prowling the yards at night, stealing chickens and pigs. Mauley, sergeant of Galtres, had been incensed by the claims. Though his immediate predecessors had performed their duties with deputies, rarely coming north – king's men, the status a gift – Mauley was often in York, biding with his daughter in the Fenton house on Coney Street. He was proud of order in the forest. Owen searched his memory for more, but he could not think clearly with Geoffrey's jabbering. He'd made his excuses this morning, asked Geoffrey to stay at Freythorpe Hadden with Magda, who was to remain behind a while. But Magda had scoffed at that suggestion. She was not always Owen's friend.

'Spare me your poetic struggles,' Owen grumbled.

Geoffrey's retort fell on deaf ears. A plume of dust on the road ahead caught Owen's attention. Riders were to be expected on the southern approach to York, but something about this pair imparted a sense of urgency. He urged his horse forward, nodding to Lucie and the children as he passed the cart.

'Are they for us?' Alfred, his former lieutenant in the arch-bishop's household guard, called out from his driver's seat as he steadied the cart horses.

'I'm riding ahead to see.' As Owen grew closer he shook his head at the strange pairing approaching them.

'Can that be Brother Michaelo?' asked Geoffrey, catching up. 'I thought he had agreed to stay as Archdeacon Jehannes's secretary. But if he is on the road . . .'

Upon Archbishop Thoresby's death his secretary, Brother Michaelo, had found himself without a home, without a purpose. A Benedictine, he had left the Abbey of St Mary's in York during the incumbency of the reasonable Abbot Campion. Unfortunately, the current abbot, knowing of Michaelo's penchant for handsome young men, and a long-ago attempt to poison the abbey infirmarian, refused to receive him back into the fold. An earlier plan to return home to Normandy and seek a place in a modest priory near his ancestral home was one Michaelo had pursued with reluctance. Seeing the monk's wretchedness and believing there must be work for a man of Brother Michaelo's experience in the city, Jehannes, Archdeacon of York, had invited the monk to bide with him for a time. He himself had need of a secretary, though the work was intermittent, not enough to keep Michaelo regularly engaged. Jehannes hoped to find other clerics who might need some of the monk's time. But Michaelo's reputation preceded him, and so far clerics proved reluctant.

'It is indeed Michaelo,' said Owen, 'accompanied by Bartolf Swann, if I am not mistaken.'

'Who?'

'Coroner of Galtres Forest,' said Owen.

'What business would Michaelo have with such a man?' Geoffrey asked a little breathlessly, as if anticipating a good tale. 'Do you suppose they are taking ship together?'

'I very much doubt it,' said Owen. 'Michaelo would drive Bartolf mad with his fussing.'

The elderly Bartolf was far more likely to be riding south to consult with Magda Digby about one of his mysterious ailments, which, according to the Riverwoman, were merely signs of aging in a man who moved as little as possible and drank wine to the point of passing out every night. Though he'd been a man of sufficient status and wealth to be appointed coroner, he had suffered a series of setbacks and had perforce handed the business to his son some time before Owen's arrival in York ten years earlier. His son Hoban had managed to restore the family fortune and, acting as his father's banker, ensured the mayor and the king's officers that his father now had sufficient wealth to perform the duties of coroner without danger of compromise – as much as any coroner for the crown. Even so, the man dressed more like a laborer except on official occasions, his clothes ill-fitting as he shrank with age, his copious white hair kept somewhat under control by a felt hat crammed low over his forehead, his pale eyes peering out through a snowy, greasy thicket. Many a widow in York yearned to clean him up – he had once cut a fine figure, when his wife was alive, and many remembered him with fondness. Today, he looked as if his horse had dragged him much of the way.

Owen dismounted. 'Master Bartolf, Brother Michaelo, good day to you,' he called out as the riders drew up beside him.

'*Benedicite*, Captain Archer, Master Chaucer.' Michaelo's delicately arched nose quivered. 'God's grace is upon us, that we should meet you on the road home. We were on our way to Freythorpe.'

Is this what Magda had seen?

While the monk spoke, his companion had scrambled from his mount and made straight for Owen, latching onto his arm. 'My son! My son! You must come at once. I've left orders that he should stay as we found him, though, God help me, it pained me to leave him lying in his own blood. But I said Captain Archer must see it all as it was. He will find who did this to my Hoban.'

'Hoban?' Owen looked up at Michaelo.

The monk crossed himself. 'His son Hoban has been found dead in the wood. I have told Master Bartolf that you are the prince's man and cannot be expected to help in this, but he'll not be swayed.'

'I am nobody's man at present,' Owen said.

'No?' Michaelo glanced over at Geoffrey Chaucer with a little sniff. 'Your friend must be disappointed. But all the better for Bartolf Swann.'

Alfred had drawn the cart up to the dismounted horsemen and had hurried round to assist Lucie in stepping down.

'Dame Lucie.' Brother Michaelo bowed to her. 'I pray you forgive us for intruding on your mourning.'

Lucie waved him silent as she joined Owen and the distraught

Bartolf. 'My dear Bartolf, you are injured. Let Brother Michaelo tell the tale to my husband while I see to that gash on your head.' He had blood caked on his cheek and in the hair over his left temple.

'What do I care about my old head, Dame Lucie, my son is murdered—'

'I insist.' She nodded to Owen as she put an arm round the old man and led him away to the back of the cart, where she kept a basket of supplies.

Owen was grateful for Lucie's graceful intercession. 'How do you come to be escorting Bartolf Swann?' he asked Michaelo, now also dismounted.

'Well you might wonder, Captain Archer. It seems Bartolf knows of your close friendship with the archdeacon and thought to engage Jehannes's help in persuading you to take on the task of finding his son's murderer. The archdeacon advised him to leave you in peace to mourn Dame Philippa, but the old man would not hear of it.' Michaelo glanced over at Bartolf with a look of distaste. 'So many years serving as coroner, yet look at him – did he believe his own seed immortal?' An impatient sigh. 'But as I saw he could not be dissuaded, I offered to escort him to Freythorpe, as I know the way.'

'Father, what has happened?' Gwenllian asked sleepily from the cart.

'Hush, my love. Some trouble in the city, nothing to do with you.' Owen kissed her and coaxed her to lie down beside her brother. 'Rest. We will be home soon.'

Lucie seemed to have noticed that Gwenllian had awakened and had drawn Bartolf farther off the road, in the shade of a tree. Alfred and Geoffrey held the man steady while Lucie cleaned and bandaged his wounds. As Owen went to join them he heard the old man muttering about dogs, his son's throat torn, a bloody clearing near his home in the forest.

The wolves circle their prey. 'He was savaged by dogs?' Owen asked Michaelo, who had followed him.

'So he says.'

'Bartolf's dogs?' Swann kept a brace of hounds at his property in Galtres.

'He is adamant that his own dogs would never harm Hoban.

But one wonders. Hoban's purpose in riding out yesterday evening was to bring the hounds back to his home in the city, where his father has been biding. This morning, discovering Hoban had not returned, Bartolf took a servant and rode out. They found him in a clearing.'

'And the hounds?'

'Gone. As is his horse.'

'Not at the house?'

'No. Zephyrus and Apollo – hounds with the names of pagan gods.' A sniff. 'Nowhere to be seen.'

'Why did he ride out in the evening? Why not wait for morning?'

'I have asked as little as possible, Captain, but I believe someone informed him his hounds were running loose, and he was wild with worry, insisting on riding out himself. Hoban thought to calm him by bringing the hounds to him. I should say that Bartolf had enough presence of mind to request one of the York coroners to record the death, knowing he could not do so with any clarity.'

'I am glad to hear that. The coroner will have left a guard over the body.'

Lucie joined them. 'I have given him something to calm him. He will soon sleep.'

Indeed, propped against the trunk of the tree, eyes closed, his breathing rough but beginning to calm, Bartolf seemed well on the way to slumber.

Owen crouched down and gently roused him. 'You will ride back to York in the cart with my wife and children, Bartolf. Alfred and Master Chaucer will accompany you.' He glanced up at Lucie. 'Brother Michaelo and I will ride ahead.'

She nodded her agreement.

Owen assisted Bartolf to his feet. 'Michaelo says that one of the York coroners was out there?'

'Gerard,' said Bartolf, his voice weak. 'Been and gone. Left his men to guard my son.'

'Has Mauley been informed?' asked Owen. 'As sergeant of Galtres he should be.'

'Mauley, of what use is he?' Bartolf whined.

'He's gone south,' said Michaelo.

'How do you know that?' Owen asked.

'I am a scribe for hire at present, Captain.'

Useful.

Bartolf clutched at Owen's sleeve. 'You will find my son's murderer? You will see that justice is done?'

'I will go to where he lies and learn as much as I can,' said Owen. 'That is all I can promise for now.'

'Do not leave me behind!'

Lucie met them at the cart. 'Bartolf, you and I must go to Muriel. Remember, she carries your son's child. She must not feel alone.'

'Muriel. Oh, my poor child.' Bartolf gave a sob of dismay. 'I meant to send for Mistress Alisoun. Pray God someone had the wit to do so.'

'He had not the wit,' Michaelo muttered as Owen drew him away. 'What need have we of a coroner for the forest of Galtres? How often is that shaggy man called upon to sit a jury and decide whether a crime is committed, and who responsible? Is that not the job of the steward of Galtres, punishing the poachers and thieves who haunt the woods and marshes? What other sort of crime is there? Why would Swann care to chase after such riff-raff?'

Many wondered that. It was a lesser post than that of the coroners of York. Why would a successful merchant such as Swann have been chosen to serve the crown in such a capacity? He received no pay for it, no lands or titles. At least, nothing official.

'I am not so well acquainted with Bartolf as to answer your questions,' said Owen. 'But as to the crimes, the small villages in the forest have their share of trouble, though not so often as in York.' And yet as the years fell away Bartolf had spent more and more of his time at his small home in the forest, leaving the townhouse to his wife and children, and, upon his wife's death, his son and heir. His trading partners had grown accustomed to dealing with Hoban rather than his father.

'Perhaps he wanted merely a quiet place to drink himself to death,' said Michaelo, punctuating the comment with a sniff of disapproval.

Brother Michaelo, a fount of information, a master of scorn. Owen urged his horse to a trot.

TWO

A Clearing in the Wood

Dappled sunshine, a pair of horses tied to a low branch, and, beyond them, their riders lifting a stained cloak over the blood-soaked body, then gently lowering it and bowing their heads. Alisoun had spied another horse and a donkey across the clearing. Gerard Burnby, one of the York city coroners, talking in a low voice to the clerk who wrote on a wax tablet propped on the donkey's back. *Dogs. Throat torn out. Hoban Swann.*

Hearing that, Alisoun had hurried away; Hoban's wife would need her. She'd taken the narrow trail along the river to save time, her heart heavy, praying for Hoban, for Muriel, for the unborn child. Had she heard twigs snapping behind her? Turn and turn again, she'd seen nothing, yet sensed a shadow. By the time she'd reached Magda's house she was out of breath, yet she stopped only long enough to add to her basket a sleep powder gentle enough for an expectant mother – milk of poppy, valerian, and various herbs to calm and cool. The grieving mother-to-be would need sleep.

Now, as Alisoun sat in the shuttered bedchamber listening to Muriel Swann's even breathing, she sipped watered wine, calming herself. She'd had all she could do to quiet the grieving woman long enough to coax her to drink a cup of wine in which she'd mixed the sleep powder. Bartolf Swann had foolishly sent a hasty message to Muriel with the first servant he'd encountered, a boy who embellished the details into a terrifying tale of snarling wolves dismembering Hoban. Alisoun had arrived to find Dame Muriel's mother, Janet Braithwaite, physically restraining her daughter, who was leaning halfway out the window. She'd come perilously close to leaping out and ending her own life and that of the child she carried.

'How can I bear to see him so? How can that not curse our child?' Muriel had wailed.

After a long struggle involving the cook, reluctant at first to touch his mistress, they succeeded in guiding the expectant mother to a chair. Alisoun rubbed Muriel's hands and talked and talked until she at last convinced the grieving woman that she had seen Hoban, and that, though mortally injured, he was whole. Once Muriel could hear it, she fell to weeping, an expression of grief far safer than a leap out the window. Dame Janet had blessed Alisoun for knowing just what her daughter needed to hear. Alisoun wondered why the woman had not shouted for assistance.

As the wine settled Alisoun, she winced at the memory of her fearful flight along the river. She'd carried her bow – why hadn't she turned and confronted her shadow? At the least she would know whether she'd imagined it. Though she had not seen him since the night she'd tended his wound, she'd feared it was Crispin Poole, who would be concerned that she would connect this attack with his encounter with a vicious dog and consider it her duty to report it. Yet why then had he not shown himself? Confronted her? She would have reassured him that she meant to keep her word. Despite her doubts about why – honor or fear – she had no intention of betraying him. He, too, had been attacked in the wood.

Though not so viciously.

The royal forest of Galtres was a combination of woodland, marsh, small farms, and villages, subject to laws that protected game, especially deer, and their habitat, and also restricted the felling of trees. Owen had convinced Brother Michaelo to accompany him as his scribe, recording his examination of the corpse and the clearing in which Hoban lay. As coroner for Galtres, Bartolf Swann was known for keeping detailed accounts of the circumstances in which a body was found; though the coroner from York would have dutifully recorded his observations, Bartolf would expect a more thorough accounting from Owen. Michaelo had not been keen, admitting that he'd never ridden through Galtres without a full complement of armed guards, as was Archbishop Thoresby's wont. Bands of outlaws were known to hide there.

'Not to underestimate your skill with the bow, Captain Archer. But you are a complement of one.'

'I should think that sufficient to guard a monk who has taken a vow of poverty.' Owen was already regretting his request. But he had a purpose in testing Michaelo's mettle.

Once past the hovels of the poor clustered close to the walls of the city and St Mary's Abbey, Owen led the way through woodland and meadows, aware of a subtle shift as his awareness sharpened, his thoughts focused. He surprised himself with the thought that he'd missed this, the search, the sense of responsibility for restoring order.

Just past Overton, he guided his horse onto a track through coppiced woodland leading toward the marsh, fanning at the insects determined to blind his one good eye as he searched for signs of passage along the underbrush. He had instructed Michaelo in what to watch for. If the attacker had come through at night with a horse and one or more dogs, the animals at least would have spilled over the trail somewhere.

'It seems to me that unless Hoban's animals fled at the first sign of danger there must have been more than one attacker,' Michaelo had observed.

The monk showed promise in his attention to detail.

They'd almost reached the Swann property when Michaelo called Owen's attention to trampled underbrush at the turnoff to a narrow track.

Observant. He might just do. Owen thanked him.

The ground grew spongy, part of the marsh in a flood, and the insects even more insistent and loud, the buzzing and whining almost dizzying, conjuring in Owen unwanted memories of fields of corpses stewing in the sunlight after battles, the ever-present droning of flies feasting. He reflexively covered his nose and mouth. But the vision passed, and he muttered a prayer of thanks as the way opened into a clearing and the insects thinned out, heading for the more interesting body covered by a blood-stained cloak. Two men stood guard, one using a leafy branch in a futile effort to fend off the flies.

'We'll walk the horses from here,' said Owen. As he dismounted, he noticed how Brother Michaelo lifted the hem of his habit and tucked it into his belt in order to follow suit, glancing down with distaste at the blood-stained weeds near his booted feet.

'Yet so far from the body,' the monk muttered.

That was important. 'Either Hoban was dragged, or he was not the only one injured,' said Owen.

He could smell it now, the strong, metallic scent. It took a great deal of blood to overpower the ripeness of the early autumn marsh. The scent spooked the horses, and it took much coaxing to lead them closer to the body. The guards had covered their noses and mouths with rags – more for the swamp odors than for the blood, Owen guessed. Some believed the pestilence came from the odor of decay.

'Tie up the horses by that stand of trees,' Owen ordered Michaelo. 'Then come and join me by the body. Be ready to record my observations.'

Lifting the rag from his mouth, one of the guards said, 'Well met, Captain Archer, well met. We did not hope to see you so soon.'

'I am here to record the condition of the victim and the surrounding woods. What are your orders concerning the removal of Master Hoban's body?'

'The sheriff is sending a cart. We are to take it to Swann's home on Coney Street.'

Michaelo joined them. 'It would be a help if I might sit to write,' he said.

The man fanning the flies nodded in the direction of an uprooted stump.

'That will do.' Michaelo waited, but when no one rushed to bring it to him, he reluctantly fetched it, dragging it a few feet.

'Closer,' said Owen. 'It is better if you see for yourself what I am describing.'

With a sigh, Michaelo bent to the work of dragging it up to where Owen stood. Brushing off his hands, he sat down with grace and drew a wax tablet and stylus from his pack.

Owen crouched beside the body and nodded to the guards to lift the cloak away. Hoban's pale gold hair was matted with blood, his comely face twisted in pain and terror above an un-natural rictus that had been carved across his throat. Michaelo breathed in sharply at the sight, but made no complaint. Nor did he gag. All good signs.

Before beginning his examination, Owen bowed his head over Hoban's body. 'O Lord, I beseech you to receive him with love, and give comfort and ease to his wife, Muriel, his unborn child, and his father, Bartolf, who have lost one dear to them,' he prayed.

Michaelo and the guards responded with 'Amen.'

Owen used the hilt of his dagger to lift Hoban's chin, gingerly, for there was little left connecting head to body.

'Large dogs. Or wolves,' said one of the men. 'Ripped out his throat.'

Quietly, for Michaelo's ears, Owen corrected the account. 'A man wielding a knife slit Hoban's throat ear to ear.' His right shoe was missing, his stocking torn and blood-stained, his foot partially gnawed, his calf clawed. 'But a dog might have brought him off his horse,' said Owen. 'We will know more once we cut his clothes away.'

Michaelo glanced up, his stylus poised above the wax tablet. 'We?'

Owen chose to ignore him. 'But we will not do that here.' He looked up at the guards. 'Let me show you how to support the head and shoulders while we wrap him in the cloak, as in a shroud.'

The guards knelt and followed his instructions, working gently, with respect.

When Hoban Swann was shrouded, Owen thanked the guards and rose to take a slow turn round the clearing to see what it might reveal. Brother Michaelo followed, wax tablet in hand.

'Two men – or more if Hoban had already collected his father's hounds – his horse, and their own animals, as well as their victim,' said Owen. He crouched beside some flattened brush, poking it with a branch, stirring up the stench of urine and blood. 'One of the animals was injured.'

'Those attacking, or one of Swann's?' Michaelo wondered aloud.

'Cannot say. But I see no hoof prints just here, so one of the dogs, not a horse.' In fact, he'd noticed only one set of hoof prints; perhaps only Hoban had been mounted. He followed the bloody trail of flattened brush to the bank of the Ouse, toed an indentation in the mud, the grass compressed. 'Keel of a small boat. Planned with care, this attack? Or did Hoban happen upon men desperate to hide their activities? The boat could move the men and the dogs, but what of Hoban's horse?' He looked round, saw no hoof prints by the river.

'Master Bartolf said it had not returned to the house,' Michaelo noted. 'Nor were the dogs there.'

'One of the men might have ridden Hoban's mount to the ford farther upriver. We should go to his home, see whether the horse simply returned by now. Or the hounds.'

Michaelo made a sound deep in his throat.

'Are the signs of so much violence hard for you to see?' Owen asked.

'Does it not disturb you? The violence, the blood.'

'My dreams are haunted by it. But I honor the dead by doing what I can to expose the darkness that took them.'

'And bring them justice?'

'Justice? No. Breathing life into the dead, undoing their injuries – *that* would be justice, but that I cannot do. I seek to prevent further violence, expose the corruption . . .' Owen's words sounded hollow to him even as he uttered them. 'It is little enough.'

'You are an honorable man, Captain.' Michaelo held Owen's gaze for a moment. 'God surely blesses your work. Perhaps this is His intent, the work through which I might atone for my sins, serving you in this endeavor.'

It seemed he had taken to heart Owen's hint of having a possible ongoing need for his services. Time would tell whether the monk embraced that challenge. 'To Bartolf's home then. I pray the servant Joss is there.'

'Do you suspect him?'

'Until I talk to him, I've no way of knowing.' But how Joss received them might help Owen understand why Bartolf had become so concerned about entrusting the dogs to him that Hoban had felt it necessary to ride out of an evening to rescue them.

The ride to Bartolf's home gave Owen more to puzzle over. The track was wet and overgrown, part of the marsh when the Ouse flooded, hardly the path Hoban would commonly take. Why had he done so as night fell? And how did Joss happen on Hoban's body? With his one eye Owen swept the narrow track, looking for anything that seemed out of place. Again it was Michaelo, following, who found it.

'An item fallen beside the track,' he called out. 'To your left, wedged in a low branch.'

Owen's blind side. He dismounted, guided to the spot by the monk, who remained astride.

'There,' said Michaelo, 'near your right knee.'

Crouching down, Owen saw it, brown and easily dismissed as a dry leaf or part of the trunk, a leather pouch that fit in his palm. He opened it, finding within a waxed parchment packet containing an oily salve. He sniffed. Betony, boneset, and something else he could not identify – but Lucie would know what it was. The combination suggested a wound and a broken bone, common enough among country laborers, horsemen. Owen tucked it into his scrip.

Michaelo leaned down. 'Is it useful?'

'That depends on who dropped it, and when.'

No smoke rose from the long, low house, no dogs prowled the fenced area to one side. The gate was fastened, the structure appeared to be complete and undamaged. No one answered as Owen called out and opened the door. Spare furnishings, bowls, and moldy bread sat on a shelf along the wall that looked out into the dogs' enclosure. Up the ladder to the loft, a pallet was piled with skins, an overturned jug and bowl.

'Had he no one to tidy and cook for him?' Michaelo said with disgust.

'If so, whatever he paid them was too much,' said Owen. 'Perhaps Joss did it all.' Or someone else was missing.

Exiting the house, Owen spied the well-worn track he recalled taking the few times he had called on Bartolf. Much wider, more appropriate for accommodating Hoban on horseback with the dogs ambling along. 'Seems to me this would have been Hoban's choice to and from the house at dusk, not the narrow track to the clearing where he was killed.'

'Perhaps the way along the marsh was not his choice?'

'Possible, though I saw no sign of struggle at the house.'

Before mounting his horse, Owen cupped his hands and called out for Joss. Waited. Called again. Nothing.

'Perhaps he often disappeared,' said Michaelo, 'and that caused Bartolf to worry about the dogs.'

'Yet he spent several days in York without concern.'

'Ah,' said Michaelo.

As he led the way down the more traveled track Owen took the right-hand side. Though it meant he must turn in the saddle to look at Michaelo, he could search the right side of the track with his good eye while his companion searched to the left. So occupied, they rode in silence for a while.

'Geoffrey Chaucer must have galloped to Freythorpe Hadden the moment he had word of Dame Philippa's death,' Michaelo suddenly said. 'One wonders how he retains his position in the royal household, he spends so much time away.' He adjusted himself in the saddle so he might glance at Owen. 'How did Chaucer hear of her passing?'

'He came north on a mission, learned of our loss from the Merchets at the York Tavern.'

'Ah. That explains much. Yes, I see. He came north on a mission for Prince Edward, did he not?'

As he was biding in the home of Archdeacon Jehannes, Michaelo had been privy to some of Owen's discussions with his friend, and knew that a visit from Geoffrey was imminent. The prince grew impatient for an answer to his generous offer. Prince Edward, the future king, hero of Crécy and Poitiers, wanted Owen in his retinue, to be his spy in the north. He would have Owen keep his ears pricked for news of the powerful Northern families – the Percys and the Nevilles in particular – and report to him quarterly, or on the occasion of something he should hear at once. Owen had first been recruited by the prince's wife while his liege lord the archbishop yet lived. But coming from the prince himself – it now carried so much weight it felt like a royal command. Chaucer understood, and had tried to soften that with visions of the great honor it would be to serve the future King of England.

'The matter of your position in his household?' said Michaelo, misunderstanding Owen's silence.

'Yes.'

'A pity that the prince uses your friend as mediator, with the risk that such coercion might cause a rift between you.'

'A rift? Hardly.' Geoffrey was ever irritating.

'My error.'

Owen turned in his saddle to look at his companion. 'I take it you have considered Jehannes's idea that you serve as my secretary should I join the prince's household?' The position would require much correspondence, and who better qualified than the former secretary of an archbishop? Michaelo was also acquainted with many Nevilles and Percys, indeed, he had dealt with all the noble families in the North, overseeing the preparations for their visits to the archbishop and accompanying His Grace to their castles and manors.

'I have, Captain. I can think of no one better suited to the task.' Owen grinned in response, but Michaelo was quite serious as he continued. 'I would be honored, should you so wish it. Though my purpose was not to pry.'

Owen doubted that. The monk was likely eager to know whether he might once again move in high circles.

'My point was,' Michaelo paused as if searching for the right words, 'I fail to see how this afternoon's task proves my capability. Your duties for the prince would not be those of a coroner.'

'I disagree. If all were peaceful amongst the great families of the North, His Grace would have no need of me. Powerful men are no more likely to die in their beds than are the citizens of York. Prince's man or captain of bailiffs, I might have need of you in investigating a violent death.'

That was the other possibility. The mayor, aldermen, and wealthy merchants of York wished Owen to take up the work of captain of the city bailiffs, a position they had proposed with him in mind; indeed they could not understand why he would hesitate – a comfortable annuity, status in the city, work that was not much different from his previous responsibilities as the arch-bishop's captain of guards. Ah, but the difference was all – except for his journeys to his and Lucie's manors south of the city, Owen would have no cause to travel far. He would be home with his family, among his friends, with never the threat of long stretches away. It seemed ideal.

Yet he hesitated. With Lucie's shop, the York house, her father's manor and his own, which had come to him by Archbishop Thoresby's gift, his family did not need the city's annuity. As a third option, Owen might occupy himself, as he had done since Thoresby's death, seeing to their land and business, answerable to no one but his family and his own conscience. But whenever he considered that aloud, Lucie asked why, then, he continued to retain two of his former men. Alfred and Stephen had helped him rid his new manor of a band of thieves, and he'd left them there for a few weeks with Rollo, the steward he'd hired. But that had been several months ago. He was bored, she said. Bored with the life he'd yearned for all the while he worked for Thoresby. The old crow must be laughing in Heaven.

Lucie had favored the council's offer until Geoffrey appeared at Freythorpe with specifics about the one from Prince Edward. The prince offered a far more generous stipend than did the York council, as well as property, status, even a knighthood if Owen wished. He most assuredly did not, and Lucie supported him in that. Nor did she care a whit for wealth or status. It was the *work* she believed would be to his liking, more varied and potentially far more interesting than keeping order in the city. No doubt. But Owen knew the prince's reputation, the brutality of his raids in Gascony, and the cold-blooded sentences he laid down on anyone who crossed him. Even now, as ill as he was, Prince Edward's reputation was that of a querulous, vindictive lord. And what about his illness? How long would he have need of Owen?

'Both he and Princess Joan hope that you would continue to work for her, and the young Prince Richard,' Geoffrey had assured him. Teasing Owen that he seemed to be weakening, Geoffrey had quickly gone on to explain how it would work. Owen already had influential friends in York and elsewhere in the shire who might be encouraged to share information with him and invite him to accompany them on visitations throughout the area, introducing him to others in the prince's affinity. 'And your delightful Lucie, daughter of a knight. The prince is keen to make her acquaintance, as is my lady. An invitation to one of their northern estates, perhaps?'

Owen thought Lucie might enjoy such an honor. And he would take pleasure in making it possible, even more in escorting her. He disappointed himself in finding the proposal tantalizing. Against all reason he missed the status he'd held as Thoresby's spy and captain of guards.

'Captain of bailiffs,' Michaelo sniffed. 'You would choose that over the prince's household?'

'I take it you would not.'

'I envy you the luxury of choice.'

*   *   *

The Swann home stood on a double messuage in Coney Street. A fine wooden archway opened into a modest yard leading to a fine hall with a grand iron-bound oak door.

'A well-designed entry that shields the hall from the busy street,' Michaelo noted. 'Much more suited to the status of the family than the house in Galtres.'

At Owen's knock, the door was flung open by a young man-servant, his red eyes attesting to his affection for his late master.

'Captain Archer. They await you in the buttery,' he said, bobbing his head to both of them as he stepped aside to allow them passage.

The hall was lofty, with a tiled floor. Near the fire circle at its heart a woman paced, her silk and velvet gown shifting colors in the firelight. A rosary swung from her hands and her lips moved in prayer. Janet Braithwaite, Muriel Swann's mother. She was a large, imposing woman.

'God help us,' Michaelo murmured. 'She has a taste for going to law, ever vigilant regarding her "due". She took His Grace to law over a perceived slight.'

'Did she win?'

'Against John Thoresby?' Michaelo sniffed.

Apparently there was much Owen did not know about the late archbishop's standing in the community.

As soon as the servant informed her of the visitors, Dame Janet turned toward them. As she approached she wrapped the rosary round her left wrist as if a bracelet and shook out her skirts as if prayer were a dusty business. Her eyes bore no signs of grief, though her face was pinched in worry. 'You have brought a monk, Captain Archer? But I summoned our parish priest.'

'Brother Michaelo is not a priest,' said Owen. 'He is kindly assisting me, recording everything for Bartolf, as he would if the victim were not his son.'

'I see.' Janet nodded to Michaelo. 'I will have the boy summon Bartolf. He is just out in the kitchen. I did not want him plucking at Hoban's shroud.'

'He is coroner,' said Owen. 'He knows not to do that.'

'When not in his cups,' said Janet. 'Which is rare these days. The men said you had them wrap Hoban with care, that it was important not to disturb him until you arrived, and I saw to it that no one did so.' She began to turn toward the servant.

'No need to summon him, not yet,' said Owen.

'The old bear will not like it that he was not told of your presence.'

'First I would speak with Bartolf's manservant, Joss. Where might I find him?' Owen preferred to speak to the servant away from his master, and then examine the body without the father's witness.

'The one who precipitated all this? The old bear cursed him and turned him out. I went after him, ordered him back to the house in Galtres where he might be of some use. It is possible the dogs might return to the house. Not the horse. Alas, the horse was a hire, according to my daughter. Hoban was in a hurry to ride out before nightfall, no time to have his readied – it's stabled across the river. He meant to hire one from a stable outside Bootham Bar. More expense for them.' She frowned. 'So you did not stop at the house?'

'I did. Joss had not returned.'

'The lout. He should have been there hours ago.'

'Would you know of a reason Hoban might have carried a salve for a wound? Or had he broken a bone of late?'

'Not that I recall, but my daughter would know. After you have examined the body, I will take you up to her.' Without further comment Janet escorted the two of them to the buttery at the end of the hall.

Hoban had been placed on a stone counter. Oil lamps and a lantern provided light, the two guards standing over him. Two servants carrying bowls of oil and water stood by, awaiting instructions. Bartolf sat in a corner, head bowed.

'What are you doing in here?' Janet demanded.

'Praying for my son.' Bartolf's voice was hoarse with grief. His eyes silenced his challenger. 'The servants are ready to assist you in cleaning the body so that you might better see the wounds, Captain,' he said.

So much for sparing the old man. 'Do you have a pair of scissors to cut the cloth?' Owen asked.

One of the servants lifted a pair, offering to do it himself.

'I prefer to begin,' said Owen. He instructed the guards in freeing enough of the cloak that he might gain purchase in cutting through the wool. It was hard work, the wool stiffened by the dried blood. His hands would ache tonight.

Janet Braithwaite's silks rustled as she joined Owen at the table.
She groaned when Hoban's head was uncovered. 'My poor Muriel
must not see this.' She placed a beringed hand on the scissors.
'Permit me to do this, Captain. A woman of his family should
prepare his body.'

Owen saw no reason to object. 'Of course.' He nodded to the
guards. 'Steady his head and shoulders as best you can.'

Bartolf stood near his son's head, his face a mask of anger. 'I
will gut Joss, the bastard. He's guilty. He's the one. Why else run
away? I curse the day I hired him.'

So he'd overheard Owen's conversation with Dame Janet.
Quietly advising Brother Michaelo to ignore any such outbursts,
Owen was answered by an indignant sniff.

When the clothing was cut away, Owen motioned the servants
to lift the body so that Dame Janet might remove the blood-stiffened
fabric from beneath Hoban, the guards still steadying the head and
shoulders.

'Now work some of the oil into the crusted blood on his face,
then his torso, using wet cloths to wash it away once it has softened.
Gently,' Janet said as the young man jostled the head.

While Janet oversaw the servants, Owen motioned for Michaelo
to record that only the one leg and foot were injured, the finger-
nails broken and possibly one finger, and one palm was crossed
by what looked like a wide, ragged wound, the sort caused when
gripping the reins with bare hands as one falls from the horse.
'When you are finished with the head and torso, clean the hands,'
he said to the servants. Someone approached him from behind.

'This is Father Paul,' said Dame Janet.

'We will not be long,' Owen told him, keeping his eyes on the
servant who cleaned the torso. As he worked, several stab wounds
were revealed on the stomach just below the ribs. The other
worked the hands. Owen saw that he was right about the reins.
So Hoban was not wearing gloves. Perhaps in his haste he had
forgotten them.

Now for the most difficult part – the men supported the head
while Owen and Bartolf – he insisted, a father's right – turned
Hoban onto his side to examine the back. Scratches, no more.
They had just resettled him on his back and adjusted the head
when Michaelo touched Owen's arm and looked toward the door.

Muriel Swann stood in the doorway, head bowed, hand to heart. All those present followed suit. She took a step forward, then hesitated at the buttery threshold, a mere whisper of a woman, her silk gown loosely hanging from a thin frame that accentuated her swelling stomach. She looked toward her husband's body with fevered eyes. The servants bowed and withdrew, but when Owen asked if she wished to be alone with Hoban, Muriel shook her head. Her gown released the scent of lavender as she moved to where her husband lay. As she beheld him a sob shook her, and Alisoun, invisible until that moment, hurried into the room, whispering something to her charge. Muriel held up a hand. 'A moment.'

Time stood still as the mother-to-be bent to her murdered husband, touching, kissing, whispering endearments. Bartolf stood with head bowed, his body shaking with sobs. Owen was about to turn away when Muriel made a sound like a long sigh and began to slump to the stone floor. He lunged forward and caught her, lifting her in his arms. Though she carried a child in her womb she had little substance. Alisoun led him out through the hall and up outside steps to a bedchamber in the solar. Dame Janet followed on their heels, moving round to the foot of an elegantly draped bed. Alisoun turned back the bedclothes so that Owen could settle his charge on the silken sheets. Muriel stirred, but did not open her eyes as Alisoun drew the covers over her.

'I told her she should not look on his face, for the baby's sake,' Dame Janet sobbed. 'I pray he will not bear the mark of the devil.'

Alisoun put an arm round the woman, leading her back to the cushioned chair by the foot of the bed, near a lit brazier, and told the servant seated near the door to pour Dame Janet a cup of wine.

Asking Alisoun to step out onto the landing for a moment, Owen showed her the medicine pouch, explaining where Brother Michaelo had found it. 'Do you know the place?'

For a moment Alisoun stared and seemed to stop breathing, but then said simply, 'I know the track along the river.'

Owen opened the pouch, holding out the salve wrapped in parchment. 'I hoped this might be your preparation, or Magda's. I am keen to know for whom this was prepared.' He offered it to her, expecting her to examine it.

But she tucked her hands behind her back. 'I am sorry, but I

cannot help you. I pray you forgive my haste, but I must attend
Dame Muriel. Her mother is of little help.'

'Surely you cannot know whether or not it is your preparation
until you smell it. I can tell you that it contains betony and boneset.'

'A common mixture,' she said.

'Might you at least tell me what the third ingredient is?' He
held it up to her nose.

She recoiled. 'You waste my time, Captain, for I do not wrap
salves this way.'

He believed that she did. But he must step lightly with Alisoun
or risk losing any chance of coaxing her to help him.

'What has this to do with Hoban's murder?' Her tone was of
one offended.

'Permit me to explain. Hoban might have dropped this – or it
might have been dropped by his attacker.'

'Oh.' The sound was little more than a whisper. 'I prepare so
many salves, Captain.'

'This would be for a wound or a broken bone. As you know,
of course.'

'I cannot tell what it contains.' She gave her head a little shake
as she stepped away from him. With her abundant hair wrapped
in a white kerchief, her head seemed too large for her long, slender
neck, giving her the look of a plucked chick. A frightened one.

'It may come to you. If it does, I pray you send word.'

'Of course, Captain. Magda – Mistress Wilton came to tell me
that Magda stayed behind to attend a birth at Freythorpe?'

'Tildy, our former maidservant,' said Owen. Of course Lucie
would have the presence of mind to alert Alisoun to the delay.

'Do you know how long she will be away?'

'Until Tildy is safely delivered. Pray God that she is, and soon.'
Alisoun crossed herself. 'May God watch over dear Tildy.'

Clearly an afterthought, which troubled Owen. A healer's first
concern should be for the patient.

'I leave Dame Muriel in your competent hands,' Owen said.
Pray God her indifference was a passing mood.

He noted how Alisoun hesitated, as if gathering her wits about
her before returning to the bedchamber. Understandable in the
circumstances, yet her demeanor troubled Owen. Alisoun being
prickly was normal. And she did carry much responsibility here in

this house of mourning, holding the lives of mother and child in her hands. But he sensed a reluctance to engage with him. He was almost certain she had recognized the pouch and the salve, yet refused to admit it. Why?

Down in the hall, Owen thanked Michaelo for his assistance.

The monk gathered his things and rose with a grimace he attempted to hide with a bow. Sore from the long ride and the discomfort of writing in far from ideal circumstances, Owen guessed. 'I will have a report for you on the morrow, Captain.'

'Rest first. Send word when I might collect it.'

Michaelo bobbed his head and departed with less than his usual grace.

In the kitchen, Owen discovered Bartolf dulling his grief with ale. From the looks of him, he was making good progress. A pity to pull him back.

'I have some questions for you.'

Bartolf squinted at Owen. 'Of course you do, Captain. 'S why I came for you, to set about finding my Hoban's murderer. How might I assist you?' His words slurred as his head wobbled over the tankard and his eyelids fluttered.

'Is Joss the only one working for you at the house in Galtres?'

Bartolf slowly shook his head. 'Nay, Cilla keeps my house. Not so young na more, but we're none of us so young anymore.' He let his head drop as if it were too heavy to support, rolled his eyes upward to peer at Owen through the bush of white hair. 'Is it true Joss has bolted?'

'He's not at the house, but whether he chose to run off is more than I can say at present.' Owen lifted the man's chin. 'Why did you suddenly worry about the dogs?'

'Zephyrus and Apollo? Because—' Bartolf blinked as if he'd just lost the thought. 'Rumor, that was it. A rumor of a wolf roaming near the house, and that lout Joss would run before he'd protect the hounds.' He closed his eyes. 'And someone'd seen Zephyrus and Apollo running loose.' A sloppy nod. 'Running loose!' He banged his fist on the table.

A wolf. Was this what Magda had foreseen? 'Who had seen them? Who had seen the wolf?'

Bartolf's head wobbled. 'Stopped me in street as I came from tavern.' His eyelids were closing. 'Didn't know him, but he knew me.'

'Someone came up to you and told you he'd seen a wolf in the forest? And your dogs running loose?'

'Zactly.'

Had one person really given him both pieces? Or had Owen just put the idea in his head?

'Did you tell anyone about this when you came home?'

'Hoban.'

Bartolf attempted to pour himself more ale. Owen took the jug and poured a small amount into the bowl, then set the jug out of Bartolf's reach.

'Were you and Hoban alone when you told him?'

'Why d'you ask?'

'I am hoping that you described the man who stopped you on the street, might even have said his name, and someone here in the house overheard.'

'What man?'

Owen closed his eye and prayed for patience. Changing the subject, he asked, 'Where does Cilla live?'

'Oh, Cilla. She works for many, not just me.' Bartolf reached up to scratch his head, found he was still wearing his hat. 'Bloody – I kept this on to remind myself to go back out there, search for Zeph and Pol.'

'My men will search for them at first light, Bartolf. Tell me, are they lawed?'

'Course they're lawed. Three claws cut off on each paw, poor fellows, but that's the rule of the forest. See? That's why I worry. Joss – he doesn't remember they can't defend themselves against wolves or dogs who haven't lost claws. Shouldn't be in the wood, not like that, but I've heard howling and I fear— Then this man, he said a wolf is about. Hoban went to bring them home.' Bartolf sucked in breath. 'My son.'

Quickly, before the man began to sob, Owen asked him who he used as a scribe.

'Elwin. He clerks at the minster. I'd send for him when I had need.' Bartolf touched his hat and began to scramble to his feet. 'My dogs.'

'I told you, my men will search for them at first light. You stay here tonight. Get some rest. Stay safe. Muriel needs you.'

'Oh, aye, the poor bairn. Aye.' As Owen was rising Bartolf grabbed his arm. 'First light? You swear?'

'They will spend the night at the Riverwoman's house and go forth at dawn. I swear.'

'Bless you, Captain. Bless you.'

Owen patted him on the shoulder and took his leave, promising again to search for the dogs. Bartolf, slumped, did not look up.

Alisoun handed Dame Janet a cup of wine and then moved to the window of the bedchamber, opening the shutters for some air. Her heart jumped as Captain Archer strode out from the kitchen, taking off his hat as he paused in the back garden and raked back his hair. The dark curls were threaded with silver that caught the late-afternoon sun. So handsome. Lucie Wilton was a most fortunate woman. Alisoun fought the urge to hurry down to catch him, tell him she'd been frightened, but she'd thought better of it and wanted him to know that she had prepared that salve for Crispin Poole after he was attacked by a large dog. The captain would do all he could to protect her, and Poole as well, if he was innocent, she knew that. All she need do was run down.

But she just stood there, watching him don his hat and stride off.

THREE

Salves, Barbers, Secrets

Home at last, God be thanked. Owen paused at his garden gate, watching his two eldest race round the tall linden in raucous play. He took advantage of their distraction to slip into the workshop behind the apothecary, hoping that Jasper might have a moment to examine the salve. It was even possible that he'd prepared it.

He heard voices, but the shop appeared empty until he looked beyond the counter and saw his son placing small packages into a basket held by a young woman. They spoke quietly, but the tone was playful, teasing. When the basket was full, Jasper took it from her arm and carried it as he escorted the young woman to the door, bowing as he handed it to her. She blushed up at him, then hurried out into the street with a soft *Benedicite*.

When had Jasper grown so tall, and so courtly? With his fair hair ever tumbling in his eyes, he still seemed a lad to Owen, but he was a man now. Eighteen.

Owen strode forward into the shop.

'Da!' Jasper looked satisfyingly happy to see him. 'Is it true Hoban Swann was felled by his own dogs?'

The rumors had begun. 'I am not certain what happened, but I doubt his dogs were the attackers. Unless Zephyrus and Apollo have mastered the use of a dagger. I would appreciate your not spreading that round.'

'That the dogs are gods, running loose with daggers?' Jasper laughed. 'Who would believe such a tale? Have you found them?'

'No. I've found precious little for my pains.' It was Owen's turn to grin. 'She is pretty.'

A vivid blush, the curse of such fair skin and hair. 'She is betrothed to a blacksmith. Fortunate man. He'll never deserve her.'

'And you would?'

'My heart belongs to a brown-haired, brown-eyed healer.'

Pity, Owen thought. 'Speaking of whom, Alisoun said this was not her preparation. Perhaps yours?' He drew out the pouch, opened it, placed the parchment on the counter.

Jasper bent down to sniff, glanced up. 'Safe to handle?'

'I am unharmed. I smell boneset and betony. What do you think?'

Jasper opened the packet. Taking a little on a fingertip, he tasted it. 'Not much else. Some calendula to soften a scar, I think. Not mine. Wrapping's wrong. A barber's stock? They set children's and laborers' limbs after falls, accidents with carts. Often the broken bone is only one of the injuries. This would serve wounds as well. And dog bite.'

'Has anyone come in for something for the bite of a dog?'

'While you were away? No. Though there's been talk about wolves in the forest while you were away.' He sniffed again. 'Calendula.' He nodded. 'Ma told me about Tildy. What do you think?'

'Pray for her, son. Magda is a healer, not a miracle-worker.' Owen picked up the packet, and was returning it to the pouch when Jasper made a sound as if about to speak. Owen glanced up, curious.

Jasper fingered the pouch. 'Any markings?'

Owen turned it over. The pouch had been fashioned from a mere scrap of leather of poor quality, worthless but for keeping out the weather. Someone had sewn it together and added a narrow strip of leather to tie it closed. A common item. 'Nothing but a long score.' He held that to the light. 'Do you recognize it?'

Jasper hesitated, then shook his head.

Lucie paced the hall with baby Emma in her arms while the nursemaid helped Kate prepare food for the older children. As Kate was Tildy's sister, Lucie had invited her to sit for a moment on her return and have a bowl of ale as they exchanged their news. The young woman had listened to Lucie's account of her sister's condition with outward calm, but her hands had shaken as she poured more ale. Soon came tears, and a flood of questions Lucie could not answer. That Magda Digby attended her sister was a great comfort, but Lucie judged it wise to ask the children's nurse, Lena, to assist in the kitchen while Kate caught her breath.

Emma had just fallen asleep in Lucie's arms when Owen returned. She put a finger to her lips as he began to speak.

He slumped down onto a chair, groaning as he stretched out his legs.

'A long day, I know,' she said softly. They'd departed Freythorpe shortly after dawn. 'Sit down, have some ale. Bess brought it when she saw we'd returned.'

'Sit with me?'

She was about to protest that Emma might wake if she stopped walking, but seeing in the shadows beneath his eyes the toll the day had taken, she relented. Lena could take over now. 'I'll be but a moment. Some bread and cheese?'

'And ale?'

She smiled, humming under her breath as Emma stirred.

When she returned without the baby, Owen took no time in launching into an account of all that he'd witnessed since parting from her on the road. A long day indeed. She was surprised that a man had murdered Hoban, not wild dogs. She'd heard the rumors. Whether or not she also felt relief, she could not decide.

'I can tell you what Bess has heard about the Swanns,' she said. 'Talk in the city is that Bartolf has become forgetful. He's been missing appointments. Muriel and Hoban feared he was drinking too much. Or too alone out there. They invited him to bide with them in the city for a fortnight.'

Owen took a good long drink. 'And he agreed?'

'Bess did not say whether he argued about it.'

'Did Bartolf mention it to you?'

'He said little on the journey back. I will ask Alisoun to keep her ears pricked for gossip in the household.'

'That would be helpful.' Owen finished the bread and cheese, washing it down with ale, then sat back, looking less drained by the day. 'The old man's mind is so muddled with grief and drink I doubt I'll learn much more from him.'

'Poor man. And Muriel – may God watch over her.'

'May He do a better job than He has so far.' Owen took another long drink. 'What do you know of Bartolf's servants Cilla and Joss?'

'Nothing at all about him. You might ask Bess about Cilla. Everyone's worked at the York at one time or another. I've heard that she considers herself a healer, though she's said to do more harm than good. Magda would be able to tell you more. Pray God she returns soon, with happy news.' She shivered, remembering Daimon holding his wife's swollen hand, whispering prayers.

'Tildy. Yes.' Owen pulled Lucie close and she rested her head against his chest. They sat that way, in comforting silence, until Hugh and Gwenllian came thundering in from the garden.

Lena quickly opened the kitchen door and herded them in.

But Lucie sat up, the moment gone. 'Will you join Geoffrey at the York this evening?'

'I'd forgotten. I'd best, or he will tell tales about me.'

Owen's distrust of Geoffrey Chaucer puzzled Lucie. Yes, Geoffrey was a gossip, but he was also a loyal friend who would never tell a tale that might damage or even challenge Owen's standing in the city. He had hurried to Freythorpe Hadden upon arriving in York and hearing of Dame Philippa's death. Geoffrey had been fond of Philippa, and she of him. While biding with them in York after the archbishop's death, Geoffrey had endeared himself to Lucie by keeping her ailing aunt entertained. Arm in arm, he and Philippa would stroll round St Helen's churchyard and down Stonegate, she telling him what she could remember of the people passing by – her memory came and went – he embellishing the bits with invented tales of their younger, secret exploits, inspiring much laughter. Philippa could talk of nothing else when he was called back to London. *Such a storyteller, he is! And wise.* Yet Owen now doubted his sincerity.

For the moment, Lucie bit her tongue, thankful that Owen asked for no response, deep in thought, reaching out to pour more ale. She sat sipping her own for a while, resisting the temptation to tease him about how eagerly he had taken up the search. She did not want to influence his decision about the future. For so long she had worried about how he would occupy himself without his work for Thoresby.

She had not pushed, knowing that he still mourned the archbishop, the man he'd resented in life. It was a hard lesson for Owen, seeing in hindsight the extent to which Thoresby had given him the freedom to go about his work as he saw fit. A betrayal and a death had cast an additional pall over his last days with the archbishop, and Lucie had suspected Owen wanted to be left in peace to grieve a while longer. But when Bartolf and Brother Michaelo hailed them on the road home, Owen had not hesitated to engage. It seemed God did not intend to allow him a moment of idleness.

The people of York would be pleased that he had taken this in hand. Their friends, the guildsmen, the city bailiffs, the mayor and aldermen, Princess Joan, Prince Edward, Geoffrey Chaucer – they had all anxiously waited for him to take the first step into his future. Especially Geoffrey, for it was he who had suggested Owen to Princess Joan. Would this investigation lead to his accepting the role of captain of bailiffs? Lucie had considered it a tame post relative to that proposed by Prince Edward, but Hoban Swann's murder seemed to suggest otherwise.

'The Swanns are fortunate to have your help,' she said when Owen seemed to be surfacing.

He frowned down at the bowl he had just picked up. 'I have learned nothing of use.'

'You will.'

His dark eye bore into her, then he suddenly grinned, melting her heart. 'Divine revelation?'

She leaned over to kiss his dimple. 'Belief in you, my love.'

'In truth I've come away with more questions than answers. Will you see Alisoun soon?'

'I can. You said she seemed troubled?'

'I did. It might be the weight of responsibility, but I would be grateful if you would talk with her.' Owen drew her up into an embrace ending with a long kiss.

'Well now,' Lucie said as they parted. 'I look forward to tonight.'

'I will not tarry at the tavern.'

'Best not.' She laughed. 'I forgot to ask how Brother Michaelo coped – the forest, the swamp, the blood?'

'Better than I had expected. He is useful. Quite useful. Observant. It was he who found the pouch.'

'So you will use him again?'

'If he is willing, I am glad to do so.'

'You secretly delight in his sardonic mutterings.'

'At present there is little of that. Too little. I could use a distraction from the grim parts of the task.'

'Then I pray he recovers his righteousness.'

*   *   *

After sending Alfred and Stephen away to spend the night in Magda Digby's home so they might begin their search for Joss, Cilla, and the dogs at first light, Owen had spent a few hours in the York Tavern with Geoffrey and his friend George Hempe, a York bailiff. Geoffrey's presence happily prevented Hempe from pursuing his campaign to convince Owen to take on the captaincy of the bailiffs. Both were keen to hear what he'd learned of Hoban Swann's murder, and to offer their opinions. Bess suggested Owen ask Bartolf's nearest neighbors about Cilla's whereabouts. As Bartolf had said, she worked around, for whoever needed an extra hand.

'But she may be of little help,' Bess had said. 'She's a queer one, that woman, speaks in squeaks and squawks, growls, hisses, and moves in prances and springs. Mark me, she's more than a little mad. Yet she's a hard worker, will take on any task and do her best, which is better than most. But God help those fool enough to call for her when they need a midwife. I've heard such tales . . .' Bess had rolled her eyes.

'May God watch over Cilla.' Lucie said when Owen told her. 'Amen.'

Even with that worry, Owen had no trouble engaging Lucie in some bed sport before sleep.

Shortly after dawn, Alisoun woke to the sounds of Dame Muriel and her mother, who had chosen to sleep the night with her daughter. Muriel talked and wept as Dame Janet stroked her hair and assured her that all would be well, she must be strong for her child. Alisoun slipped away to fetch some food and replenish the watered wine mother and daughter had sipped through the night.

In the kitchen she found Bartolf Swann snoring by the fire, the cook grumbling as he moved about his morning chores trying not to wake the old man.

'You'll be comforted to know that Captain Archer's men stayed the night at the Riverwoman's,' he said as he gathered bread and cheese for her, and filled the jug with more wine. 'They will keep trouble from your door.'

'What right had he—' Alisoun stopped herself when she saw the curious look the cook gave her. Of course he would expect her to be eased by that. 'How do you know this?'

'The master. After the household went to bed he talked and talked. Much of it jabber – pushing away the devils that haunt a man when he's gone past sensible drink. He'll drink himself into the grave. But who can blame him, poor man, his only son?'

She remembered standing at Magda's door in the deepening evening watching the broad back of Crispin Poole as he crossed over to the bank. And that other observer, standing at the edge of the wood. Had Poole dropped the salve, or had it been taken from him? Either way, she imagined him coming to the house yesterday at dusk, needing more, and discovering the captain's men there. He would be angry, thinking she had betrayed him. But why would she? What had his misadventure to do with Hoban Swann? Except – the dogs. How he'd insisted it was but one dog, though she was certain she'd first heard a pair. God help her.

She should not have used that particular pouch. She and Jasper had found the scrap of leather, making up a story about what had scored it, silly chatter. And now, when the captain showed it to Jasper, he'd see the mark and remember. Would he betray her? Of course he would, he would do anything to earn the captain's approval. He was ever talking about the time he'd helped the captain catch a thief and a murderer. That was when he'd began calling him 'da' instead of 'the captain'.

She delivered the jug of wine to Muriel's chamber. Mother and daughter were at last asleep, a small miracle. By the light coming through the shutters Alisoun guessed that Jasper might be up by now, readying the shop for early customers or sweeping the street in front. She could go to him, but he would want to know why she begged the favor of secrecy. What would she say? *I know of a man who was attacked by dogs but I'm certain he did not murder Hoban Swann*? But how could she possibly be certain? She knew little about Crispin Poole. She did not understand why she was so keen to defend him. Because she did not trust the captain to believe his innocence?

Holy Mother, help me. Give me a sign to show me the way. Alisoun plucked her shawl from a hook by the door, hurried down the steps and through the gate into the neighbors' back garden, taking the path to the York Tavern's yard, next door to the apothecary. She hurried along, letting her eyes wander round the flowerbeds and fruit trees, up to the dawn sky, but suddenly she stopped, a voice in her head warning her that hurrying to Jasper to find out whether he'd betrayed her was a betrayal in itself. He would guess it was important. What could she say? *Is this my sign, Blessed Mother?*

Turning round, she hurried back to the Swann house, her heart pounding, frightened by her own confusion.

'I've spoken with all the gate guards,' said Hempe. 'Sounds like Joss entered and left by Bootham Bar, both times in a hurry. On his way out, he pushed past a family who were in the queue, saying he must make haste, he'd been ordered back to the Swann home in Galtres to stand guard. Toby let him pass. "Thought it best to see the back of him before he started brawling," he said.'

'So he headed back to Bartolf's home but never arrived,' said Owen. 'I don't like that.'

'Nor do I.'

'And what of Hoban? Had he gone out alone?'

'Alone but for a hired horse spooking at all the folk – he left just before the closing of the gates. Said he was doing a favor for his father, fetching his beloved dogs, and the warden agreed to watch for him, let him back in. Course he never came. No one apparently following him. Nor Joss when he came in early in the morning.'

'How early?'

'Almost the first one at the gate.'

'So early,' said Owen. 'What was he doing out on that track at such an hour?'

'Might he have heard something?'

'Hoban would have died quickly,' said Owen. 'By morning there would be nothing to hear.'

'So the manservant heard him attacked in the night, but stayed put until first light?' Hempe suggested.

'I want to find Joss,' said Owen as he handed Hempe the leather packet containing the salve. 'Could you have a man go round to the barbers in the city? Ask whether this was made by them, and, if so, for whom? How long ago?'

Hempe frowned down at it.

Thinking he'd offended the man, Owen reached for the pouch. 'Forgive me. You have your own duties.'

Hempe closed his hand round the packet. 'Not at all. I'm just trying to decide who has the wits for the task.' He glanced up with a wink. 'I have it. Just the man.'

As Owen was thanking Hempe, Brother Michaelo opened the garden gate and stepped through. 'Now that's a sight I never expected to see. You move in ever-widening circles,' Hempe said, chuckling.

'*Benedicite*, Captain, Master Bailiff.' Michaelo handed Owen two rolls of parchment. 'One for you, Captain, and one for the city, if they should wish to have a record.'

Hempe nodded to both of them. 'I must be off. I will let you know what we discover,' he said, holding up his clenched hand.

Owen thanked him and turned to Michaelo. 'You are faster than I'd hoped. So. Now that you've had a night to sleep on it, are you willing to work with me again?'

'The experience was – I had not understood the burden of your work. Observing you, I felt—' Michaelo lifted his hand as if to brush aside the thought. 'I would be honored to work with you again, Captain, if it please you.'

'Good. I have not yet broken my fast. Would you care to join me while we talk?' Owen gestured toward the house.

'I do not wish to impose myself—'

'I invited you so that we might discuss business. It is I who impose.'

The monk bowed. 'I am at your service.'

Lucie observed them with some curiosity as she called to Kate to bring food to the hall. 'The children are at market with Lena, so you should not be disturbed,' she said as she moved toward the garden door.

'I pray I am not interrupting your morning,' said Michaelo.

Lucie assured him she had been on her way to the shop when they arrived. 'You are always welcome in my home, Brother Michaelo. *Benedicite*.' On a pilgrimage to St David's in Wales, Brother Michaelo had been a loving companion to Lucie's father, Sir Robert D'Arby, nursing him in his final illness. When Michaelo returned to York he had brought the news of her father's death, and shared with her all he could recall of her father's last days. He had been a great comfort to her while Owen remained in Wales.

'Ale?' Owen asked.

When Michaelo nodded, Owen poured for both of them, helped himself to some bread and cheese, and ate quietly for a moment, watching the monk study the room while he sipped his ale.

'A handsome, most comfortable hall,' said Michaelo when he noticed Owen's one-eyed regard.

'It is. A generous gift from your friend Sir Robert.'

'My—' Michaelo bowed his head. 'May he abide in God's grace.'

It was on that journey that Owen had witnessed the gentler side of the usually sharp-witted, arrogant Norman monk. A revelation. And, afterward, he'd benefitted from the man's discretion about his involvement with Welsh rebels.

'Do you know Elwin, the clerk who serves as Bartolf Swann's scrivener?'

'No, but if he is a clerk I should be able to find out about him. What do you need to know?'

'For the moment, merely where I might find him.'

They were interrupted by the arrival of Geoffrey Chaucer.

'Oh, forgive me, I—' He looked from one to the other, clearly interested.

'Brother Michaelo has already delivered the report of my observations,' said Owen.

Michaelo rose. 'I will see to the other matter we discussed, Captain.'

Owen thanked him.

When Michaelo had departed, Geoffrey took his chair and helped himself to some ale. 'What did I miss?'

'Nauseating courtesy. I must find a way to resurrect the more palatably snide Brother Michaelo.'

FOUR

A Rumor of Wolves

For a moment Owen let the sounds of a busy night in the York Tavern override the voices of his two companions, George Hempe and Geoffrey Chaucer – tankards thumping on the long tables, feet stomping on the floor in time to Tucker's fiddling, laughter rising up, folk greeting latecomers, and beneath it all the steady rumble of men's deep voices. He leaned back and stretched out his legs with a sigh of contentment.

Until Old Bede coughed out his latest conspiracy. 'The sheriff says he was beaten but he did not show us the body, did he? Wolves attacked Hoban's grandfather the hour Hoban was born. It's true. And now the wolves have returned to Galtres. The sheriff and the mayor, and some what are sitting right in this room' – his eyes slid to Owen's table – 'don't want us to know, but it's plain, eh?' The old man sucked his teeth and his eyes narrowed to slits as he prepared to hawk up his bile and spit it out.

'Not on my clean floor, Bede. Out in the alleyway with you,' Bess Merchet warned as she entered the public room in the nick of time. 'And you're out for good if I catch you spreading such lies in my tavern again.' With hand to mouth, Bede lurched across the floor, almost knocking over a man who had risen to propose a toast at the next table. 'I count on you to remind him what he risks,' Bess told the old gossip's companions. 'And it goes for all of you as well. *Dogs* attacked Hoban. There are no wolves in Galtres, nor in all of England, not any more.'

As if apologizing for her guest, Bess bobbed her head to Bartolf Swann, who had left his seat back in the corner of the tavern, where he'd been drinking with a pair of stonemasons, and was weaving his way amongst the tables, heading for the door. The old man nodded blearily as he departed.

'She would make a fine bailiff,' said Geoffrey.

To the other side of Owen, Hempe choked on his ale. 'A woman? She could never pull her weight.'

'Oh, I think you are wrong about that, master bailiff.'

Hempe leaned close to Owen. 'Master Chaucer goes too far.'

'He meant to rile you, and he succeeded. Be easy, George.'

It was not entirely true, Bess's claim. There were still a few wolf packs in England, or so it would seem. Whitby Abbey boasted wolf pelts of recent vintage, and the monks of Rievaulx Abbey had reported a wolf pack on the north moors the previous winter, feeding on sheep. Magda Digby knew of a pack that wintered in Galtres, though the warden of the forest denied it, blaming the loss of livestock on poaching outlaws.

So that part of Bede's story was possibly more accurate than Bess gave him credit for, and the rest was not entirely his imagining. Hoban's grandfather had been attacked by a pack of wild dogs, not wolves, at the very moment of his grandson's birth. The midwife had crossed herself when she heard and said it bode ill for the boy. That was long before Owen had come to York, but he had heard the story from enough folk to give it credence. Curséd old man, conjuring the horror of Hoban's murder in the presence of his grieving father.

Geoffrey rocked his tankard on the table as he observed the room with a half-smile. Owen followed his gaze to the one-armed merchant, Crispin Poole.

Curious, he leaned over to ask, 'Are you acquainted with Poole?'

Starting, Geoffrey bowed his head as if realizing how he had been staring. 'He intrigues me. As if a pirate donned the clothing and the bearing of a man of means, a prominent citizen of the city. We are not acquainted, but I hope to remedy that.'

'The prince is interested?'

Geoffrey looked at him askance. 'Why would you think that? How would His Grace know of this man?'

'You discomfited him, Master Chaucer,' said Hempe. Indeed, Poole now stood, counting out some coin. 'No amount of tailoring can hide his stump of an arm. A man knows better than to stare.'

Owen agreed. He felt a kinship with Poole. They'd had a few ales together, sharing their mutual discomfort about their appearance. Poole had seemed keen to hear about how Owen had created a new life, started a family. *I envy you, Archer.*

'I will seek him out and beseech his forgiveness at the first opportunity,' said Geoffrey.

'Oh, aye, that would surely win his favor.' Hempe made a face at Owen as if to say his companion was quite mad.

But he was wrong about that. Geoffrey's mind was sharp, focused. What was his business with Crispin Poole, that is what Owen wished to know. He would bear watching.

'So what have Alfred and Stephen discovered?' Hempe asked.

'Still no one at Bartolf's,' said Owen. 'They've begun searching all the properties nearby. A neighbor told them Cilla rarely worked for just one household, she once worked for Bess – for all of a day – but we've found no one who's seen her since Hoban's death.'

'Worked here for a day?' Geoffrey laughed. 'What was her crime?'

'More than a little mad, as Bess put it,' said Owen.

'And the taverner would have none of that.' Hempe laughed.

According to Bess, Cilla had also worked for Archdeacon Jehannes for a brief period. Perhaps he might offer some insight.

'And none of the barbers recognized the salve?' Owen asked Hempe.

'None would admit to it.'

'Would you?' asked Geoffrey. 'Such a murder, and then the bailiff's man comes round with such a question.'

'A wretched business, all in all,' Hempe mumbled into his tankard.

The sun was low in the sky and a freshening breeze had dispelled the late-afternoon warmth. Lucie stood at the entrance to the walled herb garden considering the order of her autumn chores. She had lost time with the trip to Freythorpe and there was much work ahead before the first frost. Owen enjoyed doing the digging and the heavier work, but with Hoban's murderer to find he might not now have time to help. If only Edric, her second apprentice, had stayed until after Yuletide, as originally planned. But as he'd never seemed at ease after his falling out with Jasper over Alisoun's affections, Lucie had not tried to dissuade him from what appeared to be an excellent opportunity in Beverley.

'Dame Lucie?' Alisoun stood beneath the linden.

With a fleeting thought of having summoned the young woman

with her reverie – why did such fantasies arise at dusk? – Lucie hastened toward her, noticing that the young woman shivered in the cooling evening. 'You came out without a cloak or wrap? Is it Dame Muriel? Do you need help?'

'I would welcome some advice, but I was most eager to speak with the captain. Is he here?'

'No. He's at the tavern. Might I help?'

'Did you know he gave his men leave to sleep in Magda's house last night without ever asking my permission?'

'He did not—?'

'Dame Magda entrusted her home to me in her absence. It is my responsibility. But he never thought to ask.'

Accustomed to the young woman's temper, Lucie did not take offense at her abruptness. 'He knows better than to do that,' she said. 'I will speak with him, though I do not believe he meant for them to stay another night.' She put an arm round Alisoun's slender shoulders. 'Come in, do. We will talk in the warmth.'

Lucie guided Alisoun past the table where Jasper poured over some books. 'My first husband's garden journals,' she said softly.

Alisoun greeted Jasper as she passed him, but he did not even look up from his reading. A falling out? Lucie wondered. She led Alisoun to a long bench by the window.

'Are you at ease biding in the Swann home?' Lucie asked.

'I would prefer to sleep at Magda's, but I cannot in good conscience leave Dame Muriel at the moment.'

'Of course. They are treating you well?'

'If you are asking whether they treat me with respect, yes, they do. But I do worry that Dame Muriel might need a more experienced midwife. She picks at her food – the baby cannot be getting enough nourishment.'

'Fear about her first pregnancy, and now her grief, her husband murdered – I am not surprised she has no appetite. But she must keep up her strength or the baby will grow strong as the mother weakens.'

'Will you tell the captain he was wrong to send his men to Magda's without asking my leave?'

'I am sorry he was so thoughtless, Alisoun. Yes, I will speak with him. But surely you cannot think they would wreak havoc there? They respect Magda. Fear her a little, I think, and her dragon.' Lucie took Alisoun's hands. They were still cold. 'Something warm to drink? Are you hungry?'

'No, I cannot stay long. I know they are good men, that they will do no harm.' Alisoun gestured as if at a loss to explain.

'But my husband should have told you of his plan, and asked your leave.'

Alisoun's expression brightened. 'You understand.'

'I do, Alisoun. I do.' Owen doubtless devised the plan as he spoke to the men without a thought to how it might seem to Alisoun, how proud she was of the responsibility. He needed to apologize. 'I will make it clear how he offended.'

'I am grateful.' But there was yet a shadow in her eyes. Something still troubled her.

'Is there more?'

Alisoun glanced out the window for a moment, as if searching for the right words. 'All the household is frightened.' She turned back to Lucie. 'Has the captain learned anything of use? Something that might lead him to the murderers?'

'I wish I had some encouraging news for you, but I've nothing, Alisoun.'

'Nothing?'

A momentary light in Alisoun's eyes gave Lucie pause. Relief? Why would she be relieved? Gone now. It had flickered out as quickly as it had appeared, yet it had been there, she was sure of it.

'I hoped to have something to tell Dame Muriel,' said Alisoun. 'Not that it would cheer her, but – I worry about how little she eats. Have you a powder to stir her appetite? Safe for a woman with child?'

Time to grieve, that is what the widow needed, but Lucie understood Alisoun's concern. 'Of course. I will send Jasper with a physick in the morning, if that will do.'

'That will do very well, thank you.' Alisoun took Lucie's hands, pressed them.

Hers were warmer now, but the smile was tight, forced. Had Lucie imagined that? Knowing how quick the young woman was to take offense, she resisted reassuring her that she was equal to the task. Best to say nothing. She seemed to have her wits about her, which was essential. The child Muriel Swann carried was all the more precious now that Hoban was dead. But the expectant mother's history of miscarriages did not bode well.

Bess had joined the group of friends at Owen's table, but kept an eye on old Bede as he stumbled back in from the yard. 'A round on the house for my good friends,' she told a passing servant, gesturing round the table. 'We could all use it after that scurvy pizzle spouted off,' she growled.

Geoffrey choked on his ale.

Bess patted him on the back. 'A pity to waste Tom's ale up your nose, Master Geoffrey.'

Beside them, Owen watched Bede and Crispin Poole crossing paths. Bede bobbed his head to Poole, who ignored him and walked out.

'I don't blame Poole. That old fool Bede cannot bear seeing folk enjoying themselves,' Hempe muttered.

'Scurvy pizzle, spouting off, oh, my dear Mistress Merchet, you are a poet,' said Geoffrey, wiping tears of laughter from his eyes. 'But the old man means no harm, does he?'

'He is not good for business,' said Bess. 'You saw Crispin Poole take his leave. And Bartolf Swann. And now his companions.' She nodded to the stonemasons as they passed. 'Folk come here to forget, not be minded of the day's miseries.'

'To be fair, it's common knowledge that dogs played a part in Hoban's death,' said Owen. 'For once the old gossip is merely repeating what he's heard.'

'To what purpose? That's my point,' said Hempe.

'He wants attention,' said Bess, 'and with neither wit nor charm all he has is his knack for annoying.' She slipped a hand over Owen's. 'Am I to have a bailiff living next door?'

'I will not be hurried in this decision, Bess. Not by you, nor George, nor the aldermen.'

'Or Lucie?'

'Even my beloved wife.'

Bess patted his hand, and as she rose called out to her husband, 'Tom! You have left your bailiffs high and dry.' She pretended to misunderstand Owen's protest. 'These are on the house, my friends. It is a good night and I am feeling bountiful.'

*   *   *

By the time Lucie rose to see Alisoun to the door Kate had lit the
wall sconces against the night. 'I don't want you walking through
the city without escort. Jasper will accompany you to the Swann
house.' He was good with dogs.

'Me?' Jasper did not bother to hide his irritation.

Not much more than a month past Lucie had worried that Jasper,
who was only eighteen, might be too eager to ask for Alisoun's
hand, long before he reached the level of journeyman. Even then
his earnings would be modest. Perhaps she need no longer worry.

'I hadn't meant to still be out after dark,' Alisoun was saying.

Lucie assured her it was no problem. 'On your way back, peek
into the York, Jasper, see whether your father is still enjoying
his evening with George and Geoffrey or whether he looks as if
he'd welcome an excuse to escape. If so, tell him he is needed
at home. He will come.'

Nodding glumly, Jasper closed the books and kicked back
the bench.

'I would offer you a more congenial escort if I could,' Lucie said
to Alisoun, ignoring Jasper's glare. While he was gone she would
return Nicholas's garden journals to the chest in her bedchamber
where they would stay until he apologized for his behavior.

Hempe lifted his tankard to hide his laughter as Bess glanced
back at Owen with a wink.

'You'd best make your decision soon, else she'll do it for
you,' Geoffrey noted, lifting his tankard to salute her as she
weaved among the tables.

'You would be right about that.' Owen knew only too well the
power of Bess's will.

'How many husbands has the fair Bess survived?' Geoffrey
asked.

'Tom is her third,' said Owen. 'And no, you have not a chance
with her, even were either of you free to marry.'

Hempe laughed low in his throat. 'No southerner could ever
tame that fine woman.'

'Tame?' Geoffrey feigned shock. 'I should hope not.'

Owen welcomed their banter, turning his mind from the horrific
ruin of Hoban's body.

*   *   *

This angry silence. Alisoun wished Dame Lucie had not insisted Jasper escort her. But in truth she was grateful for the company, and for the light he carried. Her footsteps pounded on the gravel path as she matched Jasper's quick pace through the garden, past the back of the apothecary, and out the gate that opened into the yard of the York Tavern. Two tipsy men stumbled past them, saluting Jasper and clumsily trying to bow to her. Something about them made her glance back. They'd not smelled of wine or ale, but something else, something . . .

'Are you coming?' Jasper waited for her behind the tavern, at the gate into the next yard.

'Did you smell—?' She stopped. The smell was stronger here. And the back of her neck tingled.

'Drunks reek. Yes, I know. Come on, then.' Jasper began to open the gate.

She touched his arm. 'Were you not to stop in the tavern?'

'I'll do it on the way back.' Jasper swung wide the gate.

Alisoun hesitated.

'What?'

'I don't know.' She fought the urge to rush back toward the well-lit, warm, raucous tavern. The night was so dark. She gathered her courage and brushed past him, into the Fenton garden. But the feeling intensified. She wanted to turn and run back to the tavern yard. It was torment to wait for Jasper to close the gate and join her.

'More light,' she implored. There were no lights in the Fenton house. The family were away in the country for the harvest.

Jasper opened the shutter on the lantern without argument, illuminating a hedge and beyond it an untended garden, redolent of rotting fruit and moist earth.

'Something's not right.' Alisoun fought down bile and the urge to touch him for comfort. 'I smell blood. On the ground just by the far gate. This side.'

He stopped suddenly, holding out his arm in a warning to stay back. 'It's a man. Beaten.'

She pushed past him. Bartolf Swann lay slumped against the gate. Blood had bubbled out of his mouth with his last breaths. He was still now, released from the pain of a knife in the heart, the clubbing that had caved in one side of his head. She knelt to him, whispering his name.

Jasper crouched beside her, shining the lantern on the battered body. 'Are you certain it's him?'

'Yes.'

'We need to fetch the captain and the bailiff from the York. Come.' He rose and held out his hand.

'I don't like to leave him,' said Alisoun.

'He's dead. There's nothing you can do. And how do we know his attacker is gone?'

'I don't sense anyone here. I'll be safe.'

'If you're wrong, I'll be blamed. You're coming with me.' Jasper took her hand and tugged.

She did not resist, but as soon as she was standing she tried to free her arm. 'I need to pray for his soul's passing, as Archdeacon Jehannes taught me to do in the birthing room.'

Jasper held tight as he hurried her away from the body, not stopping when she faltered. She had never known him to be so rough.

And then they were in the tavern yard. She blinked in the sudden light as they approached the open doorway. Jasper handed her the lantern and ordered her to wait while he went in to fetch Captain Archer.

Owen was on his feet the moment his son appeared. Even from across the room he noticed the blood on Jasper's linen sleeve, saw with what agitation he shook his head at Bess's flood of questions. And was that Alisoun he'd glimpsed holding a lantern? She'd disappeared before he was halfway across the room.

'Is it Muriel Swann?' Bess was asking when Owen reached them. 'Is the babe come betimes? Bartolf has already left. Did you not cross paths?'

Jasper shook his head as he turned to address Owen. Ghostly pale, he was.

'It's Bartolf Swann, Da. Stabbed in the heart, his head bashed in. By the gate into his yard from the Fenton garden.'

'Dead?' Owen asked, though he knew the answer by how Jasper's voice broke as he described the injuries. The lad nodded, then crossed himself.

'God help us,' said Hempe.

Geoffrey was right behind him.

Tom already waited at the doorway with the lantern.

'Where's Alisoun?' Jasper impatiently pushed the hair from his forehead. 'I told her to stay.'

Owen put his hand on Jasper's shoulder. 'How did you find him?'

'Alisoun was visiting and I was walking her back to the Swann house.' His voice shook. 'If she's returned to him, I'll—'

'Did you hear anything?'

'Nothing.'

'Fetch a priest, son.' St Helen's was near. 'Prayers must be said over the body before the soul departs.'

Jasper nodded and headed back through the yard.

Alisoun stood by the gate leading to the Swann yard, her lantern illuminating a woman on the other side.

'For the love of God, Mistress Alisoun, he is my father.' Olyf Tirwhit's voice rang out. Hoban's sister, she had married Adam Tirwhit, her brother's good friend.

But Alisoun stood firm. 'You must not move him until Captain Archer and the bailiff see how he fell.'

'Dame Muriel is desperate to come to him,' said Olyf. 'You know how weak she is, you of all people. We must carry him into the house now.' Two men stood behind Olyf, only partially visible in the light. 'You do not want to draw her out into the night in her condition.'

'That's all we need is a Tirwhit meddling,' said Hempe. 'They go to law almost as often as the Braithwaites.'

'It *is* her father on the ground,' Owen noted. He stepped into the light. 'Alisoun is right, Dame Olyf. It is important for us to see how your father fell. As soon as we have examined the area we'll bring him to the house, I promise you.'

'Thank you, Captain Archer.'

'My son is fetching a priest.'

'I've already sent for one.' The woman bowed her head. 'I did not mean to meddle,' she said softly as she turned and departed with the two men.

Jasper returned, breathlessly announcing that the priest was on his way. And then he and Alisoun began to argue.

'I'll see to the lad,' Geoffrey told Owen, slipping over, resting a hand on Jasper's shoulder and having a quiet word.

Alisoun joined Owen. 'I did not want to leave him here alone, with no one to pray over him.'

'Pay Jasper no heed. We all express our grief in different ways.'

'This puts me in mind of Hoban, such brutality,' Hempe noted. 'We need to find their common enemy.'

'Enemies. This looks to me the work of more than one.' Owen crouched down to feel Bartolf's neck. 'He's still warm.' He asked Tom to shine the lantern on the ground around Bartolf's body. But it was too disturbed to pick out prints.

'The ground's well churned as if he fought them,' said Hempe.

'If only he had lived long enough to speak their names.' Owen eased himself up and paced slowly toward the gate. There. Two partial prints, much larger than Alisoun's, facing away. So at least one of them had departed through the Swann yard, bold cur. And something more, paw prints. By the look of them he'd had a dog with him, a large dog. 'We might not have seen this had Dame Olyf and the servants come through, Alisoun.' She wrapped her arms round herself, and he saw she was shivering. 'Why don't you go on to the house and see to Dame Muriel? Jasper can walk you.'

'I can go alone. Look. There are torches in the yard.'

Geoffrey stepped forward. 'Permit me to escort you, Mistress Alisoun. I'll be of more use there, gauging the temper of the household, than standing out here trying to keep out of everyone's way.'

They went through the gate arm in arm as the priest from St Helen's arrived, dropping to his knees as he signed the cross over Bartolf's shattered head.

Hempe unclasped Bartolf's scrip from his belt and rose with a grunt. 'I get too old for this. So says my wife, and tonight I would agree.' As he handed it to Owen, coins rattled inside. 'So it was not a robbery.'

'Or Jasper and Alisoun frightened them away before they could search him,' said Owen. 'But such violence for the little he might carry.'

'Would you talk to the family, take a look at Bartolf when we have him in a lighted room?' asked Hempe. 'You've more experience with something on this order. And you saw his son's injuries. You might see similarities. I'll bring in Bartolf's body, talk to his friends.'

Now was the time to thank Hempe for the compliment but remind him he was the bailiff in York. Yet Owen felt himself nodding. Hoban, now Bartolf . . . This was an organized attack on a law-abiding family of York. He would not rest easy until the murderers were caught.

In the Swann yard the torchlight danced in a sudden breeze. Menservants stood on either side of the door of the two-story house, their daggers visible. As Owen had expected, they told him they had taken up the watch after Olyf Tirwhit had sounded the alarm.

Owen stepped into the hall. Muriel's mother, Janet Braithwaite, stood with Olyf near the fire in the center of the room, the latter giving instructions to a small group of servants. Jasper and Geoffrey hung back toward the door.

'Go warm yourselves,' Owen suggested.

Nodding, the two moved toward the fire circle. Geoffrey was talking, and, head bowed, Jasper listened, nodded. God bless the man. He might be irritating at times, but he understood that the lad needed to be drawn out of himself, away from the memory of Bartolf's shattered skull.

Olyf noticed them passing, then looked back toward the door. She nodded to Owen, the jewels in her crispinette twinkling in the firelight. Though tall and large-boned, she was a graceful woman with a way about her that caught a man's eye. She gave some last orders to the servants, whispered to Janet, then came over to Owen.

'They obey your orders,' he noted.

'They welcome someone telling them what to do at such a time.'

'Of course. The bailiff has asked me to talk to Dame Muriel and the family.'

'Alisoun is calming her. She wisely sent Dame Janet down here to calm the servants, but as you saw—' She gestured toward Janet, who still stood staring into the flames. 'It proved too much for her. I will send a servant for Muriel when father's body—' She seemed to choke on the word, and bowed her head for a moment, as if her sharp efficiency had been but an act she could no longer sustain.

'Forgive me, Dame Olyf, but I hoped I might ask you a few questions.'

'Of course.' She told a passing servant to bring brandywine.

'You want to know what drew me out to the gate in the dark.' She waited for his nod. 'I had been sitting in the hall waiting for Dame Janet – she was saying goodnight to Muriel. The fire – you can feel the heat. Too much! I stepped out for some air and saw Alisoun and the young man hurrying away across the neighbors' garden. They leaned toward each other, but walked so quickly—' Olyf glanced toward Jasper. 'I thought they were young lovers, and regretted spying on them. But then – now I know they were running for help.' She looked round. 'Where is that girl with the wine?' There were tears in her eyes. 'Ah, here she comes now.'

'I am sorry to ask you to recount such a discovery. Did you notice any movement elsewhere?'

'I was so intent on them—'

'Any sign of a dog?'

'Father's dogs?'

'Had they been his, would they not have protected him?'

'Yes, yes, they would. They are devoted to him.' She had begun to pluck her sleeve as if uneasy.

'We saw only one set of prints,' said Owen. 'A large dog.'

Her beringed hand rose to her throat. 'They said my brother was attacked by a wolf.'

'I do not give credence to the rumor of a wolf.'

'I pray you are right. For certain I cannot see how such a creature might find a way into the city— Was Father bitten?'

'We will know when we examine him.' He asked whether anyone in the house had expected trouble, whether there had been any sense of danger, a stranger watching the house, anything that caused concern.

'I know of nothing. My father and my brother were such kind men. They had no enemies, surely.'

'As a coroner, your father might very well have made some enemies. But your brother would have no part in your father's responsibilities as coroner, would he? Did he help your father in any way?'

'No. Hoban had no interest in that. I had not thought about the danger of Father's position. But he held it so long, without any trouble—'

The hall door opened to the servants bearing their master's corpse. George Hempe and the priest followed close behind. In the light from the wall sconces, Bartolf's injuries were all too horrific.

Olyf gave a little cry.

Owen bowed to her and followed the procession into the buttery off the kitchen, a place become too familiar. The servants placed Bartolf on the same stone counter where Hoban had so recently lain. Oil lamps and a lantern provided light for a pair of maidservants who stood ready to clean the body. Owen told them to begin with Bartolf's face, so that he might see the extent of his wounds.

'Bless you. Best to do this before Dame Muriel sees him,' one of the women whispered to Owen.

It was a futile courtesy. There was no way to make pretty Bartolf's ruined face, the crushed skull. One of the servants gently turned Bartolf's head to the right, to hide the worst of the devastation.

'God in heaven,' Olyf whispered at Owen's elbow.

He had not noticed her following him. 'You might wish to forgo this,' he said.

She crossed herself and hurried from the room.

Owen joined Hempe in a close examination of Bartolf's wounds. The knife had been thrust with such force it had broken a rib. Blood clogged the old man's mouth. A dog had clawed him high on his left thigh. Again, not Bartolf's lawed dogs.

'I would say a bodkin, narrow blade,' said Hempe. 'Do you agree?'

'I do. But whether that killed him, or whether the shattered rib tore through his lung—' Owen turned Bartolf's face so that Hempe could see the blood in his mouth. 'Or he might have choked on his own blood.'

'He was such an old man. Who so brutally attacks an old man?' Hempe asked. He rubbed his face. 'I am so tired my eyes want to close on me. I will send men round to warn the wardens at the gates, and the night watch. Perhaps someone will have something for me in the morning.'

Out in the hall, there was no sign of Dame Olyf. Owen said goodnight to Hempe and went in search of the servants, asking whether anyone had accompanied Dame Olyf outside when she had discovered the body. All looked toward an elderly man who seemed reluctant to admit his part. Owen drew him out into the yard.

'Dame Olyf said she heard something without. Told me to get a lantern and come out with her,' said the servant. 'The yard was empty, but there was a man out on the street with – I don't know what it was – a wolf?' He crossed himself. 'He just stood there, looking back at us, then hurried off when I walked toward him with the lantern. When I turned, she'd walked to the gate. We saw two people hurrying off through the neighbors' garden, young, must have been Mistress Alisoun and your son, and then Dame Olyf moaned to see Master Swann—' The man's voice broke. He dropped his eyes and crossed himself.

'Is there anything else?'

'She whispered, "Dogs again." And something else, but I couldn't understand it. But the dog, if it was a dog, had been out on the street.' The man shook his head. 'Then she hurried inside. Ordered us to arm and guard the house. And sent for the priest. I'd seen the man and beast before, I think, in the neighbors' garden. Early one morning. Walking away, toward the York Tavern yard.'

'Would you recognize his face?'

'Never saw it, Captain. I'm sorry for that. But the dog, he looked like a wolf, I swear he did.'

'You've seen wolves before?'

'Have I—?' The man screwed up his face. 'Long ago. In the forest. Saw two run down one of the king's deer.'

'You said *like* a wolf.'

A nod. 'Very like. But – I can't say. Seemed wrong somehow.'

'You've been most helpful.'

'Master Swann was a good man, Captain. And Master Hoban. I pray you find who did this.'

'The bailiffs and I will do our best.'

Curious that Olyf Tirwhit had not mentioned seeing the man and beast out on the street.

It grew late, and Owen had much to think about. He collected Jasper, who was pacing near the hall door. 'Geoffrey deserted you?'

Jasper gestured toward the fire where Geoffrey lay stretched out on a bench, asleep. Hempe strolled over and gave him a boot in the leg, chuckling as the man snorted and sputtered in confusion.

'I learned something that might be of interest,' Geoffrey said as they made their way through the gate, guarded now by one of the servants. 'The cook told me of a man and a large dog or wolf watching the house a few days ago.'

'Standing in the Fenton yard?' Owen asked.

'Ah. You've already heard.'

The Fenton garden again. Because the family was away? It was next to the Swann home? The owners were kin to the steward of Galtres? 'Would he recognize the man?' Owen asked.

'Said he saw his back.'

Owen cursed under his breath. 'Did you tell this to Hempe?'

Geoffrey laughed. 'That half-wit?'

'He is no half-wit, my friend. And this *is* his investigation.'

'He may believe it is his investigation, but mark me, Owen, the Braithwaites and the council will insist you take the lead.'

'He's right, Da,' said Jasper. 'When Dame Janet was departing with Dame Olyf she said as much, she would speak with the mayor and aldermen on the morrow, see that they offered you whatever you asked to solve the two murders.'

So everyone connected the deaths of father and son, even before hearing of the clawing.

Tom greeted them at the tavern door with a request to send Bess home. 'She went to warn Lucie why you would be late home.'

Owen was grateful. In the confusion, he had forgotten she would have at least expected Jasper to return earlier.

Tom nodded. 'She went for a favor and stayed for herself, it seems. I'd be grateful if you would tell her I want to lock up now.'

It was wise to lock up tonight. The city gates had been locked hours ago. Bartolf's murderers were near, within the walls.

Geoffrey bid them goodnight and disappeared into the tavern. 'He'll tell you all he's learned for the price of a pint of your best,' Owen told Tom. 'Though you might want to wait for Bess, else he'll insist on two.'

Owen felt a weariness descend as he and Jasper crossed the tavern yard toward home.

FIVE

Between the Wolf and the Dog

A n oil lamp placed between them on the window seat illu-
minated the two friends, Lucie slender and upright, her
long braid a plumb line down her straight back, Bess sitting
cross-legged in a nest of cushions, her sleeves pushed up to reveal
muscular arms, a beribboned white cap insufficient to contain
her wiry and abundant red hair, some escaping to curl against her
damp neck. The two keeping watch together – a familiar sight.
They both turned as he and Jasper stepped into the hall.

'My prayers are answered.' Lucie rose to embrace first Owen,
then Jasper. 'You are both home, safe and sound.'

Bess bade them good night, saying she must see to Tom. Now
the tavern was shut for the night he must get some sleep, morning
would come soon enough with all the chores to do for those biding
at the inn and those who would gather early to hear the latest
about the night's tragedy. She made a face at Jasper's offer to
escort her through the yard. 'And how would you defend me, I
wonder, with you about to topple with fatigue? Perhaps it is I who
should escort you to your chamber above the shop.'

But the lad was hungry, as was Owen, and Lucie sat with them
by the kitchen fire while they ate bowls of stew Kate had warmed
for them. Lucie assured them that Bess had told her enough for
now, best that they save the rest for the morrow. 'It is sleep you
need now, not stirring up.'

But Owen had a question for Jasper that could not wait, for the
lad might forget details by morning. 'When you came through
the yards, did you see anyone?'

Jasper rubbed his eyes. 'Two drunks coming from the York
Tavern, holding each other up.'

'Who?'

Yawning, Jasper shrugged. 'I paid them no heed. They were
pissing drunk, and it was dark.'

'You had a lantern. Think, son.'

Jasper shrank into himself. 'I didn't look at them. How could I know it might be important?'

'I did not expect it of you, son, I merely hoped. What of Alisoun? Do you think she might have noticed?'

'She asked if I'd marked how they smelled. Like drunks!' Jasper rolled his eyes, but then he seemed to think more of it. 'To be honest, I tried not to smell them. But Alisoun did. And then she seemed uneasy the moment she entered Fenton's garden, long before I smelled anything. Now I wonder – did the drunks reek of blood? I did not ask her.'

'I will.'

Jasper nodded. 'There is something – but I might just be telling tales.'

'You can trust me,' Owen urged.

Jasper raked a hand through his fair hair. 'Before you send someone round to the barbers, you might talk to Alisoun again. I think she lied to you, Da.'

'About what?' Owen asked. 'The salve?'

'At least the pouch. It's hers. I recognize it.'

'Alisoun's? How do you know?'

'I was with her when she found the piece of leather. We competed for the best story about how it came to bear that mark.' Jasper suddenly looked stricken by his betrayal. 'Perhaps you asked about the salve, not the pouch?'

'Is that true?' Lucie asked Owen. 'Might she not have noticed it?'

'I can't recall,' Owen admitted. 'But one of Hempe's men went round to the barbers today. No one admitted to preparing that particular salve. I will talk to her again. Thank you, son.'

Lucie rose to rub Jasper's back, massage his shoulders. 'Is this why you snubbed her tonight?'

A shrug and a nod.

She kissed the scar on his right cheek. 'Best be off to bed. We'll have a crowd in the shop in the morning, hoping for gossip.'

'I'm sorry I paid no heed to the drunks,' Jasper said as he stumbled to his feet.

'We don't know they were of importance,' said Owen. 'You were a great help tonight. You were patient, kept your ears pricked. I'm grateful. You deserve some sleep!'

Lucie smiled to see how much that meant to Jasper. He seemed his usual self as he left the hall for his bedchamber over the shop next door.

Owen took Lucie's hand and led her up to their bedchamber.

'If what Jasper overheard is true, that Janet Braithwaite is petitioning the mayor for my help, I'm going to need Alfred to guide the bailiffs' men in my methods. But I've sent him and Stephen off into the forest.'

'About that.' She told him of Alisoun's complaint. He winced as he settled on the bed to remove his boots, clearly acknowledging his transgression. 'Perhaps when you apologize to her you might find a way to show her the pouch,' she said.

'I will. Though she will realize what I'm about and be angry all over again.' Owen set his boots by the door.

That was the way with Alisoun. And yet . . . Lucie paused as she was about to climb into bed. 'If she lied, she might be apologetic.'

Owen slipped his hands around her waist and kissed the back of her neck. 'Alisoun? I would like to see that. But I admit she was a help at Bishopthorpe Palace when Thoresby was dying, and she seems good with Dame Muriel and her mother.'

'I'm glad to hear that.' Lucie turned in Owen's arms. 'What if Alisoun is lying because she fears the person for whom she prepared it? She might be in danger.'

'You are assuming much, my love. What if she dropped the pouch on the track, and fears someone will accuse her of murdering Hoban?'

'Oh, surely they would not think that.'

He'd removed the patch he wore over his scarred, blind eye and she could see a slight twitch. Magda called the twitches and showers of needle pricks on the scarred eye his gift, a knowing. Lucie guessed that he worried Alisoun was somehow implicated.

'I pray it is easily explained,' she said softly, sorry to have mentioned it before sleep.

'Nothing is easy with Alisoun,' Owen muttered as he climbed into bed.

'No,' Lucie agreed, remembering his account of their first meeting, climbing up a ladder to a loft where young Alisoun stood, aiming an arrow at him. He and Magda had been on a mission of mercy. A fisherman had earlier seen Alisoun on the riverbank shouting for help. In the house they had found her family, siblings and parents, dead of the pestilence; Alisoun had retreated to the barn, where she stood ready to defend herself, her horse, her farm. 'If she dispensed the salve, the person might return to Magda's house. Perhaps it is just as well you sent Alfred and Stephen there.'

'Unprepared.' He grumbled into his pillow.

'I had been thinking that some of Kate's siblings might be willing to watch Magda's house.' Kate and Tildy's many brothers and sisters were a treasure trove of hard, honest workers. 'Rob and Rose? One of them would be there while the other came to me with messages.' They were twins, fifteen years old. 'Though now that we fear for trouble . . .'

Owen had turned onto his back. 'I cannot think of a better pair, dauntless but level-headed. They would know to hide if someone looked less than friendly, then devise a way for one of them to fetch help.' He pulled her close. 'Bless you, my love.'

'You are so confident in them?'

'I am.'

Lucie kissed him. 'And I am glad to have found a way to cheer you before sleep.'

She settled into his arms.

'I pray God neither the Nevilles nor the Percys are involved in this,' Owen whispered.

She would prefer that to it being one of their neighbors. But she understood his dread. Powerful families made his work far more difficult, and never satisfying. They seemed above the law. 'No more talk of this tonight.' Lucie wound a leg around him. 'Sleep now. You have much work ahead of you.'

She stroked his hair. Within a few moments his breathing slowed into the rhythm of sleep.

But she lay there staring at the beam overhead for what seemed like hours, worrying about Alisoun and Jasper – if the two men in the tavern yard were the murderers, they might fear one of them could identify them. But what had they done with the dog? And what was Olyf Tirwhit hiding?

Shortly before dawn Owen woke to the sound of baby Emma's tears and Lena's sweet voice singing her back from her bad dream.

A reminder of why he did all he did, to keep the world safe for his children and his beloved Lucie. He turned over and pulled her into his arms.

She smiled sleepily as she kissed him. 'Such a sweet voice she has, though nothing like Alisoun's.' Lucie rolled over on her back. 'Poor Alisoun, plucked from the peace of Magda's rock and set in the path of danger.'

'If she did lie to me, she was already in danger.'

'True. Poor Jasper, he was so angry with her. He glared at me when I told him to escort her back to the Swann house.'

'It was not his choice to walk her home last night?'

'No. He was such a boor about it that I locked Nicholas's books away until his temper cooled and he apologized. But he had cause.'

'Not to glare at you.' He saw the worry in Lucie's eyes. 'Alisoun would be even less safe at Magda's house.'

Lucie sighed. 'I know. I'm worried that both she and Jasper might be at risk if the pair of drunks murdered Bartolf.'

'I thought of that as well. I'll see to protecting them.' Owen heard the kitchen door open. 'Kate's awake. I'll bring in some wood for her.'

She smiled. 'Kate is quite capable of bringing in the wood. But I know, you need to stretch your legs while you plan out your day.' She kissed him and slipped back down beneath the covers. 'I'll escort the twins to Magda's. Let Jasper burn off some of his temper with good honest work alone in a crowded apothecary. I will make my apologies to Alisoun later. Such a pair we are, inviting intruders into her home.'

'Why you? Why walk into danger?'

She propped herself on one elbow, reaching out to touch his cheek. 'How can I ask it of Rose and Rob if I think it too dangerous to go myself?'

'Perhaps—'

She touched a finger to his lips, silencing him. 'We have no cause to believe we will come to harm, my love. It is Alisoun who needs our protection. Don't worry about me.'

'But I do. You are my anchor.'

'And you are mine. I will be careful, my love.' Her steady gaze assured him.

Owen dressed in the soft dawn light filtering through the shutters and stepped out onto the landing to begin his day.

The rising sun touched the rooftops, but already it was disappearing behind low clouds, the sort of late-summer overcast that kept the dew and the river damp trapped, thickening the air, dragging down the spirit. Owen paused at the gate into the tavern yard, observing a woman who paced back and forth near the tavern door, wringing her hands and mumbling something to herself – prayers, perhaps. He could not quite place her. Simple dress, a faded brown with some shine at the elbow and a patch on the skirt, tidily sewn. He opened the gate, letting it squeak loudly to warn her of his presence.

She turned toward him, her hands to her heart. 'Captain Archer. God bless, you are just the man I hoped to see. Tom Merchet told me to wait right here, you would be over before long. It's my Da, Old Bede as they call him. He didn't come home last night. I've looked all the places he sometimes sleeps it off and no one saw him after he left the tavern. I'm that worried, Captain. With the murder last night, and Tom Merchet saying Da had been out in the yard, he might have seen something.' Owen recalled her name now, Winifrith. 'You must find him for me. I pray you.' She drew a penny from her sleeve. 'I've little to offer.'

Owen gently closed her fingers over the coin. 'There's no need, Dame Winifrith. Just tell me where you've looked and I'll take over your search. I need him as well.' He offered her his arm. 'Shall we talk in the tavern over a bowl of ale?'

After she'd departed, Owen sat a while with Tom and Bess.

'I wondered about him when he returned,' Bess said. 'We've danced this dance many a night and he's always walked back in with a proud glare, but not last night. He sat slumped over in his chair and said little while I had the doors locked so they wouldn't all spill out and crowd round poor Bartolf. Do you think Old Bede saw something?'

Owen told them about the two drunks.

Tom frowned down at his hand on the table, shaking his head. 'No one left in that condition last night, except for Old Bede. And Bartolf, I suspect. The stonemasons sitting with him walked straight lines out the door. Poole never drinks much, though he pays as if he does.'

Bess agreed that only Bartolf and Old Bede had been drunk. Nor did Owen recall anyone else leaving during that time.

'Nor I,' said Geoffrey from the doorway. 'I'll come with you, Owen. I've developed a fondness for the old gossip.'

'Go on, then, you two,' said Bess, 'find the old troublemaker.'

Groups of people stood out on the street, heads together as they swapped stories about the tragedy, but they all followed Owen and Geoffrey with their eyes as the two passed. All along Coney Street and across the Ouse bridge conversations halted as people turned to watch them. A few called out to Owen, asking if he needed help. He paused to speak to some, quietly asking whether they'd seen Old Bede. He saw the worry in the faces even before they answered. The old man might be a tell-tale, but he was York's tell-tale, and no one wished him a violent end. One man suggested they check a house down an alley on Peter Lane, the home of Old Bede's best friend, Timkin. Bede's daughter had not mentioned it.

They found it to be more a shack than a house, no windows, a hole in the roof that would vent the smoke if there were a fire beneath it, but the ashes in the middle of the earthen floor had been ground into the dirt by the old man's coming and going. He was huddled in a corner, snoring so loudly he did not hear them enter. Owen shook him awake.

A snort. Eyes wide. 'I didn't do it! I swear. Sleepin' it off. I'm just an old drunk, no harm to anyone.'

'Rest easy, Timkin,' said Owen. 'We're here looking for Old Bede. He didn't come home last night and his daughter's worried. Someone thought he might have stopped here, but I see you're alone.'

'Old Bede, now?' Timkin scratched himself. 'Nay. *He* has the coin for the York, but it's a long while since I could pay the Merchets' prices. Pray God he's not fallen in the river. Strong swimmer, Bede is, but not when in his cups.'

Alfred insisted on coming across the stones to help Lucie over to Magda's rock. 'They're slippery at the beginning of low tide.' Rob and Rose were already hopping across, balancing small bundles of clothing on their heads. 'Am I to mind them?' Alfred asked.

'No,' Lucie laughed. 'They're relieving you of your watch. My husband needs you.'

'Bartolf Swann's murder?'

'You've already heard about it? Out here?'

'A visitor told me. You'll want to talk to him. He's why Stephen went to Bartolf's alone this morning.' Alfred called out to the twins to wait for him before opening the door. 'I don't want to startle him,' he said. He was not smiling.

By the time Lucie and Alfred reached the rock the twins had disappeared round the side of the house. Everyone in York was curious about the strange, dragon-guarded dwelling, and they were clearly no exception. Alfred knocked on the door and called out that Dame Lucie Wilton, the apothecary, was with him, then pushed it open.

Someone wrapped in a blanket was struggling to rise from a seat close to the fire.

'I pray you, rest easy,' Lucie said. 'I will come and join you.'

Letting the blanket slip down from his head to settle on his shoulders, Old Bede greeted her hoarsely.

'God be thanked. I am so glad to see you.' Bess had told her he was missing. Lucie noticed his clothes hanging from the rafters. 'What happened?'

'I swam here in the dark of night. Upriver. They didn't think a dried old bean like meself had it in him. Faith, I wasn't so certain meself. I'm thankful it's late in a dry summer. I wouldn't have made it when the rain on the moors comes thundering downriver.'

Lucie glanced up at Alfred, who nodded. 'He was soaked through and shivering so hard he couldn't talk until he'd shed his clothes and I'd rolled him in blankets and stoked the fire.'

'Tell me what happened,' Lucie said. 'Did someone follow you when you left the York Tavern last night?'

Old Bede nodded. 'They came up behind me down on staithe, as I was doing my business. Stopped me from heading upriver to bridge. Two of 'em, big men. I reckoned I'd seen them playing drunk earlier, coming out of that very gate Bartolf Swann had gone through and died, eh? But now on staithe they've another with 'em, has a dog, all teeth and straining to break free and jump at me. Between the wolf and the dog, I was, so to speak, them or the river. With the river I had a chance. I dived in and pushed down, down. God was looking out for me, leading me to piss at staithe, where river's dredged and I could go deep. I fought current till my chest wanted to burst. They couldn't find me in night black as pitch, water such a good brown. But I can't go home now, can I?'

From the doorway, Rose said, 'We'll keep you hidden here, Old Bede. No one will know.'

Lucie nodded. Rose and Rob could do it. 'You can trust them. We'll take care of the rest. You've seen any of them before?'

'Mayhap the one with the dog. Can't say for certain. Minds me of one worked on staithe. He's been gone some time. Ran off after some trouble. Bailiff Hempe could tell you his name. Always with a dog back then, nasty. Had the devil in 'im. Not the same dog now, but those same teeth . . .' He shook his head.

For once Lucie was grateful for Old Bede's love of gossip.

As they crossed back over the bridge, Geoffrey noted how folk watched them, 'Or, rather, you. They bow to you, grateful for your protection. What is it like, having such a noble calling?'

'Burdened by their faith that all will be as it was as soon as I've caught the guilty. It won't. It can't be. Men are dead, Hoban Swann's child will never know his father, the Swanns' lives are forever changed. And how many more will suffer?'

'Ah. I am humbled.'

'No. *I* am. I've discovered nothing of use. Nothing.'

They walked in silence for a while, until Geoffrey tapped Owen's arm. 'The prickly bailiff approaches.'

George Hempe strode toward them with two of his men, his expression grieved. 'I've heard about Old Bede's disappearance after leaving the York, heading for the King's Staithe. My men will search the riverbanks up and downstream.' Owen offered to help, but Hempe shook his head. 'Janet Braithwaite awaits you at her house. Olyf Tirwhit and her husband Adam are with her, planning the Swanns' burials. John Braithwaite's expected by nightfall – he had business in Kingston-Upon-Hull. But Janet will brook no delays. She means to hire you to bring to justice the murderers of her son-in-law and his father. The mayor and council approve of her plan.'

As Jasper had said. 'I will attend her this afternoon,' said Owen. 'Lucie should be back, perhaps with Alfred and Stephen. They might have noticed something on the river.'

Hempe nodded. 'I'll set my men to the search and join you at your house. I'd like to hear what your men have to say.'

'You might ask the gatekeepers whether anyone arrived with a large dog yesterday, and whether they've left.'

'I will.'

Owen thanked him and hurried down Coney Street.

SIX

A Matter of Conscience

I n the early hours, after Dame Janet at last departed for her own home, Muriel fell into a deep sleep. Alisoun was sitting in a chair beside the bed, dozing fitfully, when one of the servants placed a blanket over her. The warmth was welcome, but steady sleep still eluded her. She'd dreamt of her parents, faceless, but somehow recognizable. Sometimes, when surprised by her reflection in water, she saw her mother in the set of her own mouth, her cheekbones, her hairline, and her father in the shape of her eyes and nose. But she could no longer put those features together into clear memories of their faces. How long would it take Muriel to forget Hoban's appearance? Would she remember that her husband was handsome, but be unable to see what made him handsome?

Alisoun gently rubbed the ribbon edging of the scrip she wore to hold her medicines. Jasper had bought the ribbon for her at the Lammas Fair, and she'd sewn it to her scrip so that it would be with her wherever she went, reminding her that she was loved. She had felt so alone since her father's death, the one person who had made her feel as if she had blessed his life. Magda was good to her, but Alisoun did not feel she had a place in the Riverwoman's heart. Jasper's love had been a revelation. She'd felt whole again. But she had ruined that when she lied to the father he respected above all others. Alone again. She tucked her hands beneath her and bit back tears, refusing to cry over Jasper. No, refusing to cry over her own fecklessness. She could think of no way to explain why she protected Crispin Poole, except that she had promised. Magda would never break a promise.

But would she have agreed to such a secret?

Was it just the promise? Wasn't it more than that? He'd been bitten. A deep, bone-scraping bite. And he'd been shaken by the experience. That was not the reaction of a guilty man.

What she needed to do was prove his innocence.

Her charge stirred in the bed. Alisoun did not wish Muriel this awakening, as the horror and sorrow of the previous evening added to that of her husband's death. She worried for the health of the baby.

'Alisoun?'

'I am here beside you.'

'My husband. His father. Was it a dream?'

She felt the question like a hand squeezing her heart and heard Magda's voice in her head, *Breathe deep. Know her pain, but do not take it on. She needs thee sound, whole, strong, unwavering.* 'No. Not a dream.' Alisoun took Muriel's hand and guided it to her stomach. 'Bring your heart here. Here there is life.'

Muriel pulled her hand from Alisoun's and turned on her side as a sob racked her thin frame. Alisoun rose to gather the herbs for a morning tisane, then opened the door to tell the maidservant to bring hot water. And so a new day of grieving began.

'Swam to Magda's from the King's Staithe? Most men half his age couldn't do that.' Owen had never believed half of the old man's stories. 'I underestimated him.'

Alfred laughed. 'I'm not saying he wasn't half dead when he washed up on the rock, and shaking so hard I built up the fire, wrapped him in blankets, and prayed he did not go from freezing to burning with fever.'

But as far as the man whom Old Bede suspected had pursued him, Hempe, who'd just joined Owen, Lucie, and Alfred in the kitchen, remembered little. 'If it is the same man.' He shrugged. 'His name was John, like half the shire. I don't know where he was from. The trouble was his dog. Big. Nasty. Trained to attack anyone who challenged his master. Mauled more than one who came at John, and some who didn't. That's several years ago or more. Do you recall it, Owen?'

'No, but I've had little to do with the staithes,' said Owen. 'Did he have any friends? Family in the city?'

It was Alfred who'd piped up. 'Now I remember. John with the wolf dog.'

'Wolf dog?'

'He called it a mastiff, but it looked more wolf than dog to most of us.' Alfred ran his hand over his bald head. 'The man was a queer sort. Dead eyes. Quiet. Too quiet.'

'Young? Old?'

'Alfred's age, more or less,' said Hempe. 'I'll ask about him down at the staithe. Maybe someone knows where he's been, and where he is now.'

'And if anyone noticed a small boat on the staithe,' said Owen, 'something that could glide away in the night, no one the wiser.'

Hempe nodded.

'What of Bartolf's servants?' Owen asked Alfred. 'Did you or Stephen learn anything?'

'Stephen came as we were leaving the rock,' said Lucie. 'No one has seen Cilla since Hoban's death. But a neighbor says he heard a woman shriek not long before he heard Swann's dogs barking the night Hoban was murdered.'

Hempe had risen from the table with a grunt, thanking Lucie for the bread and cheese. Owen stayed him a moment. 'What of Bede's daughter? Can we tell her he's safe? Do you think Winifrith could behave as if she's still desperately waiting for news of him? It would be cruel to draw out her worry, but far crueler to risk her father's life.'

'Tell her,' said Hempe. 'Winifrith's strong. When she was widowed she told her children she would not bring in a man who would beget more children on her who he would love more than them. That their granddad would now be their father. You can trust her to do whatever she must to protect Old Bede.' He bowed his head. 'I'd offer to be the one to go to her, but I don't want her to think . . . we once . . . and now I'm married . . .'

'I'd not put either of you through such agony. I'll speak with her before I attend Janet Braithwaite.'

'You are a good friend,' said Hempe. 'I've arranged for Ned, one of my men – he's not been with me long but he served you in the archbishop's guard for a short time – to join the servants at the Swann home, listen, watch. Dame Janet approved the idea, and convinced Dame Muriel.'

'Ned's a good lad,' said Owen. 'I should inform Alisoun who he is.'

Lucie touched Owen's arm. 'I'd rather you see to Janet first. She is of course fiercely protective of her daughter at the moment,

a difficult pregnancy and now such grief. Janet's factor was short
with Jasper in the shop, and if you don't attend his mistress, he'll
be back. Ah. Here's Ned now.'

The young man was bounding along the gravel walkway
and came to a skittering halt outside the open garden door.
He doffed the hat holding back his unruly hair, dark as Owen's,
to bow to Lucie, then nod toward Hempe and Alfred. 'Is it true,
Captain? You've need of me?'

Owen laughed. 'Are you so eager to escape the bailiffs'
company?'

'They seldom need me, so I'm stuck at my father's cooperage.
Back-breaking work, coopering. Is this about the murders?'

While Lucie wrapped up the medicine she'd prepared for Muriel,
Owen explained why the household needed protection.

'I'll guard Mistress Alisoun and the household with my life,
Captain. You may be sure of that.'

'Mistress Alisoun is able to defend herself, Ned, have a care
with her,' said Owen. A kindness, as there was a gleam in the
young man's eyes. So Jasper had a rival. Owen recalled that
the young man had wooed a serving maid when in service at
Bishopthorpe Palace. Perhaps it meant little.

Ned put a finger to the side of his nose and winked. 'I am aware
of Mistress Alisoun's courage, Captain. And her skill with a bow.'

Owen thought to say more, but Lucie gave him a look signaling
it was best left as it was. The four of them departed the house,
Owen and Alfred leaving Ned and Lucie at the gate of the Swann
residence, then continuing on to the Braithwaite residence farther
down Coney Street. They were announced by the barks of a mastiff
pulling against his chain near the hall door, his claws rasping on
the stones. Not lawed.

A man appeared in the doorway, followed by Dame Janet who
called out a welcome as the man crouched to the dog, softly
speaking to it while stroking it behind the left ear until it settled
back down.

'Forgive the noise, but he is an effective guard, isn't he?' said
Dame Janet.

Perhaps. But it was one thing to bark, another to know how to
attack. And how to control a dog so trained.

'Do come in.' The woman who had the previous night wept

and wrung her hands now wore an air of calm authority as she
led them into the hall. Olyf and Adam Tirwhit sat side by side on
a cushioned bench lit by the afternoon sun pouring in through a
high window. Her head rested on his shoulder and he held her
close, his head bowed. Near them was another couple, plump with
prosperity, he garbed in a dark jacket and leggings, she in a gown
a subtle shade of blue adorned with seed pearls, her hair caught
up in a silver-threaded crispinette. 'I do not believe you know my
son Paul and his wife Elaine,' Janet said quietly.

Olyf straightened and moved away from her husband as
Owen and Alfred took seats near them. Janet wasted no time.
As soon as Owen introduced Alfred, their hostess went straight
to the point. Owen would be generously compensated. He had
only to tell them what he needed and he would have it at once.
The city needed him. The mayor, council, and sheriff agreed that
Owen should take charge.

Adam Tirwhit quickly added his plea that Owen do all that
he could to bring the murderer of his wife's father and brother
to justice. Anger sharpened his words so that the plea came out
sounding more like a command.

Olyf silently nodded in agreement, her face pale, her eyes
such wells of suffering that Owen knew the image would haunt
him until he had solved this.

'They insisted on seeing the bodies of father and son,' Dame
Janet murmured, as if their emotion required explanation.

Owen expressed his sorrow for their loss, speaking of both
men's goodness, halting as Olyf's tears overflowed. 'I will do all
in my power to find their murderers.'

A brisk nod from Janet. 'May God guide you in your task.
How might we assist you?'

'I have questions. But if it is too soon—'

Adam was shaking his head. 'Let us waste no time.'

'Is there somewhere we might talk out of hearing of the
servants?'

Janet glanced back at the two servants who stood out of the way
but close enough to hear any command. 'I had not thought – I
trust them all or I would not—' She stopped herself with a finger
to her lips. 'My husband's parlor.' Rising, she motioned for her
guests to follow.

Owen began by asking about the dog now guarding the house. 'He is new to the household?'

'He is mine,' said Paul Braithwaite. 'It's a long ride. My manor is near your wife's. I thought it prudent to bring him. Protection for myself, my wife, my parents' household.' He cleared his throat twice as he spoke.

'I believe he has all his claws?' Owen asked.

A frown, then a nod of understanding. 'I never take my dogs into royal forests, no. A cruel practice, lawing.' Paul glanced at Olyf, but she held her gaze on Owen, as if drawing hope from his presence. Tearless now.

Why had Paul glanced at her?

'I brought all the staff together this morning to introduce them to Tempest,' said Janet. 'To reassure them.'

Owen inclined his head to acknowledge her, but he was more interested in her son. He'd not realized that Paul Braithwaite's manor was near Freythorpe Hadden, which was south of the city. He thought of the boat on the bank near Hoban's body. Perhaps someone had ferried Bartolf's dogs over to the south bank of the Ouse. 'It was your man who calmed him just now by the door?' Owen asked. Paul nodded. 'Might Alfred have a word with him after we've finished here? He might have some helpful advice about the dogs we're searching for – the attackers and those missing from the Swann house in the forest.'

'Of course,' said Paul.

In the end, they had nothing of use to tell him.

'When will you bury Bartolf and Hoban?' Owen asked.

All looked to Janet Braithwaite.

'Tomorrow. I prefer to wait until my husband returns, which should be tonight. Muriel is still his baby daughter, you know how it is. He will want to be there.' A nod, as if that was settled. 'We plan a quiet service in St Helen's, no great feast in their memory until their murderers are apprehended and punished. Just family.'

'Send word to me of the timing. I want the bailiffs' men on the watch.'

'I will, Captain.'

Owen stood. 'I will leave you in peace for now.' He nodded to Alfred. 'See about the dog.'

Paul rose. 'I will accompany you.'

'I would prefer you did not,' said Owen, watching the man's reaction.

Clearly uneasy, he said, 'Galbot is a man of few words, Captain. He might need my coaxing.'

'Alfred has experience questioning quiet servants,' Owen assured him, staring him into compliance.

Winifrith studied Owen's face as he spoke, as if reading there whether or not she believed him. 'He's a swimmer, my da, that is so. Proud of it, he is. Goes in the water at night, mostly, so there's no traffic, you see. So I can believe he did that. Between the wolf and the dog—' She nodded. 'So he saw he was stuck with two sorry choices. In his cups, that's not the time to swim. Not so drunk after all. God be thanked.' She made a sound between a laugh and a sob. 'There are some think he's taking up space with no good purpose on God's earth, but he's been a good father to me and my little ones.' She surprised Owen with a hug. 'Bless you, Captain Archer.' She stepped back, wiping her eyes on her sleeve. 'And bless Alfred and the young ones who are hiding him. I couldn't hope for better protection. And the Riverwoman's dragon will watch over him.' Her face suddenly tightened. 'But my little ones. I cannot tell them he's safe, they're sure to come out with it. God forgive me, I must lie to them and let their dear hearts grieve.'

'I pray it will not be for long, Dame Winifrith.'

'Find the butchers and hang them so Da can come home.'

'I mean to.' While he was there Owen thought he might as well ask if she recalled John with the wolf dog. He was glad he did.

Winifrith sent a worried glance out into the small garden where the children played. 'Is he the monster who's murdered two good men and sent my da diving into the Ouse?'

'Your father thought he might have been one of the men last night. Do you know anything more about him?'

She shook her head. 'But ask any mother along the river and she'll tell you he enjoyed frightening the children with that beast of his. He kicked one of the neighbor's boys for throwing a pebble to keep the dog away, and the dog bit the poor lad in the leg. But that was several years ago. I thought us well rid of him. God help us.' She crossed herself.

*   *   *

As they approached the Swann house, Lucie asked Ned how well he knew Alisoun.

'I saw her every day when she and Dame Magda were caring for Archbishop Thoresby at Bishopthorpe, though I spoke to her only once or twice.' He blushed and averted his eyes, looking relieved when a servant welcomed them into the hall.

'Have a care. Dame Muriel's well-being is in Alisoun's hands, and hers alone. Consult her regarding anything relating to the mistress of the house.'

'I will. And I'll keep to the shadows so she forgets I'm there.' Ned spoke with resolve.

Lucie bit back a smile at the thought of two stout wills colliding.

The house was quiet, subdued, the servants going about their work in silent watchfulness. Even Alisoun moved so quietly coming up behind Lucie that she startled her with a touch on her shoulder. She welcomed them both with warmth, noting that she'd not seen Ned since Bishopthorpe.

They smiled at each other, then both looked away.

Lucie thought it a good time to explain why he was there.

Alisoun thanked them, moving straight to a description of the behavior of the two men who had passed her in the yard, and how they smelled. 'They reeked of dog, as if they'd been rolling about in a kennel. And blood, though it wasn't until we were in the Fenton garden that I sorted that part. I smelled no ale on them.' She nodded to Ned. 'You will want to present yourself to the cook. He will tell you your duties, and where you will sleep.'

Lucie suggested she go up to Muriel. Alisoun and Ned rose as one, then he headed for the kitchen.

In the solar, Muriel sat by a small window, a bit of embroidery lying forgotten on her lap. She turned as they entered, greeting Lucie with a shake of her head. 'I said no visitors, Alisoun.'

'Dame Lucie has brought a physick to calm you and bring up your appetite, but she cannot advise me of the correct dosage without seeing you.'

Lucie sat down on a stool beside the grieving mother-to-be and took her hand. Despite the warmth of the day and of the room Muriel's hand was cold. Lucie studied her eyes, felt her pulse, sniffed her breath. 'You need food.' Lucie told the servant who waited by the door to bring her mistress some broth. 'Easily

digested, even at such a time.' Only now did she mention Muriel's
terrible loss. They sat in silence for a few moments, Lucie listening
to Muriel's shallow breathing. At last she rose to give the woman
some privacy while instructing Alisoun regarding the physick, a
small dosage during the day, more at night. Behind her, she heard
Muriel begin to weep. She pressed a cloth to her mouth, as if
trying to silence herself. Lucie returned to sit beside her, taking
her free hand.

'I depend on your husband to find the men who took Hoban
from me,' said Muriel. 'And his father.'

A shiver ran from her hand to Lucie's, who sat there a moment,
head bowed, praying that Owen might safely bring the monsters
to justice. *Safely, I pray you, Lord.* 'He is already out and about,
asking questions,' said Lucie. 'And he's placed one of his trusted
men in your home, to listen and observe, to go where Alisoun
cannot go while she is with you. You are protected.'

Muriel pressed Lucie's hand. 'Bless you, both of you.' She sat
back as the servant returned with the broth.

Alisoun added the physick, then brought the bowl of broth to
Muriel, recommending that she sip it while it was warm. Lucie
was gratified to see the woman's sunken cheeks flush with the
warmth, and accepted a cup of watered wine to sip, appreciating
the peaceful moment.

Out of the quiet, Muriel asked the servant to wait outside. As
soon as the young woman drew the door shut behind her, Muriel
said, 'I should have come to Captain Archer about my suspicions.
If I had done so—' A deep breath. 'You must tell him to look
at Hoban's circle, his sister, her husband, and my brother Paul.'
She crossed herself and turned to gaze out the window, her hand
to her heart.

His circle? Lucie glanced at Alisoun, who shook her head. She
was about to ask what Muriel meant when she gave a little moan,
pressing a hand to her stomach.

'Rest now,' Lucie whispered, stroking Muriel's back to relax
her.

But Muriel shook her head. 'They keep some secret, I've always
felt it. Hoban kept things from me. At first I told myself he protected
me, sheltered me in his love, but . . .' She caught her breath and
pressed Lucie's hand, her eyes swimming with tears. 'I do not like

to say it of him. He was so happy about being a father. And I loved him so.'

'A little more of the physick, Alisoun,' Lucie said, 'in some watered wine.'

Muriel shook her head. 'No. No first let me tell you what you must tell your husband. Since Crispin Poole returned – you know of whom I speak?' Lucie nodded. 'Since then, they've whispered and argued under their breaths. Frightened. Or angry. Both?' She rubbed her forehead. 'How can I be certain of anything when he would never tell me? Nor would she, Olyf—' She crossed herself. 'Poor woman, she has lost brother and father. I do not like speaking ill of her. But she is a shrewd one, though she plays the innocent.'

Alisoun knelt in front of her charge and took her hands, catching her eyes and holding the gaze, calming her.

As Magda would do. Lucie asked if she should go.

'No!' Muriel broke away from Alisoun and took Lucie's hand. 'Crispin Poole. As I said, since his return, they've not been the same. The captain must hear this.'

'Poole,' Alisoun whispered, so softly that Lucie almost missed it.

She glanced at her. The young woman seemed lost in herself. Crispin Poole. He had consulted Lucie earlier in the summer about pain in what remained of his right arm. The haunting of the lost hand and forearm. She had sent him to Magda Digby, who knew how to work with such soul wounds. Owen knew him better than she did. 'I will tell my husband what you have said,' Lucie promised.

Muriel nodded. 'My brother asked me if I wanted his dog Tempest here. Stupid man. A dog? After what a dog did to my husband? I've always hated his dogs.'

'Whose? Your brother's? Has Paul always kept dogs?' Lucie asked.

'Breeds them for hunting. Wealthy men come from far and wide to purchase his beasts. I believe his wife – Elaine – I believe she hates them as much as I do.' She gave a sob. 'Hoban never blamed me for being barren, ever. He was the most patient, loving man. When I told him I was at last with child . . . How his eyes lit up . . .' Muriel stared out the window, her body shaken with sobs.

Alisoun handed Lucie a cup of watered wine containing more of the physick. 'For the baby's sake you must rest,' said Lucie.

Muriel drank it down quickly, then rested her head against the back of the chair with a sigh. 'I can sleep now. Captain Archer will know what to do.' Alisoun helped her rise, supporting her with an arm round her waist as she slowly crossed the room to the bed.

When Muriel was asleep, Alisoun joined Lucie on a bench by the window, thanking her for coming. 'Your presence is a balm for her.'

Lucie noticed shadows of exhaustion beneath Alisoun's eyes. She wanted so much to ask about the pouch, but it was not the time. 'Would you like me to stay with her while you rest?'

Alisoun let her shoulders slump. 'Would you? I'll just lie down here. If Dame Janet or Dame Olyf should come—'

'I doubt Janet Braithwaite will have the time to visit her daughter today, but if she does, she can wait in the hall. The same for Dame Olyf.'

'Bless you.'

Lucie poured the weary young woman a cup of wine, then told the servant to shutter the window. In the dim quiet, Alisoun slipped out of her dress and beneath the bedclothes, and Lucie settled beside the sleeping widow, letting her mind quiet before sorting through Muriel's tearful confidences.

'Keep an ear pricked about Paul Braithwaite,' Owen told Alfred as they parted on Coney Street. 'I don't know what I'm looking for. Any gossip, any enemies. And Galbot. Find out if he's a local man. Hempe's men might know. I want to see how Ned's been received, then I'll go to see Archdeacon Jehannes.'

Alfred nodded and strode off.

At the Swann house he found Ned out in the back garden pushing a barrow behind the cook, who was picking late-season herbs for a stew. Ned excused himself and stepped aside to talk to Owen.

'They've put you to work out here?'

'I offered. I thought it a good way to hear the gossip of the household, Captain.' He grinned. 'And I have. I can tell you that the servants resented Olyf Tirwhit ordering them about last night, saying she'd never have dared if their mistress had not been bedridden. Dame Muriel and Dame Olyf – no affection there, it seems.'

'Do you know why?'

Ned shook his head, then lifted his cap and bowed to someone approaching.

'Lucie!' Owen took her hands. 'Any news?'

'I must get right back, but I saw you down here and wanted to give you a message from Dame Muriel.'

He listened with interest about Hoban's 'circle', the secrecy, the discomfort about Crispin Poole's return, her dislike of Paul Braithwaite's dogs. He had Ned tell her what the servants said about Olyf and Muriel.

'There may be something there,' said Lucie, 'though we need more.'

'Did you show Alisoun the pouch?'

'Forgive me, but she is exhausted. I thought it better to wait.'

As Archdeacon of York, Jehannes had a substantial house near the minster. Surrounded by a modest but welcoming garden, it was a place of refuge. Owen often came here seeking the counsel of his good friend. Jehannes managed to retain an innocent joy and an open heart.

A young clerk opened the door to Owen, gesturing with a finger to his lips that he must enter the hall in silence. 'As you can see,' he whispered, 'Dom Jehannes and Brother Michaelo are at prayer.'

The two knelt at *prie dieus* before a corner altar, heads bowed, hands pressed together. The clerk escorted Owen to a seat by a low window that looked out onto a walled garden, and offered him a cup of wine.

The hall was simply furnished, Jehannes's spiritual life being that which drew his attention. Yet where in the past neither hangings nor painted plaster had brightened the interior, that was no longer so. His cook had wed a stonemason who worked at the minster, and the couple, both artists, had transformed the hall. Tree boughs arched along the walls, beneath which hung large embroidered panels depicting the flora and fauna of the moors. With paint and thread they brought the beauty of the North into Jehannes's home.

Once Owen had settled, sampled the fine wine, studied the artwork, the well-tended beds of herbs and roses in the garden, he turned his mind to Muriel Swann's warning. An unexpected revelation, old friends keeping a secret, excluding Muriel, though her brother was part of it. And Crispin Poole. Might it be nothing but a cache of fear unleashed by recent, horrific events? Or was it possible that Poole's return had stirred up some darkness from their shared past? Owen searched his memory for any clues in his conversations with the man, but Poole's only mention of ill feelings pertained to John Gisburne, who had provided him with letters of introduction to influential merchants in the city – apparently at the command of a patron whom Poole declined to name. It was not done graciously, and though the letters had gained him entry into business, he'd been received coolly in society, and ignored by Gisburne's family. Perhaps it was time to dig into Poole's past.

'I sense a storm brewing in that head of yours.' Jehannes smiled as he settled across from Owen. 'More wine?'

Owen declined the offer. 'I came to ask you about a woman you once employed – Cilla.'

Jehannes frowned. 'Cilla?' He began to shake his head, then his eyes widened with memory. 'Ah, Cecelia, the odd little woman who wanted nothing to do with a secure position. I'd forgotten she preferred to be called by that odd name.' He glanced up as he noticed Brother Michaelo hovering nearby. 'Michaelo, you are welcome to join us.'

The monk glanced at Owen, who waved him to a chair beside him.

'So you remember her,' Owen prompted.

Jehannes smiled. 'Oh yes. Quite a peculiar woman, dancing about, making the oddest noises. In truth, I enjoyed her presence, though I cannot say I ever understood her. Hard worker. Alas, she likes to drift, work a few days here, a few days there, then disappear for a week or so. We parted as friends, I like to think. She left me feeling as if I might be the dullest man in the North country. What is your interest in her?'

'She worked for Bartolf, kept his house in Galtres. No one's seen her since Hoban's murder.'

'I pray she is safe. As I say, she stayed nowhere long. She might have moved on beforehand.'

'Perhaps. But the manservant who raised the hue and cry is also missing,' said Owen. 'What do you know of her background?'

'Nothing. I would not know where to tell you to search.'

'The two of you were deep in prayer. For the Swanns?'

Brother Michaelo inclined his head.

Jehannes sighed. 'That, of course. But you must know, I have just received word that our new archbishop, Alexander Neville, means to visit the minster after Martinmas. So soon!'

'And you dread it.'

'I do. He was insufferable as a prebend of the minster, but as Archbishop of York, heady with power . . . God help us.' Jehannes made an apologetic face as he crossed himself.

'God help us indeed,' Owen muttered.

Michaelo sniffed. 'I cannot believe Alexander Neville has anything to do with this tragedy. His nose is far too high in the air for him ever to lay eyes on a family such as the Swanns.'

'I pray you are right,' said Jehannes.

'And yet . . .' Michaelo paused for effect, catching Owen's eye. 'In inquiring about Elwin, the clerk Bartolf Swann used as his recorder, I learned that he has worked for several of the minster canons, including Alexander Neville. He'd had little work from him until Neville was campaigning for the archbishopric, and then his orders came from the family rather than the man himself. Kept him busy. He might prove interesting . . .'

'Thank you, Michaelo,' said Owen. 'That gives me much to consider.' Much unpleasantness. Was this a Neville battle? Why would they slaughter such a family? Michaelo was right, the coroner of a royal forest was beneath them.

'There is one more thing about Elwin. While I was talking to him, he was called to the home of Crispin Poole.'

'Oh?' Owen was interested. Poole again.

Michaelo rose. 'And I believe I might be of further use to you. A woman who goes by the name of Cilla has been biding in the minster yard for the past few days. Badly bruised face, when I caught sight of her.' He raised a warning hand as Owen began to rise. 'Not you, you are too noticeable, and not until sunset. Perhaps I might take Dame Lucie to her, to see whether there is aught she might do for the injury?'

'You are a wonder, Brother Michaelo.'

The monk bowed his head and coughed, as if to hide his pleasure in the compliment. 'I seek to serve.'

'Bless you. I will consult Lucie. If she agrees, she will meet you here after sunset. I will escort her.'

'Better that I escort her from your home, Captain. As if fetching her to someone in need.'

Owen glanced at Jehannes, who gave a subtle shrug.

'Of course. Most prudent.'

'And now I shall go see to some tasks.' Michaelo bowed to Owen, to Jehannes, and withdrew.

Owen said nothing for a few minutes, absorbing the fact that Michaelo was aware of the poor who lived in shacks pressed up against the minster walls.

'His penance,' Jehannes said, softly. 'He dons an old, threadbare habit and goes among them, offering some of his food, praying with those who ask. Difficult to believe?'

'I had no idea.'

'Nor had I. I saw him return one evening and asked what had happened – I thought he'd had some mishap, tumbled into the river, borrowed some old clothes at the abbey. He told me. Reluctantly. Since then I've learned a little from Brother Henry in the infirmary, things he learned from his teacher, Brother Wulfstan. You know Michaelo is of noble birth, Norman. One of twins. Both sons raised as if to be heir to the land, until Michaelo's brother won over his father with his martial skill and popularity amongst his peers. Still, Michaelo, with his education and noble mien, expected money to cross hands ensuring him a swift rise in the Church in France or here in England. But something went awry, and he was sent off to a distant cousin in York, abbot of St Mary's, a man of no influence.'

'Abbot of St Mary's? Campion?'

'His predecessor, who died within months, leaving gentle Campion to deal with the resentful Norman whose cousin had decided he should begin humbly and prove his worthiness.'

'It explains his resentment.'

'And his contentment in John Thoresby's service. If you do accept the prince's offer . . . Well, you see why he is so eager to prove to you his worthiness.'

It explained a great deal.

SEVEN
Ripples in Time

ost in the rhythm of grinding mother of pearl to a dust with her mortar and pestle, Lucie was not aware of Brother Michaelo's presence until she paused to sip some well-watered wine. It was a dry, dusty chore.

'Grinding pearls?' he said, from his perch on a bench by the door, one of the few cleared spaces. Harvested plants and partially completed mixtures crowded the workshop as she prepared the apothecary for winter illnesses.

'Brother Michaelo! Forgive me for not noticing you.'

'I thought it best not to interrupt. Such a fine powder, I did not wish to be responsible for a disaster. Might I ask the purpose of such a powder?'

'Curing rashes, quieting the thoughts, purifying the liver. The barbers add it to many salves.' Lucie took another sip as she blinked away the dust. How strange to see Brother Michaelo in an oft-mended, ill-fitting habit. Had Owen not warned her, she would have wondered what mishap had necessitated his borrowing a fellow monk's clothes. She took off her apron, setting it aside and smoothing down her simple gown.

'Come.' She plucked a hood and a short summer cloak from the pegs by the door, completing her costume for the mission, and picked up a basket of remedies she'd gathered, choosing them in the hope that Cilla was amenable to her ministrations.

Jasper appeared in the doorway to ask whether he should finish the work.

'No need. I will not be long.' She did not bother to reprimand him for the discourtesy of ignoring Michaelo. Jasper's deep-set distrust of the monk was not easily mended. 'I am grateful to you for closing up the shop this evening.'

As they walked up Stonegate, Lucie wondered aloud why Cilla would seek refuge in the minster yard.

'To an extent, it is a safe haven,' said Michaelo. 'The folk living there keep careful watch, knowing that at the first sign of trouble the dean and chapter will drive them off and destroy their hovels to prevent their return, so they do their best to keep the peace.'

'How terrible it must be to . . .' She was interrupted by a man expressing his thanks that Owen was to be captain of the city bailiffs.

'He will see to scoundrels and crooks,' the man said.

When Lucie explained that he had taken on his present investigations as favors to the Swanns and the Braithwaites, that nothing had been decided about Owen's future, the man seemed to wilt.

No sooner had he walked on than a woman touched Lucie's arm, shyly asking whether Owen had found Old Bede, and whether it was true that a wolf was running loose in the city. No wolf in the city, Lucie assured the woman, but Old Bede was still missing. Again, the disappointment was visceral.

'Their fear has me questioning the wisdom of escorting you to the crowded yard,' said Michaelo.

'I take responsibility for my own safety,' said Lucie. She was watching alleyways and the shadowy areas close to the shop fronts, alert for danger. 'Are the dean and chapter eager to evict the poor from their yard?'

'I have no doubt they pray for a reason to do so.'

Lamps were being lit in the homes they passed, and within the minster gates the stonemasons were saying their goodnights as they quit work on the east end, Thoresby's lady chapel.

'He would be pleased that the building continues,' she said as they passed.

'Let us pray that the dean and chapter manage to hide the funds from the grasp of the new archbishop,' said Michaelo.

'He is a greedy man?'

A sniff. 'He is a Neville. Sir Richard Ravenser would have seen it finished, and finished well.' Thoresby's nephew and the late archbishop's personal choice to succeed him. The powerful Nevilles had outmaneuvered him, winning the king's support. 'An opportunity squandered,' said Michaelo. He drew a square of linen from his sleeve as they approached the shacks huddled against the north end of the minster. Lucie caught a scent of lavender as he shook it out and held it to his nose.

And yet, as they picked their way along a narrow path between the shacks folk smiled and bobbed their heads at Michaelo as if he were a familiar, trusted figure. He nodded in turn, and responded to many by name. Wattle and daub, reed mats, piles of stones, half-burnt timbers – the folk fashioned their dwellings with whatever came to hand, and few seemed sufficient to protect them from the harsh Yorkshire winter to come.

'Did you tell Cilla you were bringing me?'

'No, I merely inquired as to her welfare, having heard that she'd suffered a fall and badly bruised her face. Here we are.' He handed Lucie the basket.

Tucked into the corner where the nave met the north transept, the shelter was nothing more than planks of wood angled against the stone edifice. Well shielded from the wind, perhaps, but little else. The sharp angle shaded it, so the stone would be cold and damp.

'If it's Cecelia you seek, you'll not find her here.' The speaker leaned on a crutch fashioned from a branch, the top wrapped round with rags as filthy as the ones that hung from his large, emaciated frame. 'Gone in the night.'

'Gone?' Michaelo looked round as if not believing him.

Lucie looked round, noticed a girl peering out from the shelter beside Cilla's. She crouched down to speak to her. 'I brought salves for Cecelia. I'd heard she was badly bruised.'

The girl's head seemed to sink into her shoulders as she shied away.

'Would you know where I might find her?'

A shake of the head revealed horrible scarring from a burn on one side of her face, and Lucie realized that the child had only one arm.

'She won't want you to find her.' Her mouth twisted as she spoke, the scar making it difficult for her to form her words.

Lucie drew out a jar of the salve Owen used to keep the skin of his blind eye soft and malleable. 'This will soften the skin on your face,' she said. 'A little each morning and each night.' She handed it to the girl. 'A gift.'

A twisted smile. 'The man with the hellhound came for her in the night.'

'Grace!' A woman plucked the jar from the child and handed it to Lucie. 'We do not need your pity.'

'Forgive me,' said Lucie. 'I am—'

The woman withdrew with the child.

Michaelo touched Lucie's arm. 'Come. We are not welcome here.'

'The child was about to tell me something.'

'No matter.' Michaelo took the basket from her arm and guided her away.

As they picked their way among the dwellings, Michaelo asked a few whether they knew where Cecelia had gone. The question was met with uneasy glances as folk shook their heads. At the edge of the camp a woman fell into step with Lucie.

'They are afraid of the hellhound,' she whispered. 'But the beast cannot harm Cecelia.'

Lucie turned to ask the woman how she knew, but she'd vanished.

'In faith, she was there yesterday,' Michaelo was saying. 'Forgive my error. When I inquired after her wellbeing earlier and heard she was away I took that to mean for the moment.'

'Who was the woman who spoke to me just now?'

Michaelo frowned down at her. 'I did not see.'

Wrapping Dame Muriel against the evening chill, Alisoun led her out onto the solar landing, walking her back and forth to work out a cramp in her calf. The landing stretched the length of the house, affording a view of the Fenton garden, the York Tavern, and, at a slight angle, Lucie Wilton's apothecary garden. Dame Janet would be horrified to see them out there, believing as she did that her daughter must remain in bed. But Muriel was no longer hobbled by the cramp, and she breathed with more ease. Even such a simple exercise might induce a deeper, more restful sleep. They continued their pacing, saying little, both lost in their own reveries, until Alisoun caught a movement near the rear door of the Fenton house. As she watched she saw a man gesture to an animal so large that as it began to dart away he hardly needed to bend over at all in order to catch it by the scruff of its neck and make it stay.

She must alert Ned without alarming the household. 'I pray this has encouraged your appetite, Dame Muriel.' She hoped her companion did not hear the tremor in her voice as she tried to lead her toward her bedchamber.

But Muriel resisted. 'A few more turns. My leg feels so much better.'

Alisoun rubbed Dame Muriel's shoulders. 'We will stay out longer in the morning.'

Muriel shook her off and stepped over to the railing. 'Is that the new servant in the Fenton garden? What was his name? Ned. Yes, like my cousin. Why would he trespass?'

Alisoun joined her. Ned was indeed stealing toward the Fenton house. The man and dog were no longer in sight. She felt a wave of relief.

'He is following Captain Archer's orders, guarding your household,' said Alisoun. 'The Fentons' house being empty, he's right to check it.'

'Bless him. Bless all of you.' Muriel touched Alisoun's forearm. 'I could not ask for more loving care. I believe I might eat something now.'

Alisoun hurried down to the kitchen herself, telling the cook what she wanted, that she would return for it in a moment. At the gate into the Fenton garden she saw no one. Hurrying to the house, she found the door ajar. She pushed it open and was stepping through when someone grabbed her from the shadows, holding a dagger to her throat.

'Be silent. You are safe so long as you say nothing. You did not see me. You were not here.'

Feeling the stump of the arm pressing into her chest, she knew it to be Crispin Poole.

He pushed her out the door and shut it behind her.

Back in the Swann yard, she vomited in the midden.

Jasper stepped out from the apothecary workshop as Owen passed on his way to the tavern. 'Brother Michaelo was here again, talking to Dame Lucie. Are you both working with him?'

His mind on other matters, Owen nodded. 'He believes he's found Cilla.'

'Oh.'

The disappointment in Jasper's voice got Owen's attention. 'What's troubling you?'

'How can you work with the man who poisoned Brother Wulfstan?' The infirmarian at St Mary's had survived the poisoning, living to save Jasper's life the following year, becoming a beloved spiritual guide to the orphaned boy while he lived.

'I believe in the power of redemption,' said Owen. 'Happens he's . . .' He lost the thought as Ned hurried through the gate. 'Trouble?'

'A man and a dog, standing beneath the eaves of the Fenton house just now.' Ned took a breath. 'Watching Alisoun walking Dame Muriel on the landing above.' Another breath. 'And then he was gone. I thought you'd want to check the house with me.'

'What did he look like?' Owen asked, thinking of Braithwaite's man Galbot and the dog Tempest.

'He stayed in the shadows so I could not see his face. A short man, or the dog is uncommon tall.'

Tempest was a large dog, but not so large as to make Galbot, who was of middling height, seem short. Still, Ned was guessing.

Jasper had ducked into the workshop and reappeared with Owen's bow and a quiver of arrows. 'I pray you don't need them.'

Owen pressed his shoulder in thanks and strode out after Ned, who had hurried ahead. Owen kept a casual gait. No need to raise an alarm.

Ned waited by the house. 'They stood right here, looking up.' He pointed to the windows on the upper floor of the Swann home. 'Alisoun was walking Dame Muriel back and forth,' he said quietly. 'I'd heard the creaking up above, came out to see who it was. Then I noticed the man and dog standing here.' He raised his hand in greeting as Alisoun appeared at the railing, but she did not respond, backing out of sight.

Owen tried the latch on the door. Not locked. In fact, the door swung inward at his touch. 'You?'

'No. I found it this way.'

Owen pushed it wide and stepped into a corridor, kitchen and pantry to either side. He stopped, held his breath, listened. He motioned to Ned to search the rooms to either side while he moved forward into the hall. Warm coals in the fire circle. The Fentons had been gone for weeks, but someone had been here today. The street door was slightly ajar. No one on the street with a dog.

'Damn,' Ned muttered at his shoulder. 'He moves quickly.'

'And unnoticed. He knows this street. Knows this house, perhaps.

At least we know he's still in the city. Warn Alisoun. But first, go to the Braithwaites – you know it, two doors away?' Ned nodded. 'See whether the dog Tempest is tied up in front of the house, guarding it. If not, ask to talk to Galbot, his handler. See whether they've been out walking.'

'But what if it was him, and he's up to no good?'

'He'll know that we noticed. Come to the York Tavern to tell me what you learn. Wait for me if you return before I do.'

'Where are you going?'

'The minster yard.'

With a nod, Ned strode out into Coney Street.

With that long, fast stride, hand resting on his sheathed dagger, Lucie knew that Owen expected trouble. She broke away from Michaelo to hurry to him.

'Owen!'

He took a moment to recognize her. Clearly she did not fit the scene he'd envisioned. 'God be praised.' He gathered her to him in a fierce embrace.

'What is it?' asked Michaelo, joining them.

'A man and a large dog watching the Swann home. They disappeared and I—' He stepped away from Lucie, shaking his head. 'I encouraged you to go to Cilla and then when I thought—'

She stood on tiptoe to kiss his lips. 'We did not find her. The man with the hellhound took her away, according to a little girl. And a woman who did not stay long enough for me to see her told me not to worry, the beast cannot harm Cecelia. I did not have a chance to ask what she meant by that. Who saw the man with the dog?'

'Ned. But he was gone by the time we searched the house. Whoever he was, he'd lit a fire there.'

'So he spends time there. Watching the Swann house?' Lucie crossed herself. 'Someone is helping them, someone with the means to hide the men and their dogs, and provide a way for them to move about the city.'

Owen nodded, walking toward the folk peering out from the hovels. But he managed only to frighten them back into their shells. He turned back to Lucie and Michaelo with a muttered curse.

'They're frightened,' said Michaelo.

'A hellhound, the girl called it,' said Lucie. 'Do what you need to do, my love. You must find this man.'

As Owen stepped through the doorway the tavern grew quiet, all eyes on him, eager for news. An old, familiar experience. He was glad he'd left his bow and quiver with Tom at the door. 'We know nothing more than we did last night,' he told the Merchets' patrons.

Someone asked if Old Bede had been found.

'We are still searching.'

Folk crossed themselves, then went back to their conversations as he made his way to the far corner where Geoffrey presided.

'Is it true?' Geoffrey asked. 'You have nothing?'

Owen settled on the bench and sighed as his back met the cool outer wall, ignoring the question.

Bess placed a full tankard before him. 'Drink up.'

She was walking away when Owen touched her elbow. 'On the night Hoban was murdered, was Crispin Poole in the tavern?'

She tucked in her chin, eyes down, remembering. A slow nod. 'Yes, he was. Tucked here in the corner. Stayed a long while, alone, drinking little. If he was waiting for someone, they never came.' To Geoffrey she said, 'Best leave the captain in peace. I know that look, he's come to think.'

'I am yours to command, Sweet Bess,' said Geoffrey, holding out his tankard for a refill.

But on this particular evening, Geoffrey's silence was the last thing Owen wanted.

'You made no mention of Sir John Holland,' said Owen. 'I would have nothing to do with him?' He did not trust Princess Joan's son by her first husband, a young man he found cruel and undisciplined.

Geoffrey perked up. 'Not here seeking peace after all? The prince has given much thought to your dislike of Sir John. Though he believes it possible you misjudge his stepson, he values you precisely because you are your own man. You would have no need to communicate with Sir John. What say you?'

'Sweetens the prospect.'

'So you accept?'

'I am considering the prince's proposal with the care it deserves.'

'Stubborn Welshman. You brought it up to torment me.'

The ale was beginning to take effect. Owen stretched out his legs and yawned. 'Muriel Swann believes that Crispin Poole might hold the key to all that has happened. You have an interest in him.'

Geoffrey narrowed his eyes. 'What has he to do with the prince?'

'You tell me.'

'Nothing, so far as I know. My interest, as you call it, is mere curiosity. The man intrigues me. He seems morose, as if regretting his return. Was it his choice, I wonder.'

'Have you learned anything?'

'How can one bide at the York and not hear about a battle-scarred prodigal son returned? But we've not been introduced.'

'Battle?' He'd not asked Crispin how he'd come to lose the arm, assuming the man wearied of the tale, as Owen did the story of his blinding. 'Tell me what you know.'

'Is that an order? Am I addressed by the new captain of York's bailiffs? But soft – you still have no authority over me. Though I am biding in your city, I'm here on the king's business—'

'Have pity, Geoffrey. Two people have been murdered, and I'm desperate for even a hint of a cause that might connect their deaths.'

'Other than blood? Perhaps you might look to their friends. Speaking of which, our friendship feels brittle of late. You are keeping things from me.'

'As you are from me. How do I know we're not working at cross-purposes?'

'Owen! You know me better than that. How could you think I would undermine your efforts to find the murderers before more harm is done?'

He did know him better than to think that. For the most part. He had decided to trust Geoffrey when Princess Joan brought trouble to the archbishop's palace of Bishopthorpe, and his trust had been rewarded. Yet there was ever a strange friction between them, and Owen found it difficult to relax with the man. Still, he had never, to Owen's knowledge, worked against him. In apology, Owen told Geoffrey what Lucie had learned from Muriel, the 'circle', the secrets, their unease upon Poole's return. 'Tell me about him.'

'Your friend the Austin canon—'

'Erkenwald?' A former soldier, he had put aside his weapons

and taken up the cross, serving for some years now at St Leonard's Hospital. Owen had once coaxed him into action to save Alisoun Ffulford when she ran away from the hospital's orphanage and straight into trouble.

Geoffrey grinned. 'Such a stout name.' He sat back, arms crossed over his belly, ready to tell a tale. 'Before Erkenwald took his final vows he accompanied an elder canon to Avignon. There he encountered Poole, a one-armed merchant catering to the English bearing petitions to the Holy See. The story there was that Poole had been felled in battle by a mace to his remarkably thick skull. He woke to find himself trapped beneath a mortally wounded destrier that was crushing his arm as it thrashed in its death agony.'

'Beneath a great beast and he lost only the arm?' said Owen. 'Most fortunate of men.'

'I sensed that the canon doubted it happened quite that way. But it is the story Poole tells. *However* he lost the arm, he seemed a merchant of some account.'

'He must have had a patron,' Owen noted.

'If he did, Erkenwald did not say. But what *I* know is that he has friends at court. And among influential merchants in the North, such as John Gisburne, who furnished him with letters of introduction to his guild members here in York.'

'A merchant with friends at court – I can see why Crispin Poole would win John Gisburne's support. Poole did mention the letters of introduction, but it appears Gisburne did that and no more. His family has ignored Poole.' Owen remembered the man's clenched jaw. He'd felt the slight. To Owen's mind, Poole was better off without him. But Gisburne's influence would be invaluable to a merchant. He was currently in Westminster sitting on the king's commission on the wool market, having once been in charge of the wool staple in York. It was said he kept the outlaws he called household guards with him there, no doubt enriching Gisburne with thievery and crooked business transactions while he concocted ways to cheat the king. Owen knew firsthand the man's ruthlessness. 'So Poole has a patron of some influence at court?'

'Talk to Erkenwald. I'm certain he knows more.'

'Why did you approach him about Poole? Does this have to do with your mission here?'

'To be honest, I don't know whether it does or no, but I saw

Poole leaving the grounds of St Leonard's Hospital, turning to nod to Dom Erkenwald.'

So Geoffrey was following him. Owen tucked that away. 'When did you witness this?'

'The day I arrived, then departed for Freythorpe Hadden.'

So quickly noted. To Owen that meant Geoffrey had known of Crispin Poole before his arrival in York.

'I swear to you that I'll do everything in my power to help, not hinder your investigation of the murders of these good men,' said Geoffrey.

'Crispin Poole's friends at court – that's your interest, eh? You are to uncover what it is he's doing for them, this one-armed merchant?' Owen believed he'd hit the mark, though Geoffrey's flinch was subtle. Was it Alexander Neville? As Owen could not guess whether Prince Edward favored the new archbishop or considered him as a threat, he thought it best not to mention him. Not yet. 'So as long as my discoveries do not inconvenience either the king or his heir, you'll allow me to bring the murderers to justice?'

'Allow? I've no such power over you, my friend.'

They exchanged smiles, saluted each other with their tankards, then drained them.

'Thank you, my friend.' Owen pushed back from the table. He would rise early and catch Erkenwald at the beginning of his day. 'One more thing. Have you ever seen Poole with a dog?'

'Ah. Back to the murders.' Geoffrey shook his head. 'I've seen no dog with him.' He nodded toward the door. 'The lad's been watching us for a while.'

Ned sat at a table near the door with Alfred.

Owen thanked Geoffrey and crossed the room to his men. Catching sight of him, Alfred rose, just raking a hand across his bald pate as if to smooth back his long-vanished hair, a nervous habit. Nothing of use to tell him, Owen guessed. Ned looked more sanguine, rising slightly and bobbing his head.

'Come to the house with me, I would have my wife hear your news as well,' Owen said, leading them out the door and through the garden gate.

Lucie rose from the window-seat where she and Jasper had been talking.

'Any news?' she asked, motioning the men to the table. Kate

hurried out with a pitcher of ale, blushing at Ned's greeting. The young man was far too generous in his attention to young women.

'I've none to offer. Learned nothing of use,' said Alfred as he settled on a bench. 'Braithwaite's manservant Galbot was reluctant to talk.' Bringing Ned up to date, he described the dog Paul Braithwaite had brought to guard his parents' home.

'A man lacking tact,' Ned noted.

'It would seem,' said Owen. 'Everyone copes with loss in their own way. And with such violent deaths, fear competes with their grief. Paul Braithwaite might feel this is how he might contribute to the protection of his family. He looked to Olyf Tirwhit, Bartolf's daughter, for approval, which puzzled me.' He glanced over at Lucie, who nodded, interested. 'I am hoping to have news about the dog and his handler.' He looked to Ned.

'I found Galbot and the dog in the kitchen, and the cook complained they'd been there a while. Not the pair I'd seen.'

'A coincidence that Galbot took Tempest off guard when another dog was in the area?' Owen wondered aloud as Ned drained his bowl and set it aside.

The young man sat forward. 'I did talk to someone on the street, asked if he'd seen a man with a large dog. He had not, but he mentioned a cart sitting in front of the Fentons' house for a time. He'd wondered whether the family had returned, but when he came out of his house it was gone.'

'He moves the dog about in a cart?' Lucie wondered.

'Clever,' said Jasper. 'Folk might not even notice the dog in a cart.'

'Was George Hempe in the tavern?' Lucie asked. 'Does he know about tomorrow's service in St Helen's?'

'No.' Owen looked to Alfred.

'I will tell him we'll need men at the two houses, and the church,' said Alfred. 'Will they bury them in St Helen's churchyard?'

'She did not say,' said Owen.

'Several of her ancestors are buried beneath the church,' said Lucie.

They spoke of Crispin Poole and of Cilla's disappearance, Jasper muttering something about a fool's errand to the minster yard, Michaelo merely seeking attention. Owen was left feeling frustrated when Ned and Alfred rose to leave and Jasper headed for his bed over the shop.

'Stay a moment,' Owen said to Alfred. 'Early in the morning, before you set up for the burial, take one of the bailiff's men and walk the route a cart would take from the Fenton home to John Gisburne's manse, ask anyone you see along the way whether they noticed a man with a dog in a cart today.'

'I thought the lad said who would notice?'

'But if someone, just one person, did—' Owen nodded to him.

'Gisburne. Aye.' Alfred whistled as he stepped out the door.

'Much as I dislike him, I see no evidence,' said Lucie.

Owen knew she was right. 'Perhaps I do it for spite, but if we learn anything, all the better.'

'We need to see the pattern in the attacks,' said Lucie as she lit their way up to their bedchamber.

'The Swanns are the center.'

'And Crispin Poole the spur?' Lucie turned on the steps to regard Owen. 'Why did he leave when he did, do you know? A falling-out with Hoban?'

'And a dog somehow involved, is that what you're thinking?' Owen could not help but grin as he kissed her.

'Laugh if you like, but it might fit the pattern.'

'And Bartolf?'

'As coroner, he might have had ideas about how his son should comport himself. Perhaps he blamed Crispin for some mischief.'

'And that led to murder?'

'You might scoff at the idea, but it all fits.'

She continued up the steps, leaving Owen to wonder why he was so quick to reject the idea. He hurried to catch up with her.

'Then you suspect Crispin?'

She paused. 'Perhaps. Or perhaps as Hoban's friend he was protected.'

'Then why leave?'

'There are gaps in the tale, I admit it. I should not have proposed it.'

'No, I am glad you spoke of this.' In fact, the more he considered it, the more he wondered whether the answers lay in the past. 'You are a wonder,' he said as she set the lamp on the shelf inside their door. He picked her up and carried her to the bed.

*　　*　　*

Stepping out onto the landing, a respite from the warm room and
Dame Muriel's snores, Alisoun stretched her arms over her head
and breathed deeply. She wished she might quiet her mind. If not
for lying to the captain, she might feel good that the grieving
widow and expectant mother in her care slept deeply tonight, that
her ministrations were effective and appreciated. She'd not set out
to lie, merely to protect by silence. But with that false step she
had begun a precipitous fall, and now she felt as if she were down
in a pit she must escape, but could find no purchase with hands
or feet, no way to pull herself out.

Something struck her arm, and again. Pebbles. Down below,
Ned motioned for her to join him in the garden. She hurried down.

'You have a good aim,' she said. 'But if I'd cried out, I would
be cursing you for causing me to wake Dame Muriel.'

'I kept waving to you, but you did not see me. I saw you out
there earlier, when Captain Archer and I were searching for the
man and beast I'd seen. Did you see them?'

'I did. I was thinking how to slip away to tell you when I saw
you go into the yard. Did you catch them?'

'No. Have a care, Alisoun. He'd lit the fire in the hall. Who
knows how long he was there, or whether he'll return? He's
watching this house.'

So Ned had entered the house. Had he seen Poole? Had
she? She was no longer certain, and the thought of what might
have happened tightened her throat. 'Why would someone watch
the house?' she whispered.

'We cannot know that until Captain Archer discovers why
Hoban and Bartolf were murdered, and in such wise. The
beasts . . . They play a role. One has been seen at the minster
yard. They call it a hellhound. Danger is abroad. I wanted you
to know.'

She needed no warning about that. But she was grateful for the
information. 'Thank you. But why are you telling me this?'

'I know you can defend yourself. I did not mean to offend you.'

This was what lying brought, a distrust of everyone, even those
who befriended her. Stupid, stupid, stupid. What was Crispin Poole
to her? He had not bothered himself about her safety.

'You did not offend me. I am grateful for this, Ned. I feel
responsible for the mistress of this house. I meant merely that I

wondered whether Captain Archer had given you leave to tell me of this.'

'Would he not want you to be safe?'

But I lied to him. Again she tripped over her own mistake. 'Of course. I don't know why I asked. I should return. I would not want Dame Muriel to waken and wonder where I was.'

'Until tomorrow.'

'Yes.' She bobbed her head and hurried back into the house, starting as she stepped into the hall and caught a movement at the corner of her eye. A cat mewed. Alisoun crouched down to pet her. 'Have a care, Viper,' she whispered, smiling at the cat's name. It was said that Muriel's brother had disliked the cat, and had called her 'viper' to irritate his sister. But she had embraced the name, celebrating the ferocity of the gray and black tabby. 'There are evil dogs abroad in the night.' Alisoun shivered as she said it, looking round the four corners of the long room.

EIGHT

Old Soldiers and Intrepid Maids

'You were thrashing about before I woke you,' Lucie whispered in Owen's ear. 'Were you dreaming of the jongleur's leman?'

She knew him so well. In times of trouble Owen's scarred left eye prickled and ached, and he relived the night that ended his career as captain of archers. In a camp in Normandy, he'd caught a man slashing the throats of the noble hostages in his care. A Breton whose life he had saved. His thanks was betrayal. Owen's fury had distracted him and he'd not noticed the jongleur's companion until she'd slashed his eye, blinding him. But that was not the unpleasantness from which he'd just awakened.

'No, wolves. Packs of them, circling a battlefield piled high with bodies. I could hear cries for help from those still alive, but trapped beneath the fallen.' Bile rose in his throat. The dream still felt too real.

'God have mercy.' Lucie brushed back his hair and kissed his forehead. 'You will find the murderers, my love. Have faith.'

How could she be so certain? 'I'll borrow yours for now, until I've made some progress.'

She kissed the scar radiating out from his left eye. 'I have more than enough faith in you for both of us. It's past dawn, my love, and you wanted to catch Erkenwald before he goes on his alms rounds. You must hurry!'

They made their way down the steps, shoes in hands so as not to wake the children. In the kitchen, Kate had set up a table by the open garden door, bread, cheese, and fruit, a pitcher of Tom Merchet's ale.

'The bread and ale are fresh this morning. My sister Rose brought the bread from Ma's kitchen. She stayed long enough to tell me the old one is on the mend, and eats more than the two of them together.' They had agreed not to mention Old Bede by name so that they might not slip elsewhere.

'No unexpected visitors?'

'A few seeking a healer, and they explained Mistress Alisoun's absence, where she might be found if they could not wait. And a man, asking whether they had seen a body in the river.'

'Did he give them trouble?' Owen asked.

'Not my Rose and Rob. They told him a tale about a terrifying beast, half-wolf, half-boar, that had chased them in Galtres, and they had sought the dragon's protection. They begged him not to tell the Riverwoman or her apprentice that they had been trespassing, but they were so afraid. He cursed them and went away. In truth, I don't know whether to laugh or pray.'

Lucie took her hand. 'They've wit and courage. But I pray for them all the day. Are they worried?'

'A little. They say there is something out there. Silences – all the birds quiet, as if on alert. Something's prowling out there. And folk in the shacks against the abbey wall have seen men with dogs as big as wolves – some claim they *are* wolves. But they keep their distance. There's been no trouble.'

'Yet,' Lucie whispered, sending Owen a worried look.

Kate did not seem to notice. 'My brother is practicing his knife throwing and has set up a butt to practice with the bow. Rob believes with such a martial display anyone with a thought to attack will think twice.' She laughed and turned to fuss with a pot hanging over the fire.

Such display means nothing to a hungry dog, Owen thought.

'And it was Jasper who brought the ale from the York Tavern,' Kate went on. 'He said all was quiet in the night, and he's opened the shop, so you need not hurry, Dame Lucie.'

'Jasper's opened the shop so early?' Lucie glanced toward the door.

Owen reached for her hand and coaxed her to sit, promising he would take the time to talk to their son before he went to St Leonard's. 'The memory of you smiling at me across the table will warm me through the day.' It worked, and he pushed all thought of the day ahead from his mind, talking instead about the garden, his plans for changes at the manor that had been gifted him, including the house, which had been neglected for a long while. 'I could use your advice about that.'

Lucie seemed far away as she broke up some bread.

'What are you thinking?' Owen asked.

'We might wish to go sooner rather than later, combine the visit to your manor with one to Paul Braithwaite's. You said he mentioned it was close to Freythorpe Hadden, so it is close to your land as well.'

'Braithwaite's? Why?'

'I don't like the handler being so quiet, so unhelpful to Alfred,' said Lucie. 'A master of hounds loves to talk hounds. Galbot was his name? It may simply be that Bartolf's beloved dogs have found a new home with him, and he fears we will tell the Swanns, who will retrieve them. But whatever it is, we should know.'

'I hope we need not call on Paul Braithwaite at his home,' said Owen, 'that the murderers make a mistake and reveal themselves before we travel south again.'

'If Alfred comes with news, I'll send him to St Leonard's?'

'Yes. Tell him that I will head to the Braithwaite home after I'm finished at the hospital.'

Lucie rose and bent to kiss the top of his head, kneading his shoulders. 'Now go on, see what our son is about.'

He found Jasper sitting on the floor of the workroom behind the shop, a large space that had once been the kitchen and hearth place of their home, before Lucie's father bought the large house across the garden for them. Jasper was pulling the bound shop ledgers from a low shelf, stacking them up.

'What is this?'

'Mother hid Nicholas Wilton's journals from me.'

'She had thought for good cause. Had you not walked with Alisoun, had she gone that way without a lantern—'

'But I did.'

'It was your manner, son. And now since she understands why you behaved so, she's been too busy to fetch it. Remind her – she won't fuss. Want to lock up and walk with me to St Leonard's?'

Jasper looked relieved, but he shook his head at the invitation.

'I need to put these away and go out to the counter to see to customers.'

'I do not know what we would do without you, son.'

A shy grin, a shrug, and Jasper busied himself with the task.

Owen left by the shop door opening onto the street, and quickly stepped back in to avoid a handcart careening toward him. A baker's boy pushed the cart piled high with bread into the yard of the York Tavern. 'Sorry, Captain!' he called out. 'This goes where it will of a morning.'

'If he weren't the baker's son—' Jasper shook his head, grinning. 'Have a care now, Da.'

Bess Merchet was giving the baker's lad a piece of her mind when Owen ventured out into the morning crowd. If the lad did not learn to control the cart he'd soon be out of work no matter that his father was his employer. Yet Owen silently blessed him for a moment of laughter in a grim time. As he headed to the hospital he was stopped every few steps. Several asked if Old Bede had been found. He lied with a shake of his head. A merchant's wife said she would take some fresh bread to Winifrith and the children. An elderly clerk noted that as long as no one found Old Bede's body, there was hope. 'After this long?' A young woman with a newborn in her arms shook her head. In Blake Street Owen came upon a man carrying a dog with a bloody rump, the lad with him weeping loudly. A red-faced woman followed them wringing her hands. 'You should know better than to let dog loose after what's happened to the Swanns. How was I to know he was your old hound, snuffling round me in the dark before dawn?' There would be more such canine injuries before this was over.

The twins' report, added to Ned's sighting of the man at the Fentons, the whispers of a hellhound in the minster yard, and Old Bede's fright at the staithes bothered Owen more and more. It was an organized siege, not just the murder of two enemies. He must find the connections so that he might anticipate the next potential victims.

'Captain!' George Hempe hurried toward him. 'Alfred told me about today's service. I will ensure there are sufficient men to protect the two families. I am turning a deaf ear on the aldermen's complaints – they say the Braithwaites are using us as their personal guard.'

Owen thanked him.

'I do not know how long I can continue to support you.'

'I know.'

'If you were captain of bailiffs . . .'

'Did they say that? I'd have their full support if I accepted the post?'

'They did, but that should not influence your decision.'

Owen heard his humorless chuckle and knew himself to be in danger of saying whatever he need say in order to keep the city safe. His city, the city in which his family and friends depended on his strategy. He cursed the bind he was in, cursed Thoresby for dying and leaving him at the mercy of city and prince.

'Where are you heading?' George asked as he hurried to keep up with Owen's angry pace.

'St Leonard's. Erkenwald might have some information for me. And then to the Braithwaites.'

'I will meet you there. Or at the church.' George touched Owen's arm. 'I will do all I can, my friend.'

'As will I. Pray it is enough.'

St Leonard's yard seemed a haven of peace, canons and lay brothers and sisters going about their chores. Spying the barrel-chested Erkenwald rounding the far corner of the church, Owen hastened to catch up with him, sending pigeons flying out of his path. The canon glanced up at them, then round to see what had startled them. A grin and a nod. 'Owen, my friend.' He gestured to a bench at the edge of a garden still colorful at the waning of the season. 'Matilda de Warrene's garden. She would smile to see it so lovingly tended.' A corrodian of St Leonard's, she had loved this garden. 'You are not come to steal me away for a bowl of ale and conversation at this early hour, and looking so solemn.'

'You would be right.' Owen settled beside him. 'I am in need of information. Geoffrey Chaucer tells me you know Crispin Poole.'

Erkenwald raised his thick brows. 'Was it for you he asked about Poole? Had I known that I might have been more forthcoming.'

'But not for himself? You do not trust Geoffrey?'

'Do you?'

'For the most part.' Owen could not lie to the good canon, a friend who had come to his aid during an outbreak of the pestilence when all the city was mad with fear. It was the death of Matilda de Warrene's husband he'd investigated then.

'Then I leave it for you to decide whether or not he can be trusted to know more than I told him,' said Erkenwald.

'You met Poole in Avignon.'

'Earlier. As a soldier. He was new in the camp, struggling to find his place, his value. With no particular martial skills, he spent his time lurking, listening. The sort I wanted nothing to do with. I was glad when my company moved on. The next time I caught his name it was grumbling about how he was rising in the ranks on the backs of his fellows. "He does favors," they said, "injuries, rumors, whatever his betters want doing," they said. He'd become skilled with a knife, even better with his hands. A strong man. He rose to sergeant, and then his arm was mangled so badly there was nothing to do but remove it.'

'Fell beneath a horse? Lay on the field all night pinned beneath the dying destrier?'

'Chaucer told me that's what he's saying.' Erkenwald's battle scars twisted his grin into a grimace. 'I didn't correct him. But the truth is far less heroic. He and his comrades stole a wagonload of wine, casks of it. They were already in their cups, and the lot who were riding in the back of the wagon tapped a cask and guzzled until they started brawling. Poole fell out over the wheel and his arm got caught in the spokes. Mangled.'

Owen winced, imagining the agony. 'Poor devil. The memory of it must still bring on a cold sweat.'

'Some did call him a devil. But I wish such pain on no man.'

Interesting how much Erkenwald had chosen not to share with Geoffrey.

'After the accident, he somehow moved into trade. In Avignon. Considering how he had risen before—' Erkenwald's expressive brows finished the thought.

'A patron for whom he did favors?'

'So I imagined. Someone who appreciated a protégé good with a knife, his hands, and ruthless. He might have lost a hand, but not his knife hand. As you have learned to compensate for one eye, so might he become proficient with one hand.' He shook his head. 'God forgive me, but I fear it was an ill wind brought him back home. You know he grew up here.'

'I do. It seems he was friends with Hoban Swann, perhaps Paul Braithwaite, Adam Tirwhit?'

'I know nothing about that. But he seems a lonely man now. A falling out?'

'I know less than you. Was Alexander Neville in Avignon at the time?'

Erkenwald studied Owen. 'You are thinking he has come to be watch and ward for the new archbishop?'

'I am thinking I must learn whether there was trouble between the Swanns and the Nevilles, though they are hardly of the same status.' He told him of the event at the Fentons the previous day, and Lucie's discovery at the minster yard. 'An organized assault stinks of the Nevilles.'

'Or some powerful family.' Erkenwald glanced round. 'We appear to have been fortunate. No sign of dogs in the hospital grounds.'

'You are indeed graced,' said Owen. 'Have you met with Crispin Poole often since his return?'

'Several times, though not by choice. He came to me, wanting me to know that he has sought forgiveness for his sins, worn a hair shirt, done endless penances – fasting, celibacy – and that he'd returned to right a wrong he had committed in running away from the city so long ago. But he discovered it cannot be righted. He can never make reparation for his lapse in courage.'

'What was the wrong?'

'That he did not say. And I did not care to ask. I am sorry to disappoint you.' Erkenwald shook his head at a lay sister bearing a basket and shears who asked if her cutting some late roses for the church would disturb them.

Owen waited until she was at the far end of the garden before speaking. 'Righting a wrong. Perhaps he came of his own accord, to settle an account with the coroner of Galtres.' He was testing the idea.

'And the first time he murdered the wrong Swann?' Erkenwald asked.

'He was in the York Tavern the night of Hoban's murder. And he was there the night of Bartolf's murder as well, though he left shortly after Bartolf did.'

'So it is unlikely he is the murderer.'

'Or he left the deed to others.'

'A man known for his skill with a knife? Would he find that satisfying?' Erkenwald laughed at Owen's grin. 'I was a soldier first.'

'You were indeed.'

'What is your impression of the man?' Erkenwald asked.

'The times we drank together in the York Tavern I found him an easy companion, well spoken, curious about events during his absence, a solitary soul, though he's living with his mother. But it might all be a careful guise donned for my benefit. If he is the one who's murdered Hoban and Bartolf, he has been careless. So careless as to suggest he believes he is above the law. I fear for York if that is so. Whose creature must he be, to have such confidence?' Owen took off his hat and ran a hand through his hair.

'That is an unsettling thought.'

'I can pray Poole is here for the reason he gave you, rather than to clear a path for a powerful patron. For all our sakes.'

'Unless his disappointment in discovering he cannot make amends led him to murder,' said Erkenwald.

'I cannot yet make sense of it,' said Owen.

'Why hesitate? Confront him.'

'If he is well backed and fiendishly clever, I will have revealed my suspicions to no purpose. He'll slide out from beneath my boot the wiser for it. I need to know as much as possible before I speak to him.' Owen cursed under his breath. 'If I were in Prince Edward's household, I might perhaps know the name of Poole's patron.'

'Is that reason enough to accept the prince's offer?'

'In truth, I doubt he will permit me the choice – phrasing it as such is a courtesy. Until I refuse. It is a command, not an offer. You see it otherwise?'

Erkenwald grunted. 'I think you are right. I will miss you.'

'Miss me? He wants me here in York, except when I am calling on the great families at their castles and manors, with Lucie on my arm. A knight's daughter. He likes that.'

'A cunning plan. Will he knight you?'

'Pray God I can refuse that.'

'And the city's wishes?'

Owen shook his head. 'I don't know.'

'Is there anything that appeals to you in his proposal?'

'I confess I do miss the access to knowledge of folk beyond the city and my family's lands. For just such moments when danger arrives from beyond my ken.'

'You do not yet know that the evil comes from without. But I understand.' A little smile. 'Righting wrongs. You cannot help yourself, can you?'

'What do you mean?' Owen asked, but he knew, he waved his friend quiet before he could respond. 'No, you are right. I missed the hunt.'

'In Thoresby's service you had both the city and the realm in your hands. To recreate that you must needs accept both offers – captain of York's bailiffs and spy for the prince.'

'I have made no decision.'

'No?' A wry grin. 'For now, I pray you restore peace to our fair city.' Erkenwald made the sign of the cross, blessing Owen. 'May God grant you the wisdom to see the way to justice.'

'Amen.' Owen bowed and crossed himself. But the blessing gave no ease. 'Justice? Nothing will bring back Bartolf, or resurrect Hoban so he might at last be the father he yearned to be.'

'No. But you must and will pursue the guilty and deliver them up to the crown. It is your nature to do so. Yours is a heavy burden of conscience, my friend. I will pray for you.'

'I count on your prayers,' Owen said. 'Do you sense that Poole has put aside his martial past? That he is now a man of commerce, no more?'

Erkenwald let out a sigh. 'I cannot say. I sensed a deep sadness in him, but whether that might move him to violence or peace . . .' The canon shook his head. 'I confess I cannot find it in me to believe him sincere, but that is my sin, not his. My earlier impression of him, in France – I cannot yet see beyond that.'

'I will talk to him tomorrow. I would today, but the requiems . . .'

'You have your hands full.'

Owen mentioned Cilla, that Lucie had hoped to talk to her in the minster yard. 'Have you met her?'

'I have. Why?'

'She worked for Bartolf Swann.'

'Ah. I do recall mention of that. She sought a post here, but chafed at the rules, wanted to work as it pleased her. Mark me, her manner might be unsettling, but Cecelia, or Cilla, as you will – she has her feet firmly on the earth. She is cunning. Scheming.'

'That is a new wrinkle.'

'I cannot speak to her purpose, but our disinterest angered her.'

Perceptive man. 'I could use your help.'

'You know where to find me.' Erkenwald's scar twisted his smile.

'I meant out beyond St Leonard's gates.'

'That is not my calling.'

'You are so certain?'

'I am. Now, Brother Michaelo . . .' Erkenwald frowned. 'No, in truth I cannot imagine him in anything but those tidy robes.'

'He has hidden depths.'

'I've no doubt of that.'

They sat for a little while in silence, watching the lay sister gathering beauty in her basket.

Alisoun stepped out into Coney Street with a basket over her arm and a list in her head of the gifts Dame Muriel wished to have ready to present to the servants after the requiem mass. A peculiar idea inspired by a dream in which all deserted her in mourning. Upon awakening, she realized how dependent she was on all who were helping her through this darksome time, even the servants, and she meant to show her gratitude. Such extreme emotions neither surprised nor concerned Alisoun, for Magda had warned her that they were to be expected, particularly as a woman approached her lying-in. But it made it no less irritating that Alisoun must hurry out as soon as the shops opened, and without a servant to assist her – for that would ruin the surprise.

Dreams had troubled Alisoun's sleep as well, dark dreams of great black beasts stalking the shadowy streets, fangs bared, their fiery eyes peering into the darkest corners, seeing all. The last thing she wished to do this morning was walk the streets alone. Though she knew it unlikely the streets were any less safe than on any other day, she could not seem to talk herself out of a strong sense of unease.

Folk greeted her with enthusiasm, lingering as if hoping she might share some gossip. After all, she was in the bosom of

the bereaved family. She thanked them for their prayers and
hurried on.

Her first call was a chandler's shop. She was just stepping
away with her purchases of oils and candles when she caught
sight of Wren, the young maidservant who had been at Magda's
home the night of Hoban Swann's murder. Her eyes went at once
to the girl's stomach, though it was far too early for her to be
showing again.

'Mistress Alisoun!'

Realizing Wren must have noticed her glance and might inter-
pret it as judgment – that Alisoun blamed her for her master's
inability to keep his hands to himself – she readied an apology.

'Wren, I—'

'I am grateful to you, Mistress Alisoun. My mistress never
missed me. I will keep you in my prayers all my days.'

'And your master?'

Wren seemed to hesitate, then leaned close to whisper, 'Master
Tirwhit has stopped his nightly visitations.'

The name caught Alisoun's attention. 'Adam Tirwhit? He is
your master?' Not her place to question, just to heal, according
to Magda, so she'd not asked the name of Wren's employer.

'So he is.'

The back of Alisoun's neck felt prickly, Providence? So her
mistress was Olyf Tirwhit, part of the circle Dame Muriel had
spoken about. 'The murders – your master and mistress have
reconciled in their grief?'

'No, it's not like that. He's accused her of having a lover. He
watches her. Angry.' She leaned close again, though they'd both
kept their voices low as they stood beneath the eaves of a house
next to the chandler's shop. 'She slips over to the house he leased
next door whenever she has a chance. She pretends it's the aged
widow Poole she's visiting, but she fusses with her hair and her
clothes before she goes.' A knowing nod.

Crispin Poole was her neighbor? Had God sent Wren to her?
Or . . . Alisoun almost backed away. Wren seemed too eager.
It was of course possible that Crispin was Olyf's lover. Or
she feared that whoever had murdered two of her kin might aim
the next arrow at her own heart, and Crispin, a former soldier,
might protect them. Though he had but one good arm . . . Alisoun

had heard Captain Archer say that a soldier injured in the field went on.

'But the troubles began after he returned, so no one else trusts Crispin Poole. Neither her brother nor her father did, may God grant them rest. I pray my mistress is not walking into danger.' Wren grasped Alisoun's arm. 'Are we in danger?'

Alisoun was now convinced that it was no accident Wren had discovered her here. Had she been scheming from the start? Coming to Alisoun the very night Hoban Swann was murdered? Keeping her from rushing out when she heard the dogs? 'I doubt you need fear for yourself. But if you see anything that seems a threat to your mistress, you might send me word.'

A hesitant nod, then more vigorous. 'I will. I want to help.'

'Bless you. I am biding at the Swann home on Coney Street. Dame Muriel is with child, and with all that has happened she felt the need of me. Her losses – her husband, his father, I fear she might succumb, and lose the baby.'

'Poor woman.' Wren wiped her eyes with her sleeve.

'She and Master Hoban waited so long for this child. But Captain Archer means to find the murderers,' said Alisoun, 'and if there is anything I might learn to help him . . .'

'So I should bring word to you about anything that I learn about Dame Olyf and Master Crispin?'

She was keen to focus on them. 'Or anything that happens at either house that does not seem as it should. Any strangers loitering about.'

'Strangers,' Wren whispered.

'Yes. Can you do that?'

'I can, Mistress Alisoun. But why are you here in the market when the Swanns are to be buried this morning at St Helen's? Does Dame Muriel not need you?'

Was that what she was after this morning? 'I might ask the same of you. Did Dame Olyf not need your help dressing?'

'She woke me before dawn to dress her, then left with the master to be with the family. Did you not see her?'

'No.'

'Oh, perhaps they went to the Braithwaite home.'

'And you are not attending her today?'

'Blessed be, no. But I must be on my way, I've much to

do before they return this evening.' She began to turn away,
then stopped, staring at a man emerging from an alleyway close
to them.

Alisoun shifted feet to see beyond the people milling about
in between. A servant's dress, patched, something handed down
from his master, a large wart on the side of his nose.

'Who is that?' Alisoun asked.

'Who?'

'You held your breath as you watched him, you know of whom
I speak.'

'I— He was out near the midden last evening. I shooed him
away.'

'He was in the Tirwhit yard last evening?' Alisoun tried to
keep her voice steady. That wart . . . She recognized him. He
had once come to Magda for savine, a type of juniper, so he
might make a paste to remove the wart, he said. Magda had
refused him, for it might also be used as a poison, offering a
paste of houseleek instead. He had brushed it away, demanding
the savine. *Tie a toad round thy neck*, Alisoun had snapped.
Red-faced and cursing, he'd hurried off, slipping and sliding
across the rocks to the riverbank in his blind fury. Magda had
chided Alisoun. *Insult a seeker with a useless charm and he'll
never return.* Alisoun had not known it was useless, though she
admitted she'd meant to insult him. What do you mean, a seeker?
Magda had looked at her, disappointed. *Thou'rt not such a fool
as to believe he was after a cure?*

'He was lurking back there,' said Wren, 'watching the houses.
Both of ours.'

There was more to the memory – Magda had muttered something about Bartolf the coroner being a fool for keeping him.
Was he Joss, the missing servant? 'You said you shooed him
away?' she asked. 'What did he then?'

'Backed away into the dark.' Wren gave a little shiver.

'Did you tell your master or mistress?'

'No. They were fighting and fussing about today, what to
wear, who would be at the church, then at the meal. Master
Adam was that angry that it was to be only kin. He said
Master Bartolf was coroner and deserved the mayor and council
in attendance. The mistress said he cared not a whit about her

father but wanted to preen before the important folk. Why? Is he important?' Wren turned to look at him, but he was disappearing between the stalls.

'Let me know if he comes back to the house,' Alisoun said, then hurried after him.

'You can trust me!' Wren called after her.

Pray God she knew better than to do that. Though Alisoun pushed her way through the crowd, she saw no sign of the man. But she knew more than before, enough to know that she must tell the captain everything. She would take him aside at the dinner later. And, after she had completed the shopping, she had a thought to take a look at the Tirwhit residence.

At the cutler she picked out a flesh hook for the cook, and a cheap rush light holder for Dame Muriel's maidservant.

Hurrying back to the house with her basket of gifts, she took her first opportunity to ask Dame Muriel how she might know the missing manservant – in case he was about in the city.

'Joss?' Muriel made a face. 'You would know him by the wart on his nose. A disgusting thing. Have you seen him?'

'I did not know what to look for.'

'Now you do. Come, set all this aside. We will present the gifts to the staff in the kitchen before the feast in hopes of lifting their spirits so they might carry out their duties on this sorrowful day.'

Alisoun made a show of realizing she'd forgotten something. 'I will not be long, Dame Muriel.' Up in the bedchamber she tucked her bow and quiver in a sack and slipped down the steps to the yard.

NINE
A Dog in the Night

O wen felt the weight of his responsibility as he parted with his friend, mulling over his words, *In Thoresby's service you had both the city and the realm in your hands. To recreate that you must needs accept both offers – captain of York's bailiffs and spy for the prince.* A double burden. Was that what he wanted?

As he made his way out of the hospital grounds the morning dimmed, a cluster of clouds obscuring what had been a bright morning sun. Footless Lane was quiet, but as Owen rounded the corner onto Coney Street he once again fielded questions about Old Bede, expressions of relief that he was investigating the deaths, and queries as to when the Swanns would be buried. Beneath it all, he questioned his hesitation about Crispin Poole. So many fingers pointing to him, a man of war, a man of violence, with retainers to carry out his blood-feud while he sat at the York Tavern. But what was the feud? What were the Swanns to him? That was the missing piece. He shook himself out of the puzzle. He must be alert, this day of all days.

On the route from the Braithwaite home, past the Swanns', round toward St Helen's, the bailiffs' men stood with hands on weapons, making a clear statement of their intent – to guard the funeral procession with force, if necessary.

Bless Hempe. Difficult to believe he and the man had begun as adversaries. But, thinking back to George's early distrust of Owen it was clear he'd simply been doing his job, protecting the folk of York from what seemed to him an untrustworthy toady of the archbishop. To Owen, George Hempe had been a bumbler preventing him from solving the murder of a midwife who had saved Lucie's life. Now he trusted Hempe, understood him, but also knew his limitations. Owen had made certain his own men were in place, Ned at the Swann home, Alfred at the church, and, once the Braithwaites departed, Stephen would be in place to stand guard at their home. Owen was just wondering where Stephen was when the man hailed him.

'Anything odd at Poole's home?' Owen asked as Stephen joined him. He'd placed him there for the early morning, out of curiosity more than suspicion. He was glad of it now.

'Quiet. All the noise came from the Tirwhit house beside him. They are a fighting couple, though once they stepped out of the house they played the loving pair. Their maidservant left shortly after they did, very early, but not with them.'

'Any cause to think the maid was heading for trouble – or to cause it?'

Stephen's craggy face drew down into thought. 'Had a basket over her arm, a light step. I took her to be a lass on her way to market, nothing more.'

'And Hempe's men are at Magda Digby's?'

'Arrived last night, they did. He chose well, Rose and Rob took to them, and they will say nothing of Old Bede's presence. Those young ones – that's a pair will never settle for quiet lives, I'll wager.'

Owen grinned at the clear admiration in the man's eyes, but it all sounded too comfortable.

'Your friend, the king's man,' said Stephen, 'Chaucer? Noticed him idling round Poole's house. Wandered on off when he saw me watching him. What's his business with Poole?'

'I wish I knew. He seems far too interested in him.'

'Ah. Then I apologize, for I followed him and asked that he take my place watching Poole's.' Stephen shook his head. 'Alfred warned me that the more time I spent in your service, the more I'd conjure problems everywhere, and spend my nights trying to solve them. There's something odd about Poole, and his taking the house beside the Tirwhits, moving his good mother from her home of many years to that large, drafty place.'

Owen had not placed someone at Poole's or Tirwhit's homes for the day. An oversight he'd suddenly regretted. 'And did Chaucer agree?'

'He did. And showed me he is armed. A surprisingly good piece of steel, that dagger of his.'

'Well done.' Who better to watch Poole than the man with such a keen interest in him?

Grinning with pride, Stephen nodded toward the Braithwaite yard. 'Polishing up the stones for the guests?'

A serving man was on his hands and knees, scrubbing the pavement where the dog had sat the previous day. 'They had a dog chained there yesterday,' said Owen. 'I wager they ignored it and the poor beast was made to sit in its own piss and shit.'

Stephen laughed. But Owen was troubled, not really believing Paul and Galbot would have neglected Tempest.

'Walk round the house, then stand guard here,' said Owen.

'As you wish, Captain.'

As Owen reached the spot he was glad Stephen had not taken him up on the wager. He smelled blood, not a dog's droppings. Indeed, the water in the servant's bucket was stained red.

'What has happened here?'

The servant started, so intent had he been on his work. 'Oh, Captain Archer! It's Master Paul's dog, Tempest. We came out this morning to find him lying here in his own blood, his throat slit, poor beast. And nobody heard a thing. Not a thing.' The man wiped his forehead, leaving a watery red smear. 'Master John will be glad to see you.'

A dog trained to bark when a stranger approached, slaughtered while the household slept. Discovered hours earlier. And no one had come for Owen, the man they had retained to investigate the murders of the Swanns? He rose to find John Braithwaite standing in the doorway, his jacket unbuttoned, gray hair wild as if he had been raking his hands through it. A corpulent man of average height, Braithwaite depended on elegant dress and a haughty manner to impress. But this morning he was merely a fat man wishing he were anywhere but where he was, dealing with a dead dog and the burial of his friend and his son-in-law.

'Captain Archer. I was glad to hear Janet had engaged you. This tragedy—' He closed his eyes and crossed himself.

Owen expressed his condolences, then asked to see the dog.

Braithwaite shook his head. 'We must hie to the Swanns and bear the coffins to the church, Captain. You've no time—'

'I might at least see whether your intruder was skilled with a knife.' *Or I might gain nothing from it but the pain of witnessing a man's brutal use of a creature bred to do his bidding*, Owen thought.

With a shrug, Braithwaite ordered the servant to leave his scrubbing and show Owen the corpse.

'Then escort the captain to my parlor.' As John Braithwaite withdrew, he called out to a servant to bring wine and food, then told him not to bother, he would fast until the service.

'I could use some wine,' said Owen.

Braithwaite nodded. 'Bring wine and food.'

Owen followed his guide back along the side of the house to a shed behind the kitchen. Someone had arranged the dog's limbs so that he seemed at rest on his side atop an old cushion. Paul Braithwaite or Galbot? It was a clean cut, no more, no less than needed for a quick kill. Tempest's slayer was likely the same man who had slit the throat of Hoban Swann.

'Who laid him out?' he asked the servant.

'Galbot the trainer.'

'Where might I find him?'

'Went off to drink himself into forgetfulness, he said. Some don't expect him back.'

As Owen followed the servant back into the hall he noticed Paul talking quietly to his mother and his wife, Elaine, all three dressed for show, though in muted colors. It might be a family occasion, but they were all aware the funeral procession would be observed.

In his parlor, John Braithwaite lifted his head from a contemplation of the floor and rose to greet Owen.

'Is it true?' Owen asked. 'The servants found the dog first thing this morning?'

Braithwaite began to rake both hands through his hair, then self-consciously lowered them, folding them on his lap with a moan. 'I could not believe it. Have we not suffered enough?'

'When were you going to tell me?'

'Ah. I thought . . . So you think the same as murdered the Swanns killed the dog?'

'I think it likely. You said you were glad your wife came to me. But you've decided not to engage me?'

'You misunderstand.' Braithwaite looked stunned. 'I was relieved to hear you would undertake the task. The city needs you, Captain. When such things happen – we pray they won't, of course, but—'

Owen motioned that he understood. 'We've little time. Just tell me what happened here with the dog.'

Braithwaite wiped his brow. 'The servants alerted us and we hurried out – it was a terrible sight. My poor Janet, the day of—' He stopped, apparently realizing he was again venturing into unnecessary detail. 'It was done so silently, so brutally. Who would do that to us? And then Paul requested, as he is in mourning for his sister's husband and his old friend . . . and the dog, he was fond of the dog, as one would be . . . He asked that we not inform you until after the requiem mass. He wishes to be quiet with his grief, pray at St Helen's . . .' Braithwaite sighed, studying his clasped hands, avoiding Owen's eye.

No doubt his anger was obvious. 'Paul's old friend Hoban was brutally murdered and he wishes me to delay finding the murderer?' Owen made no attempt to soften his tone. They needed to understand the danger. 'Does your son believe the murderer will courteously wait until Hoban and Bartolf are buried? And his own dog? Perhaps—' Owen stopped as two servants entered, laying out wine, cheese, bread, apples, nuts.

As they poured wine into two bowls, Braithwaite said to one of them, 'Ask Master Paul to step in, tell him we need to speak with him. At once.' He seemed to have regained his senses with Owen's outburst. Good. When the servants withdrew, he said, 'I hadn't thought how ridiculous it sounds. I see myself as a man of the world. But I return to such a horror – something I would never have dreamed.' John Braithwaite shook his head, his eyes glazed with the shock of the memory. 'I saw what they did to Bartolf. The ruin of such a good man. Why? I have no experience in such matters.'

Fortunate man, until now. 'Is it true that no one in the house heard anything last night? Not a bark? A growl?'

'So it seems.' Braithwaite was quiet while a servant reported that Paul had already departed. He nodded and waved the servant off. 'I am sorry, Captain. It appears he has already headed to the church.'

It would seem Paul was avoiding Owen. 'Do I detect a doubt that no one in the household heard anything?'

Braithwaite had leaned forward to pour a little water into his wine. He sat back, moving the bowl to swirl the mixture, tasted, took a longer drink. Owen waited for the man to speak.

'I do not like to tell tales, but in such circumstances polite discretion feels negligent. Though he is my son.' A pause. 'I sense that Paul is holding something back. His reaction to the slaughter of his dog was—' He leaned forward to add more wine to the bowl, no water this time, wrinkling his forehead in thought. 'He was not surprised. He'd expected trouble. Do not mistake me, he was quite shaken, and I do sense a deep sorrow in him, for my son has a passion for hunting dogs. Not long ago Bartolf sold Paul a pair of his dogs. Did you know?'

'No. I did not.'

'Ah, well, there you are.' Braithwaite nibbled on a piece of cheese, nodding, suddenly frowning. 'I see the fire in that hawk eye of yours, Captain. If you are thinking Paul committed these crimes you are wrong. He and Hoban were the best of friends. And he both respected and liked Bartolf. But, like I said, he'd expected trouble.'

'Was Tempest one of Bartolf's?'

'Tempest? Oh, no, no he descended from a line of dogs stretching back to the pup presented to my son when he began to walk. Fierce dog – I was of a mind to take it from him, inappropriate for a child, but my father chided me for protecting the lad when I should be encouraging him to be a warrior. A warrior merchant?' His eyes laughed, but his mouth twisted sideways in doubt.

'So your son favors fierce dogs?'

A shrug and a nod.

'Ever cause harm? Have there been complaints about his animals?'

Braithwaite shot his jaw forward, as if readying a verbal attack, but he checked himself. 'When he was a lad . . . A boy's mischief . . . But that is years past.'

'Anyone injured? Wounds that proved fatal?'

'No. Mischief, as I said.'

Answered too quickly. There was something there. 'It might be important. I am here to help you, not to judge.'

'One of his dogs was blinded by a muddy conger in the forest. Heartsick, he was. The lad cared for it with such tenderness . . .'

A tight shake of the head. 'I suppose the three of them had both-ered someone.'

'Three of them?'

'Olyf, Hoban, Paul – Muriel never warmed to them. She was younger . . .'

'The dog was blinded in both eyes?'

'No. Just one. Stone damaged it—' He nodded toward Owen's patch, then seemed to remember himself. 'Forgive me, I did not mean . . .'

'No offense taken.' Owen was after something more interesting.

'The hound was never right after that,' said John. 'I finally convinced Paul to put the poor thing out of its misery.' A heavy sigh.

Owen gave him a moment with the memory, then said, 'So Paul *did* take his dogs into the forest, despite their not being lawed—'

'I – yes, as a boy he did. Bartolf came to some agreement with the steward. The three of them loved to be out there in the forest.'

Owen let that be for now. 'What do you know of Galbot's background?'

'Galbot? Paul's servant? Nothing.' John paused. 'Oh, I see.'

'I must consider every possibility. As you do in a business deal.'

'Of course. Of course.' A moment of quiet. 'My sweet daughter – God help her, I pray this has not jeopardized the babe in her womb. A child will help her heal, I know it will. She has prayed for one for so long, as had Hoban.' His voice broke with emotion, and Braithwaite drank down the bowl only to refill it.

Owen rose. 'Perhaps your son was right. It is no time to be troubling your family. You will wish to ready yourself to depart. I believe Dame Janet and Dame Elaine await us.'

'You are to escort us?'

Owen told him of the precautions, the bailiffs' men along the route, Stephen staying here, Ned at the Swanns', he and Alfred at the church.

'Is all that necessary?'

'Even more so now. The killing of Tempest must be treated as a threat to your son.'

Braithwaite paled. 'A threat to Paul? I had not thought—' He crossed himself.

It was clear that he found Owen's suggestion likely to be true. That he should so quickly realize the implication, without argument – yes, there was something there.

'I am grateful,' said Braithwaite as he rose and put a hand on Owen's arm. 'You will attend the mass? And you must come to dinner in my daughter's home afterwards, you and Dame Lucie. Your wife has been such a blessing for my Muriel. And young Alisoun, of course, she is so good with her. My wife has nothing but good to say of her. Will you come?'

Owen had planned to be out on watch, but it would be useful to observe the family as the wine and ale flowed. Surely Lucie would agree. 'We would be honored.'

'God bless you, Captain. And now you are quite right, my manservant must tidy me.' He walked Owen out into the hall. 'So all of this – these deaths are all of a piece?'

'Did you ever doubt it?'

'I prayed it was not so. Help us, Captain. Find the monsters who have destroyed our happiness.'

Destroyed our happiness. Curious how the Braithwaites had taken charge, though it was Olyf who had lost father and brother. It was not for Owen to judge. But Paul Braithwaite's behavior – that *was* Owen's concern. Did he fear he might be a suspect merely because he owned dogs, or was it something more?

He noticed Olyf and Adam Tirwhit standing with Janet and Elaine, all clearly irked to be left waiting for the master of the house.

Greeting them, he asked Dame Olyf if he might speak with her. 'I promise to be brief.'

Frowning as she fussed with a flowing sleeve on her silk gown, Olyf led Owen to the far corner of the hall.

'Forgive me for intruding on your grief,' said Owen.

'Dame Janet and I are retaining you to investigate the murders of my father and brother, Captain. You need not apologize.'

He bowed to her courtesy. 'I could not help but notice that when Paul said he never took his dogs into the forest, he glanced at you. I wondered why.'

'Paul? Did he?' Her look was far away.

'I thought perhaps because you knew about the blinding of his boyhood dog?'

'His—? What has that poor creature to do with the murders of my father and brother?' Her tone was sharp, but her expression wary, one might even say fearful.

'Did you witness the attack?'

'Why should you think so? And why should you care?'

'Do you recall who attacked his hound?'

'You are not thinking that the person, so long ago . . .' She shook her head. 'If I was there, I cannot remember. We did our best to avoid the men who lurked in the woods.'

'So it was a man?'

A silken shrug. 'I told you, I don't remember.'

'According to John Braithwaite, your father arranged for the forest steward to look the other way regarding Paul's dogs in Galtres.'

'Well, yes, as long as he kept them on leads. He disliked going anywhere without a pair of them.'

'So when the one was attacked, there was another?'

'What? I've no idea, Captain. As I said—'

'No counter-attack by the hound's companion?'

'I said I have no memory of it.' She was angry now.

'On the night you found your father, did you see a man and a dog out beyond the archway, in the street?'

'I recall no one. Now I must go bury my kinsmen, Captain.' With a sweep of her skirts, she turned from him and hurried across the room.

He followed, assuring her companions that John would not be long. 'I must see to a few things,' he said, 'but I will be at the church.' He must tell Ned about the latest violence, and send word to Lucie of their invitation.

'You are deserting us, Captain?' Elaine Braithwaite cried, reaching a hand up to touch his arm. Short and plump, she seemed a child dressed up in her mother's elegant robes, until one noticed the lines crossing her forehead and radiating from her dark eyes. She'd borne five children to Paul Braithwaite, raising them in the vicinity of his aggressive dogs – that must cause some discomfort between them.

'There are guards all along the way,' Owen assured her, 'and one of my best men right here at your door.'

Janet Braithwaite patted Elaine's arm. 'Do not fret. The captain will protect us.'

'As my husband's beloved Tempest could not,' said Elaine, turning aside.

He'd never before heard the word 'beloved' spoken like a curse, but the sentiment did not surprise him.

'Enough about Paul and his dogs,' Olyf muttered, calling out to a servant to fetch the master of the house.

On his way to the Swann house, Owen ordered one of the bailiff's men to stand watch at the Braithwaites' door. Stephen was now to escort the family gathered in the hall to the Swann residence, then on to the church if Owen had not yet joined them there.

As he walked, Owen decided to include Alisoun in the discussion with Ned. He might tug at her conscience with the tale of the murdered dog. She was particularly fond of dogs, which had concerned him when she cared for Gwenllian and Hugh. His daughter would return from walks with Alisoun excited about all the dogs they had met, describing them in such detail that it was plain she had petted them. Owen objected. Anything larger than a lapdog would have been trained to guard its owners, not engage with strange children. Time and again he had made his position clear, time and again Gwenllian came home with stories of large dogs who were 'so friendly', Alisoun assuring him that she could tell a dog's nature, he must not worry. He had been relieved when they had hired a new nursemaid for the children. But he knew Lucie missed Alisoun; neither Maud, nor her recent replacement Lena, were as adept at controlling Gwenllian and Hugh by engaging them in something that excited them. That had been Alisoun's gift. In Owen's opinion it came at a price.

Unfortunately, Alisoun was away. Ned said she'd hurried off moments before. Owen told him about the dog.

He looked sick at heart. 'Two houses away, yet I heard nothing in the night.'

'Neither did anyone in the Braithwaite household, apparently.'

'Then it was done with practiced stealth. God have mercy.' Ned crossed himself.

'If Alisoun returns, tell her, but impress upon her that she must say nothing about this to Dame Muriel. Trust that Janet Braithwaite knows the best for her daughter.'

*   *   *

As the bell in St Helen's Church began to ring, George Hempe and a fellow bailiff led the procession from the Swann home, followed by the coffin-bearers – John and Paul Braithwaite, Adam Tirwhit, the two York coroners, the king's forester of Galtres, and two of Hoban Swann's household servants. The women of the households followed, and behind them, Owen, turning his head this way and that, checking for trouble with his one good eye.

Neighbors lined Coney Street and spilled into the lanes along St Helen's churchyard, heads bowed, honoring the lives of two good men of the community. As Owen passed the apothecary, Lucie appeared, falling into step beside him.

'Moments like this, all the neighbors . . .' Lucie's voice caught.

'Moving, but dangerous. If one of them rushed forward with a knife, or set dogs on the gathering, and others entered the fray to help, no matter how well-meant—' He stopped as they entered the church.

'All is well,' Lucie assured him.

Too well. He did not like this quiet.

'Here,' Lucie whispered, guiding him to the left rear corner. 'We can observe the family without too much notice.'

Bless her. Blinded in his left eye, this spot afforded him the greatest range of vision without too much turning of the head.

Muriel Swann, slender and pale, placed her hands on her husband's coffin. Her father drew her away, his arm around her, protective, loving. She shrugged him off and straightened, but in a moment her sob broke the silence. Her mother was quickly there, offering a scented linen, speaking softly to her.

'Where is Alisoun?' Owen wondered aloud.

When Lucie said nothing he turned to see what had her attention. Her gaze was fixed on Olyf and Paul, who had their heads together, whispering. As Owen watched, Elaine Braithwaite elbowed her husband. With what must have been a muttered curse and a look that spoke of more than the usual marital discord, Paul straightened. After an uneasy glance round that Owen just avoided missing, Olyf returned her attention to the priest.

The service continued uninterrupted, the families on their best behavior.

And Owen fought to keep his seat, his entire being shouting that he should be out on the streets, that the murderers would take this opportunity to deepen the family's pain. He told himself he had sufficient men on watch. But it was little comfort.

It was a subdued gathering at the long tables set up in the Swann hall, the servants silently bringing in food, wine, ale.

Lucie leaned close to Owen. 'Notice the order of the seating. A slight? Or a thoughtless error?' On the dais sat Dame Muriel, flanked by her parents, her brother and his wife. Braithwaites all. Olyf Tirwhit, daughter and sister of those they honored at the feast, was seated down the table.

'Either way, she feels the arrow,' he said, nodding across the table at Olyf, who sat bolt upright with a stiff smile as guests paused to speak with her before taking their seats.

As Muriel rose to address the gathering, Elaine Braithwaite interrupted her.

'My dear, I have just realized our error. Come, Paul, we have taken the places meant for dear Olyf and her husband. Forgive us, Muriel. The emotions of the day—' She bobbed her head and drew her confused husband from his chair, gesturing for the Tirwhits to take their places.

Muriel bowed her head as the Tirwhits and Braithwaites changed places, but not in prayer. Owen could see how keenly she watched the exchange. Elaine settled across from Owen, Paul beside her.

Lucie touched Owen's leg. 'Make use of this. Find a moment to speak to Paul Braithwaite.'

Perhaps God did smile on his efforts this day.

As she turned into Low Petergate, Alisoun slowed her pace, beginning to question her impulse, trying to recall the image that had flashed in her mind, the danger that led her to bring her bow and a quiver of arrows. Magda encouraged her to pay attention to such forebodings, though not necessarily to act on them. Beyond Christchurch she paused. She knew the Tirwhit house. She'd accompanied Magda there when Adam was ill with a fever. His wife had been a pale presence, hovering in the shadows. Alisoun recalled thinking the woman was uneasy in Magda's presence. Not unusual. She was wondering whether Adam Tirwhit's home was the one nearer the church or farther away when she noticed Geoffrey Chaucer ambling past the nearest one, then turned to walk down the street beside it, his pace slowing, his head cocked as if he were listening to something. Curious, she headed for him. As she reached the house she thought she heard a woman's cry, then – a growl? If it was a growl, it came from a large dog. Forgetting the man who'd drawn her attention to the house, she slipped into the alleyway beside it. Drawing her bow and quiver of arrows from the bag, she fastened the loose end of the string, drew an arrow, slung the quiver over her shoulder so that she could reach for more arrows if needed, and crept down toward the sounds of a struggle.

As Owen glanced round the laden table he noticed Paul Braithwaite down two goblets of wine in quick succession, whisper something to his wife, and rise abruptly, swaying as he glanced round, forcing his large, liquid brown eyes wide as if he might see more clearly, and tugging down on his short jacket as if it might assist him in balancing.

At the risk of insulting the man, Owen darted round and caught him as his first step went awry. He steadied him on his feet. 'I wonder whether I might impose upon you as an expert in hounds?' he said, nodding to the curious Elaine Braithwaite to reassure her that he would see to her husband. He guided him down the table, past the servants moving about the kitchen, and out into the back garden.

With a muttered excuse, Paul Braithwaite rushed toward the privy and into the small enclosure. Owen heard a brief, unpleasant exchange within, and a young manservant burst out the door holding one hand over his cock, the other tugging at his leggings as he hurried back to the kitchen.

Pacing the perimeter as he waited for the man to emerge from the privy, Owen greeted the bailiff's man standing at the far end.

'The lad – Ned, he's sitting on the steps to the solar, watching the Fenton garden next door,' said Hempe's man. 'Worried about Mistress Alisoun. She returned from market, fetched a pack, and left again – almost running when I saw her head through the back gardens. Toward the tavern yard.'

Owen could not understand why on this of all days she had vanished. Tempted to send Ned off searching for her, he reassured himself that with all the men set round the city and at Magda's house someone would be alert to trouble wherever Alisoun might be. 'Did she look round to see whether she was followed?'

'Nay.'

Thanking him, Owen settled on a bench far enough from the privy that the stench was masked by the pleasing scents from the kitchen, strong enough that his stomach growled in anticipation.

When Braithwaite reappeared he was still bleary-eyed, but he walked a straighter line and seemed in no danger of toppling. Though his features were regular and well proportioned, there was a morose quality to his face, with his brown eyes dipping downward toward the temples, and his mouth arching the same way. 'I am in your debt,' he sighed as he slumped down on the bench beside Owen, doffing his brown velvet hat and wiping his brow with his elegant sleeve.

'Fresh air clears the head,' said Owen. 'I do not envy you this public event on the day you suffered such a loss. It can cut as deep as that of the loss of a brother, I know. One of our herding dogs fell down a well when I was a lad. I mourned him for months.'

'My wife says I am mad to let it weigh on me, accuses me of mourning for him more than for my friend and his father.'

'She does not share your passion for the hounds?'

'Not in the least, though she enjoys spending the wealth they bring.'

'The pricked ears, the wide chest, the noble bearing – did you breed that into Tempest?'

A proud nod.

'How do you learn to raise such fine animals? An apprenticeship?'

'Of a sort, though not regulated by a guild.' He told Owen how he had befriended the master of hounds on the neighboring estate, how the man agreed to train him in exchange for his work in the kennels. He spoke as if Owen were a prospective buyer, emphasizing his long apprenticeship, the status of his customers – including a few members of the powerful Percy and Roos families, but no Nevilles. His clear affection for the hounds began to soften Owen's attitude toward him. It sounded as if he'd built his success on treating the animals with respect and love.

'Your family lived out in the country when you were a lad?'

'On our manor, where Elaine and I have raised our family, and here in the city.' He turned a little, facing Owen, and, in a much cooler tone, said, 'You waste your time pretending interest in my business, Captain. You've suspected me all along. I know you count the Riverwoman a friend. She pointed to me as a man with dangerous hounds, am I right?'

Owen did not need to act as if he were caught by surprise, for he was. 'What has Magda Digby to do with this? And with you?'

The sad eyes challenged him. 'I was but a boy when she warned me not to betray the trust of the hounds by involving them in our pranks. Her concern was for them, and her words changed how I saw them. She woke my love for them. But she does not believe I've changed, eyes me with disdain when we pass in the street. She told you none of this?'

'No. I've not spoken to her since I left her at Freythorpe Hadden, nursing the steward's wife. For all I know she's not yet heard of the murders.'

Paul Braithwaite blinked. 'Not here? God's blood, and you let me think—'

'It was you who spoke of her, not I. How had you used the dogs?'

'Childish mischief. Laughed to see folk bolt when a great hound moved toward them with seeming purpose. She warned me that folk might want to harm my dogs because of that fear, as they do wolves, asked me whether I'd thought of that, how I thought I'd bear that. I crumpled to think of it.'

'Tell her some time. She will warm to you when she hears how you care for them now.'

'So what *do* you want?'

'I sought you out as one whose knowledge of hounds might help me in finding the men who murdered the Swanns. I'm curious about this practice of lawing in the royal forests.'

'Pah. All to protect the king's hunt. His steward culls the herds of deer and hunts the boar for his own pleasure, not the king's.'

'Cutting off the claws – do the animals suffer?'

'Do they feel it, do you mean? Of course they feel it.' Paul took off his hat and raked a hand through his hair. 'I do not subject mine to that savage practice. Never will.'

'Can you think of anyone who might risk taking their unlawed dogs into the forest?'

'If I heard that anyone had done that to my dogs . . .'

Tempting to mention that he had as a boy, but Owen was after something else. 'Not yours, but someone heedless of his animals.'

'There are plenty who count them dumb beasts.'

'The Neville family? Have they ever brought such dogs into the forest?'

'I know nothing of the Nevilles.'

'Did Hoban and Bartolf have any business with them?'

'The great Nevilles own property in Galtres, so Bartolf might have encountered them as coroner, but I do not recall him mentioning the family. Hoban's trade did not put him in such company.'

'You and Hoban were good friends?'

A glance down at his hands. 'We were, though once wed, with children and work, I saw him only on occasions the family came together, or I came to the city for a civic celebration.'

'He was a good husband to your sister?'

The gentle smile previously reserved for dogs lit the long face. 'He was a man smitten to the bone, Captain. And so eager to meet his son – sure he was Muriel carries a son and heir.' His voice broke. He slapped his thighs and rose. 'Speaking of Hoban, I should say a few words in his memory.'

Owen rose with him, met his stride as Paul headed back toward the hall, thinking it a kindness to bring his thoughts back to the dogs. 'The attack on Tempest – such violence. It worries me. I've heard from your father that you favor large, powerful dogs. And you mentioned the Riverwoman's warning. Could this have been meant as retribution?'

'Tempest? No.'

'Have *any* of your hounds injured another's animals? Or a man?'

Paul began to trip, but caught himself. 'No.'

'Some folk have long memories. Anyone who blamed you or your dogs for a loss?'

Paul quickened his stride.

No challenge for Owen's long legs. 'You did not know that Magda Digby's been away all this time?'

'I told you I didn't.'

Silence through the kitchen, stumbling once as he tried to avoid a serving man carrying a tray with two steaming platters of meat.

At the door of the hall, Paul removed his hat, smoothed back his hair, set the hat back at a slight angle.

'One more question,' said Owen, startling the man, who'd clearly thought himself alone. 'Who has dogs that might be trained to attack as Hoban and Bartolf were attacked?'

'I have been wondering that myself. To so bond with the animals as to train them to assist you in attack, which this seems, yet do what he did to Tempest?' Paul's large eyes seemed black in his pale face. 'No, I know of no such monster. Now you must allow me to return to my family. My sister has suffered a terrible loss.'

Not him, his sister.

'Was Hoban party to the pranks for which Magda reprimanded you?' he asked, but too late. Paul had gone straight to his sister, leaning close, speaking to her.

TEN

Lying Dead in the Garden

Alisoun crept down the alley, prepared to assess her best aim as quickly as she might. As she walked she noticed an overturned bench where the alley gave way to the garden, a trampled flowerbed, the soil churned. Now she could hear a woman begging for her life, answered by a growl. In the distance a man cried out in agony. Holding her breath so as not to give herself away, Alisoun crept to the end of the house and peered around. Not much farther than an arm's length along the back wall of the house stood Euphemia Poole, her sightless eyes wide with terror. A brindle-coated creature – wolf? – had her pinned against the house with its forepaws on her shoulders, its head so close it might catch the woman's breath. Twenty or more paces past them two men struggled with a pitchfork, one of them bleeding, his knees beginning to give out, clearly overpowered by his tall, hefty opponent.

Suddenly a man rushed out from behind a garden shed, shouting, 'For my father's honor!' and brandishing a long, curved dagger as he made straight for Euphemia and the creature. Alisoun stepped out and drew her bow, aiming for his shoulder. But she'd misjudged his speed and the arrow skewered his neck. He threw his weapon as he stumbled and fell to the ground. Alisoun stepped out of the dagger's trajectory and reached for another arrow.

'Drop down, lass!' someone shouted from behind.

She was glancing back to see who had spoken when she caught a movement at the edge of her sight – the creature was lunging toward her. Too late to aim, too late to do anything. It threw its weight against her, pushing the air from her lungs. She let go her bow and arrow, reaching out for something to break her fall, but her legs buckled beneath her and her head hit the ground. Searing pain, the darkness blood-red.

*   *   *

Geoffrey's stomach twisted at the sound of Alisoun's head hitting the edge of the stone wall. As soon as he saw that the beast was now moving toward the pair struggling on the other side of the garden, Geoffrey went to Alisoun. Blood flowed from a gash in her head and she lay motionless, alarmingly limp. Kneeling to her, he leaned close to listen for a heartbeat, any sound.

He lurched upright as one of the pair across the garden gave a sharp whistle. His opponent was on the ground, the beast pawing him. 'Now!' shouted the man, and he and the beast stumbled away, clumsy in their haste, heading through the back gardens toward St Andrewgate.

A faint rasp of breath. Geoffrey crossed himself, leaning down, felt Alisoun's breath on his cheek, felt a pulse in her throat. *God be thanked for this small mercy.*

'How might I help?'

Geoffrey looked up into the frightened face of the man who'd struggled with the other attacker. His face and clothes were filthy. 'Are you injured?' Geoffrey asked.

'I'll be limping and bruised, but I want to help.'

Sitting back on his heels, Geoffrey surveyed the garden. Dame Euphemia lay curled up on the ground, the man who'd thrown the dagger sprawled a few feet away. No question of his causing trouble. The other man and the beast were gone.

'Your mistress?'

'Injured, I do not know how badly.'

'I am worried for her champion. What is your name?'

'Dun, sir.'

'Come here, Dun.' Geoffrey motioned for him to sit down on the path beside Alisoun. He gently lifted her by the shoulders, her thick hair coming loose and fanning out over one shoulder. Geoffrey's breath caught in his throat. He'd thought of her as a warrior, but she was suddenly a fragile, beautiful young woman whose life might depend upon him. 'Move closer.' Dun shifted. 'Sit cross-legged.' When the man was in position, Geoffrey arranged Alisoun so that her head was cradled in Dun's lap, her hair held away from the blood pooling on the path. She moaned softly.

'Where is Master Crispin?' he asked Dun.

'Called away to Master John Gisburne's home in Micklegate.

Wore his best clothes. Meaning to join the mourners at Swann's after seeing to business?' A shrug.

Gisburne. A familiar name, a wealthy merchant for whom there was no love in Owen and Lucie's household. As for Poole joining the mourners, Geoffrey very much doubted that to be the case, but as he was already headed there to find Lucie and Owen, he would ask. 'Stay right here, with your hand on her shoulder so that she feels your presence, and talk to her, tell her tales, keep assuring her that help is coming.'

'Tales?'

'Anything that coaxes her back to us. Sing, if you've a voice that won't pain her.'

'I can sing.'

To Geoffrey's relief, the man raised a competent voice in a love ballad. It would do. He left Alisoun with her troubadour and went to see about Dame Euphemia. The elderly woman whimpered as he approached, curling into a tighter ball.

'I will bring help,' Geoffrey said softly.

Dun broke off his singing to say, 'My fellow servant, Eva, she will be hiding in the kitchen. She can calm my mistress.'

'The kitchen?'

'Dogs frighten her. Even ladies' lapdogs.'

And that particular hound . . . Geoffrey found the woman under the work table beneath two overturned laundry baskets. Hardly invisible.

'The hound is gone, and his handler. You must see to Dame Euphemia.'

The woman peered out. 'The wolf is gone?'

'I have no time to waste, your mistress and the young woman who saved her are injured. Look to your conscience, find your courage, woman.' He left her with that.

Outside, Dun had paused in his singing.

'Another song,' said Geoffrey. 'I told you, sing her back to us. I will return as quickly as I might.'

As he hastened down the alleyway, Geoffrey noticed the Tirwhit maidservant standing at the edge of the street. When she saw him, she turned aside as if to pretend she was just passing. He'd come to know her on his watches, a young woman most curious about her neighbors. He would test her purpose.

He hurried forward. 'I've often observed you watching this
house, now is your chance to befriend the Pooles. Your neighbors,
are they not? Are you not employed by Adam Tirwhit?' He caught
her arm as she made to walk away.

'Is that blood on your sleeve?' she asked.

So it was. His heart ached to see Alisoun's blood on his cuff.

'I dare not—' She tried to shake him off.

But Geoffrey did not let go. 'They have suffered a grievous
trespass. I pray you, see what you might do to make Dame
Euphemia more comfortable.'

She gasped and reared back, her eyes seeking escape.

'Useless wench.' He pushed her away and hurried off.

Owen stood sharply as Geoffrey rushed into the Swann hall, his
hat awry, an urgency in the way he searched the room. So he'd
been right in predicting an attack, but wrong about the location.
Owen was out of practice, idle too long, his wits dulled.

'Blessed be, you are here.' Geoffrey wheezed out the words.
'Forgive me, it's been a long while since I ran so far. You must
come with me. And Lucie. We need her healing skills.' He tugged
on his jacket and straightened up, as if suddenly aware he was in
public in disarray. His sleeves were bloody.

Touching the cuff of one, Owen found it saturated. 'Whose?'
he asked.

'Alisoun Ffulford's, God help her.'

'My dear Alisoun,' Lucie whispered, lifting Geoffrey's arm,
'and so much blood? How? Where is she?'

'At Poole's home. Dame Euphemia is injured as well, but Alisoun
– I fear most for her, a head wound. The animal pushed her down
and she fell against a stone wall. She bleeds from the head.'

'I knew she was in danger,' said Ned, appearing from
nowhere. 'I will come.'

'You will stay here in my stead,' Owen commanded. 'Watch
the room. Note everyone's movements.'

'But—'

'I need you here.' Owen stared down the young man until he
saw him awaken to his duty and nod.

Geoffrey was straining to see all at the long table. 'Is Crispin
Poole among you?'

Owen met Lucie's gaze as Geoffrey explained why he'd asked. 'A convenient coincidence,' Owen said.

Lucie raised a brow.

'I pray you, come quickly, both of you.' Geoffrey edged toward the hall door.

The crowd had grown quiet, the guests craning their necks to hear and see what news the late arrival brought with him. Owen considered their expressions, especially the Swanns and the Braithwaites. All looked frightened.

'Come.' Owen led Lucie and Geoffrey out into the afternoon.

'Bold bastards, to strike in daylight,' Geoffrey said, rushing to catch up as Lucie and Owen hurried toward the gate through the back gardens to the tavern and apothecary.

'How many?' Owen asked.

'Two men – that I saw, and the hound. A great, slavering—'

'Did you recognize the men?' Owen asked.

'A rush of violence, no time to pause for introductions. My concern was to warn Alisoun. She was aiming at one of the men and did not notice the hound coming for her.'

'Alisoun was armed?' asked Lucie.

'Bow and arrow,' said Geoffrey. 'She came prepared for trouble.'

'How?' asked Owen. 'How did she know?'

'I know nothing of that.'

'Did she fell the one at whom she aimed?'

Geoffrey crossed himself. 'Shot him through the neck. He is dead.'

'*Mon dieu*,' said Lucie.

'And the other?' Owen asked.

'Fled with the beast. Out the back garden.'

'No one ran after them?' As Geoffrey began to defend himself, Owen said, 'I merely want to know all that you know. No judgment. Anything else?'

Coming to a halt in the Fenton garden, Geoffrey closed his eyes as if to gather his thoughts, then realized he'd lost his companions. Hastening out the gate into the tavern yard, he caught up, describing in detail all that he'd seen – Euphemia pinned against the wall, Dun and one attacker struggling, the other attacker's dagger, Alisoun aiming the bow, then being knocked aside by the hound. 'What manner of man attacks an elderly blind woman in such wise?' he fumed.

'Did anyone come to your aid?' asked Lucie.

'Dun, as I said. The man had tried to fend them off with a pitchfork. Most fortunate fool, to have survived that gambit. The Tirwhit's maidservant watched from afar. I found her at the end of the alley and asked her to help the Pooles' maidservant, Eva, who'd hid from the hound. But I've no faith the maid will do as I asked.'

'Who is with Alisoun now?'

'Dun. Cradling her head, trying to keep her awake.'

'Well done,' said Lucie. 'Go, search,' she said to Owen as they reached the gate to their garden. 'Geoffrey will help me collect what I might need from the apothecary and escort me to the Poole home.'

'Tell Jasper to keep the children safe,' Owen said. The shop was closed in honor of the funerals. Jasper was likely working in the garden.

'Hurry.' Lucie took Geoffrey's arm and waved Owen on.

Lucie plucked jars and bandages from the shelves in the workroom behind the shop as Geoffrey stood with eyes closed searching his memory for details about the nature of the injuries. He described Alisoun's head wound, realized he'd no idea of Dame Euphemia's injuries, believed Dun might have a sprained or broken ankle, and sundry wounds or bruises. So, Lucie thought, possible broken bones, sprains, bruises, open wounds, and, of course, the terror of the attack. Betony, boneset, comfrey, hawthorn in case the elderly Euphemia's heart sounded weak, moneywort, red nettle for bleeding, sanicle, walwort, wintergreen, most in mixtures Lucie found efficacious for speeding the healing of wounds, bruises, and broken bones, as well as valerian and poppy to calm. She added a potion Brother Wulfstan had devised to stimulate healing by drawing up the blood, but not in a way that would cause Alisoun's wound to open. At least Lucie prayed that was so. She was urging Geoffrey to come along when Jasper stepped through the door.

'Ma! Master Geoffrey! She said you were here, but I didn't understand—' Jasper looked at the basket of medicines and bandages. 'Another attack?'

'At the Poole home,' said Lucie. 'We are fortunate that Geoffrey witnessed it. He fetched us from the feast. Your father is searching for those who fled.' She paused, belatedly puzzled. '*Who* told you we were here?'

'Dame Magda. She has been sitting with us, calming Kate, now she's holding Emma, you know how Emma reaches out to her, always begging for Magda to pick her up.'

'You said calming Kate – about her sister? Is Tildy—'

'She will be well, but she lost the babies.'

'Both?' Lucie crossed herself at his nod. Tildy might have survived in body, but her spirit . . . To lose both babies carried all these months . . .

'Who's that for?' Jasper pointed to the basket.

'Three were injured,' said Geoffrey. 'Dame Euphemia, a manservant, and Alisoun.'

'Alisoun?' Jasper frowned at Lucie. 'You did not say.'

'You gave me no chance.' She silently cursed Geoffrey for not thinking to prepare Jasper.

'I will come with you.'

Lucie put a hand on Jasper's arm. 'I need you here with the children. Alisoun will have Magda and me, the best care, but the children have only you.'

'But—'

'Only you, son.'

A reluctant nod. 'Will you bring her here?'

'We will do what is best for her.' Lucie touched his cheek. 'I love her, too. As does Magda. Does Magda know of all that's happened? The murders? The dogs?'

'We spoke of it.'

'Could she see a pattern in the attacks?'

'If she did, she did not say.'

Which might mean anything.

As they walked into the garden Lucie caught sight of a sweet group on the long bench that ran below the large window in the hall: Gwenllian and Hugh crowding round a small figure with Emma in her arms. Magda's multi-colored robe glimmered as she rocked Lucie's youngest.

To come to them this day, in their hour of need, this was no accident. Lucie's heart steadied. All would be well. There was magic in the woman, she had no doubt.

In the hall, fierce eyes met Lucie's over Emma's sleep-tousled hair. 'So Bird-eye comes to the aid of a city haunted by the wolves of their darkest dreams.'

'Did you doubt that he would, when the time came?' Lucie asked.

Magda kissed Emma's forehead. 'He protects what he loves.' She handed Gwenllian her sleeping sister and rose, shaking out her skirts. 'Come. The king's man can describe all that he witnessed on the way.'

'I thought I was "the poet" to you,' said Geoffrey.

'Now and then.'

As they moved through the garden and out into Davygate, Geoffrey described what had happened.

'Euphemia Poole? If she is aware of Magda's presence, she might curse thee for it. But mayhap she will be too desperate to care about an old pagan healer crossing her threshold.'

As Lucie reached up to knock on the door of the Poole home it opened. A disheveled woman, a servant by her simple gown, welcomed them with such emotion Lucie suggested she sit down.

'No time. The captain said you would be coming, Mistress Wilton, though he did not mention you, Dame Magda. I am so glad you have come. Your apprentice lies injured, Dun is trying to keep her awake. Come. I will escort you.'

It was Geoffrey who led the procession through a narrow passageway to the garden door, providing Lucie an opportunity to speak with the woman, ascertain that her name was Eva, long in service for the family, as was Dun, the man who was now singing hymns out in the garden.

'My mistress – she will not welcome Dame Magda,' Eva said as they reached the open doorway.

'I will see to her, Dame Magda will see to the others,' said Lucie as she stepped out the door.

And paused, taking in the grim scene. Dame Euphemia lay to her right, crumpled against the house, one leg bent beneath her, her white hair undone, draping over her arms. Ten strides beyond, Alisoun lay with her head cradled on the lap of the singing manservant, her face pale as death. Dun sighed and fell silent when he saw them. A few strides from Lucie a man lay face down, an arrow through his neck.

'*Deus juva me,*' she whispered, crossing herself.

She felt Magda's hand warm on her shoulder. 'A troubling sight. Magda will see first to Alisoun. Thou shouldst examine the dead, in case Bird-eye missed a hint of life.' Magda took the basket from Lucie's arm.

Crouching down, Lucie felt for a pulse, a breath, but found no sign of life. She peered at what was visible of the dead man's face. Nothing about it to make him noticeable, no scars, warts, neither handsome nor repulsive. Not familiar. He had the hands of a laborer, clothes made for utility, not show, not too clean. River mud on his shoes. Brown, thick hair beneath a leather hat.

She felt Eva hovering behind her. 'Did Captain Archer examine him?'

'Much as you just did,' said Eva. 'Then he told us you would be with us soon and went off after the man and the wolf, toward St Andrewgate. Dun told him where to go.'

Lucie joined Magda, who was kneeling beside Alisoun, listening to her heart, using her hand to feel her breath. Suddenly she snapped her fingers close to one ear. Alisoun jerked, a slight movement, but her eyelids did not flicker.

Lucie took that as a bad sign.

'Master Chaucer ordered me to sing to keep her awake, but I failed,' the singer said. His voice was going hoarse with the effort.

A tisane of bark oil and horehound later, Lucie thought.

'Thou art called "Dun"?' Magda asked.

He nodded.

'Magda thanks thee for thy care, Dun. Now rest thy voice. Magda will soon relieve thee of thy charge.' Lucie watched as Magda slipped a bony hand beneath Alisoun's head to lift it, running her free hand across the blood-soaked area, grimacing at what she felt. Gently she continued, examining Alisoun's hands, wrists. Looking up at Geoffrey, who had joined them, she asked, 'No time to break her fall?'

'She dropped her weapon too late.'

Kneeling down beside Magda, Lucie followed her lead as they cleaned Alisoun's wound, dressed and bandaged it, saw to her other injuries – bruised hip, grazed elbow – and dribbled into her mouth a tisane that would calm and strengthen her. Now and then her eyelids flickered, but she did not wake.

'How she fares within . . . We cannot know until the child wakes.' Magda's pale eyes were sad.

Biting her lip, Lucie bowed her head, silently praying that God grant Alisoun her life. She might do much good with her healing skill.

'Art thou praying?' Magda asked in a soft voice, pressing Lucie's hand when she admitted that she was. 'Magda does as well, in her own way.'

'She has become dear to me.'

'To Magda as well.'

Lucie resolved to keep her mind on her work. Grief must wait. 'I will see to Dame Euphemia myself.'

'Nay. Magda will assist thee.'

'But Euphemia—'

'Who is to tell her?' A conspiratorial smile. 'She is not aware of aught at present.'

Working together, Lucie and Magda examined Euphemia, deciding how she could best be moved without causing further injury. A shoulder out of joint and a swollen ankle already bringing up a bruise appeared to be the worst of what she had suffered, though at her age such an abrupt drop to the ground might well break fragile bones. Geoffrey and Dun, who had been replaced by a thick cushion beneath Alisoun's shoulders and head, carried Dame Euphemia to her bed, assisted by Lucie. The maid, Eva, fussed over her mistress's placement. And still Euphemia did not wake. A too-deep sleep?

Magda shook her head at Lucie's concern. 'Her pulse is strong.'

In silence they set Dame Euphemia's shoulder and wrapped her ankle and her swollen knee. The elderly woman slept the while.

'When she wakes, if she protests your presence, will we move Alisoun?' Lucie asked.

'Not until she rouses. Dame Euphemia may fume in her chamber. Her inner blindness came upon her over many years, as she drew in on herself until she could see no one but her husband and her son.'

After Geoffrey carried Alisoun to the bed Eva had prepared for her in the hall, Lucie saw to the manservant, asking Dun about his own injuries. Sprains, a blossoming black eye and a gash on his cheek – the caked mud had stopped his bleeding, and a hand beginning to spasm. She thanked him for caring for Alisoun despite his discomfort. Then she set to work cleaning his hands and face in order to find the wounds and bandage them, splinting two fingers, wrapping a sprained ankle, backing off when with fear in his eyes he begged her not to sew the wound on his face.

'It will take longer to heal, and the scar will be more noticeable.'

'Folk do not see me. And I was never fair to look upon.'

'You fought with courage today,' she said. 'The Pooles should be grateful.'

'Dame Euphemia has always been a fair mistress.'

'And her son?'

'Kinder than his mother, truth be told.'

'You will need help for a while. But Crispin Poole brought his own servants, did he not?' She was prying, for they looked like retainers, not house servants.

'One of them dresses him, assists where he struggles with but one hand. The other,' Dun leaned in close, 'he does little but walk about, spying on folk.'

'They accompanied him today?'

'No, they have been away. In Galtres, I think, watching the coroner's property.'

'Why?'

He shook his head.

'How kind of him to watch over Bartolf's house,' said Lucie, storing that away for Owen. 'I will speak to your mistress about hiring someone to assist you for a time.'

He pressed her forearm in gratitude.

The hall was a long, high, echoing space with few furnishings or hangings. Not an inviting room. Magda bent over Alisoun, smoothing back her hair, murmuring to her. She claimed to use no charms, but Lucie knew she fashioned bundles of herbs, stones, feathers, and twigs, and had experienced the power of her murmured words, a deep warmth, heavy limbs and eyelids, the silencing of thought.

Sensing Lucie behind her, the healer glanced over her shoulder. 'Magda will stay with Alisoun until she is well enough to move to thy home or the river house.'

*　*　*

On St Andrewgate, Owen noticed a woman hurrying in his direction, peering back over her shoulder as she tugged her child along
behind her. He hailed her and asked whether she had seen a man
and a large dog.

The woman lifted her child up in her arms, hugging her tight.
'I did see them, though the creature was like no dog I've ever
known. The man clutched the collar of the beast with one hand,
dangling a knife from the other. I screamed and scooped up my
Jen, and others shouted. He fled into the Bedern.'

'Can you describe the man you saw, what he wore?' Owen asked.

She closed her eyes, rocking the child as she conjured the
image. 'Not so tall as you, brown hair, no hat. His clothes – a
worker's garb, leather tabard. Nothing to set him apart.'

Could it be Galbot? He'd worn a leather vest. Owen cursed
himself for not asking Paul Braithwaite how long Galbot
had worked for him, what he knew of the man's past. But by
then he'd fled, so it would have done little good. At the funeral
feast he'd had a moment with Elaine Braithwaite, nothing of note
until she said something about Tempest's death not being the first
loss Paul has suffered, his precious dogs. She'd been silenced by
John Braithwaite, who said her jealousy regarding the dogs was
unbecoming. Owen must speak to Paul.

He thanked the woman.

'You will protect us, Captain? Protect the city?'

So far he had failed at that, but, seeing her fear, how she pressed
the child to her, he did not voice his frustration. 'I have all the
bailiffs' men on the streets, searching for these men. And I have
your keen eyes.' He forced a reassuring smile. 'We will find them.
What of the dog? You said he was unlike any you'd seen?'

'He was a great beast, a wolf, I think, all black.'

'Black?'

'With fiery eyes and a long red tongue. A devil dog, to be sure.'
She bobbed her head to him and hurried on.

He had encountered wolves on campaign across the Channel,
but never black ones, though he knew no reason why one could
not exist – but fiery eyes? Unless she meant the expression. A
long red tongue? Might someone describe a dog's tongue thus?
What had Magda said? *What do folk see when they see a wolf,
Bird-eye? The animal? Think again.* Their darkest fears?

Whoever the man was, it sounded as if he had tight control of the animal.

The bailiff's man who'd gone on to Monk Bar to question the gatekeeper returned, shaking his head. 'No one's come through with a large dog today, Captain.'

Owen told him what he'd learned.

'The Bedern. Bad luck for us. If he's a churchman we'll never draw him out, the devil piss on him.'

'I very much doubt we seek a cleric,' said Owen. 'But we are not the law in the Bedern, that is true.'

The Bedern was part of the minster liberty, set aside to house the vicars choral, who said masses in the chantry chapels in the minster, and Owen would need the dean's or the archbishop's permission to search there. The bailiffs had no jurisdiction in there either. Damn Thoresby for dying. Damn him. Owen would waste precious time convincing the dean . . .

'Might have ducked in and out the far side,' said Hempe's man. 'Headed for the river. They'll spit him out when they see he's not one of theirs.'

'Pass the word along the watch to keep an eye out for this man, and a dog, likely a large one.' Owen said nothing of the woman's description of the dog. He began to suspect that what Magda had meant was that folk saw not what was there, but the beast from their nightmares. 'I'm going to take a stroll in the Bedern.'

A surprised laugh. 'You're not one for rules, Captain? Can we expect that when you're our captain?'

Owen slapped the man on the shoulder. 'If I captain your bailiffs, they'll keep to *my* rules.' He grinned, though he felt no cheer.

While in the kitchen fetching some brandywine for Magda, Lucie heard an unfamiliar voice out in the garden. Geoffrey had sent Dun to fetch a priest to say prayers over the dead man. Had the priest arrived? She should speak with him. She handed Magda the brandywine and headed out.

On her way she thought to check on Euphemia. She found her still asleep in the bedchamber whose walls were covered with small tapestries. Unfinished, Lucie realized, looking round, all religious scenes in vibrant colors, delicate, beautiful work.

'She had great skill,' said Eva.

'They caught my eye as I came to check on your mistress.'

'I am grateful for your care.' The maid reached up to straighten one of the hangings.

'You are devoted to her.'

'She has been good to me, in her way.'

'And her son? Is he difficult?'

'He is a fair man. But—' She looked down at her hands. 'I should not speak of the master and mistress of this house.'

'Even if it might help us catch the men who attacked your mistress?'

Eva toed something on the floor. 'He cannot forgive Dame Euphemia for what she did. But she did it so that he might come home. If that poacher had not been hanged for the girl's murder . . .'

Trying to sound as if she knew something of what the woman spoke, Lucie asked, 'What was your mistress's part in it?'

'If the master had kept the boy's secret, she would not have done it. And how people know that the mistress pushed him to name Warin as the girl's murderer – I don't know who told them.'

A thread of memory. A young woman's drowning, the girls at St Clements' whispering. 'This Warin was not the murderer?'

'No. He helped Master Crispin save her from drowning. Then the young master went away. No one knows why. Folk thought he might have done it, Master Crispin. Maybe he hid for a few days, made certain she was dead before she went in the Ouse this time, and then ran off to be a soldier.'

'They thought Crispin saved the young woman, then murdered her?'

'I don't know that folk knew of the first drowning. But what if he hadn't been trying to save her? What if Warin saw that?' She met Lucie's eyes, questioning. Unsure even now.

If this woman who had known him so well was unsure of his innocence . . . Was it this long-ago tragedy that haunted them now?

'And he knows what his mother did?'

A nod. 'I should not have told you, but—'

'No, I am grateful, Eva. You have helped me see.' Lucie might have gone on, but hearing once more the unfamiliar voice in the garden she remembered her mission. 'The priest is here. Do you think Dame Euphemia would like him to bless her after he's given the man the last rites?'

'I meant to say – I have seen the dead man before, watching the house, sometimes from the back garden, at night, sometimes staying in the shadow of the church. I told the captain that. And I've seen his companion as well, the one who ran.'

'Recently?'

'This very day.'

Never underestimate the importance of household servants as witnesses. 'How long has he watched?'

'Since we moved here. More often of late. Both of them.'

'You saw both men before you hid?'

An embarrassed nod and shrug. 'And I believe I saw them talking to Wren, the Tirwhits' maidservant, early this morning.'

'Thank you. Again, you have been most helpful.'

'I shamed myself, hiding from the wolf that attacked my mistress.' Eva wiped her eyes with her sleeve.

'The priest is here,' Geoffrey announced from the doorway, startling them both.

'You asked whether Dame Euphemia might wish the priest's blessing, Mistress Wilton,' said Eva. 'I believe she would.'

'I will tell him,' said Lucie.

Just before he stepped out into the yard, Geoffrey turned to Lucie. 'The Tirwhit maid, Wren. She has a great curiosity about what the Pooles are about when home. I notice her peering toward the house often. And I've just recalled seeing her earlier today with Alisoun near the chandler's shop on Finkle Street. They were talking, but Alisoun was only half-listening, glancing about as if alert to danger. I cannot help but wonder whether something Wren said to Alisoun drew her here, ready for trouble.'

'That would explain Alisoun's presence.' Lucie told Geoffrey what Eva had said about the two men watching the house, and speaking to Wren.

He looked chagrined. 'I am a poor spy if I did not catch that. Both of them. So they chose a time when Crispin was called away. By the plotters?'

'I wondered as well.' Lucie had much to discuss with Owen. 'I will talk to this Wren after we've spoken to the priest,' she said.

'If she returned to the Tirwhit home. Which, I am sure you've not forgotten, is Olyf *Swann*'s home.' He raised a brow.

A complex web indeed. 'I pray you, find Owen, tell him all this. And that Magda is here.' She was quite certain he would wish to ask Magda what she had known, foreseen.

Geoffrey did not argue. 'I will find him.'

A discreet brothel stood to one side of the alleyway to which the woman had pointed. Owen stepped inside, doffing his hat.

'Now this is a day for celebration. Captain Archer himself gracing my house.' The voice came from a settle piled high with bright cushions, but in the dim light Owen could not at once see the speaker. When she moved he found his bearings – the woman was stretched out on the settle, her gown the same fabric as the cushions.

'My apologies for the intrusion,' Owen said. 'You are doubtless closed for business at this hour.'

'There is no particular hour for pleasure, Captain. This is as good as any.' Her voice was low, melodic, her tone teasing.

He counted on the women of this house being regular clients of Magda and Alisoun, and therefore motivated to assist him. 'I am searching for a man and a dog who attacked the widow Poole at her home on Colliergate. The Riverwoman's apprentice, Alisoun, was injured protecting the widow.'

'Young Alisoun? How might I help?'

'Word is the man fled into the Bedern. Have you seen him?'

As he spoke, the woman sat up, moving with a fluid, studied grace. She was not young, but no less beautiful for the years. Though no stranger to the delights of brothels, he'd never been one to patronize those in York, for he'd lost his heart to Lucie Wilton on his first day in the city. Yet something about the woman was familiar.

'Alas, Captain, I cannot help you. But there were whispers about a wolf entering a house nearby a few nights past. A search the next morning came up with nothing. A man and his dog are nothing of note in ordinary times, but at present – no one is at ease with such apparitions since dear Bartolf was taken from us.'

The affection with which she spoke the coroner's name interested Owen. 'Was Bartolf a client?'

'Oh, we all knew the dear old man and competed for his coin – he spent freely here. He'd quite an appetite for a man his age.' A dimple appeared as the smile brightened her lovely face. 'Now for you, Captain . . . I know several of my compeers would forgo payment to lie with you.'

He felt his face redden. Her sinuous movements, the scent, her voice . . .

'I did not know that about Bartolf.'

A chuckle. 'Then you did not know him well. I can see that your mind is on your work – but the offer stands, Captain. Here, let me point out the house to you.' As she passed she caught his hand, drew him to the doorway, leaning her head against his shoulder as she pointed to a modest structure a few doors down and across the alleyway.

He was not as immune to her charms as he'd thought. Stepping away from her he forced himself to focus. 'Do you know the owner of the property?'

'Alas no, but I might inquire for you.' She placed a cool hand on the back of his neck.

He took the hand, kissed it, and gave her his most charming smile. 'I would be grateful.'

'Grateful!' A throaty chuckle, her smile teasing. 'Worry not. I know you are devoted to your apothecary wife, and I am glad for her. And for you. Lucie Wilton is wise, competent, and beautiful. But my offer holds. Come round in a day, and I hope to have a name for you, at the least.'

'I'd like to hear more about Bartolf as well.'

A nod. 'I am more than happy to spend more time in your company, Captain. I promise I'll keep my distance. You know you can trust me – or do you not recognize me out of the garb of a lay sister of St Leonard's?'

The moment she reminded him, he remembered. Honoria de Staines. She'd been a good friend to Bess Merchet's late uncle, and, yes, a lay sister at St Leonard's Hospital. But there had been secrets in her past . . .

'Dame Honoria, of course.'

She smiled and gathered her skirts, about to withdraw to her seat, when she held up a hand. 'I have remembered something I overheard. It is several weeks now. Otto and Rat – yes,' she

laughed, 'he looks like one. The two of them are unlikely sorts
to grace my house, but they did, showing me they had good coin.
When they were in their cups and ready to ascend to the bedcham-
bers they spoke between them of a young woman murdered a
long while ago, Gerta, the daughter of a charcoal-burner in Galtres.
Their money had to do with that in some way. I thought it odd,
so I made a point of remembering it.'

'And now I benefit. I am most grateful.'

She kissed the tips of her fingers and touched them to his cheek.
'I am repaid by bringing out that dimple. May God watch over
you, Captain.'

Stepping out into the alleyway, Owen took a deep breath.

'Captain?' George Hempe strode toward him from the direction
of St Andrewgate, frowning. 'A bawdy house?'

'Looking for witnesses,' Owen assured him. 'You've heard of
the attack at Poole's?'

'Man and wolf fleeing here,' Hempe glanced round, 'where I've
no jurisdiction. Nor have you. Though if Thoresby were alive—'

'—I would be free to chase them down in here, yes, I've
thought of that. But he's not. Still, I know of no law against
asking whether a man and a dog passed by, and where they
went, and we will continue to ask so that folk know it's not safe
to hide them here, for in time we could convince the dean to
allow us to take them.'

They both turned as Geoffrey Chaucer hailed them. 'God's
blood, I've run the gauntlet only to find you so close to hand.
Lucie sent me, to tell you all that we have discovered, and that
the Riverwoman is at Poole's.'

Magda was here. God be thanked. 'But not Poole? He's not
returned?'

'No.'

'Let me set some of my men to walking the Bedern while we
hie to the Poole home,' said Hempe. 'They say Alisoun Ffulford
shot one of the two men, but you've not seen him, have you,
Owen? It needs your eyes.'

'I have. No one I know. A woman saw them come this way.
The man she described – he could be Galbot, Paul Braithwaite's
man. And a man and a wolf were rumored to have been seen
entering a house down the way a few nights ago.'

'Let my man check it, the one who's watching this alley on your orders.' Hempe grinned. 'He's glad to have you as captain.'

Geoffrey made a rude sound.

'First to Gisburne's on Micklegate,' said Owen. 'Walk with me a way, Geoffrey. Tell me all you know.'

'I should accompany you – and bring some of my men,' said Hempe.

Owen agreed.

Once Geoffrey had told them all he knew, Owen sent him off on a mission. First to Brother Michaelo, to ask him to walk through the minster yard, in case there was talk of a man and a dog, or, even better, a sighting. Then to the Swann home, to tell Muriel, Olyf, and the Braithwaites all he knew, and see whether Ned needed assistance. And then to Owen's home, to bide there a while, have an ale, tell Jasper all that he'd seen and heard so far. The lad would never admit it, but Owen thought he would be grateful to have another man in the house for a time. Geoffrey had begun to protest, but Owen had not been too proud to beg, winning his agreement.

'A stranger comes to the city with a hound and a friend to attack a blind widow,' Owen said to Hempe.

'You make him a riddle,' said Hempe. 'I'd say he was hired for the job.'

ELEVEN

An Old Enemy

Owen's height, patch, and reputation preempted any plan to slip through the city unnoted. Folk called out to him, asking about the attack at Poole's home. Word had spread quickly, but the city was haunted by the deaths, the specter of great wolves prowling the streets. Owen envied Hempe. Though he'd served as bailiff for years, he was the sort of man who could move through a crowd unremarked, vaguely familiar, unthreatening. Except, of course, for those he'd arrested. One of those skittered away from them near St Crux, sliding into the shadows, but Hempe had his men drag him out.

'Brown-haired man in a leather jerkin in the company of a large hound. You see anyone like that, you find one of my men as quick as you may and I'll overlook your latest theft.'

'The purse? But there were naught in it, Master Bailiff.'

'Leave it on her doorstep and I'll forget about it – if you keep an eye out.'

A vigorous nod and the man loped away.

'He's simple, but he has an eye. The purse was valuable in itself. And he never wastes his time on those with nothing of value. He knows everyone's worth in the city.'

'You should hire him.'

'I would, but he disappears. He's plagued by fits. The Riverwoman puts a few drafts in him, gives him a cot while he sleeps it out, and he's back on the streets, bright and keen as ever.'

'The city depends on her for a great deal.'

'And you. Even in death you will be revered – your corpse will work miracles, mark me.' Hempe laughed.

By the time they reached the Ouse Bridge Owen no longer heard the questions about the attack, his mind on Gisburne, how to handle him. The man was slippery as an eel, powerful in the city and the shire, rotten to the core. That his fellow merchants and city counselors overlooked his criminal dealings confounded Owen. Lucie believed they feared what he knew of them, for his men spied on all in the city. What might he have to gain in aiding the attacks on the Swanns and their friends? Did he hope to take on the role of coroner? Surely his calls to parliament already gave him more power than would the post of coroner in Galtres. Perhaps a favor for a friend?

Owen nodded to one of the Graa clan, wealthy, powerful, and assured the man he would soon give the mayor his decision regarding the position of captain of bailiffs.

'We need you, Archer. Today's attack makes that plain. A blind widow?'

Hempe was grinning about the support for Owen as captain when Owen said, 'Crispin Poole approaches.'

The man they sought was obliging them by making his way toward them through the throng of folk on the bridge. As Crispin grew near, Owen heard people hailing him to express concern for his mother. Graa hastily took his leave.

'God's blood, they've attacked my home?' Crispin growled as he reached Owen and Hempe. 'I hope you are on their heels.'

'We're on yours, to be frank,' said Owen. 'What did Gisburne want of you this morning?'

'I couldn't say. No reason for a sudden summons.' Crispin glanced at the folk pressing round them, eager to hear.

'Move on,' Hempe called out.

'Damnable woman,' Crispin muttered. 'I feared – is my mother alive?'

Damnable woman? 'Yes,' said Owen. 'Injured, but I do not believe her life is in danger.'

'God watches over her. Heaven knows why.' Crispin's eyes flicked between Owen and Hempe. 'Are you come to escort me home? Both of you? Do you think the attack was meant for me? That I might be attacked on the way?'

'The man who came at your mother shouted something about vengeance for his father's honor,' said Owen. 'He seemed to be addressing her, according to Chaucer.'

Crispin blanched, there was no other word for it. White round the mouth, which opened a little in a prolonged sigh. 'I see.'

'Do you? We would like to know what exactly you see,' said Owen.

'It is a long tale.'

'Has it anything to do with the death of a young woman named Gerta?' Owen was rewarded by Crispin's muttered curse. 'We will talk later. At your house.'

'Not now? You are not headed there?'

'I would like to watch Gisburne's face as he's told about your mother's ordeal. You were summoned to Micklegate – John Gisburne's home, and while you were away . . .'

'You are thinking Gisburne arranged for me to be away?' Crispin looked aside, as if working to control his temper. 'I will accompany you.'

'Then come,' said Hempe, breaking his silence. 'We continue to draw a crowd.'

Owen glanced round, nodded to folk who began to ply them with questions. 'If you will let us pass,' he said, beginning to push through them.

'And how readily the crowd parts for the captain,' Hempe muttered, still amusing himself about how the folk venerated Owen.

'How did Gisburne behave?' Owen asked Crispin when they were clear of the worst of the crush of curious onlookers.

A shrug. 'Friendly. He served wine, cheese, and bread, asked how I liked the house in Colliergate – with the air of having arranged it for me.'

'Had he?'

'No. Olyf . . . Dame Olyf and I met by chance in the market a while after my return. I complained about the damp in my mother's house and she mentioned that their neighbor was letting their house. Large, airy, empty.'

'You and she were childhood friends?'

A glance as if checking Owen's meaning, then a nod.

'So what was the urgency?'

'None that I could tell. He told me he will be in York for at least a fortnight, likely longer, and he means to fulfill his promise of introducing me to the prominent merchants in the city, see to it that I found satisfactory trading partners.'

'Promised *you*?'

'No. I'm of little value to him in myself. Who do I know? What luster might I add to his crown? No, he promised . . .' Crispin seemed to be surveying the crowd with a worried frown.

'Promised whom?' Owen asked. 'Is it Alexander Neville, His Grace the Archbishop of York?'

Crispin looked at him, startled. 'You knew?'

'I guessed.'

'I see why the prince and the city want you to spy for them.'

'Spy for the city?' Hempe grunted. 'We've no need of spies.'

Oh, but they did, with worms such as Gisburne and Neville about. Owen was sorry to be right. Neville and Gisburne. Now that was a pairing to turn a sour mood bitter.

'A Neville,' Hempe said, as if things began to make sense to him.

'What are you to Alexander Neville?' Owen asked.

He did not like Crispin's reaction to the question, how he sped up and averted his eyes, pretending sudden interest in the fish-mongers on the south end of the bridge.

'Why should Neville care how you are received in York?' Owen guessed, of course, but he was keen to hear how Crispin would phrase it.

'I am a member of his household, in a sense, here to smooth the way for him with the citizens of York, provide him a list of those with influence.'

'And Gisburne has presented himself as one who should appear on that list?' Owen asked.

A small smile. 'He has. But His Grace wishes an independent assessment.'

'Then Gisburne would hardly cause you trouble.'

'I would think not. I – he did impart some news. I suppose he wants me in his debt . . .'

'That would be his way,' said Owen. 'This news?'

'He traveled here in the company of the archbishop's secretary, Dom Leufrid. On the archbishop's barge.'

'And this Leufrid could be expected to inform you of his arrival in York in short order?' asked Hempe.

'Not before he has received all the gossip available from the prior of Holy Trinity across from Gisburne's house.'

'So Gisburne did you a favor,' Hempe noted.

'He does not do favors, he makes deals,' said Owen.

'Might this attack have nothing to do with the recent murders?

Bartolf and Hoban?' Hempe wondered aloud. 'You are aware that Gisburne retains an unusual number of armed servants, Poole?'

'So I am told,' said Crispin.

'The man is a menace,' said Hempe.

'Even so, this attack on my house, I fear – in truth, I am quite certain it is related to the Swann murders. I will explain later.'

'Something to consider,' said Owen. 'One of Gisburne's household servants might have let slip your impending visit to someone who decided to make use of your absence.'

'Hence your curiosity about Gisburne's purpose,' said Crispin. 'I see. I have much to learn about the undercurrents in the city.'

'It seems you are being forced to learn quickly,' said Hempe.

Still standing at the southern edge of the bridge, Owen had begun to question his motive in confronting Gisburne himself. Hempe might handle it, allow Owen and Crispin to return to the scene of the attack.

'Let us leave Gisburne's household to Hempe and his men, Poole,' said Owen.

'And where will you be?' Hempe asked.

'At Poole's house.'

Hempe grinned. 'Good plan. It will be my pleasure to discomfit King John.'

Michaelo was expected back momentarily, Jehannes's servant informed Geoffrey, and the archdeacon was also away. He invited Geoffrey to wait in the hall. When he'd left, Geoffrey turned slowly, absorbing the beauty of Jehannes's hall, the painted vines, the hangings, and then, out the window, the garden planted with a thought to pleasing the eyes. He had never guessed the archdeacon a man of such refined taste.

'Master Chaucer.' The monk startled him.

'You do like to steal up on a man,' Geoffrey exclaimed. But he smiled, ever charmed by how Michaelo floated rather than walked.

'I understand there has been another attack?' The monk's nostrils quivered on the last word.

'No deaths this time, much thanks to Alisoun Ffulford, who shot down one of the attackers, routed the other. I witnessed her courage, and that of Dame Euphemia's manservant. The surviving attacker ran off with the hound. Captain Archer asks you to walk through the minster yard as he believes it your custom to do of an evening, offering comfort. While you do, keep your ears pricked for any whispers of a man and a hound, wolf, whatever they call it.'

Such a smooth, etched face, homely when in repose, but now, as the monk's pleasure in being called to serve lifted all the corners – why, he could be quite handsome. Geoffrey had never seen him look so – beatific. He had an amusing thought. Owen Archer was a handsome man in his own way, certainly the women behaved as if he were uncommonly alluring. Was Michaelo smitten? Oh, now that would be delicious.

'And if I learn anything? See anything?' the monk asked.

Geoffrey prayed he'd not smiled. How to explain? 'My mission, after speaking with you, is to inform the mourners at Swanns' of the state of the victims at the Poole home. Then I am to await Archer at his house. Come to me there.'

Michaelo tucked his hands up his sleeves and bowed to Geoffrey. 'I will do as the captain asks.'

Geoffrey had no doubt he would.

Brother Michaelo saw the king's man out the door. How the captain could entrust that man on such a mission . . . Perhaps he'd merely meant to keep the blankly smiling fool out of the way, and out of earshot. For the captain knew that Chaucer was a gossip. A prudent ploy? Yes, that must be it. Michaelo was moved that Owen recalled his practice of providing spiritual counsel to those living in the minster yard. Dame Lucie perhaps described his reception. He wondered when they shared such moments in their day. In bed before sleep? What must it be like to have such a companion?

He shook himself. Such thoughts did him no good. He had work to do.

Chaucer . . . Geoffrey Chaucer had not mentioned stopping first in the Bedern. Michaelo wondered whether that part of Chaucer's route concerned his own official mission for the prince. One must never forget. Several of the clerks residing in those lodgings were used by officials in the city as messengers to London and Westminster. Paired with the matter of the stranger who had arrived at the abbey staithe last night in the company of Archbishop

Neville's secretary, the former intending to bide at the abbey, the
latter at Holy Trinity Priory in Micklegate, there might be treachery
afoot. The captain should know of these developments.

The thought of the new archbishop's secretary brought on a
headache, and Michaelo paused, composing himself. Of all the
clerics in the land, that Neville should choose Michaelo's cousin
Dom Leufrid, the thief who stole the money Michaelo's family
had intended would buy him a comfortable position in a wealthy
abbey in the south of England. Because of Leufrid's greed Michaelo
had wound up in York, so far north, with little to offer the abbot,
a distant cousin. Leufrid, the bastard, now secretary to the worm
who had stolen the archbishopric from Thoresby's worthy nephew,
Richard Ravenser – infuriating.

Michaelo prayed for the compassion to forgive, but deep in his
heart he yearned to ruin the loathsome Leufrid.

Hereby lies a tale, Geoffrey thought as he hurried down Stonegate.
The blind goodwife and the wolf. Pity it wasn't a fox, but what
of a wolf dressed as a man? The wolf fools all but the blind.
She 'sees' him for what he is and cunningly turns the tables . . .
Pah. He had more immediate concerns on which to train his
mind. He ordered his thoughts as he cut through the yard of the
York Tavern and passed through the Fenton garden into the yard
of the Swann home.

As soon as he stepped through the door conversations halted,
servants carrying platters turned to look at the new arrival, and
the musicians ceased playing. He'd hoped for a quiet word, but
that was clearly not to be.

In a rush of silk, Olyf Tirwhit was upon him.

'Is Crispin injured? I should go to him—' Her breath was
sweet with wine and she staggered aside as her husband stepped
between them.

Geoffrey was relieved to see Muriel Swann and Janet Braithwaite
in the man's wake, John Braithwaite, Paul, and his wife not far
behind. Ned brought up the rear, hurrying in from the kitchen.

'I suggest we step into another room,' Geoffrey said. 'All eyes
in the hall are upon us. You can then decide how much information to share with your guests.'

Janet led the group into the buttery, a morbid venue, Geoffrey thought, remembering Bartolf's bloody corpse on the table, and no doubt Hoban's before that.

'I heard from the bailiffs' men, and much has passed round the hall,' said Ned. 'Is it true that Mistress Alisoun shot a man between the eyes?'

'Neck.' Geoffrey touched either side. 'As if preparing to roast his head over a fire.'

The young man's grimace halted Geoffrey from further comment.

'I pray you tell me, is it true that Alisoun is mortally wounded?'

Geoffrey patted Ned's shoulder. 'Magda Digby and Lucie Wilton tend her.' The young man gave a cry like a whimper. Seeing his distress, Geoffrey regretted speaking while distracted.

'Is she?' Ned asked.

Geoffrey could hardly soften it for the lad when he was about to share the ugly details with the rest of those gathered in the buttery. 'I pray you, patience. I hope to make one report to all here.' He patted Ned's arm.

By now the Swanns, Braithwaites, and Tirwhits stood assembled before Geoffrey. Clearing his throat, he recited the tale plainly, with no bardic embellishments – though he had considered some poetic phrases.

He watched their reactions. Owen would ask. Olyf's cry of relief when she heard of Crispin's absence won a poke from her husband and a disgusted look from Muriel. Paul Braithwaite looked drained of blood and teetering, but they all reeked of sweet wine, so it might mean nothing. To their credit, though in their cups the group listened with interest and concern. He noticed that none asked for details of Dame Euphemia's injuries, none cried out at the profound cruelty of attacking a blind, elderly woman – he'd been wise to omit his embellishment regarding her snowy white hair falling down round her shoulders, one long strand dipped in her would-be murderer's blood. It would have been wasted on this audience. However, all expressed amazement at Alisoun's courage – and that of the manservant – and dismay about the extent of the young woman's injury, tempered with relief that Magda Digby and Lucie Wilton were there to nurse her.

'Oh, my dear Alisoun.' Muriel Swann looked as if she might faint. 'She has been so kind, so caring. What can I do?'

'Continue with the regimen she has prescribed, daughter,' said

Janet Braithwaite. 'Give birth to a healthy baby she will delight
to see when she is able.'

As an argument ensued between mother and daughter, Geoffrey
took the opportunity to slip away. Opening the garden gate, he
lingered at the spot where Bartolf had been murdered. Except for
the hours spent in his company on the way to York, Geoffrey had
not known the man. Nor had that encounter allowed insight into
his character. On that day he'd not been the respected, perhaps
feared coroner of Galtres, but a mere mortal man shattered by the
violent murder of his only son. What had he been like the day
before? Geoffrey would never know.

Owen and Crispin headed back across the river, both alert for
the missing man and dog.

'So Gisburne is not to be trusted,' Crispin noted.

'In my experience, no.'

'He behaved in such wise when you were Thoresby's man?
Did the archbishop do nothing?'

'He would allow Gisburne to make a generous donation to
the fund for the minster's lady chapel.'

'But John Thoresby was highly regarded. A saint compared
to Neville.'

'He was no saint.' Owen glanced at Crispin. 'It would seem
you are doing more than making a list of influential citizens for
Neville.'

The man pressed his lips together, eyes fixed on the street ahead.

Owen grew impatient. 'So you choose not to speak.'

'No. I – I would be your friend, and so I hesitated to tell you.
The city dreads the arrival of the new archbishop. His reputation
being what it is, they see him as a wolf, not a shepherd of souls.
And I'm to be to Neville what you were to Thoresby. I will
have few friends here.'

Worse than Owen had guessed, but fair warning. 'You have
my sympathy. And I would say that even were it not Neville.'
Though had it been Richard Ravenser . . . But there was no point
in such thoughts.

'But you said— One night in the York Tavern you admitted to
missing Thoresby.'

'The man, yes. And the knowledge, the support, the authority

I enjoyed. But he could be maddening. Powerful men are, in my experience.' A grunt of agreement. 'You are at ease with Neville?'

A bitter laugh. 'No one is at ease with the man. I've yet to hear anyone speak of him with any affection.'

'This Leufrid?'

'Alexander Neville and Dom Leufrid are two of a kind. Cold, ruthless.'

'Men of the Church.'

'Ambitious men for whom the Church was the way to power.'

Owen liked the way Crispin thought – to a point. But as Prince Edward's man or the captain of the city, Owen would need to watch every word, every gesture when in Poole's company. Pity. They might have been friends, in another time.

'I should tell you, Gisburne spoke of another man on the barge, a Moor, he did not name him, but an emissary from Prince Edward.'

A Moor? Owen wondered . . . 'Emissary to—'

'You, as I understand it. Apparently the prince is keen to add you to his household. Quite an honor. But I thought Geoffrey Chaucer was seeing to that.'

'His Grace grows impatient?' Owen shrugged, though his mind was racing. Might it be his old friend? 'What had Gisburne to say of that?'

'That you were Icarus, in your arrogance flying too close to the sun.' Poole chuckled. 'By the rood, the man envies you.'

'He must have little experience of His Grace the prince.'

'That is what I said.'

Yes. They might have been very good friends. But back to the matter at hand.

'When I told you of the attack on Dame Euphemia,' said Owen, 'you called her a damnable woman, said you'd feared – what? What does your mother have to do with the murders? Why would the man who lunged at her shout something about his father's honor?'

'You implied her injuries were minor. But if he lunged at her – who intervened? She sees only the faintest shadow in the best light. She could not defend herself.'

'Alisoun Ffulford.'

'The Riverwoman's apprentice?'

Owen told him what she'd done, how serious her injury.

Crispin looked far more stricken than he had when told about his mother. 'How did Mistress Alisoun come to be there?'

'I don't know.'

'Did she – has she mentioned me?'

A curious question. 'She has not awakened.'

'I mean, before. Anything about – I see from your expression she kept my secret. May God watch over her. If she should die – God knows, I am to blame. I take full responsibility.'

Owen wanted to hear about that.

'You should also know that the serving man did his best to protect Dame Euphemia,' said Owen. 'Injured as well, but he's able to walk and tell you what he witnessed.'

'Old Dun? Then I have misjudged him.'

'What of this Gerta?'

'When did you connect that with all this?'

'Not me. Two men were overheard speaking of her. They had come into some money and were spending it on good wine. Too much good wine. Their good fortune was somehow thanks to her. Or her murder.'

Crispin had stopped in front of Christchurch, staring at Owen. 'Recently?'

'Several weeks ago.'

Crispin nodded. 'Come.'

TWELVE
Gerta

I n Crispin's hall, Magda watched as Lucie dripped some liquid into Alisoun's half-opened mouth. Owen might find it a comforting sight had Alisoun been fussing, or gazing round with her usual wary expression. First Magda, then Lucie glanced up to see who had arrived, then, with nods, went back to their work. Crispin led Owen down a narrow passageway past Dame Euphemia's bedchamber, where the elderly woman lay in a deep slumber or faint, Owen could not say, and brought him to the garden.

Owen nodded to Dun, who sat watch, pitchfork in one hand.

As Crispin approached, the old servant rose abruptly. 'Master.'

'Sit, I pray you.' Crispin expressed his appreciation for Dun's years of service to his parents, and his gratitude for the man's courage this day. Dun bobbed his head.

Intent on his own mission, Owen crouched down and pulled back the cover from the dead man's face. 'So, Poole, do you know this man?' How Crispin played this part would reveal much. Owen had no doubt the man was known to him.

'Difficult to say . . .'

'Is it?'

'The young woman has a remarkable aim,' said Crispin, as if he had not heard the question.

'That she does,' Owen agreed. He waited. Would Crispin lie?

Easing himself down in a crouch by the body, Crispin turned the man's head so that he might study the face. 'Avenging his father. Of course he would. But how did he know who falsely accused him?'

'So you know him?'

'We have met. And I knew his father. A farmer fallen to poaching in Galtres, but a good man. My mother – accursed woman—' Abruptly rising, Crispin nodded to Owen. 'We will talk. But first, despite all, I will sit a moment with my mother, then join you in the hall to explain.'

Crispin's was a tidy house, spacious, though an odd choice for a blind woman and a one-armed man, narrow passageways and the indoor steps to the solar narrow and steep. Owen supposed Crispin might make use of the stump of his arm for balance as he took the steps, but it would be awkward. He could not imagine Dame Euphemia climbing to the solar; perhaps that was the very reason Crispin had chosen the house, a chance for solitude when he retired to his chamber. He was clearly not over-fond of his mother.

The hall was spacious, making the bed in which Alisoun lay seem tiny, albeit with a thick mattress and an abundance of pillows. She lay with her brown hair fanned out round her, supported by enough cushions that she was almost sitting. Long lashes were dark against her white cheeks. But as Owen drew near he noticed her breathing was quiet and steady. A good sign.

'A brave young woman,' said Magda.

'And fortunate in her healers,' said Owen, nodding to Magda, kissing Lucie's forehead.

'Did you find the man?' Lucie asked.

'No, but I've much to tell you. And if he is honest, Crispin Poole is about to tell me about a young woman's death that might somehow be the core of these troubles.'

'Eva mentioned something about that,' Lucie said, telling him what she'd gleaned.

'A false accusation to protect her son?' said Owen. 'I begin to understand.'

'I hope you talk here, in the hall,' said Lucie.

'I will make certain of that. And I pray you, listen.'

He knelt beside the bed. Was it his imagination, or did Alisoun's eyelids flutter? 'I am, as ever, impressed by your skill with the bow,' he whispered to her. 'I am not certain I would have caught him so, with him in motion.'

'Not aiming to kill him.' Breathy, weak, slow, but Alisoun spoke.

The room grew very quiet.

Owen kissed Alisoun's hand. A tear rolled down her cheek. His heart heavy, he looked to Magda.

She tapped her head with a bony finger. 'Hard as her will.' The hint of a smile did not reach her eyes.

Owen pressed Alisoun's hand. 'Use that will to return to us,' he whispered. Looking back to Magda, 'Might I ask you some questions?'

Lucie took her place.

Stepping aside, near the brazier where it was warm in the draughty hall, Magda began by describing Alisoun's and Euphemia's injuries. Owen interrupted her to ask whether the hound had clawed Euphemia.

'No open wounds, but marks of claws raking her shoulders. Not one of Bartolf's, Bird-eye. All claws intact.'

She finished with Dun's injuries. All this he might have learned from Lucie, but his next question, about how Magda had known of Hoban's murder, was his reason for taking her aside.

'Magda recognizes the signs, not how or why this or that is revealed to her. She has no answers for thee, Bird-eye. This is *thy* conspiracy of wolves. Thou hast the charge, Magda merely warned thee. *Thy* task. Open thine eye.' She tapped the place between his eyes, then pressed there.

Sensing her finger sinking into his skull, Owen jerked away in confusion.

But Magda's hands lay idle in her lap.

He felt a shower of needle pricks across his blind eye. 'I don't understand. Had I the Sight I would have known what was to come, I might have prevented Hoban's murder. And Bartolf's.'

'Not *fore*-seeing, *clear*-seeing. A gift to all who count on thy protection. Trust thyself. Thou seest far more clearly than most.'

Her answer frustrated him. Clear-seeing? Once perhaps. But he was sorely out of practice. He tried another approach to the question.

'A conspiracy of wolves – what did you mean by that?'

'That is for thee to discover. And how thou must move forward.'

'The prince or the city? Is that what you mean?'

'That as well.'

'You speak in riddles.'

'Thou'rt a riddle-breaker.'

No, he was not, though people thought it of him, expected him to find the answers, he had no gift for this. Never had.

'What did you mean by the question about what folk see when they see a wolf?' Owen asked. 'How could it not be the animal?'

'A riddle for thee, Bird-eye.' Magda rose, shaking out her multicolored skirts. 'Magda has work to do. And thou must hear One-arm's story.'

'It cannot be easy for you to see your elderly parent the victim of a violent attack, no matter your differences,' said Owen, settling back in his chair after tasting the wine and finding it to his liking – a welcome blessing on such a day. 'We who took up arms in our youth, we come to believe we are hardened to violence, that we can bear anything. But if we've come away with our souls intact, tarnished but whole, we know there is no hardening that can blunt our hearts to the suffering of those we love.'

'Love,' Crispin mumbled, then drank down his cup of strong wine in such haste it might fell a smaller man. Rising from his seat, he turned his back to Owen, facing the window. 'Love my mother? Pity her?' He flexed his shoulders. 'As a boy I prayed for the wisdom to remember to tell her nothing of petty slights as friends fell away, wary, untrusting. I could not blame them. She said she was protecting her family. Protecting. Pah. She was the death of my father, and as the fruit of her womb I am cursed. Soldiering did not harden me, she did. Sympathy for her injuries? She knows better than to look to me for that.'

Owen sat silent, absorbing this bitter speech, so unexpected. He was glad that Magda and Lucie listened from across the room. He might later doubt what he was hearing, the anger, the long resentment.

'She brought it upon herself,' said Crispin. 'The blindness? She'd seen nothing but the poison in her soul for so long, it did not matter.' He returned to his seat, poured another cup of wine, drank it down, poured another, sat looking into the cup. 'I thought I could return, right the wrong, make amends. Too late. God help me, but I almost wish it were she lying there in the garden, that the Lord God decided we'd enough of the spiteful, hateful woman, and Gerta's and Warin's kin would have their revenge.' He moved the cup in his hand. Owen could imagine the wine swirling within, how the movement caught the eye, held it, pulled it down. 'Forgive me. You must think I speak in riddles.'

'Not riddles, but a tale begun midway. Why don't you begin with meeting the man lying in the garden? Tell me about him.'

'It will make little sense without all the rest.'

'Begin with what might help me understand what has been happening, and we'll see.'

'As you wish.' Crispin considered. 'Perhaps a week before Hoban's murder, I walked out to Bartolf's house in the forest at twilight, in the company of my men. I hoped the old coroner could help me clear a man's name. But he refused to talk. Told his hounds to take a good sniff and attack me if I dared return.'

'Bringing your armed men with you might have suggested a less than friendly purpose,' Owen said.

'I had them stay back, out of sight.'

'How did you approach? By the main track or along the river?'

'Why?'

'Can you recall?'

'Along the river. Much shorter when on foot.'

'You know that track well?'

'I did as a boy.'

'Was Bartolf standing outside, aware of your approach?'

Crispin paused, his eyes far away. 'No. A man – I took him to be a servant – he shouted toward the house that someone was coming down the path.'

'How did he come to see you?' Owen asked.

'Now you ask, he was on that trail, as if waiting.'

'When Bartolf threatened you, did you leave at once? Or did you challenge him? Did the dogs attack?'

'I could see he was drunk, as usual, and there is no reasoning with an adamant drunk, so I left. And, no, *his* dogs did not attack.'

Noting the emphasis on the word 'his', Owen drew out the pouch he'd carried for days. 'I ask because of this, a salve for a dog bite. Someone dropped it on that trail. Recently. It had not been out in the weather when I found it.'

'I *was* attacked – and bitten – that night, but not by Bartolf's dogs. Another. On my way back. There was a man crouching down on the bank, and near him, in the shadow of a tree – well, I thought it a wolf, and that the man might not be aware of his danger. I called out to warn him. It was then the beast turned toward me. Leapt at my throat. I shielded my neck with my useless arm and drew my knife, but it was so quick. Its teeth were in me. My men were rushing him, they tell me, when the man whistled and the animal let go. Just like that. Man and beast backed away, the man shouting that he would avenge his father, and then they vanished.'

'His father is the one whose name you hoped to clear?'

'Warin, yes.' Crispin cursed. 'This will make no sense to you.'

'Did your men give chase?'

'Tried, but by then it was dark and the marsh dangerous.'

'It was you who had chosen the marsh path.'

'My men are not from here.'

'Where were your men today when your mother was attacked?' Owen asked.

Crispin had been watching Owen, no doubt guessed he was aware of his reluctance to be forthcoming. Now he made a face as if conceding. 'I've had them watching Bartolf's house in the woods for several days.'

'Why?'

'It all began there, or near there.'

'You mean Hoban's death and all that's happened since?'

'Yes.'

'And have your men observed anything?'

'Nothing. No one has come to the house, nor have the dogs or the horse returned.'

'Did it not occur to you that folk should be warned of the man and his wolf? If not that night, then at least after Hoban was attacked in the same place, with a beast involved?'

'I told you, none of this will make sense without all that went before.' Crispin averted his eyes.

'A lone man and his dog could not do all this,' said Owen. 'Today two men attacked.'

'I have no idea who the other might be.'

'So that night, you were bleeding, and near the home of the Riverwoman.'

'She was away. Mistress Alisoun tended me. And I am grateful.'

'She prepared this pouch of salve for you?' Owen dangled it by the cord.

'Yes.'

So Alisoun *had* lied to him.

'It seems there is a limit to your gratitude, and your trust. I recall you asking whether she'd spoken of you. And you said you felt responsible for her injury. Did you swear her to secrecy?'

'I did.'

'Why?'

Crispin winced. 'Neville. I did not know when I accepted the mission that I would find I was so reviled by my old friends. I expected resentment – I escaped, they were still here. But there was much I did not know. So much.'

'And now you do?' Owen asked.

A nod. 'I should not have come.'

'The old friends you speak of?'

'Hoban, Paul, Olyf, Adam.'

Muriel's trio plus one. 'Alisoun saw to your arm and you swore her to secrecy so that Alexander Neville would not hear of this trouble and have no more to do with you.'

Clenched jaw. Good. He might forget himself.

'You deride me,' Crispin said.

'Not without cause. Go on. What did you do next?'

'I came home.'

'After curfew? You have a friend at Bootham Bar you counted on to let you through past curfew?'

'I told a tale of my widowed mother, blind, worried for me. Folk believe I returned to care for her. I make use of that.' Crispin took off his velvet hat, wiped his brow. His hand trembled. 'Why did Bartolf not accuse me of Hoban's death? I waited, expecting it.'

'Because he threatened you with his dogs?'

'He was not so different from my mother, ever one to use his position as coroner to deflect blame from his family and his powerful friends.' Crispin's full lips curled in disgust.

'And you? You knew of the danger and warned no one. Not even Alisoun.'

'That's not the same.'

'No?' Owen glanced at Magda, who shook her head. *Let it be, Bird-eye.* 'So this man who attacked you, was his complaint against Bartolf?'

'To an extent, but that particular sin *I* lay at the feet of the woman who bore me.' Crispin looked over at Alisoun. 'I was wrong to put myself ahead of that young woman. I have grievously wronged her.'

'And others.'

'Might I have a moment with her?'

Owen did not feel the man deserved it. But he agreed, rising to stretch his legs.

Lucie joined him. 'Come with me. There is something you must hear.'

Crispin Poole bowed his head over Alisoun. He meant to pray, but he was too aware of the Riverwoman's keen regard, feeling her eyes, blue, sharp, seeing through to the rot at the core of him. Raising his head, he met her gaze.

'I have sinned against this young woman.'

'And thyself. Lives might have been saved with timely warnings. Is that not so, Crispin Poole?'

'Yes.'

'Tell all to the captain. From the beginning.'

'Will she live?'

'Live? Alisoun will rise from this. But the damage – it is too soon to tell.'

'Damage,' he repeated to himself. 'I have been a coward.'

'Go. Speak to Archer.'

Rising, Crispin found that Owen had left the hall. Moving down the corridor he heard voices in his mother's bedchamber. They were there, Owen and his wife the apothecary, speaking with his mother. Euphemia sat up against a pile of pillows telling Archer and his wife that Crispin was her only child. She'd merely meant to protect him. He was the archbishop's emissary now – surely she had been right, his life was worth more than a poacher's.

Loathsome hag. 'What is this? Has she been—' Crispin checked himself, sensing the Riverwoman in his mind, warning him to put all else aside and tell Owen all he knew so that he could judge what might yet be salvaged. 'Come, Archer. I have a tale to tell. You will find it quite at odds with what you've heard here.'

'Your mother—'

'Lies. She twists the tale to her purpose. Come, both of you. Let me tell you what happened, as far as I know it.'

To Crispin's astonishment, Owen thanked Euphemia for her willingness to talk to him, saying that she had been a great help.

*   *   *

Lucie welcomed Crispin's invitation to join the conversation about to resume. When he and Owen had first talked, she'd intended to listen, but Eva had summoned her. Her mistress was awake and wished to speak with Lucie.

Magda had motioned for her to go on.

Dame Euphemia had sat propped up in her bed, her hair now tidied in a long braid. She'd gestured for Lucie to come close.

'I would touch your arm as I speak. To know you are here, listening.'

Lucie had obliged her, moving a stool close to the bed where Euphemia might comfortably reach her arm. Imagining she was about to hear a complaint about Magda's presence, Lucie was surprised when Euphemia asked, 'Is it true that the Riverwoman's apprentice saved me from the madwoman? And that she's badly injured?'

'Alisoun Ffulford shot the man coming at you with a knife.'

'I know nothing of a man. What of the madwoman?'

'Do you mean the hound that pinned you to the wall?'

'Hound?' Euphemia shook her head. 'She had a smell about her, but she was quite human, I assure you.'

Lucie thought of Magda's words, the ones that had puzzled Owen. *What do folk see when they see a wolf, Bird-eye? The animal? Think again.* As soon as the hall went quiet, Lucie had asked permission for Owen to join her at Euphemia's bedside. The woman had agreed to speak with him. Once Lucie fetched Owen, she'd asked Euphemia to repeat all she'd told her. She'd done that, and more.

As they followed Crispin back out into the hall, Lucie and Owen spoke softly, sharing their impressions of Euphemia, a mix of understanding and horror at the coldness with which she had condemned a man whom she did not know for certain to be guilty of the crime for which he stood accused.

Lucie accepted with appreciation the offer of the high-backed chair. Her day had begun in the apothecary, preparing the autumn salves and potions, which she'd abandoned to join the funeral procession, standing through the mass, sitting for a while at the funeral feast, then rushing to collect what she might need to come here and assist Magda. Her back complained. Accepting a cup of wine, she set it aside, not wanting to miss any part of Crispin's tale.

Now she watched Owen sit forward, hands on thighs, head turned slightly to the left, training his good eye on Crispin, who sat with his shoulders curled subtly inward, as if protecting his heart. She did not yet have a clear sense of Crispin Poole. Emissary to Neville – that did not speak well of him. Yet Owen liked him – or he had. She watched Crispin squirm under Owen's keen regard. That was good. The more intimidating he found her husband, the more likely he would speak the truth, and answer all questions.

'Why do you and your mother have a different version of the tale?' Lucie asked.

Crispin seemed relieved to turn his attention to her. 'I don't know how much you heard earlier.' He rubbed his forehead with his one hand, glanced out into the hall, his eyes meeting Magda's. 'It is best that I start at the beginning. The true beginning.'

'Do, I pray you,' said Lucie.

Owen settled back, arms crossed before him, ready to listen.

Crispin began softly, describing the close circle of friends, all eager to escape the bonds of their parents, considering themselves old enough to take their places beside the adults – Paul Braithwaite, and Hoban and Olyf Swann. 'I should say Paul and his hounds. We teased him that he felt naked without a pair flanking him.' In summer, the Swann family would spend much time at the house in Galtres, away from the stench of the city. The four friends liked the green spaces outside the city walls, though Paul was uneasy moving too far into Galtres, worried about his dogs as they were not lawed, and he'd no intention of subjecting them to such pain. Bartolf Swann had a word with the sergeant of Galtres about the unlawed hounds, promising that the boy would never allow them to run free while in the forest, and that John Braithwaite would pay generously for any damage they might cause. The sergeant, Richard Goldbarn, had agreed.

In the long, slow days of summer the four of them enjoyed the woods, the river. At first, that last summer was no different than those that went before. Until they noticed Gerta, whom they knew to be the charcoal-burner's daughter, following them.

Her family had been known to them for a long while, shunned, as their kind were, their skin tanned and stinking of fire and ash. Yet that last summer, Gerta bloomed, her light-brown tresses streaked with sunlight, her skin a warm olive, glowing with health – it was impossible for the three lads to think of her as one to shun. She seemed curious about them, following them at a distance, watching. Olyf tried to shoo Gerta away, once even tossing the basket Gerta wove as she sat and watched into the river, but the boys enjoyed the attention. It did not matter to them one whit that she was of lowly status. They adored her.

Lucie asked softly, 'What did Gerta do when Olyf threw her work into the Ouse?'

'Nothing. She began a fresh basket with what reeds she had left.' He paused a moment, as if remembering. 'There was something about her, how she settled down with a task – baskets, darning – and watched with the ghost of a smile that dimpled her cheeks. Her eyes were dark and deep, they seemed able to bore into us. And we lads felt she found us empty. It made us compete all the harder for her admiration – running, climbing, hefting rocks and logs to show off our strength. God's nails, we were fools. Now and then she taunted us – "Idle boys," she called us, "pampered princes." Or yawned, which was most maddening. The more she discounted us, the harder we worked to impress her. And the louder Olyf cursed us, cursed Gerta. Even worse, Gerta favored me, catching me away from the others, asking questions. And once she asked me to take off my clothes, she wanted to see a boy's body. I did, but only when she started taking hers off as well. We touched each other. God's blood, I wanted her so badly. But she picked up her clothes and ran from me. The others found me stumbling into my clothes, my hard cock making it difficult. Hoban accused me of forgetting I was meant for Olyf.'

'Were you?' Owen asked.

'I'd known for a long while that Olyf believed it to be so, but my mother laughed at the idea, insisting I must make a better marriage than that. Far better. To her, the Swanns were nothing. But she'd never explained why until she overheard me arguing with Hoban about Olyf being my intended. After he left, mother told me that she knew things about Bartolf Swann, that he was a lecher, using his power as coroner, as did his friend Richard Goldbarn his power as the sergeant of the forest, to ensnare the daughters of the tenants in the forest, use them until they conceived bastards, then toss them to the Riverwoman and wash their hands of them. And Bartolf took bribes regarding jury selections.' When Crispin mentioned Magda he glanced up sharp, looking to her. But Magda had her back to them, mixing something over the fire.

Goldbarn's part did not surprise Lucie – he had been the subject of much gossip, though it was his use of forest resources for personal gain that had ruined him. But Bartolf Swann?

'Did you have such feelings for Olyf?' Lucie asked.

'No. Never. She was so like Paul, quick to anger, slow to forgive. I never felt at ease with her.'

'And now?' asked Owen.

'She has not changed,' said Crispin. 'Not a whit.'

'Forgive my interruption,' said Lucie. 'I pray you, continue with the story. Your mother had warned you about Bartolf . . .'

'Assuming that my mother meant that Gerta was no virgin, I am ashamed to confess I was emboldened, sought opportunities to catch her alone. Only then was I aware of her silence and clear unease whenever Paul's hounds wandered her way. And I made another discovery. Something followed her overhead, up in the trees. It was more than the rustlings of birds or small animals. I caught glimpses – a foot quickly withdrawn, an arm, fingers wrapped round branches. Gerta was never actually alone. She had a companion, a girl who dressed as a boy – short tunic and leggings. She hid up in the trees watching, occasionally dropping things from her high perch to frighten away the dogs.'

'So Gerta had a witness to your encounters,' Owen said.

Crispin's frown deepened, dark brows pressing together, his focus sharpening, as if Owen's observation had yanked him from the past. 'Yes.'

'Gerta's younger sister?' Lucie asked.

'I thought so, but later, something Warin said . . .'

'I did not mean to interrupt,' said Owen. 'Go on. You'd noticed her unease about the dogs.'

'Yes. The next time I managed to speak with her away from my friends, I asked why she feared them. Why her sister abused them. "Wolves", she called them. She told me that in her homeland they prowled the forests and ate children. She swore it was true. I told her they were hounds, not wolves, and I would keep her safe. But she would not go near them.' He bowed his head. 'I should not have told the others. I don't know why I did. They could be so cruel. Hoban and Olyf encouraged Paul to let the dogs off their leads the next time Gerta appeared. She threw pebbles at them, then ran, saying she would set her brother on them if they did that again.'

'A foolish thing to do, if she feared them so,' Owen noted.

Crispin looked away. 'I admired her. Even when confronted with what she most feared, she defied us. What courage. But if there is any blame in this, it is mine. I should have kept her secret.'

Lucie was keeping a tally. So far he'd mentioned another girl and a brother.

'The next day Bartolf informed Hoban and me that Paul could no longer bring the hounds into Galtres. Hoban insisted I accompany him when he told Paul. While Hoban talked, Paul groomed his bloody hounds, whispering to them that he would let them eat her tender flesh, cooing to them about how they were strong and faster than any girl.' Crispin poured himself more wine, but set it aside. 'We'll get her,' he said. 'We'll get the bitch.' He picked up the wine and drank.

'An ugly tale,' said Owen.

A curt nod. 'But then we did not see Gerta for a long while. Autumn came, then winter, a time when we seldom went out into the forest. And then, in spring, when the river swelled with the snowmelt from the moors, Hoban caught sight of her walking by the river. He saw her there several days in a row, at the hour when he was walking home from school.'

'His family was not living in the city that year?' Owen asked.

'No. Bartolf was failing as a merchant. The family was forced to sell land and lease their big home in the city – it fetched a good rent.'

'So he discovered the place she walked in the afternoon,' said Lucie, guiding him back to the story.

'Yes. We found her at last. And no sign of her companion in the trees.' Crispin closed his eyes for a moment. 'I make it sound like an innocent game. But I knew it was not. It felt wrong to me. Frightened me. Their idea arose out of anger, and a desire to hurt a young woman who made them feel foolish, and who had bested them, finding a way to forbid Paul to bring his hounds into the forest unlawed. I wanted to excuse myself, but I feared they would turn on me.'

'Did you try to talk to them?' Owen asked.

'Or warn her?' asked Lucie.

'No. This thing with Gerta, it changed them. I was with them because I wanted to keep them in sight, make certain they weren't coming after me, and the only way to do that was to be part of it. They meant to hurt her.' He closed his eyes for a moment. 'I should have warned her.' He stared at the floor.

'You had found her,' Lucie prompted.

A nod. 'We left school early and hurried out into the forest with two of Paul's largest hounds – by now he had seven of them. She was right where Hoban had said she'd be, walking, singing to herself, looking so content. I could have shouted a warning. But I didn't. I was a coward. As we moved closer Olyf stumbled over a rock and cursed. Gerta heard it, turned toward the sound, and Paul chose that moment to let loose the dogs, shouting the order to attack.'

Crispin had gestured with his stump, and now, frozen in the air, he glanced at it with loathing. Lowered it. 'So many penances – my crippling, my duty to my mother.'

'What happened?' Owen asked.

'Gerta screamed, threw a stone at them, then turned and jumped into the river. From the moment she hit the water it was plain she could not swim. And even if she could, the current was so strong. I dived in after her. So cold, and the water so dark – I hadn't thought about how impossible it would be to see her in the choppy current. I had never been in the river in a flood. Something hit me and I went under. I thought I was dead. I could not tell which way was up. But I was pushed against the bank and caught on to a branch, pulled myself up along it. I was catching my breath when I saw her red skirt. And then I saw her hand. I swam out. Death would be better than to live knowing I'd given up trying to save her, save her from the death I brought on her. I don't know how many times I went under, lost sight of her, saw her again, then lost her, but she'd caught a log and was managing to keep her head up. I kept swimming toward her. When I reached her I thought, at last! But she was draped over the log, limp. Alive? I could not stop to check, just worked on pulling the log to shore. But then – if I climbed out first, I had to let go of the log and risk losing her. And there was Warin, the poacher, crouching down, lifting her out.'

'He put her on the ground face down and pushed the water from her lungs. When she began to cough and retch, I sank to my knees and thanked God.'

'God watched over her,' said Owen.

'Did he?' Crispin looked doubtful. 'She was so close to death.'

'How did Warin come to be there?'

'He said she lived with his family, his daughter's close friend. His daughter had come to tell him what had happened. "Your friends won't thank you," he said, "but I do." I told him they were not my friends and I didn't deserve thanks. I wanted to come along, help him with her, but he told me to go home.

'I followed anyway, for a while, until she woke and ordered me away. "Richard must not know about you," she said. Warin growled at her, told her to be quiet about that ungodly man. "Don't call him that. I love him. We are to wed." Warin cursed and she ordered him to set her down. I asked who she was talking about, who she was to wed. Warin said Richard Goldbarn had been calling on her, bringing her gifts, filling her head with ideas. He cursed him. Gerta slapped him. I – I stumbled away, my heart breaking. The sergeant of Galtres – that old man and my Gerta? God help me, I loved her. I'd begun to think— When I reached home I told my father all of it, and said I wanted to go off to be a soldier. He locked me in my room. I found a way out, and left. I never saw my father again.' Crispin's voice broke. 'All that while I had not understood what I felt for Gerta. I should have protected her.'

Lucie allowed herself a sip of wine as they sat for a moment in silence.

'And then what?' Owen asked.

'Years later, in a camp before a battle, someone who had been in York at the time told me that a few days later her body was pulled out of the Ouse by a fisherman. She'd been dead before she went in the water, strangled, her head cracked open – maybe in the water, maybe by her strangler. The coroner's jury – Bartolf's jury – found Warin the poacher guilty, and hanged him at the crossroads.'

Euphemia's accusation now made no sense to Lucie. Nor to Owen – she saw him shaking his head. 'Warin?' Lucie asked. 'But—'

'Of course it didn't make sense,' said Crispin. 'Until my father wrote to me – once I left the fighting and was in trade, I let him know where I was, and he wrote to ask my forgiveness. He'd told mother all I'd told him. Then, when Gerta was murdered so soon after I'd fled, she feared I would be accused – they'd say I did it and ran.'

'You would be the obvious suspect,' said Owen.

'I wish she had let it lie. Father could have warned me to stay away, and I would have. My return has brought no joy to anyone. But Mother prayed for my return. So she had Father go to Bartolf and tell him that Gerta had told me she feared Warin, he had an unholy lust for her. It suited Bartolf. He must have been frantic for his friend Richard Goldbarn, fearing he'd be blamed, and how could Bartolf defend him.'

'You believe Goldbarn murdered her?' Owen asked.

'I do.'

'Why?'

'Who else might it be?'

'You describe her as quite beautiful, wandering the forest alone, or with another young woman. Crispin, it is not at all obvious Goldbarn was guilty,' said Lucie. 'Have you ever heard any proof of it? Any witnesses?'

'I had Elwin check the coroner's report. Very little is said other than that Warin was seen bending over her a few days earlier, then carrying her, apparently in a faint, through the wood.'

'When you carried her out of the water, were Paul, Hoban, and Olyf there?' asked Owen.

'If they were, I did not notice. The next time I saw any of them was this summer, on my return to York.'

'So they'd not run downstream to help you?' asked Lucie.

Owen surprised her by asking before Crispin could speak, 'Did you sense at any time that someone was watching you and Warin? Other than his daughter, Gerta's friend?'

Crispin looked from one to the other. 'Are you asking whether they hid from us, but watched? And they were the ones who blamed Warin?'

'Or part of their witness was used against him,' said Owen.

Crispin palmed his eyes, shook his head. 'A darkness that has shaped my life.'

'Do you know anything about the blinding of one of Paul's dogs?' asked Owen. 'His father said he was a boy when it happened.'

'Not while I knew him. I learned of it on my return.'

'Who told you?'

'Why do you ask?'

'I rule out nothing as unimportant at this point.' Lucie heard her husband's frustration in his comment. 'Was it Dame Olyf?' he asked.

A strangled laugh. 'Olyf? It is one of the few things she will not speak of.'

'So you asked her about it?'

'I did. And the look on her face – I would have guessed she was the one who had crippled his beloved hound. But she and Paul are still friendly.' A shrug.

'Do you have any idea who might have done it?'

'None.'

'Is that Warin's son lying in the garden?' Lucie asked. 'Avenging his father?'

'Yes. He was the man in the wood, with the dog or wolf that attacked me. I don't know his name. There was another brother, and the daughter, but I never knew their names.'

To Lucie's surprise, Owen rose. 'I have heard enough for now. I must return to the Swann home.'

'Shall I come?' Lucie asked.

'No,' said Magda. 'Hast thou not heard the cart on the cobbles?'

Owen had walked over to the window. 'It's Jasper, with Bess's donkey cart.'

'The lad comes for Alisoun,' said Magda. 'Good.'

Not so ready as Owen to cut off the conversation, Lucie turned back to Crispin. He stood looking about as if uncertain what he should do. 'Dame Euphemia accused an innocent man?' Lucie asked, hesitated, then added, 'Knowingly?'

'She did,' said Crispin. 'Plucked his guilt out of the air and embroidered a tale to fit it, then gave my father not only the tale, but a list of folk who should sit on Bartolf's jury. Ask Janet Braithwaite. She threw that in my face when I called at the house. It killed my father, I'm sure of it. He could not live with the guilt. Monstrous woman. She-devil.'

Owen had turned to listen. 'You said you saw the coroner's report. Did they list the names on the jury?'

'No. They seldom do, unless one of the members added

information, argued a certain point.' Crispin frowned. 'My father
was on it. He mentioned John Braithwaite, Will Tirwhit – Adam's
father, and the master of hounds who was training Paul at the time
– I cannot recall his name . . .'

'Was John Gisburne on the list?' Owen asked.

'He did not mention him, and I thought at the time it was
unusual for men of Braithwaite's and Tirwhit's stature to sit on a
coroner's jury; they rarely do. My father had sat on a few, but it's
usually those hoping to make a name for themselves, not those
who've sat on the council.'

Someone knocked on the hall door.

'That will be Jasper,' said Lucie. She crossed the hall to welcome
him.

He bobbed his head to her as she opened the door. 'I thought
Alisoun would be more comfortable in our home. And you would
not need to be away.' Jasper's eyes pleaded.

Magda joined them at the door. 'Alisoun agrees.'

Jasper's face brightened. 'She is awake?'

'She will be more at ease in thy home. Thou shouldst attend
her, Lucie, settle her. Magda will soon join thee.'

Lucie stepped back, inviting Jasper in. 'But who is with the
children?'

'Master Geoffrey and Brother Michaelo.' He nodded to Owen
as he approached. 'They both have much to tell you. Will you be
there soon?'

'Let's move Alisoun, and then I will talk to them. Did Geoffrey
say whether the guests are still gathered at the Swann home?'

'They've gone. Dame Muriel felt ill.'

Crispin followed them to the door. 'I will send for my men. I
can at least ease you of the burden of concern for us. If mother
needs help, I will seek your advice, Dame Lucie.' He thanked
them both, and Magda, for all they had done. 'I owe much to you,
and especially Mistress Alisoun.'

'Do not let down your guard,' Owen warned. 'Nothing is
resolved.'

THIRTEEN
Bitter Words

A s they followed the clattering wagon down Low Petergate to Stonegate, Owen and Lucie compared Euphemia's version of Gerta's story to Crispin's.

'To accuse Warin,' said Lucie. 'I would have bid her good day, but I did not trust myself.'

Nor had Owen. 'We have a name now. Hempe says the dead man went by the name of Roger.' Hempe had arrived just as they were about to depart. He had no news, but it was helpful to have a name.

'Roger, son of Warin,' Lucie said softly. 'Is this all about vengeance for their father's wrongful execution? Certainly the attack on Euphemia would make it seem so. She seemed to think what Geoffrey saw as a beast was a woman.'

'So is that what Magda meant?' Owen wondered. He found it difficult to believe. 'Could Geoffrey be so fooled?'

'A person wearing a skin, some claws – fear can twist our minds to see what we expect,' said Lucie.

'How do you think he, or they, chose the order, and how they attacked?' Owen asked.

'If it is vengeance, Roger – and perhaps his brother or a cousin – considered Bartolf as much to blame as Euphemia – or more so. First her son was attacked, but the way he described it, it was a gesture, meant as a warning. Warin might have told his children the tale of Crispin's brave rescue. Then Bartolf was made to suffer his son's murder – or perhaps that was a mistake, corrected the next night when Bartolf was taken. Paul's dogs were the spark, so he lost a dog. Then Euphemia, but Roger had not counted on Alisoun. The Tirwhits' maidservant Wren is a puzzle. If she watched the house, had Roger placed her there? Was it she who learned of Crispin's summons?'

They were interrupted by passing folk telling Lucie that they prayed for Alisoun. She reassured them that she and Magda were caring for her. A few asked after Dame Euphemia. More were concerned about their own safety. Owen told them that he and George Hempe had their men searching for the man and dog. As happened since Bartolf's murder, some folk reported sightings of fearsome beasts in the streets, or, more typically, in the alleyways. Owen had come to disregard them after Hempe's men exhausted themselves hunting down phantoms. And if the beast were a woman in costume . . .

At the house, Geoffrey rose from the floor, where he had been entertaining the children. Brother Michaelo sat on the bench outside the long hall window, in the shelter of the linden.

'Escaping the children,' Lucie quietly commented to Owen. 'He winces when they speak, as if their high voices offend him.'

'Our children might just save his soul,' Owen said, winning a surprised laugh from Lucie.

But levity soon vanished as the children observed Alisoun being carried in, their faces puckered in fear, while Geoffrey attempted to report all he'd observed. Lucie hugged Gwenllian and Hugh and whispered assurances.

Owen rubbed the scar beneath his patch, the familiar shower of needle pricks joined now by a pressure between his eyes, as he listened to Geoffrey's description of Paul Braithwaite's face when he heard about the men who'd attacked Euphemia Poole. Owen could not quite gauge Paul's part in all this, but it felt more significant than an old resentment regarding his dogs. Michaelo wanted to tell Owen something, in private, something he thought important. Owen put him off, telling him he hoped to return within the hour, asked if Michaelo could stay that long.

'I could, I've little else to do, but I would rather be of help than stand about waiting for a moment to speak.'

Lucie looked up from Alisoun's pallet. 'I've a favor to ask. Would you inquire about Muriel Swann? Find out whether she needs me?'

'As you wish,' said Michaelo, following Owen to the door. 'And while we walk, I can briefly give you my news.'

Moving out into the garden, Owen said, 'I take it you did not want someone in that room to hear what you have to say?'

'It touches on Geoffrey Chaucer.'

Owen listened with interest as they walked. Geoffrey visiting a lodging in the Bedern that housed clerics used as messengers between the religious houses in York and Westminster, London, Canterbury, and elsewhere was interesting, but not unexpected.

'And one thing more,' said Michaelo. 'Dom Jehannes had word of an important visitor biding at Holy Trinity Priory – the new archbishop's secretary, Dom Leufrid. He arrived yesterday in the company of an emissary from Prince Edward, Antony of Egypt, who is biding at St Mary's Abbey.'

Forgetting himself, Owen slapped Michaelo on the back. 'So it *is* Antony.' An African scholar and military genius, Antony and Owen had enjoyed each other's company at Kenilworth when Owen was in Grosmont's service.

'This means you are pleased?' Michaelo asked.

'I am indeed.'

'But I tell you nothing new.'

'I was not certain it was him. All I knew is that Gisburne traveled with Leufrid and a Moor in Prince Edward's service.'

'A Moor?' A shrug. 'There is one more item. Dom Leufrid is my kinsman. The one who robbed me of the money my family had provided to buy me a position of responsibility in one of the large abbeys near London and Westminster, set me on the path to become a prior or abbot.'

'This man you despise is our new archbishop's secretary?'

'As I was to John Thoresby, he is to Alexander Neville.' Michaelo laid a land on Owen's forearm. 'If you mean to protect York from this Neville, I would use all my knowledge, my connections, and my diplomatic skill to assist you. And I might dare say, I have been known to hold my own in a physical encounter.'

Owen had not forgotten how he did so on a dangerous journey long ago.

'Whether you work for the prince or the city, I wish to serve you, Captain.'

Seizing the moment, Owen asked, 'Might you find it in your power to shake off the penitential gloom, approach it with more mischievous glee?' He grinned.

Michaelo removed his hand. 'I offer you assistance and you insult me?'

Owen threw up his hands. 'I mean it as no insult. I am in earnest.'

Michaelo sniffed. 'I seek only to redeem myself in working for the community.'

'You would not take delight in hindering the loathsome Leufrid?'

'You are not listening to me. I seek to atone for my sins. Pride, ill-will – what you suggest, that way lies damnation.'

And who was Owen to push him from his path? 'I meant only – your wit is refreshing. Laughter is a balm most welcome in my work.'

Michaelo gave him a long look down the length of his noble nose. 'My expressions of scorn amuse you?'

'Oddly, yes. I miss the Michaelo who scoffs at fools.'

'Even when you are the target? You, the one on whose broad shoulders all would lay their burdens?'

'Would it not be virtuous to tutor me in humility?'

A pause. 'I will pray over the matter.'

Owen was glad to hear a lighter note in Michaelo's voice for he might be quite an asset. It amused Owen that all the while he'd thought Thoresby kept Michaelo as a penance, he had in truth harbored a bloodhound.

'So Antony of Egypt is your friend?' asked Michaelo.

'He was the old duke's good friend. I knew him in the field. An expert on obscure weaponry. I suppose the prince finds him useful. Or did in Aquitaine. But what is he doing here?'

'If Prince Edward knows of your friendship, I would guess Antony is here to improve on Chaucer's efforts to recruit you.'

'You don't trust Chaucer.'

'I trust few men, and even fewer women. Children, not at all.'

Owen chuckled, a gift on such a trying day.

'I am pleased you are amused.' Michaelo sniffed.

They had reached the Swann home.

'If you learn anything I should hear at once, come to me at the Braithwaite home, two houses away,' said Owen.

'I know the place. Shall I drop a line in the water, see what bites?'

Already taking Owen's request to heart? Owen told him about Wren's apparent connection to Roger and his fellow attacker, how she had been seen talking to them. 'It has me wondering about all the servants. Galbot – I will ask about him. See if you can learn when Joss and Cilla joined Bartolf's household. And when the Tirwhits hired Wren.'

With a bow, Michaelo glided into the yard of the Swann home.

Skirting the hall, where John and Paul Braithwaite were loudly trading insults, Owen followed the servant to the garden, where Elaine Braithwaite sat beneath the graceful limbs of a young oak, straight-backed and bristling as she watched the house.

'Captain?' She began to rise, attempting to shake out the wrinkles in her costly gown, a futile effort that almost toppled her. She might just be drunk enough to speak freely.

'Might I join you for a moment?' Owen slipped onto the bench beside her and stretched out his legs with a sigh. 'May we soon see an end to this troubling day,' he muttered.

'Has the widow Poole proved ungrateful for your interest?' A slight slurring of words proved Owen correct about Elaine having availed herself of the fine wine at the feast. 'Watch yourself with that one,' she said. 'People pity her, a widow, blind, her son returning a cripple, but she is sly, cruel.'

'You consider Crispin Poole a cripple?'

'Do I offend you? Surely you do not see yourself in him. The loss of one eye is a small thing – and that scar and patch only enhance your appearance.' She reached toward him, as if to touch his cheek, then remembered herself. 'But a hand, a useful arm.' She touched Owen's forearm. 'Such strength. Your wife is most fortunate – I see how you regard her, the warmth in your eyes, how the two of you lean toward each other, sharing your thoughts, laughing at each other's wit. Paul thinks only of his precious hounds. Heavenly Mother, what is it with some men and their hounds? I love my children, Captain, never doubt it, but Paul is the bane of my life.'

'He is caught up in grief over the killing of Tempest?'

Elaine squeezed his arm. 'You would think it had been his child the way he moans and tears up at the mere mention of the monster. But it's only the latest.'

Only the latest. This is what he'd come to hear about. 'Tempest was not the first to die?'

'Oh, no. A fortnight past a pair of his prized mastiffs went missing. You would think—' A shrug. 'As I said, he regards them as his children.'

'A pair went missing? Did he search for them?'

'I am surprised he did not think to hire you – but you were – oh, forgive me, you have a recent loss. Dame Philippa. She was a kind, God-fearing woman.'

'We do grieve her passing,' said Owen. He let the silence fall. Patience. Then, 'Has Galbot returned?'

'Galbot.' A snort. 'He is almost as mad regarding the hounds as Paul, though it is his job. No. He is still on the loose.'

'How long has he worked for your husband?'

'A year? No longer than that. Ungrateful wretch. Paul hired him as a favor to Bartolf. He came with the dogs, you might say. You know that Paul recently bought a few dogs from the old man? Wolfhound bitches, Aphrodite and Circe. Such names!'

'So they were not the pair that went missing?'

'No. Not Bartolf's beloveds. May his soul rest in God's love.' She crossed herself. 'Bartolf had no need for a servant dedicated to the two dogs he had left. Galbot needed work. Paul hired him.'

'How had Bartolf come to hire Galbot?'

'The servant Cilla coaxed him to hire the man. I only know because Paul made such a fuss about him, how his previous master's loss was Paul's gain, the man was so good with hounds, how he wished to thank Cilla.' She rolled her eyes. 'I know no more of him. I have nothing to do with the kennel.'

'The two who went missing – did Paul hold Galbot responsible?'

'*I* did. But the man knew how to please his master, wailing almost as loudly, rushing about searching for them. He beat his chest, he was responsible, having trained them.'

'So he thought they'd run off?'

Elaine frowned, swaying a little. 'Perhaps that is what he meant. I didn't care. Two less, good riddance.'

'Did he find them?'

'Bones. Burnt bones left at the gate a few days after they went missing.' She stopped, forced a smile, and rose.

Owen turned to see who approached.

'My dear.' Elaine's voice was suddenly sickeningly sweet. 'I have just been asking the captain about Dame Euphemia.'

Paul Braithwaite walked toward them with the exaggerated care of one who fears falling flat on his face. But where Elaine simply seemed wobbly, he seemed on the verge of a faint. 'And how is the old bitch?' he slurred, blinking at Owen.

'Husband! You shame me with such speech.' Elaine excused herself and swept off to the house.

'Bitch. She despises everything that puts all that silk and velvet on her fat shoulders.'

'She tells me that Tempest was the third of your hounds to die of late.'

'Did she? Bitch.' Paul slumped down beside Owen. 'Though it is true.'

'Burned,' she said.

'And the bones left at the gate. Handsome mastiffs. How I will replace them I know not. Already paid for. I'd just completed their training.' Paul groaned. 'And now Tempest. Someone threatens my kennels. I leave in the morning. I'm worried about the others.'

'And you did not think to tell Hempe or me?'

'Hempe. Pah. He's already chosen Crispin as the mind behind all this. He might be elevated to the council with this one.'

'Tell me about Gerta.'

A choked silence. Paul turned on the bench to stare at Owen. 'That pathetic— Crispin told you. Of course he did. Saint Crispin, rescuing her from the flood. He blamed me, but he was part of the plan. We meant only to teach her a lesson.'

'How do you know he blamed you? He says he did not see you again until he returned this summer.'

'His bitch of a mother told me, didn't she? She threatened to tell the tale if Father did not agree to be on the coroner's jury when the filthy little whore was found strangled and tossed into the Ouse. All Euphemia cared about was that the blame didn't fall on her precious Crispin. You can't blame me for Gerta.'

'What I think is of no concern to you. It's Warin's son Roger and his accomplices.'

'Warin?'

'His son attacked Dame Euphemia.'

A stunned silence. Paul had gone gray. 'God help us.'

'The other escaped. I don't know who he was.'

Paul tried to rise, but he was shaking too hard. 'I must see to my hounds.' A sudden retch, and he doubled over, spilling out his spleen.

Elaine Braithwaite burst from the house, running to him. 'Help me carry him into the house, Captain.'

As Elaine and her maidservant fussed over Paul, Owen took John Braithwaite aside.

'I wondered. What is your memory of the coroner's jury in the death of Gerta, the daughter of the charcoal-burner in Galtres?'

Braithwaite had been sitting at ease with a cup of brandywine. 'Who?'

'Shortly after Crispin Poole went away.'

'Oh, that vixen. Why bring up that old story?'

'What do you remember?'

'She'd been leman not only to the poacher but to the sergeant of Galtres. Tasting the high and the low, that girl. But her death, that was not right.'

No slurring. That was a relief. Dealing with two drunks was more than enough for one day.

'Did you believe the evidence against Warin?' Owen asked.

'Believe? He pretended to foster her, Archer, and then took her. Goldbarn learned of it from her. She was so frightened. But he did not act swiftly enough.'

So that was how they'd framed it. 'Goldbarn claimed she told him this and he'd meant to protect her?'

'Do I detect disbelief, Captain? On what grounds?'

'Did he have evidence?'

'You know how coroner's juries work. Warin was judged a danger to the community.'

'So said Goldbarn, who might have otherwise been suspect. Or was there someone else?'

'Goldbarn? Well, the man was a rogue, it's true, but . . .'

'Anyone else?'

'I suppose Crispin Poole. It was his father who presented the charge.'

'As for that, would it not have been easy enough to prove Crispin had already departed when this happened?'

'Tricky. She was murdered just a few days after he is said to have left the city. But he might have lingered in the forest.'

'To what end? He'd risked his life saving her the first time.'

A frown. 'The first time?'

'When your son frightened her with his dogs.'

'Paul? What had he to do with this?'

'You didn't know she'd almost drowned a few days earlier?' Owen told him of the cruel joke.

'Paul?' Braithwaite was far away for a moment, then shook his head. 'I cannot recall his behavior at the time, except that he was angry with Crispin. So angry.' He stopped, as if something had occurred. 'I did wonder whether an argument among the friends had sent him off, fuming. You know how passionate youth can be about nothing. Or perhaps – I thought it might have been Crispin who had blinded Paul's hound, though my son never named him.' Braithwaite drained his cup. 'But why are you asking about this?'

'Because one of the men who attacked Euphemia Poole was Warin's son, Roger. He's now dead.'

A jerk, as if John felt the news as a physical strike. 'Warin's son? Warin had a family?'

'Why would you presume otherwise? A man desperate to feed his family – that is the usual cause for breaking the law of the forest among the common folk.' Owen made an effort to speak without rancor, though the man had raised his bile.

'I never wished to sit on the jury.'

'But you did. Why?'

'I did it because Edmund Poole—' Braithwaite frowned at something on the ceiling. 'Now I think of it, he threatened to reveal some mischief our sons had got into. Or so Euphemia told my wife.' He returned his attention to Owen, leaning toward him. 'These attacks— Is Paul in more danger?'

'I cannot say. You might have mentioned the dogs that had gone missing earlier, the burnt bones left at your son's gate.'

'What are you talking about?'

'Paul said nothing to you of the dogs gone missing before all this began? A few days later their burnt bones were left at the gatehouse?'

Braithwaite was breathing too hard. 'It began with Paul?'

'John, are you—'

Pressing his hand to his heart, Braithwaite struggled to rise, but collapsed back on the chair, breathing shallowly. Owen knelt to him, asking how he could help.

'Brandywine. Table by the window.'

As soon as Owen saw that John Braithwaite was able to lift the cup to his mouth and sip, he went in search of Janet Braithwaite, who was ministering to her son.

'Your husband is ill. His heart, I think. Should I send for his physician?'

'Because your wife and the Riverwoman dare not leave Euphemia's side?'

'No, because they are in the process of settling Alisoun Ffulford in my home,' Owen answered in a quiet voice. 'I thought your physician might come more quickly.'

Janet looked chastised. 'Forgive me. I don't know where to turn first. I will send a servant for Master Saurian. Do the job I hired you for, Captain. Find the monsters who would tear us down.'

'I will explain later, but I warn you to be careful of any servants who have not been in your household, or your daughter's, a long while. Watch them, say nothing of importance in their presence.' He nodded to her and withdrew.

'It's Galbot, that's who he speaks of,' he heard Elaine say. 'If that scoundrel returns, lock him in the cellar.'

It was with a sense of escape that Owen stepped out of the Braithwaite home into the gathering twilight. He paused at the spot where Tempest had bled to death. What might motivate a man to slit the throat of an animal entrusted to his care? The unjust execution of his father might carry him to such an act. It was possible Galbot was Warin's son. If so, the brothers had sustained a long simmering anger, waiting almost twenty years for Crispin's return, and then planned a slowly unfolding series of attacks to sate their hunger for vengeance. That required great discipline.

His conversations had opened up new questions for Owen, and what he wanted most now, besides the comfort of his home, was quiet in which to gather his thoughts.

'Captain!'

Stephen and Alfred came striding toward him.

'A servant went running past,' said Stephen. 'Has there been another attack?'

'Summoning a physician. John Braithwaite's heart gave way to the news that his son might still be in danger.'

'Not dead?'

'No, God be thanked. The long day took its toll. I told him far too much at once. He could not cope.'

'What did you tell him?' Stephen asked.

'The captain needs a rest,' said Alfred, poking Stephen in the ribs. 'A better question is what would you have us do now?'

'Find Hempe, tell him to have a few men watch this house.'

'You think they're next?' asked Stephen.

'I believe they were the first.' He told them about the mastiffs, the bones.

'Burnt the hounds?' Alfred whistled. 'Why?'

'A clever choice if they wanted to use the dogs in these attacks. The bones might be those of any animals. Who will look so closely? It was enough to make Paul call off the search. My guess is Galbot slipped them away to his brother.'

'Galbot's in this? He's Roger's brother?'

'I believe so. Or some relation. He pretended to search, then set up the bones to end it.'

'Clever,' said Stephen.

'And Tempest? He slit his throat as well?' asked Alfred.

'That's my thought. I've much to tell you. When you've seen to Hempe, come to my house. Brother Michaelo might have more for us.'

Lucie greeted him at the door, finger to lips, and slipped back outside with him. 'Jasper was talking to Alisoun, apologizing for his behavior, when she began to sob and— What you need to know now is that she is convinced Wren prevented her from going to Hoban's aid the night he was murdered.'

'Wren? So she *was* part of this.'

'Alisoun believes so,' said Lucie. 'She will tell you the whole story when she's able. And something about Joss – that he'd been watching the Poole home. But as it was Wren who mentioned it to Alisoun this morning, I do not understand her purpose. He watched for his own reasons? Or perhaps she meant to betray him? But why mention it to Alisoun?'

'Difficult to hide Joss's wart?' Owen suggested. 'So they might distance themselves from him for that reason. God's blood, Lucie, I am grasping at the merest hint.' Owen leaned his head against the house, trying to steady his thoughts. He told her what he'd heard at the Braithwaite house, and what he'd done to John Braithwaite.

Lucie stroked his cheek, kissed his forehead. 'You say he was not slurring his words, but it still might have more to do with rich food and much wine today. Or that he has harbored doubts all this while. They sent for Master Saurian? Good. He is in the city.' She smiled and kissed him again. 'We will hear all about it in the morning, no doubt.'

'Did Michaelo bring word of Muriel?'

'Dame Janet told Dame Muriel's maidservant her mistress needs rest, the day was difficult and her mistress found it hard to let the other women take charge. Jasper delivered something to help her sleep tonight, and a blood-strengthening drink for morning.' She rubbed his back. 'For you I prescribe food and rest.'

Owen wrapped his arms round her and held her for a moment. 'You are my solace.' He kissed her. 'How is Alisoun?'

'Jasper was right. This move was good for her. Come and see. One more thing. She is not certain what attacked Dame Euphemia – a wolf, a hound – her attention was on Roger, but she said when it knocked her over she felt confused by it.'

'As do all who see it. Perhaps Euphemia is right. A blind woman is not so confused by a hide. How did Magda respond to that?'

'As if it were to be expected. You smile? So did I.' Lucie touched his cheek. 'Jasper sat with Alisoun for a long while, but has now returned to the shop to prepare for early customers – there will be much gossip about the events of the day, and folk will hope to hear it from us.'

Stepping across the threshold, Owen felt hopeful. On a small bed by the fire, Alisoun leaned back against a stack of pillows as she listened to Gwenllian and Hugh telling a story with much gesturing. Magda sat at the table holding Kate's hand, no doubt telling her about her sister's ordeal, the lost twins. Geoffrey slumped down over a cup, apparently sleeping – wine, no doubt, one cup too many. Brother Michaelo sat bolt upright near the fire, his face turned toward Owen, clearly waiting to tell him something.

'Food first, I pray you. And a moment of quiet. Sit, be at ease, I will join you when I am refreshed.' Owen headed to the kitchen, where he might eat in peace.

But the walls were not so thick that he could not hear the arrival of Hempe, Alfred, and Stephen, all talking at once. Let them settle. When he was captain of archers, he would often call his men together, then excuse himself to fetch something forgotten while they greeted one another and moved through their usual insults and challenges. By the time he returned they were present and ready to listen. So long ago now. It had been a long while since he had heard of any of his former comrades.

While he ate, he walked through the day – it seemed an eternity – reviewing the events and the knowledge he'd gleaned. That all this began twenty years earlier – was that possible?

A quiet knock on the door. He guessed it to be Michaelo and called to him to step inside.

'Forgive me, but I find it difficult to pray in there. The children's voices, so shrill . . .'

'I have kept you from all your other tasks long enough. My wife told me about Muriel. What else did you learn?'

In a marvel of conciseness, Michaelo painted in sharper lines what Owen had begun to suspect. Joss had joined Bartolf's household a few years earlier, and Cilla had begun to do small chores for Bartolf shortly after that, coming with increasing regularity about a year later. Wren had not been long with the Tirwhits. Combined with what Owen had learned about Galbot, it looked as if they were a group.

'The one who still puzzles me is Paul Braithwaite,' said Owen. 'Geoffrey said that he looked as if he might collapse when he heard the news of the attack at Poole's.'

'But he was the least affected by all this. One dead dog.'

Owen told him about the others. 'And the dogs seem to be everything to him. Losing three. Even if I'm right about the burnt bones, *he* believes they're gone.'

'You are thinking that Roger and Galbot, perhaps both Warin's sons, plotted this revenge? But what about Gerta? Had she any family left?' Michaelo asked.

'I don't know. Josh? Cilla?' Owen rubbed the scar beneath his patch. 'Or is she Warin's daughter?'

'How are the hounds moving through the city unseen?'

'How indeed?' Owen was not ready to claim there were no dogs in the city, only a woman dressed as one. 'Hempe or I would hear about it. Since the murders of Hoban and Bartolf, folk are on the watch. After Old Bede's flight I wondered whether they might be going by boat, but they'd still need to move through the city streets to reach the river. Speaking of Old Bede, I want him to see Roger's body, find out whether he's the man who threatened him.'

'Send your would-be warriors Alfred and Stephen?' Michaelo suggested. 'They might sleep there, return with him on the morrow.'

Owen agreed. 'He's not been troubled at Magda's house since an initial try. It's as if they've forgotten him.' He rubbed his head. 'In the morning, I will go back, try to learn more about Galbot. By then Paul Braithwaite should have a clearer head.'

Michaelo rose. 'I will leave you to speak with the others, and then get some rest. You and Mistress Alisoun will be in my prayers.'

A fresh wind stirred the autumn leaves, sending up a rich scent of damp, turned earth mixed with the powdery scent of leaf mold. There was a sharpness to the breeze, a sign of autumn catching hold. Owen and Magda sat on a bench far back in the garden, near the grave of Lucie's first husband, Nicholas.

'Her life was quieter then.'

'Clear thy mind, Bird-eye. Be at peace for a while.'

He tried, turning his attention to the sounds of the night garden, animals on the prowl down below, a cat slinking along the top of the wall, a great winged creature swooping down, the cry of its prey, the draft from its wings as it flew away over Nicholas Wilton's grave.

'What am I not seeing?'

'Be at ease. Thou art close to understanding.'

He did not believe it.

'Tell Magda what thou hast heard, observed. Spin the pieces out onto the night winds. In the morning thou canst collect them, after a dreamless sleep.'

He doubted he would sleep at all, anticipating a night fighting with the order of things, weighing the possibilities. But Magda was here, and willing to listen, and so he told her everything that had happened, all that had been revealed, doing his best to recount it in order without too much repetition. She gave him her full attention, staring into his eye, all the while so still he could not even hear her breath. When he was finished, she turned away, gazing out on the garden.

'How did you know that Cilla, or some woman, was the beast folk see in the city?' he asked.

'Ah. So that is the answer to the riddle.'

He waited for more, for at least a chuckle. When he could no longer bear her silence, he asked, 'What do you think?'

'For the children of Warin to carry such hate for so long . . .' Magda bowed her head for a moment, then turned to Owen, her gown flickering in the moonlight, as if her power wrapped round her as she moved.

Owen had been so keen on discovery he'd not stopped to think of the pain motivating the tale as he saw it. If his theory was correct, Warin's children meant for the Swanns, the Braithwaites, and the Pooles to experience as much pain as they'd suffered. 'What about Gerta's family?' Owen asked. 'Do you remember Gerta, the charcoal-burner's daughter?'

'Hard workers far from home. Two children they had, a boy and the girl. The lad was content to learn his parents' art – for it takes skill and practice, building the frame for the fire, gathering the correct wood, tending the burning so that it is slow but does not burn out.'

'But Gerta?'

'Pretty Gerta hungered for a man who would adore her and take her away. But who would desire a lass who stank of the burning and was coated in ash and soot? She begged Warin and his wife Mary to take her in, let her be Cecelia's sister.'

'Cecelia,' Owen felt a chill. 'Cilla?'

'Mayhap. She was a wild one, dressing like her brothers, fleet-footed and strong, scrambling and climbing, watching the birds and beasts, learning their calls. All three were children of the forest and the river, at ease anywhere, ever following Magda while she harvested herbs, roots, and bark, seeking to learn all they might.'

It sounded like the woman. 'Were you here at the time of Gerta's death?'

'Nay. It was flood time, when Magda tucks her belongings in the rafters and goes up on the moors, tending those too far to come to her. By the time Magda returned, the families were gone, fled when Warin was hanged.' She was quiet again. And then, softly she said, 'Hard times scatter families. Like wolves, together when the hunting is good, scattering when prey is scarce. Yet these came together a score of years later?' A grunt.

Wolves had not the leisure to spend their days plotting revenge. They needed to hunt to fill their bellies each day. But men . . . 'Had it been my da who'd taken in a young woman as his own and then been wrongly executed for her murder I might sit round the fire with my brothers and sisters plotting a way to punish the privileged pups and authorities who'd murdered him.'

'Mayhap thou hast more insight into such passion than does Magda. Prince Edward must think so, to trust thee to protect his family from the Northern barons.'

'I'd not thought of it in that light.' But he suddenly saw it as she did. 'Protecting the privileged pups.'

Magda chuckled, but then turned to Owen, taking his hand. 'Such trust is an honor, if thou dost consider the royal kin honorable folk. Do not make thy decision based only on what thou thinkest of the prince.'

Owen felt the tingling in the center of his forehead. Would he ever understand her power? Did he wish to?

'If I ponder that I will never sleep this night,' he said.

'Magda digressed. Thou hast more immediate concerns.'

He returned to what she'd told him of Warin, Gerta, and their families. 'But who then are Joss and Wren?'

'This is how Bird-eye catches murderers? Shaping a tale out of scraps?'

Is that what he did? Surely it was more than that?

'Might Joss be Gerta's brother?' he asked.

'The lad was ever covered in soot and ash, Magda would not know him now. But he was gentle like Joss. And when Joss came to Magda for the juniper he seemed perhaps familiar.'

'Juniper?'

'To remove the wart, he claimed. He asked for savine, in particular, *that* juniper. Magda offered houseleek instead. He cursed her and left.'

'Angry?'

'Desperate. Magda thought he meant to kill himself. Oil of savine is a potent poison.'

Owen knew of it. 'You did not try to comfort him?'

'Magda does not presume.'

FOURTEEN
Into the Flames

As Honoria de Staines slid beneath her bedcovers a few hours before dawn she prayed that God would look past her many sins this night and bless her sincere intention to save a young woman's life. Though this was her usual hour to rest, the guests having departed, stumbling home to their cold beds, and the women of the house sleeping off their long evening, this had been no ordinary night, and she lay with her eyes open, listening for intruders.

Early in the evening she had agreed to shelter the young woman before hearing her tale, moved by her appearance and the terror in her swollen eyes. By the time Honoria understood the danger in which she'd placed all the women who depended on her for their safety it was too late to toss young Wren back out on the streets; she'd made the young woman's safety her mission.

In danger, wanting to hide. Honoria had taken Wren to the storeroom off the kitchen, kept reasonably warm by its proximity to the hearth and oven. A pallet and blankets were ever ready there for women, often just girls, who needed a place off the street.

'Who beat you?'

'My da. One of my uncles is dead because of me.'

Her uncles. Honoria remembered how Wren's mother had bolted the very day her brothers had paid a visit, leaving her child behind. 'I cannot promise to keep the little one safe,' she'd said. 'Find her a place in a good home.' When Honoria asked whether Wren's father might care for her, at least take her in as a maidservant, she'd laughed. 'You think he is a wealthy customer? He's with my brothers, as cursed as the three of us.'

'No one will bother you here tonight,' Honoria had told Wren. 'No one in this household.'

'You don't want to know what I did?'

'Are you likely to kill another?'

'I didn't kill him, Mistress Alisoun did. But she was there because of me. And Da saw me talking with her.'

Had it been earlier, Honoria would have taken her to Captain Archer. Wren had information he needed. But it had been her busiest time of the evening. She must see to clients. Now, lying in bed, she was alert to every creak and sigh as the house settled into a predawn calm, and cursed herself for not taking Wren to the captain.

Enough. She rose, dressed, went to the kitchen to fetch the bailiff's man she'd bribed to sleep there, guarding Wren. She'd offered him a free tumble with the woman of his choice if he would stay, explaining the situation. A youth eager to prove his mettle, he'd readily agreed.

'We're taking her to Captain Archer.'

The young man was bleary-eyed. 'Is it morning already?'

'Almost.'

'He will not be pleased if we wake the family.'

'Until he knows who it is we bring before him.'

In the pale gray before dawn Owen woke to pounding on the street door. He stared out the unshuttered window and vowed to remember to close it from now on. There was an autumn chill in the air.

Lucie groaned. 'So early.'

Striding across the room, Owen glared down from the window at the trio standing before the door, one of them about to pound again.

'Don't you dare.'

The man started, then backed up to see who was there. 'It's Corm, Captain. Bailiffs' man. Trouble in the Bedern.'

Two cloaked figures stood behind him.

'I am coming.'

Lucie sat up now, her hair tumbled about her bare shoulders.

Owen kissed her. 'One of Hempe's young men.'

'I heard.'

Dressing as he headed to the door, Owen was opening it when something hit him in the shoulder. His eye patch.

Lucie smiled. 'You don't want to frighten them.'

'He deserves it.' Hurrying down in his bare feet, Owen nodded to Magda, who stood at the bottom of the steps. 'Trouble in the Bedern.'

'Trust thyself, Bird-eye.'

The cloaked figures preceded Corm through the door, the taller one throwing back her hood.

'Honoria.' Even at such an hour, she had a grace to her.

'I have someone you will want to talk to. I warn you, in the night she painted herself. But though she looks it, she is not the king's fool, I assure you. Might we sit down? I have a tale to tell.'

Painted herself? Owen took them into the kitchen so as not to disturb Alisoun and Magda in the hall. Kate was already stoking the fire. As they settled round a table, the smaller figure pulled back her hood. He thought she looked more like a cat than a fool, the skin round her eyes darkened with face paint that arched upward toward her temples. Her nose was painted a pale brown. It was one way to disguise blackened eyes and a swollen nose.

'And you are?' Owen asked.

'Wren, sir.'

'Adam Tirwhit's maidservant,' said Honoria. 'But she was born in the brothel, before I owned it. Cilla is her mother, father unknown until last night, when Wren pronounced him to be Joss, who had found her and beaten her for betraying her uncles.'

'Let me guess. Roger and Galbot?'

'Yes. He blamed her for Roger's death, and that because of her Euphemia Poole had escaped serious injury and her home is now too well guarded for them to remedy that. So today they intend to deal with Gerta's murderer, then return for Euphemia after Crispin Poole lets down his guard.'

Owen took a moment to digest this. So many pieces of the puzzle, yet the most important— 'Gerta's murderer. Did she say who that was?'

Honoria's raised brows expressed her surprise. 'You know this Gerta? I was at a loss.'

'A young woman murdered twenty years ago. An innocent man was hanged for it. Bartolf Swann gathered and presided over the coroner's jury who condemned him.'

'Bartolf,' said Honoria. 'I see. No wonder Cilla left when they appeared.'

'When was that?'

'More than a year ago. Galbot and Roger – they are kin to the condemned man? Or to Gerta?'

'A tale for another time.' Owen had been watching the young

woman, how she looked round the kitchen, smiled at Corm, who grinned back like an idiot, but did not help Honoria with her narrative. 'What I need to know is where your father and your uncle are headed, Wren,' he said, leaning toward her. 'Would you tell me?'

She looked up at him, blinking the cat eyes, shrinking into herself. He had that effect on some people.

Honoria turned to Corm. '*He* says it's Paul Braithwaite who is in danger.'

'Why do you think that?' Owen asked Corm.

'Wren mentioned the killing of a guard dog – Tempest? – being just a warning. When I asked her what she meant she went quiet, said she'd already talked too much.'

'When did the two of you talk?' Honoria demanded.

'She came out for some ale when I'd come down from – you know,' said Corm. 'I told her who I was. We talked a while.'

So that is how they became so cozy. Owen hoped it was just talk.

Kate set a jug of ale and five cups on the table. 'To fortify you.'

All four helped themselves, thanking her for her thoughtfulness. Owen wondered about the fifth cup, but understood when Lucie stepped through the door.

She carried his bow and a quiver of arrows. 'Magda said you might need this. Was she right?'

'She was. Bless you.'

Lucie kissed him and then laid the bow and quiver on the table as she welcomed Honoria to their home. As Owen introduced Wren and Corm, Lucie nodded. 'Magda would like Wren to come into the hall, speak with Alisoun.'

'She is awake?'

'Yes. And she wishes to speak to you,' Lucie said, holding Wren's gaze. 'I've sent for Brother Michaelo. I believe we might like a written account of all we learn from this young woman.'

Puzzled, Owen took Lucie aside. 'How do you know so much?'

'Magda. Do not ask me how she knows these things. I cannot explain.'

Wren rose, asked to be taken to Alisoun. 'I want to ask her forgiveness.'

Kate offered to escort her. As they left the room, Lucie turned back to Owen. 'She is in danger?'

'Wren is injured. The paint covers it.' He told her what he knew so far.

The young woman was soon back in the room. Her posture had changed, straightened, her gaze direct.

'Brother Michaelo is here,' Kate announced, stepping back to allow him in.

'How did you come so quickly?' Lucie asked.

Michaelo bowed to her, shifting a pack he wore slung over one shoulder. 'I was at prayer. Jehannes believed it wise to interrupt me. It is urgent, I trust?' He glanced round the room, stopping at Wren. 'This is not some jape?'

Owen and Lucie assured him not as they escorted him and Wren to the table. Owen introduced Honoria and Corm, explaining all as briefly as possible. Had he not sensed time was of the essence he might have been amused with Michaelo's obvious discomfort about dealing with a bawd and a painted girl. But he prayed the monk simply settled to his work.

Shifting a little on the bench, the young woman watched as Michaelo took a seat across from her and a little to one side and pulled from his scrip a quill, an inkpot, and two stones to weigh down the curling parchment, which was the last item he drew out, smoothing it and placing the stones with care. As he sharpened the end of the quill, he asked Wren's permission to record what she said.

'You'll write down my words?' asked Wren. 'Just as I say them?'

'Perhaps not every word,' said Michaelo, 'but the essence of what you say. Even when I was secretary to His Grace the Archbishop of York I . . . took care to make clear his meaning.'

'Why are you doing this?' Wren asked Owen.

As Lucie settled on the bench beside Michaelo to assist him, Owen chose his words with care. Everything depended on gaining Wren's trust. 'Am I right in thinking that much of what has happened with the Swanns, the Pooles, and the Braithwaites arises from your family's anger at the lies told about them, about how Gerta died? The lies that killed your grandfather?'

Wren gave a noncommittal shrug.

'This is your chance to record what truly happened,' said Owen. 'If we present such a record to the king's officials we might protect you from any judgment against your family.'

'No one has ever questioned grandfather's guilt. None but us.'

'I would not blame you for doubting my word. But I swear to you that I mean to help you if I can. Would you tell me what happened yesterday?'

'Da beat me.'

'Why?'

'He says I betrayed him. He saw me talking to Mistress Alisoun. I told her too much and she went to the Poole house, murdered my uncle Roger.'

'Alisoun was protecting an innocent victim.'

'The widow Poole lied about my Granddad. Had him hanged.' Owen could not deny that. 'Da says I can never go home.'

'Where is home?'

Wren tilted her cup from side to side, watching the ale slosh about.

'Why don't you tell me your family's story about Gerta and your grandfather?'

Silence.

'Your kin have used you, haven't they?' Lucie asked. 'Forced you to work for the Tirwhit family and spy on them and on the Pooles?'

Wren looked up, chin forward. 'I liked it there. They were nice to me.' She pushed the ale aside. 'If I tell you things, could I go back to them? The Tirwhits?'

'If they agreed,' said Lucie. 'If not, I would do my best to find you work in another household.'

'But you won't promise. What of you, Captain?'

'I have no such power,' said Owen. 'Would you not wish to be with your parents if we could find a way?'

'They made me lie to Mistress Alisoun, tell her Master Adam laid with me.'

Not an answer to his question. Or was it a no? 'Is that why you told Alisoun your father was watching the Poole home? Because they made you lie about a man you respect?'

Wren looked away, her chin trembling. 'Lying's a sin.'

Owen reached out for Wren's hand, meaning to comfort her, but she twisted away.

'Were you angry with him?' Owen asked.

'He's not a bad man. But bad things happened to his sister, and he can't forget.'

Lucie gently touched Wren's forehead above the black eye. 'He is cruel to you.'

A shrug. 'Don't know why I told her.'

'You're angry with your kin?' Lucie asked.

She gave Lucie a look as if to say it was a daft question, of course she was. 'They killed the Swanns. And the dog. That's not right. The priest said in church that a wrong done for a wrong isn't a right.' She wiped her face with her sleeve, smearing the paint and staining the fabric. 'The Riverwoman will put a curse on me for leading Mistress Alisoun into danger.'

Owen knew Magda did not dabble in curses. But no matter. 'Did your parents and uncles have any help?' he asked.

Wren picked at the paint on her sleeve. 'Otto and Rat.'

Owen glanced at Honoria, who nodded. 'Tell me about them,' said Owen.

'I don't like them. This was about our family honor. Now we're just outlaws.'

'Who are they?'

A shrug. 'They know the city well. Helped us hide.' She reached for Lucie's hand. 'I did need Mistress Alisoun. I used a drink to rid me of a baby – something my mother gave me – but then I kept bleeding. It wasn't Master Tirwhit's I carried. Rat and Otto—' She bit her bottom lip, averted her eyes.

Honoria moaned and went to Wren, crouching beside her, taking her hand. 'I am so sorry.'

'Born in a brothel, wasn't I?'

'That means nothing,' said Honoria.

'You will find me a place, Mistress Wilton?'

Lucie touched Wren's cheek. 'I will, I promise. Now will you tell me what you know of Gerta's death, and what your family and those men have done to avenge her and your grandfather?'

'Would you like more ale?' Honoria asked as she lifted the jug.

'I would.' After Honoria poured, Wren took a long drink.

Her tale was much like Crispin Poole's, though the lads and Olyf were painted in a much less complimentary light, and the lechery of Bartolf and Goldbarn, the sergeant of the forest, was held up as proof the three lads and the girl were up to no good. As the ale dulled Wren's guardedness and she spun the tale of the two families united in their grief and despair, Owen was glad of

Michaelo's pen scratching away, Lucie helping him open more of the parchment as sections filled, for it was a tale the coroner should hear in full.

'But what of Gerta's murder?' Owen asked. 'You've not told us the real story.'

Wren glanced out the window. 'As my ma tells it, the one with the hounds, Paul, he came alone to the wood that day, 'cept for the animals. Beasts, they were, taller, more frightening than those he'd brought before, and he hunted Gerta.'

Dawn now. As Owen looked out at the garden he realized he wasted precious time. He knew now who had murdered Gerta. He rose. 'I must go to the Braithwaite home. I am grateful, Mistress Wren. You are brave to tell me all this. I pray you, tell the remainder to my wife and Brother Michaelo. Then rest here. You will be safe.'

Lucie and Honoria bent to each other, whispering. Owen watched them out of the corner of his eye as he tugged on his boots, slung the quiver over his shoulder, tucked his unstrung bow in his belt. So at ease with each other. He'd not expected that.

'Rain is coming,' said Honoria. 'I smell it in the air.'

'All the better,' said Lucie, rising from the table. 'I've no time for the garden today. Let it drink its fill. Take a cloak, my love.' She plucked a short cloak from the hook by the door and draped it over Owen's arm, then handed him a small pack. 'In case you use the arrow and want your captive to live. You know how to use these.'

Owen looked into his wife's steady gray-blue eyes. Her medicine pack was sacred to her, a thing all in the household knew not to touch. 'Thank you for entrusting me with this. I will use it wisely,' he said.

She searched his eyes, touched his cheek. 'I know you will, my love. Come home to me whole and well. May God watch over you and all your company.'

'Amen.' He kissed Lucie, held her tight for a moment.

'Shall I escort Old Bede home?' Lucie asked as they moved apart.

'Let Crispin host him until I return. But you might tell Winifrith where he is. And have Michaelo take Alisoun's account as long as he is here. Bless you for thinking of that. I know the coroner examined Roger, but I will feel better that he knows as much as possible before he assembles a jury.' He whispered a blessing, then slipped out the garden door with Corm.

'Dame Lucie and Dame Honoria?' Corm chuckled as they crossed the York Tavern yard.

'Both honorable women,' said Owen with a look that silenced the young fool.

Honoria and Wren asked if they might accompany Lucie and Brother Michaelo when they moved into the hall. Alisoun was reclining against a pile of cushions and sipping from a small wooden bowl as she watched Magda pacing before the long window that looked out on the garden. It was Lucie's favorite feature of the hall, the long window, actually several smaller windows separated only by strong timbers, stretching half the length of the room. Owen was keen to glaze them with the rents from his new manor, but Lucie was content with the fitted shutters. When they were opened, she welcomed the freshening breeze bringing the scents of the medicinal garden.

'Might we speak with you a moment, Alisoun?' Lucie asked.

'Dame Honoria?' Alisoun frowned. 'Are you caught up in the troubles as well?'

Honoria asked if she might sit beside her, looking not only to Alisoun but to Magda as well, who motioned for her to do so. Settling on a stool beside Alisoun's pallet, Honoria took her hand and briefly told her of the night's events, while Michaelo settled himself at a small table nearby.

'I did not mean to take his life,' Alisoun whispered.

Lucie, seated at the foot of the pallet, assured her that they all understood. 'If you would just tell us what happened, as you remember it.' She was disappointed to hear how little Alisoun had witnessed, yet she repeated what she'd said the previous evening, that as the hound fell into her it felt wrong somehow.

'I wish I could say how. A feeling that it was not what it seemed and then I was trying to catch myself before I fell. I am sorry.'

Honoria squeezed Alisoun's hand. 'You saved Dame Euphemia's life, I think.'

'If you are not too weary of speech, would you tell us about the night Crispin Poole came to you, after he was bitten?' Lucie asked.

Alisoun obliged.

Honoria winced at the details, hissed at his request for secrecy. 'He might have prevented all this.'

Lucie was not so certain. Vengeance taken twenty years later? Would she have guessed it?

Suddenly Alisoun struggled to sit up, her eyes moving as if she were debating with herself. 'The beast pushed me over, not as a great animal would do, a sort of leap, but pushed.'

Thinking of Euphemia's comment, Lucie asked, 'So it might have been a man or a woman?'

Alisoun met her eyes. 'That would explain it.'

Hempe was already in the hall apologizing to Janet Braithwaite, who was wringing her hands. The bailiff's wife, an early riser, had shaken him awake with the news that two of his lads had been left on their doorstep, all trussed up and swearing they'd been attacked by wolves.

'Tied up by wolves. Nothing between their ears, nothing,' Hempe growled. 'Sleeping is what they were doing instead of standing watch.'

When Owen and Corm relayed their news, Janet Braithwaite's face was ashen. 'How could this happen? How could he be such a fool to go with Galbot?'

Owen cursed beneath his breath. 'With Galbot? Paul went willingly? Did you see him?'

'The cook says Galbot woke Paul, told him he'd been following Joss and Cilla, had heard them planning to attack the kennels at the manor, and my son decided he must leave at once. He would tell the guard at Micklegate Bar it was an emergency. They'd gone down to the kitchen so as not to wake Elaine, though she followed soon after, and cook overheard them talking.'

Apparently John's collapse the previous night had so shaken the household that the servants had forgotten that Galbot was not to be admitted. Or someone had forgotten to issue the order.

'Elaine insisted on accompanying Paul. Cook says she muttered about being ruined as she gathered food for the journey. They were away before John and I wakened.'

'Is there someone here who knows the way to your manor?' Owen asked. 'Knows it well enough to leave the main road?'

Janet gestured to a manservant who had stepped forward. 'Alan grew up on the manor. You are welcome to take our horses—'

'I can provide them,' said Hempe. 'This is my fault. I chose the lackwits who bungled the watch.'

'My husband would assist, but . . .' Janet's voice caught.

'Was Saurian able to help?' Owen asked.

'He made him comfortable, but said John must have a long rest.' She waved away any further comments. 'You must be off. Save my son!'

Out in the yard, Alfred waited, eager to give Owen the news that Old Bede had seen the body at the Poole home, and had identified him to Burnby the coroner as one of the men who had threatened him on the staithe the night of Bartolf's murder.

'Any trouble bringing him into the city?' Owen asked.

'None. Whoever might have wanted him . . .'

'They are on the road to Paul Braithwaite's manor, or already there,' Hempe said.

Alfred looked from one to the other. 'Are we off to the country, Captain? Shall I round up a few more men?'

'Where is Stephen?'

'With Poole, awaiting further orders – what to do about Old Bede, for one, and Bartolf's dogs. Poole's men found them wandering near Bartolf's house in Galtres, injured and half-starved. They brought them to Poole.'

'Run, fetch Stephen, and meet us at the stables outside Micklegate Bar. Tell Old Bede to stay at Poole's house until we return. As for the dogs, I don't know what to do with them.'

'Bring along any of my men you might see,' said Hempe. He ordered Corm to stand guard at the Braithwaite house. 'You do know how to defend yourself?'

The young man straightened and his eyes went cold as he drew his knife.

Hempe grunted. 'You'll do, though I do wonder. All that practice at the butts of a Sunday and Captain Archer's the only one who thinks to grab a bow and quiver of arrows when trouble arises? If he becomes our captain, I pray he'll have you men practicing daily.'

It was a thought. For his part, Owen was glad he'd done some hunting with the bow while at Freythorpe. He knew how easily he could lose his form.

The gate captain at Micklegate Bar recalled the Braithwaites departing with their cart of goods. 'The pair were bickering some-thing terrible.'

'How many in their party?' Owen asked.

'The Braithwaites and their servants, a man and a woman.'

'No one else? No one who seemed to be following them?' Owen asked.

'We opened the gates for them only, Captain. They'd word of trouble at their manor.'

The hope was that the cart would slow Galbot, Paul, and Elaine sufficiently that Owen's company might overtake them long before they reached the manor. It was a half-day's ride, slightly less than the journey to Freythorpe Hadden. As they began their journey, Hempe muttered about time wasted interrogating Gisburne's household. Owen still believed someone there had gotten word to Roger and Galbot, but to say so would be to insult Hempe, who needed to be sharp for the day ahead. And it might have been Wren, though she had not mentioned it.

When they'd had no sign of their quarry by midmorning, Owen asked the servant, Alan, if he knew a way that might bring them to the manor more quickly than by the road.

'I know a way for men on horse, willing to jump the becks and go by hill and dale.'

'We will follow you.'

The rain began just as they left the road. A cooling drizzle at first, increasing to a soft rain. The horses perked up away from the dust and noise of the road and by early afternoon the manor was in sight. From the crest of a hill Alan pointed out the main house and buildings. A substantial house, the base stone, the upper story timber, it looked much like Freythorpe Hadden just miles beyond. The stable and barn were large and well kept, the gatehouse just visible down a long, winding lane. 'Over the next hill you will see the kennels. The mistress wanted them well away from the house and chickens,' said Alan.

'It's too quiet,' said Hempe.

Owen agreed. It was so still that the breath of men and horses, leaves catching the breeze, and the patter of rain were the loudest sounds. 'Even in rain one would expect to see folk moving about between the buildings, right, Alan?'

'Something is very wrong, Captain. It is never so quiet.' Alan moved as if to mount his horse.

'You will move when I give the order.'

Alan glanced round at the others. 'I am worried about my wife.'

'We're here to protect them,' said Alfred.

Owen nodded his approval to Alfred. 'Besides the gatehouse entrance, there must be others, for farm wagons, the kennels?' he asked Alan.

'The farm wagons go through the gatehouse entrance,' said Alan. 'There's a narrow track coming up from the south, unguarded, but fit only for a man on foot or mounted. No carts.'

'And the kennels?'

'Over the next rise, you'll see the lane that leads to the kennels. Almost as wide as the main way, and smooth, to impress the wealthy coming to purchase hounds for their hunting packs.'

They remounted and moved on with care, riding down into the yard before the house. A small dog came rushing from the stables, barking a warning.

'The mistress's pup,' said Alan.

Horses whinnied in the stables, some chickens clucked. So quiet. But no. Was it a trick of the wind? Or were those voices in the distance? Raised voices?

Owen motioned Alfred and one of Hempe's men to find the source of the sound. He dismounted and entered the house with Stephen, Hempe and the others standing guard without. A substantial hall, old as that at Freythorpe Hadden, deserted but for an aged cat curled up near the fire circle. As he and Stephen crossed the room it reared up and hissed at them.

A voice called out from the passage leading from the hall to the service rooms, 'Is someone there? I'm in the pantry, collecting pots for water.'

Following the voice, Owen startled a girl about Gwenllian's age, causing her to drop two large wooden bowls on the rush floor. He held up his hands, showing her he had no weapon.

'Might I pick those up for you?' he asked.

The fierce look in her eyes reminded him of Elaine Braithwaite.

'I am Owen Archer, captain of bailiffs in York.' Not that he'd decided, but he thought it might reassure her. 'And this is one of my men. We are here to help. Are your parents here?'

'Why do you ask?'

'They left York early this morning with a man from the kennels. Galbot.'

'The kennels.' The girl sobbed. He noticed now that the scarf that held back her fair hair was damp as if she'd been out in the rain.

He approached with care, crouching down to pick up the bowls, setting them on a shelf beside her. Then he took her hands, looked up into her eyes. 'What has happened here, child?'

'Men took the hounds this morning and set fire to the kennels. We're trying to put it out before it spreads to a hay barn nearby. My brother took some men to search for the hounds. We can hear them. The fire has frightened them.' Her voice broke.

'But the hounds are clear of the fire?'

'Must be.'

'Are the strangers still here?'

'Don't know. Will they hurt us?'

'Not now that we're here. Where were you going with this – what is your name?'

'Alice. Everyone on the manor formed a chain from the fishpond to get water to the fire.'

'How far is it, Alice?'

'Just over the next hill.'

'Were the strangers on horseback?'

'Yes.'

'Courage, Alice. My men will go to the kennels.'

'God watch over you!'

Stephen was already hurrying back out through the hall, calling out to Hempe what he'd heard.

Alfred was out there, telling a similar story, but he'd heard that three men – and a beast that walked upright – were still at the kennels, watching the approach. He'd sent his companion to alert the water line that they were coming, not to interfere.

The seven set off at a gallop.

From the next rise the burning kennels were visible, smoke filling the valley, and now Owen could hear the dogs, barking, though not frantic. He ordered Alan to take one of Hempe's men and follow the sound, find the dogs.

'Do not confront anyone,' Owen ordered. 'Report to me at the kennels.'

Alan chose Pete, and the two rode down into the dale.

'Why are we hesitating?' Stephen asked.

'The wagon,' Alfred noted, pointing to a point far from the kennels. 'Two men running toward the fire.'

'Three men on horseback await them,' said Hempe.

Otto, Rat, and who? Someone from the manor? Cilla?

'What is that?' One of Hempe's men pointed to a figure joining the three men. Hairy, yet walking upright.

'I believe that is our beast – the wolf all have seen in the city,' said Owen. 'More likely a human wearing skins.'

'The world's gone mad,' Hempe said.

Owen noticed that Alan and Pete had changed their course, heading somewhere back beyond the burning kennels.

'Right. Arms ready,' Owen called. 'Alan and Pete will see the dogs are safe. Our goal is to disarm everyone and keep them down on the ground, alive.' He'd already strung his bow, though his aim would be challenged by the smoke as they descended into the dale that cradled the kennels. The curse of a single eye, a blink and he was blind. If only the rain would come down harder and douse the fire. He reminded the others to be aware that their mounts might react to the blaze. 'If they appear to shy, dismount.'

As they rode down into the dale, Owen was able to distinguish the runners – Paul Braithwaite out ahead, Galbot right behind him. Did Paul not realize the dogs had been moved? Reining in his horse, Owen dismounted, aimed, and hit Galbot in the shoulder. As the man slowed, Owen drew out another arrow, aimed, hit him in the leg. Galbot was down.

But Paul was almost to the group awaiting him.

And then something in the kennels collapsed, billowing smoke masking the drama.

Alfred, on foot, paused by Owen. 'Bad luck.'

Owen cursed.

'I'm for the riders,' said Alfred. 'No, look, one's dismounting.' He broke into a run, barreling into the man.

The other mounted man began to charge Alfred, who was rising after punching his target into stillness.

The smoke cleared just enough for Owen to recognize Joss on the horse. He aimed, hit his shoulder. Joss crumpled over the saddle, then slipped to the ground, where Alfred caught him, dragging him over to his companion.

Owen strode toward the burning kennels, hoping to find Paul Braithwaite. He dodged abandoned horses that milled about, panicked. Two of Hempe's men tried to guide them away from danger. Seeing a man raising a blade toward Stephen's horse, Owen took aim, caught him in the arm. The man dropped his weapon and Hempe rode him down, then rode after the horses and one rider heading south. One of his men caught an abandoned horse and followed.

As the rain and wind picked up, Owen was able to pick out Paul Braithwaite, still heading for the kennels, though stumbling, as if he'd been injured or overcome by the smoke. Hoping to halt him, Owen took aim. Just as he let fly the arrow, the one wearing skins jumped onto Paul's back and took the arrow in the back of the right leg. Paul shrugged off his attacker and, stepping round the fallen beam, walked into the kennels.

Owen plucked up Paul's pursuer. She cursed and pummeled him as he carried her away from the mouth of the fire, dropping her near Alfred.

'God help him,' Alfred groaned, staring back at the kennels.

It was Paul, stumbling out of the mouth of the building, his clothes and hair alight. Seeing Alan and Pete rounding the side of the building each holding a sloshing bucket in his free hand, Owen shouted, 'Braithwaite!'

After a moment of confusion, both of them emptied their buckets of water onto the man, who'd dropped down and was rolling along the ground, just missing the woman, who had made it to her knees. Cilla, the wolf, he guessed, her painted face showing beneath the wolfskin hood.

'I'll bring more water,' Alan called, riding off.

Pete jumped from his horse, rushing to Braithwaite as Owen and a man with a blanket reached them. The man opened the blanket and threw himself on Paul, attempting to smother the flames. Out of nowhere, Cilla jumped on him, pulling him away from Paul. Beyond them, another large beam fell in the entry to the kennels, sending out flaming splinters. One fell on Cilla.

Owen grabbed her up, pulling her away. 'You're burning!'

He struggled to contain her thrashing arms and legs, gave up and pushed her down to roll her along the muddy ground, but the arrow in her leg prevented that. With a knife, he tore at the skins, splitting the seams and tearing them away. Beneath, her shirt and leggings were filthy, but not on fire.

'Step away, Captain!'

As Owen did so, Alan tossed a bucket of water on the skins. Cilla tried to crawl away, but collapsed on her wounded leg, snarling and cursing, thrashing about, trying to remove the arrow. The way she moved was more animal than human.

Owen blinked away the smoke, looking at Alan. 'Thank you.'

'Everyone on the land, servants and tenants, has formed a line from the fishpond, passing buckets and pots of water. The building's gone, but they hope to contain it.' He shook his head at the woman writhing on the ground. 'Who is she?'

'Cilla.' Owen went to Paul, sinking down on his knees. Blackened, bleeding, the man's breath came in rasps. A woman from the manor came with a wineskin, crouched down and poured wine into Paul's open mouth before Owen could stop her – he was breathing through his mouth, he would choke. Paul coughed, convulsed, and the rasping ceased. Owen crossed himself, then closed the dead man's eyelids.

The woman began to sob. Owen handed the skin to her, told her to take it to her mistress out on the cart.

Rising, Owen tossed Alan the blanket. 'Cover Cilla. Take her aside. We'll move them in the wagon.'

Alfred joined him. 'All secured.'

'Fetch Galbot.'

'He's not going anywhere, thanks to you.'

'Oh yes he is.' He'd worked here long enough to know the terrain, and he'd worked with the dogs.

Alfred dragged the man to Owen.

'You heard them barking. You'll have an idea where they are.' Owen yanked him up, pulled down his shirt to pin his arms to his sides and tied the sleeves behind him. 'Lead us there,' he commanded.

'I can't walk,' Galbot protested.

'We'll assist you,' Alfred growled.

Owen told Stephen to guard the rest. Passing Pete beside the burning building, Owen ordered him to help Stephen. 'The kennels are lost. Let the household do what they wish with the fire. You see to the men.'

Some folk on the line passing buckets and pots of water called out to them, asking what had happened. Others cursed Galbot for betraying the family. But Owen and Alfred kept their attention on their prisoner, who hobbled along between them, coughing and cursing. He led them through a copse of trees and out into a clearing at the end of the dale. A wattle fence huddled against the rising hill. The dogs were within. As Galbot approached they began barking excitedly, a welcome. Of course they would know their trainer. Three men stood guard with pitchforks, lowering them and pointing them toward Owen, Alfred, and Galbot.

'Master John Braithwaite sent us here,' Owen called out.

One of the three stepped forward, shouting, 'Galbot, you traitor!' He was younger than Owen had at first realized, and from his clothing it was clear he was not a laborer.

Owen jerked on Galbot's arms. 'Who is he?'

'Adam Braithwaite, Paul's son and heir. Good with the dogs. And those are the men who care for the kennels. You're tearing my arms from my shoulders.'

'Are you Captain Archer?' Adam demanded.

'I am.' One of the rare moments when Owen's scarred face and patch could be counted a blessing.

'Where is my father?'

'We will speak of him.' Owen gestured toward where Alfred crouched over a man lying outside the enclosure, a torch jammed down into the mud still smoldering beside him. 'Who is he?'

'One of this traitor's men. He meant to set fire to the fence, kill the dogs. I thought you cared for them, Galbot.'

Owen tugged on Galbot's arms. 'Who is he?'

'Bastard,' Galbot growled as he averted his eyes from young Adam's glare. 'No wonder the others had me bring the Braithwaites. I didn't know they meant to torch the dogs.'

'No love for them?'

'I'm the only one cares for them.' Not Tempest, Owen thought. 'Cilla and Joss would have killed them first. Only Paul Braithwaite was to die here, the final tally, the most important. He murdered Gerta to avenge the blinding of his hound.'

'How dare you accuse my father of murder!' Adam cried, stepping forward.

'Because he was a murderer,' growled the man on the ground. Alfred grasped the man's shoulder and shook him.

FIFTEEN
A Conspiracy of Wolves

Elaine Braithwaite stood at the door of the manor house, her arms wrapped round her as if to keep her still. Stepping back to allow them entrance, she stood transfixed as Owen and Alan carried Paul Braithwaite's litter past her, into the hall, as if she could not believe the horror of her husband's body. Her son Adam walked behind them, shoulders back, eyes trained ahead as tears rolled down his cheeks.

Hempe had returned with the horses, and he and one of his men had helped Elaine and her maidservant from the cart, bringing them up on their mounts to return to the manor house.

'Brother.' Alice, who stood holding a baby, bobbed her head at Adam, then motioned to the two girls beside her. Paul's children solemnly led the litter-bearers through the hall and down a corridor to a small chapel, comporting themselves with dignity despite their muddied clothes and damp hair.

'Set him down before the altar, awaiting the priest and the coroner,' Elaine said from the doorway.

When the litter was placed on the stone floor, Owen asked the widow what else they might do to help.

Her composure crumbled, and she bowed her head, sobbing. Owen put his arms round her, holding her until she quieted. The children looked on with grief-stricken expressions.

Wet, weary, Owen felt the chill settling into his bones. He was grateful when at last Elaine took a deep, shaky breath and backed away.

'What must you think of me?' She dabbed at her face with a linen, then shook out her skirts. 'You will forgive me. It has been such a day.'

'Of course.'

'We are all in your debt.'

'I failed to prevent your husband's death.'

'I watched from the wagon, Captain, I saw him walk into that burning building.'

'The hounds—'

'He walked into the flames for his sins, Captain. I was beside him in the wagon when we saw the flames, then heard the baying. When I cried out – no matter what I thought of his passion for them, they were God's creatures and I quaked at their danger – he patted my hand, assured me that they must have been rescued from the fire.' She kissed Owen's cheek, then went to kneel beside her husband's body.

Owen withdrew to the stables to see to the injured.

Joss, Galbot, and Cilla huddled in a corner away from four others, talking quietly. When Owen appeared, Galbot called down curses on him and his family. Owen ignored him as he called Stephen and two of Hempe's men over to help him hold the man down while he removed the arrows, cleaned the wounds, packed them with the paste Lucie prepared for deep cuts, bandaged them, all to a litany of curses.

Next he saw to Cilla's leg. She no longer struggled – he'd slipped a bit of poppy juice in the wine he told her to drink before he pulled out the arrow. But she muttered to herself, and something she kept saying intrigued him enough that he tried to talk to her.

'Is that what you were doing, playing the wolf?'

'I am cat, hear me hiss at you.' She did a fair job, baring her teeth as she did so. The paint was quite like her daughter's.

'Who is the wolf?'

'And I am wolf.' She growled. 'Goldbarn told Gerta the privileged four were a wolf pack, bent on ruining all for us. Conspiring to destroy all that we gleaned from the wood.'

'Richard Goldbarn said this?'

'Gerta thought he meant to wed her. My beautiful Gerta.' She whimpered, tucking her chin in her chest. As Owen wrapped her leg she made animal sounds, little cries and yips. A chilling performance.

He moved on to Joss, his face bloody, one eye swollen shut, and, of course, the arrow in his shoulder. He told Stephen to hold Joss down.

'Righteous ass,' Joss muttered.

'I thought this was all about family vengeance, yet you beat your own daughter.'

'She betrayed us. The lying hag lives.' Joss spat, though he took care to face away from Owen.

'Only a coward beats his children,' Owen said, and yanked out the arrow.

The man howled. Cilla took up the cry, howling beside him, and continued all the while Owen bandaged Joss's shoulder. When he moved on to Joss's eye, Cilla batted him away.

'Come,' Owen said to Stephen and the others helping him, 'we'll leave him until she's asleep. Let's see to the others.'

Rat was obvious from his appearance, though his face was bloodied and his eyes were blackening. He said nothing, staring off to the other side of the stall where his companion, Otto, lay beneath a blanket. He'd fallen from his horse and broken his neck. One death.

The man who'd been about to set fire to the fence had burns and a broken arm. He remained stoically silent, nary a whimper, while Owen tended him.

Another man had plenty to say while Owen set a broken finger and smoothed salve on a wrenched ankle.

'Galbot tricked me. He said you were coming for the hounds and we had to defend them.'

'You worked in the kennels with him?'

A nod. 'No more.'

'No, you set fire to them.'

'To fool you! But the mistress will never believe me. And Master John – he'll see me hanged.'

'You will have a chance to state your case,' Owen assured him.

Elaine Braithwaite insisted that Owen, Hempe, and their men stay the night before returning to the city in the morning with their prisoners. Her hall was open to them.

They were more than happy to accept. It had been a long, tiring day, and two of Hempe's men were in no condition to ride this evening, one limping badly and the other with his eye bandaged after being struck by a burning cinder. Minor casualties for a job well done. Except for Paul Braithwaite's death.

Owen, Hempe, and their hostess dined at a small table in the hall. The other men sat at a long board nearby. The company was hushed, the food plentiful and hot, the wine much appreciated.

'My son said there was a woman among them, and that she had been wearing a wolf's hide,' said Elaine.

Owen explained who she was.

'Bring her to me. I would speak with her. Afterward she may rest in the warmth of the kitchen. I have set some dry clothes for her by the door.'

'You know that she is not innocent of the charges?' asked Owen. When he had returned to Joss, thinking Cilla asleep, she cursed as he confessed for all of them. *Why now?* Owen had asked. *They'll be singing a ballad about us this winter, mark me, the wolves of Galtres*, Joss had said. Cilla had howled at that, and Joss had joined in. 'And I cannot vouch for whether she'll appear animal or human.'

'Even before this, folk in York thought her mad,' said Hempe.

'It is what I wish,' said Elaine.

Hempe went to give the orders.

While waiting, the widow spoke of her husband, his love for the children and the land, and the hounds. 'I hated Bartolf Swann for encouraging Paul's passion for the hounds. Nothing was so important as those curséd dogs. I always feared they would be the ruin of him. When he told me what he'd done to that young woman so long ago, I knew I was right.'

'He told you?' Owen had not expected that.

'After Crispin Poole's return Paul feared to sleep for the nightmares. He thought if he confessed to me, and also made his confession to a priest, he might be free of the demons.'

'Did it work?'

'I believe it did for him, until the trouble began. For me – I will ever carry the darkness of his monstrous act in my heart. He told me he crushed her head with a stone, strangled her for good measure, and sent her floating in the Ouse – all for blinding his favorite hound. I will never understand. Devil dogs. They possessed his soul. They were his undoing, yet he clung to them, as if his devotion would absolve him. I want them gone. My son loves them, but I cannot bear to have them here.'

Cilla appeared leaning heavily on Hempe's arm, her head bowed, a much-patched gown rendering her more human in appearance.

'Come. Sit with me and tell me what you remember of Gerta,' said Elaine.

An unexpected request.

Cilla raised her eyes to the widow. 'What game is this?'

Elaine held out a cloth. 'No game. But first, wipe the paint off your face.'

'Does it offend?' Cilla smirked.

'If you wish me to believe anything you say, you will wipe that off.' Elaine pushed a bowl of water toward the woman.

To Owen's surprise, Cilla dipped the cloth in water and began to work at the paint, at first merely smearing it, but, as the water grew dark, her features emerged.

When Elaine was satisfied, she gestured to the bench beside her. 'Now sit and tell me of this young woman my husband murdered.'

Owen and Hempe withdrew.

'I need to stretch my legs, breathe the night air,' said Owen, heading for the door.

'It is raining.'

'Even so.' The day had wearied Owen in body and soul. Almost he wished he had ridden home tonight. But he thought better of that. He would not inflict this mood on Lucie and the children. Let the rain wash it away.

In the morning, Owen sought out Dame Elaine to express his gratitude for her hospitality.

'I will pray for you and your children,' he said.

She thanked him for the sentiment, but assured him that the family would derive satisfaction from the crown's justice. 'For the perpetrators will hang.' Her flinty eyes challenged him, as if he might suggest a different outcome.

'Cilla's words did not move you?'

'That wretch?' Her lips curled in disdain. 'As for Paul, he was but a boy when he killed the charcoal-burner's daughter and might have been forgiven, but he chose for himself an honorable death. Our children can be proud of that.' Again, she watched Owen, her eyes daring him to object.

To take one's own life was a mortal sin. She knew that, yet chose to ignore it. Would her children be so confused? And what of compassion? Cilla, Galbot, and Roger had lost their father because Paul had not the courage to admit his crime. Joss had lost his sister to the man for the blinding of a dog.

As he rode out with Hempe and the others, Owen felt sullied by his part in taking the prisoners they now escorted to York. He was not at all sure that justice had been served. His companions were likewise quiet, as were the prisoners. Otto's body remained behind, awaiting the coroner's examination.

In late afternoon they entered the city, heading straight for the castle.

'Leave them to stew overnight,' said Hempe. 'I'm for home, and Lotta.' The name brought a smile to his beaky face. 'Bless that woman. I've not once worried about the business through all of this, knowing she had it all in hand. God's grace brought her into my life.'

'God's grace? It was a murderer threw you together as I recall.'

Hempe poked him with an elbow. 'You know what I mean.' As they reached the York Tavern, the bailiff hesitated. 'One before we part?'

'Bess will want to know all,' Owen warned.

'Ah. I've no mind to talk of it tonight. I will come by after I've been to the castle in the morning.'

'You'll not be charging the girl?'

'Wren? I see no cause. But she'll be alone. They're all for hanging, Owen. They've more than disturbed the king's peace. And whether or no they wielded the weapons, they assisted. When you're captain of the bailiffs, this will be your task.'

'If I accept I'll not be a bailiff. My understanding is that I would not be called upon unless your men cannot cope.'

'We'll work you hard, Owen. Never doubt it. But so would the prince. Your skill with the bow yesterday was worthy of a captain of archers. If His Grace should hear of that . . . I'll not be the fool to speak of it, but it will be all over the taverns of York tomorrow.' Hempe slapped Owen's back and continued on toward Stonegate and home.

Gwenllian and Hugh came running to greet Owen as he stepped through the door. He'd come through the kitchen, loath to leave a trail through the hall.

'We'll pull off your boots, Da,' Gwen offered. 'Sit thee down.'

Ah. A budding Magda Digby. 'Wouldst thou?' he asked, grabbing her up and tickling her.

'Hugh, too!' his son shouted.

'Alisoun has company,' said Kate as she handed him an ale. 'Master Crispin and Dame Muriel.'

'Together?'

'No. But, well, if I were to wager— Oh, Hugh!'

The lad had fallen onto the flagstones as the boot he tugged on released unexpectedly. His face crinkled as he felt the pain, and his mouth opened, releasing a loud howl.

'I met a couple who howl like that together,' said Owen, leaning over to pick up his son with the fiery hair and the powerful lungs. 'And she was wearing skins, had her face painted like Wren's.'

That got Hugh's attention, and he quieted, even began to smile as Owen tickled him.

Over the boy's shoulder Owen looked at Kate. 'Is Wren still here?'

'She is, much to Mistress Alisoun's discomfort. She would do everything for her, and you know Mistress Alisoun, such fussing is most unwelcome.'

'My friend says you shot people with your bow and arrows, Da. Is it true?' Gwenllian's voice broke a little on the question.

He set Hugh down and crouched to his daughter. 'I did so to prevent them from causing more harm, and to slow them down so that I might catch them and bring them to answer for their crimes. I do not kill unless it is the only way to save others.'

'Alisoun killed.'

'She did not mean to. The man moved too quickly.'

'Master Burnby the coroner came to tell Alisoun she should not bring her weapons into the city. A girl has no business with such things.'

'He said that to Alisoun?'

A grave nod. 'She does not like him.'

'I doubt she does.'

'But he said, "Captain Archer has power now, so he'll defend you," and then he left. I thought you should know.'

So Owen and the coroner had a problem. 'I am grateful for the warning, my love.'

'I think he wishes he had her courage.'

'I do, too!' Hugh shouted.

How had Owen's children grown so wise so quickly?

An afternoon and evening with his family did much to restore Owen. Once the children had gone up with Lena, Jasper had retired, Alisoun and Magda had moved their pallets into the kitchen, Wren insisting on sleeping on a pallet at the foot of their bed, Owen and Lucie settled in front of the hearth fire.

'I cannot recall the last time we were so alone,' said Lucie, 'except in bed.'

'Do not say it! You will jinx the moment.' Owen laughed as he pulled her close, kissed her. 'I hated being away from you.'

'I am glad you did not try to ride into the night. But the bed was so cold.' She kissed him back, rubbed his hands.

He asked her how she was coping with the loss of Philippa, the aunt who had become so much a part of their lives. He watched her lovely face as the emotions rose, and held her close as she spoke with love of her aunt's big heart, her strength, her quiet support.

'Yesterday I found Gwenllian curled up in Philippa's cape, whispering to herself,' she said. 'And Hugh seems confused about whether or not she'll return. He seems to think that good souls resurrect, and he is certain she qualifies. At any moment she might appear on our doorstep.'

'The worst time for them to see their beloved Alisoun bedridden,' said Owen.

'I know. Of a sudden they see that those they love can be hurt, or even die,' said Lucie. 'As I did with my mother.' Her mother had died when Lucie was quite young, her father so devastated he sent her to Clementhorpe Nunnery while he went off on pilgrimage.

'They have us,' said Owen.

'Yes.'

As Lucie rose to poke at the fire, Owen told her of his conversation with Gwenllian regarding the coroner and Alisoun's prowess.

'It is rumored that he often dines with John Gisburne,' said Lucie. 'Need you know more?' She kissed Owen as she returned to her seat. 'We've nothing to fear from Burnby.'

'Fear, no. But he will find ways to annoy me.'

'Here's something to cheer us. I went to Winifrith, to tell her that her father was safe in York, and would soon be home. She told the children right then and there. The joy on their faces, the happy shrieks – how they love him. Old Bede is home now, the coroner happy with what he had to add. He's asked him to sit on the jury.'

'God help us. We will never hear the end of that at the tavern.'

'While I was there, Olyf Tirwhit was sitting with Euphemia, the two of them trading insults and accusations. I learned from Crispin that Adam Tirwhit had known of his plan to return almost two years ago, when Neville first realized Thoresby was dying. He wanted Crispin here to clear the way. Word had passed round among the merchants. That must be how Joss and Warin's children learned of his imminent return. In the end Crispin was delayed, giving them ample time to be in place.'

'Such a complex plan.'

'Such a long-simmering hate.'

'Crispin and Muriel. Kate believes they may become a couple.'

Lucie smiled at the fire. 'I noticed it as well. I do not know whether to wish them that joy. Olyf Tirwhit will never forgive them.'

'We know Crispin and Olyf could never be. And for the child about to be born to have a father, that would be a blessing.'

Lucie took his hand. 'Yes. Crispin is nothing like Hoban, and perhaps that is all for the best. I wish them joy if they choose each other. For another couple, I see stormy seas ahead.'

'Alisoun and Jasper?'

'Magda tells me that while I opened the shop, giving Jasper some time with Alisoun this morning, Ned came to call. With flowers from the Fenton garden.'

'Ned?'

'I knew nothing of what had happened, but when Jasper stormed into the shop to begin his day, tossing his jacket with such force I rushed to save a jar from crashing to the floor, I ordered him to sit down in the workroom and say ten Hail Marys before coming back into the shop.'

'Did he confide in you?'

'He spoke of how he wished to model his life after his beloved Brother Wulfstan.'

After the infirmarian of St Mary's Abbey sacrificed his life to tend plague victims, Jasper had talked of taking vows. It was a recurring theme, especially when their son questioned his feelings for Alisoun.

'It will pass,' said Owen.

'If Wren has anything to say about it, he will have an alternative.'

'God protect him.'

'Olyf Tirwhit has asked her to return to their house.'

'Will she accept?'

'Muriel has also expressed interest.'

'I begin to distrust Muriel's intent.'

Lucie sighed. 'As do I.' She turned to Owen. 'So? What have you decided about your future?'

SIXTEEN
Diplomacy

In the early morning, Owen called on Hempe at his home, eager to report to the Braithwaites and the Pooles and then move on with his day.

'It's been good to partner with you again,' said Hempe. 'Will we be working together in future?'

'You had best say yes, or he will hound you forever,' his wife Lotta teased.

'If the prince's emissary is amenable to my proposal, yes.'

Hempe slapped Owen on the back. 'You've given me hope, my friend.'

'Bless you, Captain,' said Lotta.

'Shall we go?' said Owen. 'Get the unpleasantness out of the way?'

As Hempe lived so close to Crispin, they stopped there first to assure him he need no longer worry about a repeat attack.

He was looking haggard. 'Olyf seems unable to stay away, plying my mother with unwanted remedies. My mother suspects she means to poison her.'

Owen saw an opportunity. 'Is Dame Olyf here now?'

A curse and a nod.

Excusing himself, Owen went in search of the woman. Finding her seated beside a sleeping Euphemia, he asked her to step out into the garden, where he told her of Paul's death, and how all the recent violence stemmed from his long-ago crime, the murder of Gerta.

'Paul – may God be merciful.' She slumped down onto a bench against the back wall of the house, bowing her head.

'You were there, I think. You witnessed what he did to her.'

She reared up, such a tall woman she almost looked him in the eye.

He took a step backward.

'Paul told you, didn't he? I knew he blamed me. Claimed I'd been the one who insisted he make sure she was dead. That I gave him the stone, helped him drag her to the water. Is that what he said?'

Owen slowly shook his head. 'No. We never spoke of it.'

A cough. Olyf spun round and beheld George Hempe and Crispin Poole standing in the doorway.

She turned back to Owen. 'Well, good, then. Because I never did any of that. I begged him to leave her alone.'

'Get out of my house,' said Crispin, in a quiet voice. 'And stay away.'

'I will oblige you with that,' said Hempe, stepping forward to take Olyf's arm. 'She will come with me to the castle.'

'I will not,' Olyf declared.

But Hempe's grip was strong.

So it was that Owen went alone to report to the Braithwaites, heart heavy. Janet suggested that they not disturb John. She would pass on the news to him when he was stronger. Owen agreed that was best.

She listened with bowed head, occasionally murmuring a prayer, and wept to hear of Olyf's part in Gerta's murder. 'I cannot help but think Hoban was the one made to suffer for her sin. He was such a gentle soul. So unlike Olyf . . . and my Paul. Muriel always said they were two of a kind. I do not even want to know whether my daughter knew of any of this.'

'From what she told my wife, I doubt it,' said Owen.

'Do you think Cilla witnessed all of it?'

'Perhaps. It would explain the brutality of their attacks on Hoban and Bartolf.'

'But why was Olyf spared?'

'Was she?'

Janet crossed herself. 'I should send a messenger to Elaine.'

Owen was not home long before Geoffrey appeared with a message from Antony, his fellow emissary. 'He awaits your pleasure in St Mary's hospitium. He will expect your decision, you know, whether you will accept the prince's commission.'

'That is likely his purpose, I agree,' said Owen.

'And? What will you tell him?'

After the activities of the morning Owen prayed he had the presence of mind to argue his case with Antony.

'I will share my thoughts with you in exchange for a favor.'

Owen caught Lucie's smile as she slipped past them on her way to the apothecary. 'No misgivings on my part,' she whispered.

He had confided his heart's desire to her as they sat before the fire the night before, and she had given him her support. They had agreed that if they woke without misgivings, his choice was made. Now he must convince Antony of the wisdom of his proposal.

'Come, walk with me,' he told Geoffrey. 'I will collect Brother Michaelo. He will await my invitation to come in after Antony and I have spoken. I would like Dom Leufrid to arrive while Michaelo is waiting. Such a summons would be best coming from you. Would you escort him to the abbey?'

'What if we are delayed?'

'Antony and I are old friends. We have much to talk about. Knock thrice on the door when all are assembled. I count on your powers of diplomacy to keep both Leufrid and Michaelo in the same room.' He told him of the relationship.

'You have set me quite the challenge, Owen.'

'Do I ask too much of you?'

Geoffrey laughed. 'On the contrary. I welcome the opportunity to prove myself up to the task.'

Owen counted on that.

Brother Oswald, hospitaller of St Mary's Abbey, greeted Owen warmly. 'We are honored that Prince Edward's emissary chooses to bide within our walls on this visit.' The monk smiled as if to thank Owen for his patronage and escorted him to a room off the main hall of the guest house, knocking at the door, then withdrawing.

'Enter.'

Owen grinned at the deep, resonant voice, which had been so effective in a room filled with arguing captains and commanders, and easy to hear at noisy feasts. Opening the door, he found Antony standing with his back to him, gazing out a window that faced the river. It was a small room furnished with several high-backed chairs and a table on which stood a flagon of wine and two mazers.

Antony turned round, his expression wary. 'Owen?'

'Have I changed so much?'

'Forgive me, I think of you as you looked out in the field. I'd forgotten the scar, the patch.' A grin. 'Though now I recall how the ladies flocked round you – the scar and patch made you mysterious. Dangerous.'

The men embraced, stepped apart, studied each other.

Antony was a striking man, taller even than Owen, with dark olive skin, tightly curling black hair, deep-set eyes – much like Thoresby's but tawny, and though he was a scholar of warfare rather than a participant, he had the posture of a soldier. In the past, he'd favored dark robes, undecorated, almost monk-like. But today he wore a tawny velvet houpelande to match his eyes, embroidered with exotic birds, decorated with pearls. His hat was a velvet turban of the sort much favored by merchants on the Continent, the color red.

'You look the part of an emissary from Prince Edward, heir to the throne, my friend,' said Owen.

'His Grace prefers me this way. And look at you, a little gray at the temples yet still broad at the shoulder and narrow at the waist. Still an active man, I see, though the father of three and married to one of the most beautiful women in the city, I am told, and accomplished in her own right.'

'Lucie is that and more, Antony. And we must count Jasper, my eldest son, for he is as dear to Lucie and me as if he were of our flesh.'

'For a man who cursed the fate that sent him north, you have made a life here, and a good one. I have heard much about you from Abbot William.'

'I trust he has not turned you against me?' Owen did not have the warm relationship with the current abbot that he'd come to enjoy with his predecessor.

'He much admires you, and worries what my arrival might mean for the city if you were to join Prince Edward's household. He has told me all about the recent troubles, and how the aldermen and sheriff counted on you to resolve them. Have you done so?'

'There are yet a few pieces on the board.'

'Come. Let us sit, drink wine, and talk.'

They settled in the high-backed chairs, moving them so that

they faced each other with the small table between. Antony poured, handed Owen a mazer.

'They are talking about your skill with a bow in all the taverns of the city. So you have regained your prowess.'

'To an extent, I suppose I have.' Owen did find it satisfying.

'Tell me about these outlaws. I understand they committed these crimes as vengeance for their father and a young woman?'

Owen tried to be as brief as possible. 'They will hang, of course. But Bartolf Swann misused his power as coroner, as did the steward of Galtres.'

'A common complaint.'

'We are at the mercy of the king's whim in his choices for such positions.'

'A king uses such posts as favors to those who served him well, yes. But it has ever been so. You cannot expect such a man as the king to think long on the talents necessary for such minor posts.'

'Minor to him, not to the community.'

Antony sat back, his expression quizzical. 'You have learned much since last we met, my friend, but you have not lost your fire.'

'No? I wonder.'

'Trust me, you have not. Nor have I.' Antony refilled his mazer. 'I imagine you are wondering how it is I am no longer with the Duke of Lancaster.' He sat back, giving Owen an account of the years since they had last met, moving among noble commanders until he caught the attention of Prince Edward. 'He can be a difficult man, but he has a keen mind and is curious about the world. We enjoy each other's company. And you? Tell me about how you met your wife. I have heard rumors, but I would rather hear the truth.'

Owen found in his friend a rapt audience. But when Antony began questioning him about his duties for Thoresby, which were varied and ever-changing, with increasing responsibility, Owen finally asked why he was so curious. He hoped it was not too long before he reached the moment when it would be appropriate to introduce Antony to Michaelo. And Leufrid? Geoffrey had not yet knocked.

'His Grace is interested in the extent of your talents. That should

not surprise you. My mission is no mystery to you, though Chaucer
was not privy to all I have to tell you.'

'Hence your presence.'

'That, and there is the matter of your taking so long to decide.'

'The prince is impatient.'

'He has ever been so. But at present he has cause. His father
the king is ailing, vulnerable, prey to such as Richard Lyons, Alice
Perrers – I will not bore you with the list, though should you join
his household you will soon be apprised of those he most distrusts.
In the North, it is the Neville family, a concern heightened by the
appointment of Alexander Neville as Archbishop of York.'

'A Neville in charge.'

'As it were.' Antony tapped his long fingers on the table. 'For
my part, I believe this might benefit us. In war it is preferable to
have the enemy out in the open. But Prince Edward dislikes his
father's decision to hand the North to the Nevilles. The Thoresby/
Ravenser family were more tractable.'

'Did the prince support Richard Ravenser for archbishop?'

Antony cleared his throat, glanced toward the ceiling. 'Tractable,
but, unfortunately, weak when it comes to armed might, and therefore . . .'

'Richard Ravenser would be good for the Church, but not the
realm?'

Antony inclined his head. 'Forgive me if I insult a friend. But
if the Scots cause trouble, or one of the powerful Northern families
thinks to take advantage of an aging king, the Thoresby/Ravenser
clan would be of little use.'

He had a point. 'Who would His Grace have chosen for York?'

'I don't know. He had made no decision, believing there was
more time. He thought – unwisely in hindsight – that his wife's
visit would do Thoresby much good, extend his life.'

Owen bowed his head.

'Yes. I know it caused you much pain, my friend. The woman
. . . Your man . . .'

'You know much.'

'I thought I should learn as much as I might. You have made
an impression, a good one, on many powerful people. And some
enemies . . . I have heard Wykeham is your nemesis, and Thoresby
made that puzzling choice to coerce the Bishop of Winchester into

deeding you a valuable manor near your wife's. Now he might consider you beholden to him. However, if you are of Prince Edward's household, all your enemies will think twice about crossing you. The prince protects his people.' A pause as Antony studied Owen, who worked hard to keep his expression neutral. 'My wish is to convince you that this post in the prince's house-hold is an honorable undertaking, and to your benefit and that of all your family. And I believe with all my heart that is so. But I will not insult you with claims of His Grace's perfection or ease of manner, for I know you are aware of his prejudices and sharp temper.'

'And, knowing that, I do not for a moment believe I have any choice in this. I am commanded to serve.'

Antony raised a brow. 'You know him well. But I can imagine you choosing to defy the prince. Is that how you wish to play this?'

Owen stood, walked to the window. 'It has a certain appeal. And were I not a family man I might try his patience.' He turned to face Antony. 'I have a compromise in mind. I would be both the prince's man in the North and captain of York's bailiffs.'

'Torn between two masters?'

'I do not see it that way, but as a means to protect my family from within and without the city. Knowledge of the kingdom at large, the conflicts amongst houses, some status, and a seat at the table here in the city would, as you say, be to my benefit and that of my family.'

'So little?' A smile. 'Not a knighthood?'

'No, not that.'

'I did not think so. But if ever you should change your mind, His Grace would be well pleased to count you among his fighting men.' Antony shrugged. 'He might do so in any case.'

'I am too old.'

'Yesterday's victims might disagree.'

'Ah. That is so.'

Antony's laughter was loud in the small room, and Owen could not help but join in.

Brother Michaelo had spent his time exploring the hall of the hospitium, standing by an open window breathing in the cool air.

It would rain again, perhaps by evening. He'd just turned, attracted to the sound of the emissary's laughter. Such a sound bespoke a man at ease in the world, a good sign.

'He is a man of good humor,' said Chaucer, stepping into the room. The captain had warned Michaelo that he might appear.

'So he appears from this side of the door.' Michaelo watched with interest as Chaucer glanced back toward the entrance to the hall. He sensed in the man an unease. He ignored Chaucer's attempts at chatter, returning to his contemplation of the garden.

Antony grew serious. 'The prince is aware that the citizens of York look to you for protection. He encourages you to accept the position. Pleasing the worthies of the city is all to His Grace's advantage. We are establishing a foothold to watch the Nevilles, and they are certain to put some effort in influencing the mayor and his council. The dean and chapter as well. You are the perfect mediator and spy.'

Owen agreed, but he had not anticipated the prince's encouragement. 'How is it that I am so trusted by His Grace?'

'You have my lady to thank for that. You remind her of her first husband Thomas Holland, a brilliant soldier and a most honorable man.' Antony laughed. 'So, you see? We are not sparring. What you propose is much to His Grace's liking. Now come, sit, my friend. I have much to tell you. It was no accident that I traveled here in the company of Neville's secretary.' As Antony replenished their mazers, he expressed his delight that they would be working together.

'So you will be my contact?' Owen asked.

'Either me or Sir Lewis Clifford, whom you have met. And respected, am I right?'

He was indeed.

'Neither John Holland nor his elder brother are involved. Indeed, considering that Crispin Poole was in John Holland's service, and would yet be there, doing his nasty work, had it not been for the loss of his arm – well, I advised His Grace that we might regret his involvement.'

Holland and Poole. 'I am glad to know of that connection. Is that why Chaucer was so interested in Poole?'

'He did not tell you? So he can hold his tongue when ordered.

I am glad that is so. Holland let Poole go the moment he ruined his career as an assassin. Nevertheless . . .' Antony smiled at Owen. 'Clifford and I both regard you as an excellent judge of men.'

Owen began to protest. He had made his share of mistakes, tragic ones. But Antony waved away his argument.

'We are none of us gods, Owen.'

The hall was quiet, so much so that Michaelo heard his cousin Leufrid greeting Brother Oswald on the lawn.

'I pray you did not invite Dom Leufrid to attend us here,' he said, moving toward Chaucer with murder on his mind.

The man rose, hands up as if ordering Michaelo to halt where he was. 'Captain Archer planned this. I merely carried out his orders. I was to escort him, but the man hired a chair to carry him here.'

A chair. God help him. Michaelo stopped close to Chaucer, looking down at him. 'If you are lying to me, you will regret it.'

'Then I have nothing to worry about. But why do you so despise your cousin?'

'He is a thief. He betrayed me in order to line his purse with my family's silver.'

'Yet without him you would never have served as secretary to Archbishop Thoresby. Nor would you now serve Captain Archer.'

'Like the phoenix, I rose from the ashes. But that does not exonerate the one who threw me on the pyre.'

The creak of the heavy oak door heralded the arrival of Brother Oswald, Dom Leufrid close on his heels. Michaelo smirked to see the result of his cousin's appetites, so corpulent as to prevent his arms from hanging at ease as he entered the hall, the movement something between a waddle and a trundle. How appropriate that Leufrid's greed would be his ruin. No wonder he'd hired a chair. Never a comely man, his wide, flat nose was now lost in his pillowing cheeks accentuating his overlarge nostrils, and his eyes seemed beady in the midst of so much flesh. The hair round his tonsure was so thin as to seem a mere suggestion. And his habit. Michaelo wrinkled his nose at the soiled hem – of course the man could not see it, he'd likely not seen his feet for years, his belly protruded so far. It was difficult not to laugh as Michaelo stepped forward, bowing to Leufrid in welcome.

'We meet again, cousin.'

'Michaelo?' The frog turned to glare at Chaucer. 'What is this? I was told I would be meeting with Master Antony.'

'That is correct,' said Chaucer. 'He is presently meeting with Captain Archer, an old friend. Brother Michaelo is the captain's scribe.'

Scribe. Michaelo was more than a scribe. But this was not the time to argue the point.

'I will return at another time.' Leufrid turned round, startling Brother Oswald, who stood close behind, watching with interest.

Chaucer stepped to block Leufrid's way. 'Master Antony wished you to meet his friend. He will be most disappointed should you miss this opportunity.'

'Meet him? To what purpose?'

'He will explain that. I pray you, sit.' Chaucer looked up at the hospitaller. 'Might we have some wine while we wait?' He stepped over and knocked thrice on the door.

When the signal came, Antony was just telling Owen that John Gisburne had paid a visit to Neville's secretary, attempting to besmirch Crispin Poole, offering to provide him with a better spy in the city.

'But Dom Leufrid informed me – he dined at the abbot's table yesterday – that he is pleased with Poole, particularly his connection with you. Though having heard your tale I wonder at his impression of a bond. It would seem the new archbishop hopes to learn much from Thoresby's spy.' A grin. 'Much we might learn from him.'

'It could be of use,' said Owen. 'And now, if I might introduce you to the man who will be writing to you, and traveling with me as my scribe, Brother Michaelo.'

A raised eyebrow. 'The late archbishop's personal secretary?'

'The same.'

'An excellent choice.'

'I also asked Chaucer to send for Dom Leufrid.'

'To alert him to your new role?' Antony nodded.

'Not only that.' Owen explained the tense relationship between the former archbishop's secretary and the present one.

'Pray, spare their lives, call them in at once.'

SEVENTEEN
A New Beginning

L ucie studied the handsome man standing in her doorway, tall as her husband and with a similar temperament, it seemed. His elegant robes warmed the entryway, and a subtle smell of spice added to his exotic presence. His eyes were warm, his voice deep and rich, and his smile began from his heart – one not only saw it, but felt a deep sense of well being.

'How shall I address you?' she asked. 'Master Antony?'

'Perhaps *Dom* Antony,' he said, bowing over Lucie's hand. 'I am master of none.'

'You are most welcome in our home, Dom Antony. Might I introduce you to the children?'

'I was hoping they would be present. I want to meet all your family, Dame Lucie.'

Shy at first, Gwen and Hugh quickly warmed to Antony, taking his hands and giving him a tour of the garden. Owen put his arm round Lucie and watched them moving along the paths.

'He has been eager to see it, though you will be a better guide. And he wants to see your shop as well, learn all about your physicks.'

'Is that how you first became friends? Discussing healing herbs in the camps?'

Owen seemed surprised by the question, but then admitted that is what they discussed in the beginning. 'He also wishes to meet Magda.'

'She has agreed to join us for dinner, though she insists Alisoun remain in the kitchen, resting for her short journey home to the river house on the morrow.'

Owen grinned. 'It is a good thing, to have Antony here.'

Seeing Owen's contentment, Lucie let go the months of worry over what the future might hold without John Thoresby. At last she could let her mind settle on her day-to-day concerns.

* * *

Bess glanced behind Owen as he appeared in the doorway of the York Tavern. 'Are you alone? The latest emissary from the prince is too grand for my inn?'

'Another evening, he promises. But tonight he is drinking in the wisdom of York's finest apothecary and Dame Magda. I could not entice him away.'

'He is a healer?'

'A man hungry for knowledge about every corner of our world.'

'Corner? Hmpf. He does not know the earth is round?'

Tom joined them, putting a full tankard of ale in Owen's hand. 'Drink up, Captain. Your friends are ahead of you.'

'They are indeed,' Bess noted, nodding toward her handsome neighbor's favorite table back in the elbow of the room. 'And they are a jolly pair, George and Geoffrey. You've chosen to accept both positions, have you?' Well, she had already known that, truth be told. She and Tom had delivered several jugs of his latest ale to Owen's home and heard the news.

'I did, yes,' said the captain absentmindedly as he took in the unlikely sight of Old Bede dancing a jig to Tucker's fiddling, the crowd clapping him on.

'He's cock of the walk for one night,' said Bess. 'Free tankards all round to toast his courage, and you see the result.' She laughed. 'I never thought to do such a thing for that old gossip. But the tavern wasn't the same without him.'

'Soft in the head, wife,' said Tom. 'He'll expect it every night.'

'So he will,' said Owen. 'Would you join us for a tankard, fair Bess?' He turned to her with that intoxicating smile, and how could she refuse?

Tom handed her a tankard and a jug for herself and the table. As she turned, the music quieted for a moment, the customers raising their tankards to Owen.

'Help me up, husband,' said Bess. Once she was on the stool she raised her tankard and called out, 'To Owen Archer, finest Welsh bowman in the land, and captain of York!'

Across the way, Lucie raised her head, hearing the cheers.

'They are celebrating their new captain,' said Antony. 'I am glad for him.'

'Bird-eye is well loved,' said Magda.

'Oh, that he is,' said Lucie.

Author's Note

Writing this book was a homecoming for me. A few of the series characters could not wait for my return and infiltrated my other series set in medieval York, the Kate Clifford mysteries, but in Kate's world they are a quarter century older, so not quite the same. I hope those of you who are returning to the series enjoy being back as much as I do. And for those of you new to Owen and Lucie's world, welcome!

With the death of Archbishop Thoresby in *A Vigil of Spies* my sleuth was out of work. What next for Owen? A period of mourning, perhaps returning to his earlier interest in apprenticing to his wife as an apothecary, a survey of the manor Thoresby had directed William Wykeham, Bishop of Winchester, to cede to Owen in gratitude for his considerable efforts on his behalf – all this might occupy him for a year or two, but I could not imagine him staying idle. Nor would the people of York (and Princess Joan's household) forget his skill in solving crimes.

But who could I find to replace John Thoresby, whose patronage brought Owen to York in the first book of the series? Theirs was a prickly partnering. It was not long before Owen was questioning the wisdom of choosing to serve Thoresby rather than John of Gaunt, Duke of Lancaster. He'd expected a churchman to be far more ethical than a duke of royal blood, but he realized that was not always so. The ensuing friction between Archer and Thoresby added a tension that was a gift to me, the writer. A gift that ended with Thoresby's death. Who would now be Owen's foil?

In *A Vigil of Spies* Thoresby recommends Owen to Princess Joan, wife of Prince Edward, heir to the English throne. But I did not want to shift the main stage to the royal court. What to do? I briefly flirted with his working for Alexander Neville, the new archbishop, but failed to find a plausible scenario in which

Owen would agree to serve him; nor could I imagine Neville trusting Owen, who had worked so closely with members of the Thoresby/Ravenser clan. R.B. Dobson captured the character of Alexander Neville, Thoresby's successor as Archbishop of York, in referring to him as 'so stormy an ecclesiastical petrel.'[1] A younger son of the patriarch of the increasingly powerful Neville family, the new archbishop saw rivals everywhere, and he was infamous for his aggressions against the powerful Bishop of Durham, the chapter of Beverley, and even the treasurer of York Minster, among others. He particularly disliked the 'stranglehold on the exceptionally lucrative canonries there exercised by members of the great Thoresby clerical affinity.'[2] Dobson sums him up: 'Neville suffered in his confrontations with the highly professionalised clerical elites of late fourteenth-century England by being every inch a *non*-professional.'[3]

The Nevilles arrived in England in the army of William the Conqueror, establishing themselves in the Northeast and rising through political and military service, as well as strategic marriage alliances. Alexander was born in Raby Castle, the family seat at Staindrop. His father, Ralph, was the hero of Neville's Cross, his mother, Alice, the sister of the Earl of Gloucester. With three older brothers, it was natural that Alexander and his twin Thomas sought careers in the Church. Family influence brought them early preferments. When Thomas died young, Alexander bene-fitted by becoming the focus of his family's ambitions in the Church. But he proved to be a man never satisfied, aggressively fighting for the offices he felt he deserved, which led him to the papal court, where he sought the pope's favor and influence against the hierarchy of the English Church, a majority of whom he had alienated. His efforts were rewarded when he won the vote of the chapter of York to become their new archbishop. No

---

[1] 'The Authority of the Bishop in Late Medieval England: The Case of Archbishop Alexander Neville of York, 1374-88', in *Church and Society in the Medieval North of England*, R.B. Dobson, p. 186

[2] Ibid. p. 191

[3] Ibid. p. 192

doubt his being a member of one of the two most powerful families in the north appealed to the canons, as well as his connection with the court – his brother John was steward of the royal household and brother-in-law to the chamberlain. The chapter would regret their decision. And therein lies a delicious tension for the ongoing series.

But what of Owen?

In 1374, King Edward III was in failing health, as was his heir, Prince Edward, who suffered a debilitating illness – a perilous situation for the realm. The crown depended on the Northern nobles, particularly Percy and Neville, to keep an eye on the border with Scotland, but in the circumstances such dependence could be construed as weakness. Prince Edward would want spies in the North, especially now with a Neville at the head of the Northern Church, and who better than Owen Archer, who had served the previous Archbishop of York for a decade. In the years since writing *A Vigil of Spies* I have delved into the history of Edward III, his family, and his court. Where I once thought of Thoresby's recommending Owen to Princess Joan as a compliment, I now realize he was throwing his captain and steward into the lion's den. Prince Edward was not a man to tolerate rejection. Owen would know that the prince's offer was a command.

So you see, when he lost Thoresby, Owen gained two antagonists – Prince Edward and Archbishop Neville. But I anchored him in York by using the tension of the times to motivate the city to seek Owen's help in keeping the peace as the series moves forward.

Speaking of keeping the peace, the inspiration for Bartolf Swann, coroner of Galtres, came from Sara M. Butler's book *Forensic Medicine and Death Investigations in Medieval England* (Routledge 2015). Ever on the lookout for the telling detail that distinguishes the past from the present, I was struck by the medieval emphasis on the communal interests in the juries' considerations. Although the coroner was an official ostensibly seeing to the crown's best interests in criminal investigations surrounding sudden and unnatural deaths (including suspicious and accidental deaths as well as homicides), the coroners' juries made their recommendations based on what was best for the community, predicated on what they understood as truth. Paraphrasing Butler's comments in an interview on my blog, the jury was not so interested in the details about the crime itself as they were with the character of the perpetrator. Did they feel remorse? Were they repentant? If they were acquitted would their return to the community restore peace and harmony, or would they commit more crimes?[4] Of course, being a crime writer, I was interested in the ways in which this process might be exploited by the more powerful members of the community.

I gave Bartolf the position of coroner of the forest of Galtres, which is just north of the city walls. The royal forests were established to provide good sport for the king, and a complex institution of laws and officials protected the animals and their habitat. The word 'forest' can be confusing in this context, because within the boundaries of the royal forests were villages, manors, towns, even castles such as Sheriff Hutton in Galtres. What distinguished these properties was their placement in the jurisdiction of a particular body of law, forest law. (Though there are exceptions.) Tales of Robin Hood made familiar the strict poaching laws in royal forests. Slightly less well know is the law that dogs inhabiting the forests larger than, say, lap dogs were to have three claws removed from their forefeet to prevent their attacking deer. This rendered them 'lawful', from which we get the term 'lawing'. Technically, only the nails were to be removed, but the process inevitably took off a portion of the toes as well, and sometimes the pads, maiming the dogs. A horrific practice. The dogs were to be checked every three years by officials known as regarders. As with the poaching laws, loopholes and opportunities for corruption abounded.

And what of wolves? Magda Digby asks – or rather prompts Owen: *What do folk see when they see a wolf, Bird-eye? The animal? Think again.* Down through time the wolf has become symbolic of our fears as we walk through the night glancing back over our shoulders. Although it is generally believed that wolves were hunted to extinction by the end of the Middle Ages, the exact

---

[4] 'Q&A with Dr Sara M Butler: Forensic Medicine & Death Investigation in Medieval England' https://ecampion.wordpress.com/2017/12/20/qa-with-dr-sara-m-butler-forensic-medicine-death-investigation-in-medieval-england/

dates are still debated. In his book *Wolves and the Wilderness in the Middle Ages*, Aleksander Pluskowski cites 'a marked decrease in the number of documented wolf hunts in the fourteenth century and the last reliable reference to wolf trapping in England is dated to 1394-6, from Whitby Abbey in East Yorkshire.'[5] Officials boasted of wolf-free territories, but folk still feared them, especially in hard winters. We still do.

[5] Boydell Press 2006, p. 30

Acknowledgments

My deepest gratitude to Louise Hampson, Joyce Gibb, Mary Morse, and Jennifer Weltz for thoughtful readings and insightful suggestions.

Thank you to Laura D. Gelfand and Thomas Thorp for their inspiring presentations in a session *Werewolf? There, Wolf* at the International Congress on Medieval Studies at WMU and follow on communications regarding Magda's question – *What do folk see when they see a wolf?* Extra thanks to Laura for permission to use a quote from her talk as an epigraph.

For all domestic canine details I am indebted to Molly Gibb for sharing her considerable expertise.

Thanks to Kate Lyall Grant for inviting me into the Severn House family, and all the team, including Sara Porter and Natasha Bell, who have taken my manuscript and turned it into a beautiful book.

I am grateful to all the fans of Owen, Lucie, Magda, Michaelo and all the cast who kept asking for a new chapter in their story. Thank you for your patience!

Deep appreciation to my partner Charlie Robb for the beautiful maps and so many other graphic and logistical solutions. You are my light, my love, and my anchor.